THE E WINTER

TEARING THE DARKVEIL

Book One

Jaques Smit

To Mike
Thank you for
the support. Love
your reviews on the
channel, awesome
effort!

PAUL SMITH PUBLISHING
London

Published by Paul Smith Publishing London 2024

A CIP catalogue record for this title is available from the British Library

ISBN PB 978-1-912597-29-1
ISBN eBook 978-1-912597-30-7
ISBN Audiobook 978-1-912597-31-4
ISBN Hardcover 978-1-912597-41-3

Paul Smith Publishing

www.paulsmithpublishing.co.uk

To Laura and Liam, who inspired me to keep writing

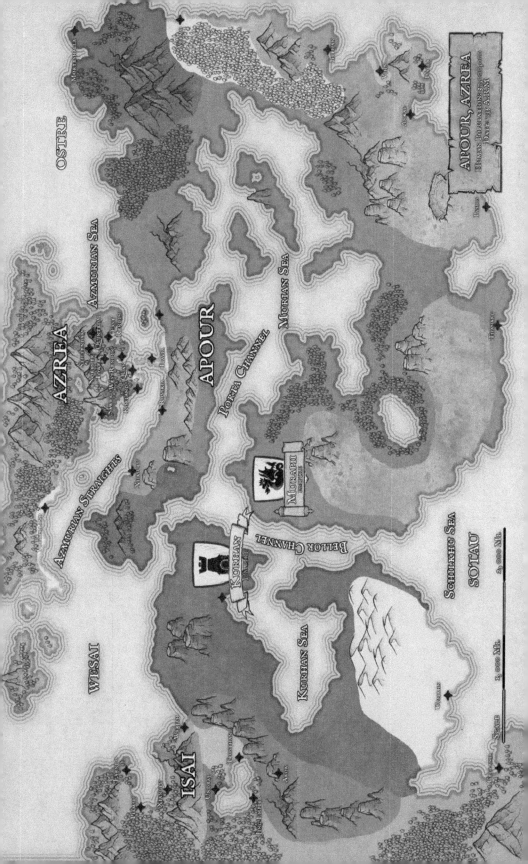

"I believe in the Magpies' Code. It says that you should always help those who cannot help themselves, if you are able. I am able, and no one can prove otherwise. I won't let anyone else control my destiny but me. So, here I am, ready to add my bones to the pile too." –
Birger

Prologue

AUTUMN, 733A.R.M.
A.R.M. (After the rise of Murapii)

"Pants…" Caoimhín cursed, tossing 'Ymir's Breath' onto the sunbathed-table. The blue crystal bounced once and rolled over, a tornado swirling inside, its eye a mocking stare.

Despite the fresh mountain breeze, sweat trickled down his temple, but he was too stressed to care. He had been at work for hours. Now, Duke Londel, the ever-overbearing investor, was on his way to demand answers, but Caoimhín still had so much to do.

The ladies curse Londel for rushing me! he thought. *Do I even want him to get his grubby hands on this?*

Kallen chuckled. "You sound frustrated, father."

Caoimhín glowered at his son over his gold-rimmed glasses.

"I swear this artefact cut right through the cliff face this morning." Caoimhín huffed, the scent of mud pungent in the air. "But now the best I can do is sprinkle cold water."

Kallen's mid-length blond hair swooped up from his cowlick. A few loose strands framed his sky-blue eyes that matched those of his father. He donned a navy-blue surcoat over chain mail, with an imposing two-handed sword strapped to his back. The boy had the muscular stature and bearing of a career soldier.

"That fool Londel is threatening to replace me if I don't have a detailed report ready when he gets here," said Caoimhín. His neck heating with renewed anger, he ran his hands through his short blond hair.

"Over my dead body." Kallen's lip curled into a sneer.

"Yes," Caoimhín swatted at a fly buzzing around him, "that's what I'm afraid of." He righted his sweat stained navy shirt and brushed down his tan trousers.

Oh, pig poops, he thought when he noticed mud splattered onto his fine leather shoes.

The pair stood among rows of artefacts stacked on tables protected by sun canopies. Caoimhín had already catalogued most of them, and it had taken several months.

What was Londel planning to do with my work, anyway? he wondered. *That man is a snake. Whatever it was, it couldn't be good.*

Caoimhín's anger settled when he reflected on the achievement. On these tables lay a wealth of lost knowledge. And he had found it. His life's ambition achieved.

"What'll you do?" asked Kallen, squeezing his father's shoulder.

"I don't know...but it feels like I sold my soul when I took that foul Duke's money." Caoimhín huffed and poked at Ymir's Breath to make it roll over. "All I wanted was to find this place. Just think about all the good this power could do. The lives we could save."

"Can't Queen Armandine buy him out?" Kallen suggested.

Caoimhín smiled at his son. He was right. So far, the Queen had been the counterbalance. "Unfortunately, the Queen's done all she can," he said. "Dukes from East Rendin don't take it well when the Queen of West Rendin orders them around."

Caoimhín turned back to his collection. The power here could change the world. Increased mining efficiency, food production, and even reduce the cost of curing deadly disease. But Caoimhín was pretty sure that wasn't Londel's plan.

"Do you think Londel would attack us if you refused him?" Kallen asked, his face twisted with concern.

Caoimhín took a deep breath and allowed the scenic location to ease the tension in his shoulders. A group of log houses nestled against the cliff to the north near their excavation entrance.

The high escarpment gave him a breathtaking view of Sawra. A billowing dust cloud drew his attention west, where a shrub-filled ridge led back to civilization – if Anthir could be called civilised.

"There comes the devil now." Caoimhín shook his head and sneered. "I wish I were better at thinking under pressure." Caoimhín rubbed at his forehead. "This is the reason I'm no good at court politics."

A chilling wind gusted from the ice cap of Heaven's Peak behind them. Caoimhín shivered and dropped into his chair, snatching up his quill to update his notes. The familiar grate of the paper always helped to calm his nerves.

"Whatever happens, father," Kallen took a step forward, "we'll face it together...but that's not a Ducal escort."

Caoimhín jerked his head up and saw a horde of figures on horseback galloping towards them. They wore black armour and had their swords drawn. A woman with burning yellow eyes led the group. Her long, red hair fluttering over crimson armour.

"What do you suppose they want?" asked Caoimhín, his head tilted to the side.

Kallen drew his sword. "It's an attack!"

"Attack?" Caoimhín narrowed his eyes. "What do you mean, attack?"

"They're bandits, father. Move! They outnumber us. We need to get to the mine!"

A pang of panic ran through Caoimhín and his eyes stretched wide. *I can't let all my findings get trampled!*

"But...my work!"

"There's nothing we can do." Kallen grabbed Caoimhín by the arm and hauled him out of his chair. "Come! Now! Our only chance is the mine entrance."

"But...but...this is history, son!"

Kallen let go of Caoimhín's hand and whipped his massive sword forward to defend against a sweeping cavalry attack. Caoimhín heard the clash of steel, followed by an agonizing scream behind him. He whipped his head around, fear for his son filled his throat, but it wasn't Kallen who got hurt.

Thank the ladies! thought Caoimhín. The stench of blood washed over him, and his stomach turned. Holding back the sick, he began snatching up as many relics as he could get his hands on. He couldn't allow the bandits to take them.

"Father!" Kallen let out a grunt of pain. An explosion of splintering wood followed and Caoimhín saw his son's massive two-handed sword flying by.

"Kallen!" Caoimhín swung around, his whole body trembling.

Kallen lay sprawled among the overturned tables, blood running down his face as he scrambled to get up. Glaring, the woman in red, turned her horse for another pass. She grunted in frustration at the scattered tables that blocked her from charging Kallen. She dismounted and drew a pair of short swords from her belt.

Kallen was frantically searching for something to defend himself. Caoimhín's heart pounded in his throat. He couldn't bear to lose his son, but what could he do? Caoimhín wasn't a soldier.

The woman's two razor-edged blades licked out and Kallen leapt back to avoid them. Stumbling over a chair, he landed on his butt. He grabbed a golden plate the size of a shield and threw it at her face. She barely ducked under it.

Kallen needed help. Caoimhín found the sword named 'Belmung' and snatched it up. Forgetting to shout a warning, he lobbed it at

9

Kallen. Luckily, his aim was off and it thumped off a fallen table. Kallen rolled under an attack and dove for Belmung. The woman followed and struck down with both swords. Kallen blocked. The force shattering both her weapons.

She fell, tumbling into another table. Kallen wasn't fast enough to stop her from rearming with… Caoimhín's heart sank as he recognised the black-bladed daggers of 'Kazamung'.

Blue lightning danced across Kallen's new sword, and red ran up the pair of daggers into the woman's forearms.

Caoimhín gasped. "By the All-Mother…what have we started?"

The two flew at each other, and the weapons met in an explosion. The force knocked a group of black-clad riders from their horses and several tables flipped.

Caoimhín cried out, "Not the artefacts!" His limbs turned cold with fear.

A dust cloud rose to envelop the area, and Caoimhín blinked it out of his eyes. *Oh no!* The force had cleared the way between him and the enemy.

The bandits were already recovering. Caoimhín had to do something fast. He reached into his pocket. Out came his quintri-day-night-goggles.

"No." He tried again. Finding his golden pocket watch.

"Also, no." The bandits stalked towards him.

Time's up. He reached in for the last time and found his instant-scaffold.

"That'll do!" he celebrated.

A hand sized disk with a dial lay in his palm. Caoimhín tuned it to align the symbols.

"Kallen! Get back!" he shouted.

Kallen shot him a glance amid the fierce exchange. Then he kicked the woman in the chest, hard enough to send her tumbling.

Caoimhín prayed to Aeg that his plan wouldn't backfire and pressed the central disk down. He cast it between them and the enemy. A translucent wall burst from the device, stretching twenty feet high, forming an impassable wall across the ridge. As it extended, several bandits and a few of Caoimhín's precious relics went flying off the cliff.

Caoimhín cried out as he watched his life's work being scattered, broken, or stolen.

Tears brimming, he barely suppressed a sob. But, Caoimhín had ensured his son's safety.

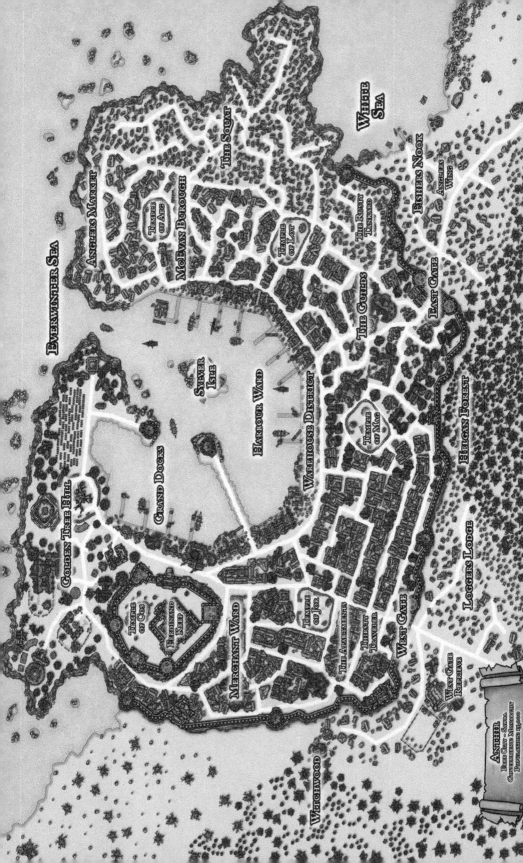

EVERWINTER SEA

WHITE SEA

ANGLERS MARKET

TEMPLE OF ARC

McEVAN BOROUGH

THE SQUAT

TEMPLE OF LOT

THE RUSTY TANKARD

FISHERS NOOK

ANGLERS WING

EAST GATE

THE GUILDS

SILVER ISLE

HARBOUR WARD

TEMPLE OF MAG

WAREHOUSE DISTRICT

HELGAN FOREST

GOLDEN TREE HILL

GRAND DOCKS

LOGGERS LODGE

TEMPLE OF COS

FERDINAND KEEP

MERCHANT WARD

TEMPLE OF JOR

THE APARTMENTS

THE OLD TRAVELLER

WEST GATE

WEST GATE REPRIEVE

WIGHWOOD

ANTHIR

FIVE CITY SAGA
COMMISSIONED MAP XX
PUBLISHED IN MMXX

1

BURGLAR OR BEGGAR

"In all things, we must seek balance, lest entropy claim that for which it hungers."   Jing Mindweaver Wakhi Illu

"Not a sound from here," Birger whispered, his heart pounding with anticipation as he held one finger to his lips.

A beautiful girl crouched next to Birger, her clear blue eyes sparkling as the moon slipped past its thick cloud cover. She wore brown leather armour, fitted close to her lean frame, and a dark grey cloak draped over her shoulders. Reddish brown hair, rendered black in the dark, licked out from under her hood, which was pulled tight over her head.

Wynn mouthed, "Can I breathe?"

"No," Birger mouthed back mockingly, "just turn blue and pass out."

Birger gave her a wry smile. The cherry sweet perfume she had stolen from the market a couple of weeks before came wafting to him on the breeze. He tried dissuading her from wearing it to the burglary, but she proved resistant to his advice.

Wynn had talked him into 'teaching' her to be a thief a little over six months ago. Whilst she learned quickly, she didn't listen and had a bad habit of being loud when she should be quiet.

Birger was only nineteen himself. Older Magpies argued he was too young to take an apprentice. But what did they know?

He had high cheekbones and deep brown eyes that were so sharp they could've belonged to a bird of prey. His sand-brown hair was mussed under his grey hood, which cast a shadow over his square jaw, button nose, and full lips.

The pair were similar in height and clad in matching outfits, to look identical at a distance. Of course, the illusion wouldn't hold up close, but that wasn't the point. All they needed was for potential witnesses to describe them as generic burglars.

It was the perfect cover amidst Anthir's sea of thieves.

The grit of the tiles beneath Birger's boots felt more familiar than his own bed. Other thieves often used the same way through the

Apartments, and though encounters were rare, they were perilous. His guild, the infamous Magpies, weren't the only Thieves' Guild in Anthir. This was the true source of his anxiety. He was planning to steal from said rival.

Birger looked up at the looming limestone wall ahead. The narrow balcony jutting out from the steep roof resembled a slice of giant multi-layered cake, adorned with carved-stone candles.

Birger beckoned Wynn and braced his back against the wall as he joined his hands in a sling. She came at him with a quick trot, and he shot her up to the balcony where she effortlessly flipped over the rail. Wynn offered him a hand, and he grabbed it, quickly scaling the last obstacle before their destination.

Behind them, the Free Duchy of Anthir slept soundly under the frosty night sky, with the chilly wind wafting the smell of salt and fish from the docks. Birger took a step closer to the window. It had a wood frame and divided into two sections – a larger side-hung pane at the bottom of a smaller top-hung window.

"Watch this." Birger began to kneel, but his rapier caught the ground awkwardly; he was forced to shift it aside before he could complete the movement.

He tried to hide the flush of embarrassment in his cheeks at the less-than-agile display. Birger swallowed and unrolled a leather pouch across his knee, displaying an assortment of thieves' tools. He uncoiled a long, fine wire before shoving the pouch back in his belt next to his large canvas satchel.

Wynn watched him with the rapt attention of a child tracking a leaf boat down a river. He bent one end of the wire into a loop and reached it through a narrow slit in the top window to unlatch the other.

The slight gap wasn't poor design or a mistake. A major downside of mistreating your housekeeper is that it makes them more likely to help potential burglars. A fact that was bolstered by Birger's recent help with Eliza's debt collectors.

With his way in secured, he closed the top window. It wouldn't do for the entry point to be traced back to her. Look after the poor, and they look after you, that's how the Magpies worked.

Birger winked playfully at Wynn, saying, "Okay, keep a lookout for any undesirables."

"You mean other than us?" Wynn asked.

"Yeah, cheeky, other than us."

A few snowflakes settled on Wynn's hood, and his belly tingled. *Aeg, she's got a lovely smile,* he thought.

14

The moonlight pooled in her eyes and touched the curve of her cheek. He caught himself grinning at her like a fool and stopped. A pang of guilt struck him. She was his apprentice. Falling in love with her would be a mistake.

She gave him a sharp nod but kept watching him.

I'm being too soft on her, aren't I, Birger considered.

Crestfallen as he was, the will to argue with her seemed like a slippery fish he just couldn't get a handle on. Birger sighed, turned, and climbed in through the window.

Playtime's over, he reminded himself.

Inside the typical merchant's apartment, Birger moved through the room as silently as a ghost ship through the mist. The thrill of danger igniting a primal sense of fun within him. Here a single mistake could get you caught.

He looked around the spacious study. It smelled like old dusty books, and the east wall held a stocked bookcase with an overstuffed leather reading chair in the corner. Next to it was a small round table holding a golden candlestick and a fat blue book. On the opposite wall stood a sturdy red-wood desk with paperwork neatly arranged on one side.

To the south, Merchant Foss' snoring rattled the bedroom door. It was loud enough to conceal the timber floor's creak as Birger stalked forward, searching every nook and cranny for secrets.

Birger thought the desk looked like one of those flat-topped kennels that rich people owned, but instead of a dog, a high-backed chair lounged inside.

A set of drawers flanked the countertop. He judged the desktop too thick in the middle, so he ran his fingertips over the wood, searching for a hint.

Mmmh... Birger thought with satisfaction as he came across an unusually straight groove. *A classic hidden compartment.*

He usually preferred his marks to be more creative with their hiding spots; it made the job more interesting, but he would take what he could get. That said, this wasn't a time for rash actions. A wrong move could cut the caper short, ending in disaster, so he proceeded with care.

Being patient reminded him of Sten's fate and how risky the job was. It made him question the decision to bring Wynn along. *Was it too reckless?* Shoving the thought aside, he murmured, "I won't make a mistake."

Like most Magpies, Birger took pleasure in stealing from the Blood Queen's mutts. They were a plague on society; they had no honour, unlike the Magpies, who had a code and a purpose.

The Magpies helped the poor and avoided killing where possible. It was terrible for business, anyway. The Black Wolves, on the other hand, trafficked in blood and human misery. From racketeering and slavery to assassinations; they were rotten to the core, and Foss deserved to freeze in one of Lot's icy vaults for being in their pocket.

Thinking about the goddess of death, Birger drew a spiral over his heart to ward off her anger. She probably didn't care what he was doing, but he didn't want to take any chances.

Birger took his time, studying the device built into the counter carefully. It was a box of eight inches by six inches with no visible handles or latches.

Maybe it's a push-to-open mechanism, but what sort of alarm did it hide or what trap?

Unscrupulous people often use dangerous means to protect their valuables. He peeked at the door, which held back the rasping snores of his host, and then he glanced to the window, where he saw Wynn watching him instead of being a lookout.

No surprise there, thought Birger.

With exaggerated pointing, he indicated she should be on guard. She put her hand to her mouth to mime 'oops'.

Wynn turned away from the window, but Birger knew it wouldn't last long. For now, he dismissed the worry. He needed to focus, and he was well aware of how quickly their situation could turn nasty, even if the girl wasn't.

He pressed on the box with the tip of his dagger, expecting it to move under its weight. It didn't. Ultimately, it wasn't what he had expected, and there was a moment of disappointment.

What had he missed? The box was there; he was sure of it. *What if...*

Birger slipped the chair out, dropped to one knee and checked under the desk, sweeping the wood surface with his hand until he found a shallow finger-sized hole. Too narrow for his dagger.

Aeg, please don't let this be a trap that chops my fingers off, thought Birger. Despite the nervous sweat trickling down his neck, he used his least favourite finger and pushed.

He heard a metallic click.

2

TRAPPED

Birger released his breath. The loud rasp of Merchant Foss snoring in the next room was all-enveloping. The old crook's personal office, with its ornate furnishing, felt oppressive. A bead of sweat trickled down Birger's cheek, and the weight of the box under the desk felt heavy in his hand.

Birger repeated his plea for luck. Although Aeg was unpredictable by nature, the Great Dragon goddess of the oceans and mistress of chance had always favoured him in the past. And the other four ladies were a poor match for his line of work. Except for Lot, whom he totally respected and definitely didn't want to offend.

Focus Birger, he scolded himself.

Lowering the tray carefully revealed a thin copper wire spanning the narrow gap. A trigger. This was where things got dicey. Making sure not to drop the box, he retrieved a pair of long, thin clippers from his belt pouch and extended it into the opening to cut the wire.

Click.

Birger licked his lips, took another deep breath, and slowly lowered the box.

When nothing bad happened, relief mixed with delight, and his entire body tingled upon seeing inside.

He grinned.

Benny's intel was always reliable. The Shade had sold the information to Benny at a reasonable price, and Birger was indebted to pay it back when he made the score.

This wasn't the first job Birger had done with the Shade, either supplying the information or brokering the theft on behalf of someone else. Their dealings had been lucrative so far, and long may it continue.

Six fist-sized leather bags lay beside four scrolls and an onyx wristband. On examination, the bags held gold, gems, and jewellery. Birger revelled in the clinking sound of coins when he hefted the bags. Glittery things made this job worth it, and the take would be more than enough to pay for the information ten times over.

Excitedly, he broke the seal on one scroll to unroll it, hoping to find artwork. There was a spot above his bed where he could hang something nice.

Alas, it looked like orders, and Birger frowned. He recognised the seal, a crying wolf, the insignia of the Blood Queen – the ruthless leader of the Black Wolf gang. She was a scary human being, and even thinking about the redhead in her crimson armour sent a chill down his spine.

Any order coming from her would cause pain and suffering for someone, so taking them could save a life or buy someone a day of freedom. That said, considering her reputation, only a madman would steal from her, and as the older Magpies kept telling him, Birger wasn't a man, he was just a boy. And taking these sounded perfectly reasonable to him.

The corner of his lip curled into a wicked smile as Birger thought, *Besides, when this goes missing, a high-ranking mutt will end up in a lot of trouble.* Satisfied, he pocketed the lot.

There was no space in his loot bag for the armband, but his need for spite outweighed the monetary value of the onyx. Birger did like the look of it and found that it fit when he slipped it onto his arm.

He inspected the bracelet in the moonlight. There were symbols carved along its edge. The writing was foreign to him, and a long serpentine dragon wove between it and the left edge.

The craftsmanship is impeccable, Birger thought. *It could be valuable after all.*

He shut the hidden compartment carefully. Aeg willing, the theft wouldn't be discovered for a few days. He secured his tools and put everything in the room back the way he found them.

Once he was satisfied that all was in order, he turned to the window. Out of the corner of his eye, he caught Wynn snapping back to her guard duties, feigning diligence. Birger shook his head.

Having an apprentice was hard.

We'll need to work on her discipline, he thought. *I'm not good at this master and apprentice thing. Leaders tell people what to do and punish them for not listening. But I really don't want to get that strict with her. How did Sten do it with me? Well, I guess, for one, Sten didn't care if I liked him or not.*

Thinking of his old mentor sent a pang of loss through his chest, but he pushed it aside. Life in the Squat was ruthless, and only the tough survived. *I'm not doing her any favours by being nice. Perhaps I'm not cut out to be a teacher.* Birger shelved the thought. He would work out what to do with her later.

As quietly as he had entered, Birger slipped out of the apartment, a cold wind burning his cheeks. After two attempts, he finally got the window latch to drop into place.

With a curious sparkle, Wynn asked, "What did you find?"

Birger turned to face her. "Why do you think I found anything?" He continued fastening his kit.

"I saw you!"

"Shush! You'll wake Foss. Anyway, your job was to keep a lookout, not to watch me."

The wind dropped out of Wynn's sails; her cheeks flushed bright red, and she hung her head. Instant regret made Birger feel like a horrible person.

He scowled and sighed. "Fine, here's your share. Never say I don't cut you any slack."

Birger took the lightest pouch from his satchel and handed it to her. It was probably more generous than the Code dictated, but he knew she was struggling, and needed the money.

"Thanks!" Wynn bounced, pointing at Birger's arm. "And that?"

Her smile returning warmed his heart and made his belly tingle.

Being gentle wasn't so bad, was it? Birger wondered, trying to convince himself.

The more cynical part of Birger disagreed. *Eventually, she'll run into the dark side of a thief's life, and she won't be prepared.*

Shut up, he told his cynical self. *Let me enjoy my moment of victory.*

"I thought it looked nice on me." Birger popped his eyebrows and fluttered his lashes. "Let's move before you get us in trouble with all that noise." Beneath the humour lurked genuine anxiety.

Wynn responded with a coy tilt of her head and followed him over the balcony ledge.

She's clearly still under the impression that we're invulnerable, thought Birger's cynic.

I told you to shut up.

As they dropped quietly to the roof, Wynn asked, "So, what're you planning to do with your share?"

"I haven't decided yet. I'm saving for a big job, and I'll need a lot of equipment."

"Really? What job?"

Birger smirked. He hadn't told anyone about his big plan before and wasn't sure he should.

Ah, why not, he decided, "I'm going to steal the Livery of Ferdinand."

"You want to steal the Duke's chain of office?"

"Hush! We aren't out of danger yet. You'll wake someone."

Wynn covered her mouth with one hand and then said more quietly, "Are you out of your mind?"

Birger smiled. "I don't think so. I just need a challenge, something exciting I've never done before."

That wasn't true, and Birger knew it. It was spite that drove him to target Duke Roar Fordson. There was a history between them that Birger learned not to talk about long ago. Most didn't believe him when he claimed to be the absent Duke's illegitimate son, and those who did tried to exploit him.

Wynn looked alarmed. "They would never stop hunting you. Birger... what you plan to do is suicide."

"Don't you worry about that. I can take care of myself. Besides, that's why I need to save. Once I do the deed, I'll need to lie low for a while."

"No kidding! You would need to climb into a hole in the forest and stay there. And what would you do with the thing? Benny wouldn't touch it with a ten-foot barge pole. No fence would!"

"I don't plan to sell it," said Birger dismissively.

"Then why steal it?"

"Like I said, I need a challenge. And frankly, I can't think of anything more challenging." Birger glanced at his pocket watch. "Let's move. We need to get back to Ichman Road to climb down. The street'll flood with traffic in under an hour."

Wynn shook her head, but she dropped the subject.

Maybe I shouldn't have said anything, thought Birger. He trusted Wynn, but now she would be a liability if he pulled it off.

Voices in the distance drew Birger's attention, but he found nothing. He figured it must've been drunks out too late. Something felt wrong about tonight. Birger couldn't make sense of the feeling, but his gut was practically screaming at him to get moving.

I'm probably paranoid because of what Benny said.

20

3

MISTAKES

The rising sun illuminated the clouds, giving Birger a chance to appreciate the rugged beauty of the sleepy coastal city. Millions of fine white snowflakes twirled in the wind, collecting in small mounds wherever they found a crevice to settle.

Chimneys puffed smoke, working against the encroaching chill. Ferdinand Keep guarded the nobles of Golden Tree Hill on one side, while Heaven's Peak pierced the skyline like the tusk of a giant sleeping boar on the other.

The Apartments that they were passing through housed Anthir's upper-middle class, the merchants. Their insecurity in being not quite the wealthiest in the city led them to play a childish game of my house is taller than yours. It turned them into a patchwork of colourful buildings that stood at different heights, even those with the same number of floors.

"Hurry, Wynn," said Birger in a hushed tone. He did his best to hide the nervousness he felt. "We mustn't be up here when morning traffic starts."

Wynn didn't answer, but he could hear her steps quicken.

While Birger yearned to celebrate the evening's success with her, it wouldn't be wise until they were out of danger. Black Wolf scouts frequently patrolled this area. Still, his exhilaration had to go somewhere – and he wanted to show off – so Birger added more acrobatic flair to his journey.

'Lot's Northerly' – as the locals referred to the wind – howled through the alley below. Lot was the goddess of life and death, winter and summer.

Being so far north, winter was like Anthir's local street bully. It always appeared ready to pelt you with snowballs whenever the opportunity presented itself.

By the crisp chill, Birger could tell she was building up her stocks for a big assault. Not that he was calling the goddess of death and winter a bully. *Certainly not,* he reassured himself; he had no wish to become a permanent ice-block.

21

Next to the All-Mother Cos, Lot was the most revered and feared. From the income earned by performing lavish funerals of the rich, her temples helped the poor with food and medical care. He supposed that made the temple of Lot much like the Magpies.

Birger glanced back to check on Wynn. They ran along the flat pitch of the roof close to the eaves, the steep section near the ridge offering them some cover.

He checked on Wynn's footing. The tiles were tricky because they were designed to fly off during a weavestorm. This made them liable to grind or crack under a misstep, or worse still, tumble down to the cobbled streets with a clatter.

Aeg forbid we encounter a weavestorm, thought Birger.

The storms were unpredictable things that appeared without warning and caused unspeakable damage. Birger wasn't sure how they came about, but the books said they happened when the 'Weave' or Realm of Magic collided with the physical world.

Most common folks simply believed magic users triggered them. This led to a general mistrust of any who weren't clergy, who were immune. Suspecting your spiritual leaders was distasteful after all.

Birger stopped after jumping across a wider gap between the buildings to look back at Wynn. He smiled at the childlike glee on her face. City life hadn't taken the innocence of a farmer's childhood from her yet. He found it incredible that she still had that sparkle, even though he knew it couldn't last.

Wynn's family were victims of the sickness that swept the region, and for an eighteen-year-old girl, tending a farm on her own was impossible. That brought her to the biggest city in Sawra and set her on the path to Birger.

She looked beautiful sailing across the gap, and he felt that treacherous flutter in his stomach again. *She's my apprentice. I can't think of her that way.*

She made it across, and they resumed their run. Ahead, the roof incline was steep. Birger leapt up, kicked off the taller adjacent building and landed on the ridge.

After a glance to confirm Wynn had seen his stunt, Birger flew down the other side.

He smiled.

A chimney surprised him, and he felt his rapier fly wide, threatening to tap the bricks. He grabbed it to preserve their stealth, but the canvas satchel bag tucked behind his arm slipped out with a flurry. It just missed the stack.

An involuntary sigh of relief escaped his lips as he imagined it plucking him off his feet. Birger heard a snigger coming from Wynn, and his cheeks heated.

Adopting a more cautious pace, he distracted himself from his embarrassment by mulling over the evening's events. The increasing distance between them and Foss felt good.

Another successful job, a little more coin and reputation. Reputation was currency to a thief. Some doors simply wouldn't open without it.

He glanced at his old pocket watch again. Winding it before he slipped it back into a belt pouch. Sten gave it to him when he started his training. The thing barely worked, but watches were expensive.

A barrel dropped onto the cobblestones below, drawing Birger's attention to a shopkeeper already beginning their day. Soon, these streets would swarm with people making deliveries.

They slowed, and Wynn asked, "What is it?"

Pensively, Birger said, "The shops are preparing to open."

"Are you worried about the guards?"

His expression turned serious. "More about the mutts... They act like the Merchant Ward is theirs."

"Oh really? I thought they only had the Harbour Ward and the Warehouse District?"

"They've been growing. A few weeks ago, I saw their Blood Queen returning to the city from Heaven's Peak and... she looked scary. Real scary."

"Scary how?" Wynn asked.

"I don't know; I can't explain it. Darker, more menacing."

"How does a woman look darker?" Wynn challenged.

"Well, for one, her armour was covered in blood, which was bad on its own, but that wasn't all... There was something wrong. When she glanced in my direction, it felt like my legs locked up, and I couldn't move." He shuddered at the memory.

"Your legs locked up?" Wynn scrunched her nose. "That's weird."

"Yeah, I know. Anyway, since then, the mutts have been claiming more of the city, and I heard Ulfhild's shacked up in the Duke's castle."

"The Blood Queen is living with the Duke?" Wynn's eyes stretched saucer-wide and worry lines crinkled her forehead.

Wearing your feelings on your sleeve isn't very thief-like; it can get you conned or caught, thought Birger. *Another thing we have to work on.*

"Maybe the Duke just needed a dash of street spice in his life," Birger joked, attempting to ease the tightness in his chest. It worked a little, but his history with the Duke invoked other feelings.

Like the other cities in Sawra, Anthir declared its independence during the Rendinian Civil War ten years before. While Anthir had never boasted a pristine reputation, things had deteriorated further.

The Duke didn't care about crime and poverty. That was why the Magpies were strong here. The same reason Birger supposed they spread across the continent more rapidly than a storm off the Everwinter Sea. They looked after the poor to balance the scales.

Birger realised Wynn was laughing. *Cos, she has beautiful lips,* he thought, and a goofy smile appeared on his own face.

Wynn's mirth died away, and she asked, "What do you think is going to happen?"

"I don't know. The mutts will get stronger, we'll get smarter, and soon we'll steal from them instead of merchants trading with them."

"But would that mean war between the guilds?"

Birger shrugged, "The Magpies have dealt with worse."

"What if we escaped to live in Gelreton?"

"Gelreton is a small town. A thief needs a city." Birger spread his arms wide and let his grey cloak ripple in the wind as he moved. "I'm a city barnacle, living on the haul of others with no other useful skills! …And, besides, old Hamish counts on me for money. He can barely get to the market to buy bread in his condition. You're not thinking of leaving, are you?"

"Don't worry, I'm kidding. I can't leave Neffily here on her own. I just miss the farm life. The forest and the animals, hunting and swimming in the river…" Wynn's playful tone shifted to a profound sadness, "I miss a lot of things."

Wynn's loss was still quite recent, and Birger realised for the first time how close to the surface that pain lurked. He shuddered as he recalled how he went rogue in the months following Sten's disappearance.

Wynn never even let it show or slow her down. Perhaps she was more stoic than he gave her credit. Maybe that was why he took her as an apprentice? They had that pain in common, and Birger wondered if focusing on her had given him an escape?

"Bleh!" Birger mimed vomiting, "I can't imagine anything worse! Forests are filled with things that want to eat you or trick you. No, thank you!"

"Unlike Anthir?" Wynn asked sarcastically.

Birger grinned and said, "At least here I can see them coming, and I'm the apex predator in these woods. Stick with me, and I'll make you one, too."

Wynn smiled and shook her head.

Birger put a hand on Wynn's shoulder. "Besides, Neffily needs you. Without your wisdom, she would get spirited away on the lies of the first drunk merchant that came by!"

Birger forced his grin wide, hoping to put Wynn's dark thoughts to rest.

"I owe Neffily a lot more than she owes me. I wouldn't have survived here for long if not for her. Do you...?"

The crack of a roof tile breaking echoed in the morning gloom, cutting her off. Instinctively, Birger pulled Wynn into a crouch beside him, motioning for her to lie flat on her stomach.

Aeg, help us, he prayed.

Birger's mind raced. It was hard to see in the twilight, so they might not have been spotted. Though if he was wrong, whoever it was could be heading towards them. He had to know.

Birger signalled for Wynn to stay down. He peeked over the roof ridge. His eyes breached the rim, and he muttered a curse.

Two men clad in black leather armour were advancing on them, and to his surprise, he recognised one.

4

BLOOD QUEEN

Birger's fingers danced on the nape of his neck, his brow creasing as he thought, *What should I do?*

Bo was a mutt captain with a bad temper and a worse reputation. Even though the approaching pair weren't aware of Birger and Wynn, they would inadvertently stumble onto them.

Think of something! Birger urged himself. *If I were alone, I could slip past them and pick Bo's pocket for a laugh,* he mused. A naughty grin flashed over his lips. *That's not helpful. I'm not alone.*

He checked the rapier at his side. He had never killed anyone and didn't want to find out if he could. Regardless, he was well-trained with the weapon and practised daily. He could keep himself alive in a duel if it came to that. *Bo's a moron, but he's a competent swordsman. And facing two of them... well, Wynn didn't even have a weapon.*

I could give her mine, Birger considered, *but that would leave me with only a dagger. And taking a knife to a sword fight is suicide. Could we jump?*

No, from this height, we would break our legs, and the only safe place to climb down is on Ichman Road, directly behind the mutts.

What else?

Running was another option, but if we got recognised, it would connect us to the Foss theft, even if we got away. To make matters worse, the sun was rising, and soon, the light would make it hard to hide.

Think Birger, think!

Chewing on his lip in frustration, he pulled his cloak tighter against the cold.

Maybe... It was all he had, so it was worth a try. He could double back, rely on the snowfall to help them hide while they waited for the mutts to move on.

It's decided then. Birger huffed. He knew it was a gamble, but then when wasn't he gambling with his life?

He signalled for Wynn to follow and stay low.

She nodded and pushed up into a crouch.

Turning to sneak away, a chill ran up Birger's spine when he heard the grating sound of a roof tile. He glanced at Wynn's feet. She clearly failed to place them correctly.

Inwardly, he cursed himself for bringing her, but kept his face passive. This wasn't the time. She needed to be focused. *Make it fun,* Birger thought. She didn't need to know that this was life or death.

Spurred by the drumming of approaching boots, Birger put on a smile and said, "How about a game of catch me if you can?"

Wynn stared back, her eyes and mouth competing to see which could stretch wider. The two bad guys came running over the rise.

Birger swept his cloak clear of his legs, shouting, "Bolt, now!" and he shoved Wynn into a head start.

With adrenaline pumping and the calls for them to stop blurring into the background, Birger ran, blinking snowflakes out of his eyes. A cacophony of roof tiles slipped and shattered under their feet as they went. The only way to escape now was to outmanoeuvre the pair and hope for the best.

He rushed up the slope of a steep red roof, slid down the other side on his thick leather greaves, and bound into a run by kicking off a limestone chimney. It felt good. Usually, he loved the heart-pounding excitement of a chase. But the fun was dampened with Wynn's life also hanging in the balance.

Birger's mind kept circling back to what could happen if the wolves caught them. Bo would kill Birger, but he would do far worse to Wynn. For a rash moment, he even considered ditching the loot, but decided against it. Getting caught empty-handed would only add torture to the morning activities.

Wynn's grey hood whipped back and her red-brown hair fluttered free. She moved with surprising speed, which gave Birger hope. He had to believe they could make it out. If no one recognised them, it was even possible to avoid long-term consequences.

Birger spotted a large group milling in the street–thugs armed with swords and crossbows. Among the roughly twenty black leather-clad ruffians stood a slender woman garbed in crimson. Her fiery hair was tied back, and she was knocking on Foss's front door.

It was the Blood Queen and her mutts come to see their fence!

Birger didn't have time to wonder what she was doing there so early. Her entourage had already spotted them dashing across the rooftops, and crossbows were being drawn.

In a throaty roar, Bo shouted, "Stop, Birger! There's nowhere to run, you street rat scum!"

28

Hearing his name sent a jolt of panic through Birger's chest. *So much for avoiding long-term consequences,* he sighed.

A crossbow bolt smashed a window right in front of Wynn, and Birger shouted, "Turn right! Get away from the road."

With fear and desperation pumping adrenaline into his blood, Birger followed Wynn, darting across the rooftops of the Merchant Ward. A few seconds felt like an eternity when your lungs burned and your muscles ached with fatigue.

Another bolt flew over Wynn's head, and she tripped, spilling out on the rough tiles. She nearly slipped over the edge, but Birger, grabbing her under the left arm, hoisted her back to her feet. Her hands bled from dozens of minor cuts.

Despite an overwhelming desire to stop and rest, Birger shouted, "Go! Go! Go!"

The sun emerged lazily peeking out from the comfortable blanket of white clouds. Soon, the roads below would become flooded with traffic to disappear in. Unfortunately, that wasn't an option yet, and they still needed to find a way down without getting pin cushioned.

The burden of keeping Wynn safe weighed heavily on Birger. A harrowing image of them being captured and tortured flashed through his mind. Wynn's tear-stained eyes looking at him, asking why he let this happen to her. It took a force of will to push the image aside.

Think! Birger urged himself, and then he saw something that sparked an idea.

Accelerating to catch Wynn, Birger seized her by the arm at the next turn and shoved her into a narrow recess between two towering buildings. He signalled to be quiet.

Tucking into the space behind Wynn, Birger hung over a three-story drop that was only marginally wider than their shoulders. And he was acutely aware of her closeness.

The smell of sweat and cured leather mingled with a cherry sweet perfume. Wynn stole it from the market as part of her training a couple of weeks before. He had felt so proud of her at the time.

Focus! Birger chastised. He stole a glance at Wynn. Her face was red with exertion, she breathed heavily and tears glistened in her eyes. She was scared, but she hadn't let it slow her down. He gave her a nod of reassurance, mixed with approval.

They were in a precarious position, straddling the outer beams of the neighbouring floors that weren't quite adjoining. Luckily, the snow hadn't made the surface slippery yet.

Birger turned to look outwards, bracing his arms against the rough brickwork. He shifted his weight, testing the stability of his precarious perch to ensure he was mobile. Then he waited.

Bo, his red hair following him like a cloud, was the first to zip past. The next building was a distance away, and the tiles cracked as the big man kicked off.

The second mutt to arrive had to pause and wait for the other side to clear before he could have a go. It was a long jump, and he needed a run-up, so he stood only inches away from Birger's hiding spot.

The man carried a good deal of muscle, and his skin was the signature deep brown of a Korlander. They were a merchant empire bordering Sawra to the south, and quite a few lived in Anthir. The big man scanned the area as he waited, and Birger heard another crack of tiles followed by a grunt. Bo was across, and at that moment, the Korlander sniffed the air, his nose wrinkling like a dog that caught a scent.

The man's head snapped to Birger a split second before a push kick connected with the Korlander's chest. His fingers grasped impotently at Birger's heel, but too slow, and soon he was in free fall. The cries of pain made Birger sigh with relief. The drop hadn't killed the man, but it should be enough to keep the mutt from coming after them anytime soon.

Swayed back into a secure position, Birger half-turned to Wynn, and exclaimed, "Come!" as he slipped back onto the roof at speed.

Bo was out of sight, but his alarmed yelp said that he heard the scream.

At least, Birger figured, *not knowing where the threat lurked would slow him down.*

The low sun cast harsh shadows across the landscape of brick cliffs and tiled hills, which gave Birger another idea, and he started scanning the area. He caught the scent of tar from a recently repaired section. The varied height of the buildings combined nicely with a dormer's drip edge, creating just enough overhang and at just the right angle to hide someone.

Birger stopped and grabbed Wynn's arm. She snapped her head back at him with a questioning glare, then he shoved her into the shadow. Wynn's face said that she didn't enjoy being manhandled, but she didn't resist him.

With grim determination in his eyes, Birger said, "Use your cloak for cover and hide here."

"But what about you?"

"There's no space. But don't worry, they call me Light Foot for a reason." Birger winked. "Just this once, please, do what I ask." He sold it with his best puppy dog eyes.

Wynn's cheeks flushed, and she returned a hesitant nod. Birger gave her a reassuring smile, but the gesture was a lie. His legs trembled with the ice-cold fear flooding through his body. A cavernous pit formed at the centre of his stomach, and time was running out, but it didn't matter how scared Birger felt. Her fate was his responsibility.

The cloak, combined with the stark shadow, made for excellent cover, but Bo would still see her if he were paying attention.

This is my best bet, thought Birger. *I'll have to ensure Bo is too distracted to notice anything out of the ordinary.*

"No matter what you hear, stay hidden. I'll meet you at Benny's this afternoon," said Birger, then he turned to zip off without waiting for a response.

He paused at the ridge and looked back. Bo appeared two houses away. Birger waited until Bo saw him and then darted off at full speed. A renewed rush of adrenaline and the sharp bite of the icy wind helped him focus.

Fighting his anxiety with faux bravado was a trick Birger had learned from Sten. The man carried himself as if Aeg had his back.

But I guess in the end, she didn't, Birger lamented.

He shoved his doubts aside because he couldn't afford the distraction; then he darted over to the next building. He rounded the corner and skidded to a halt, his heart dropping as he realised he had reached a dead end.

31

5

DEAD END

Birger panted for breath, a white cloud pluming in the cold air around him. The snow collected in heaps wherever it could find space to settle. He stood on the red roof of a three-story building in the Merchants Ward, hemmed in by walls on two sides.

Birger thought the pockmarked brickwork in front of him looked an awful lot like a mocking smile.

To his left was a three-story drop, and at the bottom he had a choice between cobblestone and a lone hay-cart.

Birger weighed the chancy jump but lost his nerve and thought, *maybe I've got time to double back?*

He turned around and saw Bo standing behind him. The bulldog-faced man had scruffy red hair and a short beard that fanned out into a mane.

Bo held a short-sword in his hand. He was tall, had broad shoulders, and wore beaten-up black leather. A crudely carved wooden doll with a mess of straw hair poked out of his left hip pouch. The kind meant for little girls.

Birger felt terrified, but he tried to hide the trembling in his hand as he drew his rapier in ready defence. "Now come on, Bo, can't we talk about this?"

"Sure, we can. Lay down your pigsticker, and we can go have a casual chat about that time you booted me into the harbour." Bo's eyes blazed with menace.

Birger feigned surprise. "That? What makes you think that was me?"

"Ha! you take me for a fool, is that it, boy?"

"You, a fool? Never! But you are as dumb as a brick in a sock."

With his cheeks burning bright red, Bo lunged at Birger, who was ready, and responded with a riposte that nipped at Bo's flank. Steel flashing, their conversation became more aggressive.

There wasn't much room to manoeuvre on the narrow ledge, and although Birger was faster, his opponent was a head taller, stronger, and more experienced. Lunge, parry, and riposte. The two lashed out at one another in a vicious melody of clashing swords, caught in a stalemate.

As one thought his opponent was caught in a pattern and tried to exploit it, the other seemed ready with a counter. Soon, both fighters were lathered in sweat. Birger was tiring, and he felt like the bigger man was toying with him.

Then another concern presented itself. Birger heard tiles clacking under many feet, which meant that the Blood Queen's helpers were close.

His options for survival were evaporating under the early morning sun. Even if he somehow bested Bo, it would still leave him trapped. He glanced at the lonely hay-cart below. It was a long drop, but his choices were few.

Pain flared in the back of Birger's hand as cold steel bit into him. He sucked air with a hiss, and Bo showed his yellow teeth in a cruel smirk.

"Give up, Birger," Bo said, with the surety of a bully that knew he and his friends outnumbered their victim. "You have nowhere to run, and the others will be here in seconds. Face it, you lost."

Birger popped his eyebrows. "Look at you, using your words. I didn't know you could string this many sentences together. Sure, they're short and lack substance, but everyone has to start somewhere, right?"

Bo glowered at Birger from under his thick brow. "Jokes? Maybe you need help to realise the seriousness of your pred... prodi..."

"Are you trying to say 'predicament?'"

"Oh, sod off. Let me help you understand. If you surrender now, maybe we won't go visit that fat slimeball Benny you like so much."

The threat landed, and Birger felt anger and fear roil in his guts. Benny was more than just someone who liquidated his loot. The older man had been there for Birger, looked out for him and been a mentor, especially since Sten's death.

He knew Bo was just goading him, though. Going after Benny would be an outright declaration of war on the Magpies.

Regardless, anger took hold and Birger burst forward with lightning speed. Bo fell back, probably waiting for Birger to burn himself out in the flurry, and, Birger realised, it was working. Sweat stung Birger's eyes and his chest heaved for air. His legs, weak from all the running, he stumbled, dislodging a row of tiles, which slid out from under him.

Gullshite! thought Birger as he was ripped to the eaves, narrowly avoiding a counter attack from Bo, he was forced to dive away to avoid his throat being flayed open. Birger's new onyx bracelet dug into his arm as it plucked him to the left.

When he jerked his head back to see how that happened, he was rewarded with a view of the hay-cart below. Guiding his momentum as best he could, Birger veered towards it.

Rolling in midair, the flight took a subjective eternity. The motion was disorientating, and it felt like his stomach was rolling in over itself. Desperately, he prayed to Aeg for help. *Please don't let there be any random hard objects like pitchforks hidden in the straw,* he added for good measure.

Birger's luck held, and he made his body limp as the soft, grassy bed connected with his back. The fall knocked the wind out of him in a full-body punch, and then the hay embraced him like a jagged, lice-filled blanket.

The cart creaked under the impact, and Birger rolled out of it, coughing. He briskly dusted himself off to get the worst straw out of his hair and jerkin. It itched! He checked to make sure he still had everything.

Birger shouted, "Next time, Bo!" with a cheeky wave as he headed west down Hir Boulevard.

Bo stared down at Birger in utter disbelief. He warily considered the jump before his nerve gave in and started looking for another way down.

Behind Bo, Birger saw the Blood Queen step into view, brandishing her wicked-looking daggers. Her red hair was speckled with snowflakes and crimson fire leaked from her eyes.

When Ulfhild stared at Birger, he froze in terror. All he wanted to do was surrender right there.

Noticing the scary woman, Bo's face went pale. Ulfhild looked like she was on the verge of stabbing him, but she put her evil weapons away, grinned, and snatched Bo's wooden doll. Her lips moved, but Birger couldn't hear, and then she hurled Bo towards the cart.

Bo bounced off the hay, shattered the vehicle, and rolled clumsily onto the cobbles. Coming to rest less than a hundred feet from where Birger stood.

Birger realised he was standing still. He shook his head to clear it and cursed at himself. *What are you doing? Go! Run!* It took every ounce of will he had to make his legs move, but they did, eventually.

Birger needed to get back to the Squat fast. When he reached Cylch Crescent, it was already bustling with traffic bound for the docks, so he slowed down to slip into the crowd. He unlaced his cloak, flipped it to the ragged brown side and retied it.

The sheet draped over his back was now a patchwork of crude needlework and false holes that made it look like it belonged to someone from the rough side of life.

Birger would've added a limp but it came for free. As did the coughing and wheezing, thanks to exhaustion and hay dust that clung to the back of his throat.

The search for Birger expanded quickly. City guards and mutt packs were everywhere by the time he reached Short Kent Street.

Guards!? wondered Birger, alarmed. *Why in Lot's name are guards searching for me?* He spiralled his heart with the sign of the goddess of death to ward against her anger. Another thing bothered him. He had never seen the Blood Queen pursue a thief herself. Oh, she often partook in the punishment but never the chase.

Birger took a shortcut through the guilds, which allowed him to reach Mysery Close with minimal exposure, and that brought him nearly home.

I hope Wynn gets back alright, he worried. *She's resourceful, and I taught her a lot about keeping a low profile over the last few months. Besides, I'm pretty sure they're looking for me. I can check in with Benny later. If she reaches him, he'll take care of her. If she doesn't...*

That's not worth thinking about.

Birger felt a sense of relief when his boot soles hit the Squat's pale dirt roads. It was Magpies' territory. Home ground. The Squat was what the thieves, beggars and paupers called their own piece of Anchorhall.

Most of the Squat was a collection of ramshackle lodgings, but the buildings were more substantial here where it merged with the Guilds district.

A blind, weather-beaten old beggar sat on a pile of rags in front of a tall building with a rounded timber roof. Its walls were covered in tan plaster that had burst to reveal grey brickwork underneath.

"Top of the morning to you, Hamish," said Birger.

He extracted a leather bag from his satchel and plopped it in the old man's open hand. It was a more significant cut than the Code dictated, but some of it was meant for Hamish.

Old Hamish gave him a toothless grin, and his face crumpled with happiness. "And tops to you, Birger. What be this then?"

"A little something to share with the people and spruce up that cave you call a home. Be careful, though. Mutts are on the prowl. You don't want to get caught with that. Would you mind getting the guild's cut to Noxolu for me?"

36

Hamish nodded. "Oh, Birger, what have you got yourself into this time?" His voice carried the weight of genuine concern.

"Nothing I can't handle. If anyone asks, you haven't seen me."

"I can't say I saw anyone," said the blind man.

Birger smirked and moved past his friend into an alcove of crates and garbage. It shielded the wall from the street. He pulled faux bricks back to reveal a small door barely big enough to crawl through. Birger fished a key out of a pouch and unlocked it to slip inside. Then he pulled the facade back into place and locked the door.

Inside, it looked like an abandoned warehouse. It was empty and spacious. Lit by the sun that shone through six dust-caked skylights. It smelled of mildew, but it was Birger's dust and mould, so he didn't mind.

Birger walked over to another door on the far side of the space. It led to the building's former office. He extracted a rusty old key from his belt pouch. There was a satisfying click as the key turned to unlock the sturdy door, and his shoulders sagged with relief.

He couldn't remember the last time he had felt so bone-tired. The cut on his hand throbbed.

Birger lit the lantern that hung just inside the entrance, revealing the small office interior. A feeling of security embraced him when the door was locked behind him, and he rested his back against it.

The room's only window was bricked up, and tables were set along the three walls. Two had burglars' equipment carefully laid out on them, and one was set up as a space for planning.

Birger slumped to the cold compacted floor, exhausted. He had never seen a response like this after a botched job. Thank Sten for leaving him with little gifts like this hideout. However, with this much heat on him, Birger might need to leave town.

I'll get some sleep, thought Birger. *For Wynn's sake, I can't stay here too long. Just until the afternoon. Hopefully, the search would've died down by then. Aeg guide Wynn home safely.*

Birger allowed himself to relax. He felt something break inside, and fatigue flooded in. The need to fight was gone, and he was utterly exhausted. Before the blackness overwhelmed him, he thought, *I have to get to Benny soon.*

6

BARRELS

Packs of roving mutts and their pet soldiers were still turning Anthir upside down. On every street corner, a poster illustrated with Birger's face was plastered on the wall. Seeing the bounty placed on his head, stopped Birger in his tracks. A year's wages for the average fisher.

Damn, thought Birger, *I wonder if I could scam them into giving me that reward?*

But he decided against it. Cons weren't his thing. He was a terrible liar. Too many things to keep track of, or the whole thing would come unravelled.

What did I steal to justify that? wondered Birger. *I would worry about my own people claiming it, but the Magpies Code wouldn't allow it. Maybe Benny knows?*

Birger was shuffling along with his tattered cloak draped over his shoulders and his face hidden deep in its hood. A biting, chilly wind rustled Birger's dark hair as it hurried the weak autumn sun over the horizon. The snow had stopped somewhere during the morning, and the noon sun must have done away with the evidence.

Birger had been so worn out from the previous night's events that he slept through the whole day, only sourly waking up a couple of hours ago. Since then, he had focused on crafting a disguise, a gratifying part of his job that he would usually take a lot of time to plan. He had been considering this disguise for some time, and part of him yipped in excitement to try it out.

For the smell, Birger wrapped a rotting fish in linen and loaded it into a special fold in his cloak. Next, to sell the look, he wrapped linen bandages around his face and hands, which he covered in reddish mud that dried to look like seeping wounds. Finally, he checked his mirror to ensure it said leper, which it did.

It was the perfect disguise for keeping guards from looking too closely, but it came at a cost. Playing the role of beggar slowed the journey to Benny's shop in the Guild District considerably. He frequently begged people he passed, spending extra attention on the rich-looking ones because he could count on their revulsion.

There was also the limp, but that wasn't entirely put on. He must've injured his right knee when he fell into the hay-cart. The injury wasn't bad. He had worse in the past; running and jumping roof to roof wasn't exactly safe, but the damage was annoying and would make him less nimble.

Birger entered Lot Road and saw two guards wearing the green and burgundy of Anthir marching towards him. They were both young, and there was a hopefulness in their eyes that Birger never saw in veterans. More evidence that they were recent recruits was in how they tried to stay in lockstep with a rough-looking, red-haired woman in the black armour of the mutts. It looked ridiculous.

Birger faked a stumble so he could turn away from them. He rested his shoulder against the wall of the simple clothing store on the corner of Dead End. Looking back down the street, the temple of Lot towered over the semi-squalor of the market that bordered the Squat. The temple was a gorgeous marble edifice with a vaulted roof.

Several locals in the street went about their daily business, trying very hard not to look in the patrol's direction, except for one. A barefoot boy whistled as he made his way down Lot Road. He wore torn yellow clothes and carried a small wooden box filled with bread. Lot's temple seal was stamped on the side of the crate.

Her clergy did much to support the poor in the Squat, which was why Birger rated Lot almost as highly as Aeg. In his line of work, Aeg's luck seemed a higher priority than Lot's blessings in death. But should it fail him one day, which inevitably it would, he ensured he remained in good standing with the Great Winter Wolf.

Every goddess had a domain, but each also had an avatar representing their nature. Lot was the Great Winter Wolf, symbolising the harsh reality in the circle of life and death. And of the avatars, Lot's was the most cuddly, which tells you something about the religion known as the Cult of the Weave.

Aeg was the Great Dragon of the Ocean and Air. Sailors favoured her for obvious reasons, but so did thieves. There was something inherently appealing about having a goddess that could bless you with unthinkable treasure – or roast you in their fiery breath at a whim. At least, for people that liked to live on the edge.

Jor was the flying serpent, and no, that isn't just another way of saying dragon. She was actually a snake with feathered wings that commanded land-shaping power. Jor and Lot worked together to maintain the wilderness, or at least, so the theologians of the cult say.

Then there was Mag, whose avatar was an enormous spider that built its nest in the realm of magic, otherwise known as the Weave.

Wizards weren't at all common, and Birger had never even met one, maybe because they were feared.

They weren't like priests who could practice magic safely. Wizards were known for causing weavestorms, so most towns didn't really want them around. However, every city still had a temple for Mag, and rich people would go there to study. Which meant Birger had never been in her temple.

Finally, Cos, the All-mother, only appeared as a woman of alien beauty.

The boy stopped next to Birger and asked with genuine concern, "Are you alright, sir?"

Oh no, a good person, thought Birger.

He nodded and grumbled, hoping to fend him off. Good people were unpredictable. Sometimes they did entirely irrational things, like trying to help you even if you didn't ask for it. This one's interference could lead to Birger getting exposed.

"Here," the kid handed Birger some bread with a kind smile. "You look very sick. Have you visited the temple today? The healers have an extra bed ready for you."

Birger stole a glance at the approaching threat.

Oh, Cos, no. They're coming straight for me. I don't want to take the kid's food, but if I don't, they'll never believe I'm a beggar.

Birger reluctantly accepted the offer and bowed his head in thanks.

"Lot's healing upon you, sir," said the youngster cheerfully.

Birger sensed the patrol approaching. *They didn't buy it,* he thought.

He relaxed his body, preparing to roll out of a grasping hand and run for his life. He hoped his busted leg wouldn't slow him down too much.

The hand came, sheathed in a brown leather glove, and caught the boy by the arm before plucking him into the road. The box went flying. It shattered on the cobbles, and the food spilt out.

A brown mongrel dog zoomed past to snatch a loaf of bread, and several gulls swooped in to claim the rest. At the clatter, storefronts abruptly slammed shut, and the people on the street vanished into side alleys.

That's what you get for being a good person, thought Birger.

The odd trio loomed over the boy with the mutt taking the lead, and up close, the woman had the leathery red skin of a heavy drinker. She held up an illustrated parchment next to the boy's face, where the other two guards restrained him.

"Looks like him. To the wagon." Her voice croaked as if she smoked too much pipe-weed.

"What, no, sorry, I didn't d..." with a cracking backhand, the woman cut the boy's protest short.

The guard said, "That'll be enough outta you."

"He looks nothing like the picture to me," said the other guard sceptically. "This kid doesn't even have dark hair."

"Close enough," the mutt replied. "Let Ulfhild decide what to do with him."

Blood ran down the boy's cheek from a cut on his eyebrow, and a tear followed behind.

Curse them, thought Birger. *She thinks this kid is me.*

Birger saw his mother's disappointed eyes staring at him from beyond the grave, and he had to catch himself to avoid speaking out.

If I confessed, they would take us both, but I can't let this kid take the fall. He tried to help me, for Cos's sake. The Code says I should help if I'm able. Yes. Sure, but am I able? Doing the right thing is so damned troublesome sometimes, thought Birger.

The two guards half-dragged the boy along. The kid made another attempt to explain, but the smack of a spear shaft to the head ended it, and the youngster sobbed as his will to resist broke.

Screw it, thought Birger. *There must be a way.*

He surveyed the street for ideas and saw that the next store down was a barrel maker. Six were on display, heaped in two rows on a table. A wedge kept them secure.

Timing is going to be critical, he thought, and hurried. His knee ached, but he pushed the pain aside.

He noted that they weren't looking at him. *Good,* thought Birger. He was counting on that.

When he was in position, Birger slurred, "Shirsh."

The barrel maker's store was now near his left.

"Shhowee, good guardshfolk." They slowed to turn, annoyance clear to see, but he pushed on, "Are yoush paying a reward for shish un?"

Birger was a terrible liar, but he had lots of practice looking drunk and didn't plan on keeping up the con for long. He continued stumbling forward and sped up a little.

The guard ordered, "Get back, wretch!"

"But, I did catch'd your fhief! Ack!" Birger belched, pointing a bandaged finger in the man's face and then stumbled into the left-most guard.

The soldier barked, "Get off!"

Stars burst in front of Birger's eyes, and his ears rang with the high note of a head injury. There was a moment of disorientation where Birger forgot what he was doing, and the entire world blurred.

His senses came rushing back as he splayed on the frosty cobbles like a starfish and his sore leg smashed into the table holding the barrels. The stopper shot out, letting the payload roll free. They jounced once or twice before barreling into the guards.

Luck! Birger celebrated, but the boy wasn't moving. *Good people have no survival instinct. Cos damn him,* thought Birger. *What do I have to do, carry him?*

Birger willed his legs to move. His right knee throbbed even more and his head joined in. Thanks to the disorientation of the head injury, he wouldn't need to fake the stumbling this time. Instead, he would have to keep himself on his feet long enough to stumble at the right time.

The two guards and the mutt were wrestling with the barrels, and Birger timed his approach as best he could.

"I'm shhowee," he slurred as he bumped and bumbled, hitting the woman bodily.

Thank Aeg, it was at the right angle. She knocked into the other two, sending the trio to the floor again in an awkward spill.

Birger whirled around to the boy. "Run!" in a harsh whisper.

"Huh," the boy looked at him, dumbfounded.

Birger steadied himself and kicked a barrel, sending it crashing into the three, and again, he said, "Run, you idiot!"

The boy finally got it and bolted.

The woman shrieked, "Stop!" She recovered and started after him, but Birger put himself in her way. She shouted, "Pathetic drunk scum!" and hammered a fist into Birger's cheek, which knocked him to the ground.

She packed a huge punch, and Birger's head rang again. What happened next was hazy, like experiencing it through a dream. It was the effect of being hit in the head multiple times, but he appreciated the carefree moment that came with it.

Birger heard one of the guards say, "He's gone. This mollusc needs to be taught a lesson."

Then stars flashed, and pain flared as blows rained down on him. The impact of a kick to his ribs forced the air from his lungs, and he crawled into a ball to cover his head with his arms.

"By Cos, he stinks!" said the other guard. "I'm going to be sick."

Points for the rotten fish.

More pain exploded in Birger's back. "Wretch!" it sounded like the woman, but Birger couldn't be sure. The pain and buzzing of his senses were too overwhelming.

By Aeg's luck, they left him without killing him. Birger lay there for a while as his mind struggled to break through the din of aches.

He checked himself for damage and found blood flowing freely from his nose and a cut on the side of his head. He thought nothing was broken, but he wasn't sure.

That's what you get for helping, thought Birger. *At least the kid got away.*

He picked himself up, nearly tripping as his right knee refused to cooperate. It still had some mobility, but it was painful, and he could feel the bones moving each time he lifted it. *That's not good.*

Long Kent Street was a busy road with all the workers from beyond the East Gate pouring back into the city while the dock workers flowed home. Anthir's population was primarily Sawran, with light eyes, fair skin, and reddish hair. However, many Korlanders and even a few dwan or quintri traded their wares in the city.

A grumpy-looking dwan, sporting a long red beard and wearing miner's overalls, waved his tree-trunk-like arms in the air. His ivory skin, marbled with pink, flared to red as he exchanged heated words with two guards, who were accosting a young boy.

The dwan seemed to take issue with them, snatching up whomever they wanted. Despite being two heads shorter than the guards, the dwan still somehow loomed over them. While Birger shared the dwan's sentiment, he didn't stick around to see who won.

He was fresh out of fight for today, but then Birger scoffed at himself. *What are you thinking? That wasn't a fight; it was a beating.*

Up the road near the docks, Birger saw the haggard-looking red-haired woman and her two pet guards. They join a large group of soldiers, walking alongside a cart hauling a steel cage. Inside sat twelve young boys, all from the Squat. In the distance, another cart, filled with even more boys, rolled past the intersection of Long Kent and Ferdinand Street.

Birger had saved one, and the dwan might save another if he didn't get himself arrested or killed, but there was nothing Birger could do for these.

It was hopeless, and guilt gnawed at Birger's gut. Those kids were going to suffer for his crime, and there was nothing he could do about it.

I've lost too much time, thought Birger. *I need to move.*

7

THE FENCE

Birger's heart raced as the pair in burgundy and green guarding the front door snapped their heads around to look at a loud noise coming from inside. The large window had a black frame and the words 'Benny's Precious Bits and Pieces' were spelt out in gold leaf across the glass.

Dusk was settling, and Birger couldn't see what was happening inside. He sat on the corner of Pont Avenue and Kent Street while he considered his options.

To sell his beggar disguise, Birger jingled a copper coin in a bowl and placed it between his feet. He surveyed the scene from the privacy of his cowl. The two guards eyed the pedestrians, scowling at each as if they might be revealed as a witch in disguise at any moment.

Benny's shop was classy enough to suit this part of town, but not so classy as to draw too much attention. Next to the door, a hip-high dark wood board invited visitors into the store in big chalk letters with too many flourishes. A steep moss-green roof capped the grey brick walls, and its chimney leaked plumes of black smoke.

Despite the light fading, the area bustled with activity as the guilds finished their business for the day. Down the road, an assortment of homemakers visited the fountain to collect water for their evening cooking, bathing, and cleaning.

Sombre expressions on the people's faces showed that the sinister activity in the streets wasn't lost on them. They noticeably circled the patrols and hid their children from the guards.

Birger rubbed at his temples to ease a building headache. At least it distracted him from the pain in his knee, but this wasn't the time to feel sorry for himself.

He eyed the guards outside Benny's shop wearily and wondered, *Should I take the initiative?* Bo's threat lingered in the back of his mind. *If Benny is in trouble, I might not have time to act.*

A myriad of horrible possibilities played out in Birger's head, and he found the experience unbearable. Worry was worse than fear. You could be brave against fear. Stepping up to face a dangerous situation

45

allowed you to feel in control, even when you weren't. Bravado was Birger's default.

A hinge whined, and a bell tinkled. The shop door opened, and Bo was fuming as he limped out. The bulldog-faced man roared with a spray of spittle. He snatched up the wood sign and hurled it through the window. Jagged glass shards rained down with a clatter.

Birger jerked in surprise. Anxiety clutched his heart when he saw Bo's face and hands were a gruesome red mess. Birger barely stopped himself from leaping to his feet, but luckily, the noise had drawn all eyes away from him.

Was that blood? he wondered.

Bo stomped down the street. The two guards in burgundy and green followed in his wake. A string of curses from Bo fluttered over their heads like a flock of seagulls screeching for food. If Birger wasn't so concerned about Benny, he would've taken pleasure in the thug's frustration.

When the trio turned the corner, Birger made sure it was safe before he approached the storefront, and he could hear his heart pounding in fear of what he might find. With a great deal of heaviness, he pushed open the door to Benny's Precious Bits And Pieces.

Near the back of the room, there was a bright red spray that painted the beige wall and wooden countertop at the cashier. The fluid still dripped to a puddle on the floor with a steady tap, tap, tap. He found no dead body, only a broken cash register.

Ah, a red dye trap, smirked Birger.

Broken furniture littered the floor, and the sign that previously invited patrons inside, now lay on a bed of shattered glass. A torn painting with a broken frame hung skew on the wall, and after a moment, the red satin curtain at the back of the shop moved aside.

Curious dark eyes fixed Birger in a crossbow sight. Then the curtain flung open, and out poured Benny's round body. He looked almost comical in his overstuffed white shirt and high-waisted black pants.

"Birger, is that you?" Benny asked.

"Well, it isn't the Duke," Birger said, while unwrapping a layer of grimy bandages from his face.

A squat man, Benny was a little shorter than Birger but three times as wide. His jowls jiggled as he spoke, and flop sweat plastered his short black hair to his head. He always wore suspenders to keep his pants up, and no one had ever seen the man in any colour other than black or white. At least, no one would talk about it if they had.

Benny was a kind soul, one of the best, and well-loved in the Squat. Before Noxolu came around, Benny was the Magpies Guild leader.

Some wished he would do it again, but Benny always said he had his run, and Noxolu was better suited for the job. Despite Noxolu being among those urging him to take over.

"You smell like death, boy," Benny said, putting the crossbow on an unbroken table. "Throw that rotting fish outside and come back here. Cos-damned good disguise. If I weren't expecting you, I would never have guessed."

Being called boy didn't sit well, but Birger knew there was no malice behind the words, and he let it go. He grabbed the smelly carcass by the tail fin to avoiding touching the gore-soaked wrappings and flung it through the broken window.

Birger pushed the satin curtains aside to follow, being careful not to get his mess on them. Benny got this bolt of satin from a Korlander who stopped in Anthir after visiting the distant kingdom of Warjah. It wasn't made in Warjah. They were only an intermediary for the even more distant Jing Empire, which controlled the silk trade.

Benny's backroom was set up for carpentry and furniture restoration. A sturdy workbench held a deconstructed rocking chair at the centre of the room. The walls were lined with carpentry tools, and several barrels of linseed oil were parked in the far-left corner. A black iron lantern sat on the workbench, and another hung from a hook next to the back door.

Pointing at Birger's limp, Benny asked, "You hurt or just really committed to the act?"

Birger grinned. "Little of both."

Now safely hidden from the street, Birger got to work undoing the rest of his bandages. Benny brushed his thin hair over his bald spot before snapping up a large wooden bowl. He plodded off, disappearing through a second door that led deeper into the building.

Birger noted the furrowed brow and thoughtful silence, which told him Benny had something to say. But Birger figured it would come out in time, so he focused on cleaning away the disguise. It had to go for two reasons: first, the beggar look would be out of place after dark, and second, he needed to clean his wounds before he caught a fever.

In short order, Benny returned with a bowl of swirling fresh water and plopped it in a clear spot on the workbench. He tossed a linen bag filled with beans across the table. Birger caught it and found the beanbag ice cold to the touch.

With a look of concern, Benny said, "That'll help with the swelling. You'll need to be mobile tonight." He kept watching until Birger applied the cold to his injured knee.

Then Benny started decluttering the workbench, moving the chair frame and tools onto the floor. Finally, he lay down a brown towel and stood back, watching Birger intently. Conscious of the look, Birger cleaned the mud from his face with the water.

He saw Benny's jaw tense and his mouth open. *Here it comes,* he thought, bracing for a tongue lashing.

"Heard you had a run-in with some mutts," Benny said. "They're looking for you, you know."

There was a hint of anger in his voice, and Birger remained silent. Benny puffed out his chubby cheeks and parsed his lips into a pout.

After a moment, Benny added, "Get clean, then we'll talk." Birger could see Benny was upset and processing how to best approach the conversation.

In their business, keeping your mouth shut when you didn't like what a teammate did was an excellent way to get killed. Starting a fight every time you didn't like something would get you killed faster. Dealing with conflicting views was a delicate balance. Birger would expect nothing less than for Benny to take his time finding the right angle of approach. But that didn't make the anticipation any easier to bear.

"Thanks, Benny." Birger smiled and pressed on, "I saw Bo leaving."

"You did, did you?" Benny raised a big, bushy eyebrow. "By Cos, you look like you went ten rounds with a bruiser. I had Wynn pay me a visit too, and thank Aeg, she left not two hours ago. Before that knuckle head and his pet hounds showed up."

"Wynn made it back?!" Birger knocked the bowl, sloshing water over the edge, and nearly tipping it over. His own strong reaction surprised him. After all, he knew she would come to Benny, since he told her to. "Is she well?"

"I can't believe you would be such a fool taking that girl to burgle Foss."

"You don't have to tell me off, for Cos's sake," Birger looked down and resumed washing his hands with more zeal, imagining it might wash away his guilt. "I wasn't expecting this kind of response, alright. I know you said it was risky, and she wasn't quite ready, but I figured I could get her out of any jam. How could I know the bloody Queen of mutts would show up so soon? And I *did* get her out of that jam."

"Bluster doesn't keep your friends safe, boy–I sent Wynn home to clean up and lie low for a while. She'll come back when the buzz around the city dies down. She wasn't hurt, aside from her pride at being stashed like some ill-gotten gains."

"Yeah, lying low would be the best thing to do right now."

"Birger..." Benny stopped as if searching for the words. "I'm worried about you, son."

"I'm alright, Benny."

"No, no, you aren't," Benny walked over and put his hand on Birger's shoulder. "You've been getting worse."

"I'm not in the mood for this talk again, Benny." Birger resumed cleaning the wounds on his face.

"You're never in the mood, and it needs to be said. Since Sten died, you've been getting more and more reckless, taking bigger risks with each job."

"I–"

"No. Keep your mouth shut and listen to me. What happened to Sten was tough on all of us, but it wasn't your fault, and getting yourself killed won't bring him back."

Birger looked up at Benny, and his eyes became blurry. There was an ache in his chest that had nothing to do with getting kicked, and his nose started running. He wasn't about to cry; it was just the mud. Some must've gotten in his eye.

Benny smiled gently and said, "You need to slow down, son. Loss takes time to heal. You need to give it that, or it will fester like any wound."

"This isn't about Sten." Birger shook his head, and lied, "That's all behind me, Benny. I don't even think about it anymore."

"Blocking out the pain and giving it time to heal isn't the same thing, Birger. All you've done is distract yourself to stop thinking about it, and now look at you. How long before it gets you killed?"

Neither of them responded for a while. Birger nodded and Benny backed off. He couldn't argue with that. It was his way of dealing with things, and Birger knew it full well. He didn't like to sit still and let things boil in his belly. The truth was, Birger couldn't let himself think about what happened to Sten.

"When Sten vanished, I thought it was because he was upset with me," confessed Birger. "I botched that Golden Tree Hill job pretty bad, and the last time I saw him, we had a big falling out about it."

"It wasn't you, son. And about that." Benny sighed and adjusted his belt.

Birger stopped cleaning his hands and looked up at Benny. "You found something on Sten's death, didn't you?"

"I discovered who had him while he was gone, and you aren't gonna like it."

8

NEXT STEPS

The night had turned dark outside, yet Benny's workshop was well lit, casting shadows on the walls lined with tools and carpentry materials. The small room felt crowded with Benny and Birger stuffed in amongst the large table, oil barrels and the half-built rocking chair. The scent of sawdust hung in the air, and Birger could tell Benny had been hard at work during the day.

Birger removed the last of his bandages and stopped washing mud off his face. A simple linen bag of ice-cold beans lay limp next to the water bowl. Anticipation made Birger's skin tingle as he waited for Benny's answer. He had been looking for information about Sten's death for months, with no success.

"Who was it?" asked Birger and held his breath.

Benny adjusted the collar of his white shirt and unbuttoned it to make room for his second chin. His hands were large and calloused from years of hard work.

Birger's own hands were slender, but equally calloused. Climbing walls, as he regularly did, wasn't easy.

There was pain in Benny's voice when he said, "That slug Bo – who just visited me – had him."

Birger closed his eyes and sighed. "I could've killed him on the roof this morning. If I had known..."

Benny grimaced. "That's no way to think. Revenge won't heal the wounds, son."

"No, but it would make me feel a lot better," Birger admitted, feeling chilled by his own words.

Could he murder someone, even if they had taken away his friend...his mentor? Bitter anger was burning in his heart, and a big part of him wanted nothing more than to be washing Bo's blood from his hands.

"How sure are you?" Birger asked.

"Trusted source, and I confirmed it when he was just here. He came to hurt me, but I used it to get in his head, and it landed. Gave me enough time to pull the crossbow on him," Benny smiled with no humour and said, "I don't know if he did the deed himself, but he was there. I'm sure of it."

Birger snatched the beanbag off the table and smacked it hard on the countertop. His anger flared bright red in his cheeks.

Birger sneered. "We should kill that scum. He deserves worse."

Benny raised his eyebrow. "With all this heat? You would be lucky if you stayed out of a castle dungeon while walking down the street."

He's right, Birger thought, *it's better to be smart and live to fight another day than fight without thinking and lose.*

"Gullshite!" Birger cursed, hurling the bag of beans against the far wall with a dull thud.

His anger faded in the face of the current reality.

"You're right. I might even have to be leaving town until this passes." Birger pushed the anger down and focused on the issue at hand. "Where is all this coming from? What did I steal? They're acting like it's the Duke's favourite moustache comb or something."

"I don't know exactly, but it's something important. The Shade didn't specify what it was, but he did tell me that the mutts and the Duke are in cahoots," Benny eyed Birger with concern before shaking his head. "As evidenced by the response, that part seems true enough."

"Cahoots? What did the Duke and the mutts have in common, other than both being scoundrels?"

"I don't know. Did you bring the stuff with you? I'm curious to discover the answer myself."

"Benny, we've made some good coin from the Shade in the past, but this one..." Birger sighed. "I'm not sure how to put this, but do you think we were set up?"

Benny considered the question for a long moment, then said, "The Shade is a friend, and he would never violate the Code."

Sceptically, Birger asked, "But how can you be sure? I trust in the Code as much as any Magpie, but people are still people."

With steadfast certainty Benny said, "I know the Shade; he wouldn't go against the Code if it killed him. Trust me on that. The Shade is a good one. Come, let's figure this out together."

Birger nodded pensively. He cleaned himself off, dried his hands, and then opened his satchel to retrieve the remaining jewel pouches and the four scrolls. Benny cleared space on the bench. He retrieved a copper-rimmed pince-nez from his pocket and placed it to his right eye before he upended the bags on the table.

The contents spilt across the wood surface, and an enormous emerald rolled off the table's edge. Birger snatched it out of the air with lightning-fast reflexes and placed it back on the bench. The sudden movement made the scab on his hand bleed, but he ignored it.

"Thanks." Benny inspected the lot. "A small fortune, but not enough to pay for all the feet stomping cobbles out there." Benny shifted the coins and precious stones to the side and unrolled each of the four scrolls. "My guess is that the Shade hoped for us to take these. That's Ulfhild's signet on the seal."

Birger pulled the lantern closer to the scrolls and he leaned in.

"I had a look already." Birger pointed at one document. "This one has orders to nick a sword in West Haven wearing Anthir's colours. The mark's name is Sir Kallen du la Rent and they say to kill him if needed. But the others look like they were written by a mad crab with a gull feather."

"Encoded." Benny picked at his nose as he considered the scrolls. "Du la Rent. The mutts sure are brazen if they go after a knight with that family name."

"Isn't that a royal name?"

"Yes, it's the Rendinian royal family name. Having that name means you're a direct descendant or close relative of the founding king and queen. What sane Duke would want to be linked with something like this? If Anthir was implicated in an attack on the West Rendinian royal family. It would mean war."

"Do you think our dear Duke aspires to be crowned the new king of the west?"

"If he did, killing a knight would be an odd play," Benny puckered his lips and shook his head. "No, I don't think your dad's interested in that."

A pang of rejection, old hurt, and hate shot through Birger, but he swiftly pushed the feelings away, a skill honed from years of practice.

Benny continued, "Something else is happening here. The Duke has no familial claims to the throne, and killing a knight, even one in line for it, wouldn't do him any good. Also, the order seems to suggest the actual target is the sword. Killing is if needed. It seems more like misdirection. If it were me, I would take the sword south or east after stealing it, knowing the people looking for me would be headed west to war with Anthir."

"Would the risk of these orders being sent to the Rendinians be enough to get the Duke to send every guard in town to the streets?"

"I don't know. Maybe the Duke wanted it all to look like a bad frame job he could blame on the East?" Benny looked up as he turned the thoughts over in his mind.

"What about this crab scratch?" Birger's curiosity chafed at him. "It must hold something even more important. Why else would the messages be encrypted?"

"You may be right. But these are beyond me to crack, and we don't have time. Bo might come back here with more to search for you." Benny's contemplation shifted into purpose, and he asked, "You said you might have to leave town earlier. What were you planning?"

Birger tilted his head and formed a half-smile. "You have something in mind?"

"I do. West Haven. I think it's time you met the Shade in person. He can help you decrypt these messages. It'll be tough to reach him." Benny scratched his round chin, then continued, "You can start with Renate Couture. She is usually at the Barrel Side Inn along Fishmonger's Corner. Show her your Dagger and Bird."

Benny tapped his left shoulder, showing the location of his tattoo, the one every initiated Magpie on the continent bore. If you broke the Code and got expelled, it got burned off first. That meant having one intact indicated you were a thief in good standing with the guild.

"Tell her Benny of Anthir said she should take you to the Shade. When you meet him, tell him everything you know, show him all four scrolls, and let him figure out what to do next."

Shocked, Birger asked, "West Haven! You want me to take this to the Rendinians?"

"Don't worry about that. You can trust the Shade with your life. Besides, he can crack this. The man has tons of influence on the continent, and he'll know what to do with these documents to stop a war from coming to Anthir."

"Right, but what about Wynn? I can't leave her to whimper in the wind back here?"

"She would be home. Why don't you stop by and see if she wants to go with you," Benny rubbed at his hair, then said, "Mind, they were looking for two boys, not a girl. I don't think they're after her. Regardless, I have a ship setting off to Welden at midnight. You *must* be on it."

Birger gathered the treasure and the scrolls, returning them to his satchel. Benny grabbed a piece of paper, a feather pen, and a pot of ink from under the worktable. He dipped the pen into the inkpot and started scribbling away.

"Benny. What actually happened with that block-faced dolt out there before he left?" Birger asked, pointing towards the front of the shop.

"The moron came in here shouting, making threats, and smashing up the place. I told him I knew nothing and warned him to be careful."

A humorous smile carved a valley in Benny's face as he said, "The simpleton took a swing at the cash register. You know I like to keep a harmless red dye trap there."

Benny fought down his laughter. "Well, he set it off, so his face will be bright red for weeks! Turned pretty dark after that, though. When he pulled his sword and tried to kill me, I used head games to buy time. That was when I asked him about Sten. He reeled like I had clapped him on the cheek. That allowed me to grab the crossbow I keep under the counter. Never let a predator see weakness, Birger, never."

Birger and Benny exchanged grim smiles.

"Here," Benny said, handing Birger the finished note. "That'll get you on the ship. It's the Airy Bell. Captain Frida will keep you safe until you reach West Rendinian soil. Now, go see Wynn."

9

WITH LOVE

There were guards everywhere, but Birger's dark brown leathers and grey cloak allowed him to glide through the dusty evening gloom safely.

Wynn lived in a tiny hovel in the Squat opposite the Rusty Tankard, which was the centre of all Magpies' business in the city and their primary source of recreation. The familiar, shoddy, old tavern, with its tan roof and oft-replaced windows, was precious to Birger. Part of him wished he could go in and greet everyone, but he couldn't afford it. He was on a schedule.

The soup kitchen at the back of the building fed many hungry beggars every night. It was a great place for thieves to collect intel on future marks by simply milling around that crowd. The beggars saw everything that happened in the city, and no one saw them in return.

Noxolu was standing at the open tavern door. The dark-skinned Korland innkeeper was the local Magpies Guild Leader.

There was a red and white striped bandana tied over her shaved head, a thick gold chain around her neck, and a white shirt that plumed from under her leather jerkin. She wore red trousers, held up by a big-buckled belt, and her leather boots were decorated with half a dozen straps running up to her knee. A golden scabbard dangled from her hip, holding a rapier ready to draw.

She stood deadly still, looking at someone Birger couldn't see. Something about that stillness made her look like a snake coiled to strike.

With no telegraphing, her hand lashed out. A barrel-chested man with greying hair staggered into view. Noxolu spun into the blow. She caught the man by the scruff of his neck and, almost effortlessly, propelled him out of the doorway.

The man landed heavily in a mud puddle, which definitely wasn't water. Rain wouldn't pool in one spot, leaving the rest of the soil dry, and Birger could smell the tang of urine in the air.

Noxolu shouted, "And stay out!"

The man scrambled to his feet, cursing and swearing under his breath. Birger stepped into a shadow to avoid him as he stomped by. Noxolu remained at the door to watch the man clear out.

A girl around Birger's age appeared from behind the building, pressing through the mill of people waiting in line for food. Her long, mouse-brown hair fluttered briefly in the wind, and she wore a red-brown dress with a bodice and a white frilly elbow-length shirt. It was Neffily, Wynn's friend, and she carried a large clay jar that bent her back with its weight.

Noxolu made space for her to enter the tavern and shut the door behind her as they returned to the evening's business.

Birger smiled and thought, *I wonder what the man did to get his butt kicked like that? Getting on Noxolu's bad side was unhealthy. She was the Guild Leader for a reason.*

Instinct made Birger duck and prepare to run for shelter as a flash of purple and teal light arched through the northern sky. The brightness dimmed a moment later into a steadily pulsing cloud that swirled and lashed out at random.

Thank the goddesses the weavestorm was out to sea, thought Birger, and relaxed his stance.

Masses of seawater and billowy clouds flowed into the colossal mess of colour. Freezing cold radiated off it–as if Anthir needed help in that department.

The city was cold year-round; winter or summer was marked by deep snow or sloshing rain. Autumn and spring were the best, since they mostly had neither. A weavestorm was as deadly as it was beautiful, and they were the reason docked ships in the harbour were chained down on all sides.

The richest of the city had large underground shelters attached to their homes. But in the Squat, your only choices were reaching the Rusty Tankard's underground shelter or running to a temple. The goddesses protected the sanctuaries from the weavestorms, which was probably why the temple of Cos was in Ferdinand Keep.

How long the storms lingered varied, and they didn't move often. So, once it had done its initial damage, one could usually avoid it.

Every year, hundreds of people got caught in the awful pull of the weavestorm. If this one was any closer, Birger's plan to escape via ship would've been done for.

He looked away from the deadly show and back to the Rusty Tankard. A cold pint to take the edge off called Birger from within the cosy tavern, but he ignored it.

On the clock, Birger reminded himself.

58

Wynn's place looked like most others in the Squat, crude construction with a thatch roof. Like the walls, the door was made of plain beech wood. These homes could hardly qualify as shelter, especially given Anthir's extreme winters. People did what they could to keep the wind out, stuffing the gaps with straw-reinforced mud, but every year many froze to death in their beds.

Birger knocked on the door.

"Who's there?" asked Wynn.

She sounded cautious.

Birger said, "Just a thief in the night."

The door swung open, and Wynn yanked him in.

"Hey," Birger complained, "what was that?"

Wynn's hovel was as simple inside as outside. There were two straw bunches in the corner for sleeping. A broken chair lay on the floor, and a mouldy piece of bread sat in a bowl on a small table.

She was still wearing her leathers from the night before, but not her cloak. Her hair was mussed, and she looked like she had been crying. She put a rusty old dagger down on a footstool next to the door. It looked like it might break if she used it in an actual fight; however, it probably helped with her sense of security.

People want to feel in control, even if that control is an illusion.

Wynn glowered at Birger. "What am I doing?! What're you doing waltzing about not even wearing a disguise?"

Birger gave her a know-it-all expression and asked, "What do you mean?"

"Haven't you seen? They're looking for you. They know your name and have posters of your face stuck all over the city."

"Yeah. It's not my first day on the job, you know." Birger shook his head. "Disguises are for daytime. At night, your normal gear, the ones that blend into the dark, work just fine. A disguise would make you a target."

"Shut up with your constant speeches! You look like you've been kicked by a horse, and they're interrogating people. Heavy-handed like!" Wynn burst into tears and pushed Birger without genuine commitment, her reddish-brown hair falling over her face. "I was terrified for you."

Birger opened his mouth and then closed it again. He stepped forward, brushed her hair back, and hugged Wynn. His heart ached. Her leather armour felt coarse, and she smelled like fear, but her hair was soft.

I was scared for you too, thought Birger.

Wynn pushed out of the embrace, and Birger let her go, while keeping his hand on her elbow.

"What're you going to do?" she asked.

Tears brimmed and swelled until a single bead slipped down her cheek. She sniffed and wiped it clear.

"I can't stay in Anthir. If they know who I am, I have no choice. I'll have to go. Benny and I discussed it, and my best option is to go to West Haven. I found something that I need to show to someone there."

"But Anthir is your home?"

"Wynn, this is bigger than the Magpies and the Wolves. I don't know exactly what's happening, but Anthir's in major danger. Besides, I'll come back, and the Code says you must help if you are able, and I'm able."

Birger lowered his eyes, thinking about all those he had failed to help that day. Boys dragged away from their families, shoved in carts and enduring who knows what kind of treatment in the dungeon.

He looked back at Wynn. "Will you come with me?"

"I... I can't. I'm already having trouble with life in Anthir, nevermind a far off place like West Haven. Besides, Neffily. I can't leave her here. I owe her."

"Neffily has her work at the Rusty Tankard, and Noxolu will take care of her. She'll be fine. You aren't safe here, and I need you." Birger gently took Wynn's hand, and he felt a pang in his belly as the potent feelings building for her over the last few months came alive.

Wynn looked down at his hand. She touched the onyx bracelet on his wrist, picking at the etched symbols with her nail, and then looked up into his eyes.

"No, Birger, I can't go with you." She lifted herself onto her tip-toes and kissed him on the cheek. "I care for you, but I can't." She took her hand out of his and said, "I could never leave Neffily behind. You've done a lot for me, but she only has me, and I owe her."

Birger felt embarrassed.

After a long moment of standing quietly, he said, "If this thing turns out to be what I fear it might be, it could cause a war between the West and Sawra. I was young, but I still remember the civil war."

Images from his childhood, an urchin begging or stealing by the docks to survive, came flooding into his mind.

"I remember the soldiers coming home crippled," said Birger, "the families crying for the fallen, and the constant fear the city would come under siege. Anthir was an afterthought back then because the West had bigger fish to fry, but it would be different this time. The war won't be fought on the shores of Lake Water Heart or skirmishes at sea."

Birger cast his eyes towards the docks that lay somewhere beyond Wynn's front door.

He cleared his throat. "The West will come to our gates, our home, with all their force and no concern for the East attacking the other front. If I go, I can keep you, Neffily, Benny, old Hamish and even Noxolu safe." He put on a smile and jested, "You had better practice while I'm away, or I'll have to go all strict teacher on you when I get back."

With that, he turned and grasped the door handle.

Wynn whispered, "Birger…" and he paused.

He could see second thoughts in her eyes. *Maybe it would be safer for her here,* he thought. *Odds were that she made the right call.*

"Don't worry about it, Wynn. I'm Birger Light Foot. There isn't a guard in the land that can catch me, and I'll figure this mess out before it comes to Anthir," he smiled, looking back at her from the door. "You keep safe too, Wynn Feather Touched. I'll miss you."

"I'll miss you too." She looked at her feet. "Thank you for everything, Birger."

He nodded and opened the door to leave. His heart was tender with rejection, and he paused, hoping she would call him back. When it didn't come, he left.

Birger shut the door behind him and walked towards the docks. Wynn's response was nothing new. After all, he was just a fin, abandoned by a father that was too good for him. Birger's mum was the only one that really loved him, and she was long gone.

Street rats who took what wasn't theirs deserved no less. The nature of the world was that people stuck with you if there was something in it for them. That was what made the Magpies Code so important to him.

The Code was a safe place in a chaotic world, and many other Magpies believed in it the way he did. Not all, mind you, but they rarely lasted long, kicked out or running off to join the mutts. The Code gave him a place in the world. People he could rely on, if not trust, and it gave him a purpose.

Maybe that wasn't entirely fair. Benny has been there for me more than he needed to be under the Code. Who am I kidding? He's always given me more than I deserve, thought Birger, and smiled.

Birger placed his hand on his wrist, where Wynn had touched him, a wistful memory of her lingered.

The bracelet! He hadn't asked Benny about the bracelet.

The night was still young. He had time before the Airy Bell would make berth. The docks were on the other side of the guilds, and Birger could pop by on the way to ask Benny what he knew.

"Birger?" the high-pitched voice plucked him out of his thoughts like cold sea water splashing into his face.

He snapped his head around. There stood a three-foot-tall white-haired girl with transparent skin that glowed in the moonlight.

10

LOSS

Tension was thick in the air. The moon hung at half-mast, and the weavestorm illuminated the Squat with bright teal and purple light. There was a drift of pale dust, and Birger heard laughter coming from inside one of the nearby shacks.

His stomach rumbled at the delicious smell of cooking fish. It even overpowered the pungent musk of urine and vomit that lingered outside the Rusty Tankard. The typical noises of a bar room drowned out the chirping crickets. And the melodic tone of a lute suggested Noxolu had hired a bard for the night.

Initially, Birger thought he saw a child's ghost drifting through the Squat. Quintri weren't uncommon in Anthir, and this particular quintri had a veteran's hardness in her red eyes.

She wore a purple silk shirt with an open collar, ties running down the front. The shirt was tucked into green trousers, and she wore high-heeled boots with a wide cuff that ended halfway up her shin. Her lean muscles visibly wrapping over the bone under her transparent skin.

Birger had read that quintri originated from the Weave and were at least partially made of magic. He wasn't sure if that was true, but he could't help but wonder if this quintri was responsible for the weavestorm. Although he had never heard of a quintri working for the Duke or associating with the mutts, he eyed her suspiciously, ready to run.

"You're Birger, right?" asked the quintri again in a high-pitch.

"Yeah, that's me," he replied, panic rising in his chest and his hand landing on his rapier. "Who're you?"

"Did I catch you by surprise?" Her red eyes sparkled, and she lifted an eyebrow. "It's just your local quintri trader. The name is Captain Fridarium Pastuli Werareta Mumsinu Technochal Ruwal, but most people call me Captain Frida."

"I'm Birger Light Foot. So you're the Captain of the Airy Bell?"

How did she find me? Birger wondered.

"That's right," she said, nodding sharply. "Benny sent me to get you. We've gotta leave early. We heard they're preparing to block the harbour tonight."

There was a mechanical chirp. Frida pushed her sleeve back to reveal a device on her wrist. She clicked a gear over, and the chirping sound died down.

"We should get going. Seems like they're on schedule."

"Who is?" Birger checked his pocket watch. It was still around dinner time.

Frida regarded him with a sour expression and said, "The harbour-master. He just gave the order to prepare the chain. We have two hours, then no one will go anywhere."

"I have to stop at Benny's. I need to ask him something."

"Alright, it's on the way. Let's move."

She spun on her heels and stomped off towards the Guilds. Despite her determined stride, her short legs were no match for Birger's longer ones, and he easily kept pace with her.

They saw a commotion at Benny's when they reached Long Kent Street. Two dozen mutts stood guard outside the store in their black armour, and all the other businesses along the road were shut. Frida tapped Birger on the shoulder and led him into a nearby alley. All Birger could see inside the shop were shadows dancing on the walls.

"We should go in and help Benny," said Birger.

"Are you nutty? It's just us two against twenty of them. What's your plan? Tire them out by letting them beat us to death?"

Birger blushed and blurted, "I don't know! We could distract them, or maybe get them to chase us?"

Frida stared him down. Her skeptical eye was among the most formidable Birger had ever encountered.

With faux patience, she said, "In case you haven't noticed, I'm three feet tall. Even the elderly stand a good chance of outrunning me."

The conversation was cut off when the shop door swung open, and Benny came tumbling out, blood gushing from a head wound. Bo came out shortly after with his face still stained red. Combined with the torchlight, it made Bo look like a demon from beyond the Darkveil.

The Cos-damned thug must've returned with friends to mend his pride, thought Birger. As he started forward, Frida grabbed his arm.

I must save Benny, thought Birger with frustration, but Frida fixed Birger with a firm eye and shook her head.

The doorbell tinkled again, and Birger looked up to see Ulfhild, the Bloody Queen of the Black Wolves, walk out. Her crimson armour was cruelly back lit from the store. She knelt next to Benny and her red hair brushed over the round man's face. Her wicked, matching daggers crisscrossed over Benny's throat.

Birger saw red flames flicker in her eyes without scorching her eyebrows, and absolute, palpable terror washed over him. Like a giant hand grabbing him, his body locked up, and his vision filled with Ulfhild's face, leaving him unable to look away.

Ulfhild spoke, but Birger couldn't hear the words; Benny stared at her with disdain. She rose and gave Benny a vicious kick to the jaw, snapping his head back, spinning his body around and sending him skidding several feet on the cobbled road. The impact had set Benny's jaw at an unnatural angle. From freshly opened wounds, more blood gushed down the older man's broken face.

Hot emotions burned in Birger's chest and neck as he struggled against the fear holding him in place. The strength of Birger's will pushed against the panic, and he managed to take a step. Frida still held onto Birger's arm with surprising strength for her size. He strained against her but knew he couldn't risk making a scene.

If Birger had any chance to help, it depended on surprise. So he relaxed his resistance until he felt the steel grip loosen and plucked hard to free himself.

When Birger took a step, his eyes locked with Benny's, and his friend stared him down. He had somehow noticed them lurking in the shadows, and the old Magpie gave Birger a simple message with a single head shake.

A pang of guilt, regret, pain, and a new kind of fear threatened to rip Birger's chest apart. It was helplessness, being out of control, and watching your friend suffer. Nothing was worse than witnessing someone you love in incredible pain, knowing you were unable to help.

Frida whispered from behind, "You dying won't save him."

"I have to do something!" Birger insisted.

"No, you don't. The Code says if you are able. We aren't, and if you put my crew in danger by pulling me into it, I'll kill you myself." Something in the way she said it told Birger that she wasn't joking.

"Screw the Code and screw you!" hissed Birger as he looked back to Benny.

Ulfhild stood behind Benny, her daggers poised to strike. Suddenly, she stabbed both blades into his back. Only years of training and habit kept Birger from screaming. The realisation that he was too late hit him like a loose yardarm on deck.

Birger wanted to think that it was Benny's rebuke or Frida's urging that kept him locked in place. Maybe even the tangible force of fear that Ulfhild wore like a suit of armour, but he felt like a coward who had failed his friend, anyway.

65

A flicker of red light burst from the wounds, and what followed would be seared into Birger's mind forever. At first, Benny's skin paled from apparent blood loss. Then, his eyes and mouth turned black, his cheeks hollowed, and his once-plump body shrank as if sucked dry like a waterskin.

Painful screams escaped from Benny's husk, and then everything fell silent.

EAST GATE

MANOR HILL

PARLIAMENT HILL

ROYAL GATE

UP TOWN

MARKED WARD

WEST KEEP

DUFA RENT PARK

MERCHANT WARD

LITTLE SAWRA

DOCK WARD

FISH-BOTTOM

HARBOUR WARD

WEST GATE

WEST HAVEN
CAPITAL CITY · WEST REACHS
GOVERNMENT MINISTRY
PREPARED IN 54,969

11

BARREL SIDE

"Giving one's life to save another is the greatest honour, one that wins us a more secure future." Jing Council Member Renla Padri

I must find a way to stop Ulfhild, Birger thought for the millionth time since that horrible night. While his motivation was partly vengeance for Benny; stopping the war that she would unleash on Anthir was much more concerning. And all Birger had was a vague hope that the Shade could help.

He sat at a small table with his back to the wall. His hair had grown long during his journey. He brushed a few strands from his face. As the deep circles around his eyes testified, he hadn't been sleeping much, and the tiredness made him paranoid.

Birger gripped the unsheathed rapier on his lap tightly, feeling the leather creak under the strain. He pulled his grey hood over his head and eyed the ragtag assortment of patrons in the inn's common room.

The urge to reach the Shade burned like a fire heating his seat. He tapped his foot on the wood floor in an attempt to redirect the nervous energy. Had he beaten Ulfhild's lackeys to West Haven? Or was he too late?

A distant thunderclap broke the steady drumming of the rain on the building's roof. The open common room bustled with early evening chatter. Men and women, weary from their day's labour, settled in for a pint. Others, well-rested, were getting ready to start an evening in places they didn't belong.

The Barrel Side Inn reminded Birger of the Rusty Tankard. This was a Magpies Guild operating centre, and these folks were Birger's people.

Thanks to the language they shared, West Haven felt familiar. But it was much larger than Anthir. The city was an intimidating black fortress with wide canals and a marble heart.

The culture was another major difference. Kissing an Anthirian on the cheek would get your lights punched out, while the

Rendinians seemed to like it. Sawrans prized stoicism, whereas the Rendinians were expressive and loud. These differences were why Sawrans never saw themselves as part of Rendin, even before they were split by the civil war.

Cos, Anthirians got awkward about handshakes. Maybe the Rendinians had fewer diseases to worry about? Birger guessed.

There was a small stage on the far side of the large room where a pair of entertainers in bright and colourful clothing prepared their instruments. Sturdy wooden tables filled with patrons were set up around a small dance floor.

Servers carried drinks and food that smelled like beef or lamb. Birger wasn't sure which it was, but it wasn't fish. He could really go for some whole roasted bream with potatoes, olives and some of those chilli flakes that Noxolu used at the Rusty Tankard. His mouth started watering at the thought.

Just a few hours ago, Birger had still been on the road coming from Stella. His feet ached. Exhaustion from the days travel would win him over eventually, but for the moment, anxiety kept his head swivelling.

It had been four weeks since he snuck out of Anthir's Harbour on the Airy Bell. Four weeks since...Birger gulped down a big lump in his throat. Benny's death was still raw, and it weighed heavy as a cog's cargo load in his heart.

Barely a night passed where he didn't wake in cold sweats. He shook his head, trying to clear those thoughts, and rubbed his tired eyes.

Benny would want me to move past this, thought Birger. *Why can't I?*

Because it was your fault. You reckless moron. Benny would still be alive if you didn't think you were invincible.

Drained like a waterskin, empty eyes sinking away... he had a flashback to that horrible night and forced it aside.

Birger couldn't argue with his cynic.

I shouldn't have taken Wynn to Foss, and I should've killed Bo when I had the chance. I should've helped Benny, I should've, should've, should've, but should'ves don't bring your dead friends back, thought Birger.

The music started playing. It was something jovial, and his rumination turned to irrational annoyance. He longed for a hot meal and a bed. At least he found Renate Couture. She sent for the Shade directly after Birger told her what happened.

Maybe that bed wasn't so far away. What's taking Renate so long? Birger wondered, and he looked over at the bar.

Behind the service counter, a giant barrel filled the room floor to ceiling. This feature was where the place got its name. The inn looked like it had been built onto the side of a humongous ale cask.

A foppish young man with a head of blond curls was upholding a longstanding tradition of slumming by nobles. He wore a purple silk doublet and sidled up to the bar. He looked as out of place in the rough common room as a hammerhead shark caught in a rowboat's fishing net.

Three armed bodyguards followed in his wake, eyeing the other patrons with obvious suspicion. It was a scene Birger had witnessed more times than he cared to count.

The fop had his elbow on the countertop and tipped his hand in a flourish, saying something to the lovely blond woman waiting there.

The woman he flirted with was Renate Couture. She was middle-aged, with blue eyes and a faint white tattoo of a bird's wing etched into each of her cheeks. She had a slim build and looked almost clumsy as she leaned on the bar. Renate wore a bright blue dress billowing out from her tiny waist and a matching jacket embroidered with white floral patterns.

She smiled pleasantly at the nobleman. Her response was drowned out by the din of people talking. She ran her hand over the young man's cheek, and he blushed.

A well-muscled strawberry-blond woman, the innkeeper, stood behind the bar. She wore a sleeveless blue shirt with the Dagger and Bird tattoo clearly visible on her left shoulder, sending a simple message 'this is a Magpies tavern'.

She opened a tap protruding from the enormous barrel and poured a hoppy golden fluid into a stein. Birger imagined the chill on his lips and the bitter taste of the hops in his mouth. He realised how badly he needed a refreshment.

The innkeeper plopped the steins in front of Renate, and the nobleman slid a gold coin across the counter with a broad smile. Renate hugged the young man, kissing him on the cheek, and he beamed from ear to ear. An expression that turned to shocked confusion when she snatched up the tankards, turned and walked away.

A moment later, Renate placed a large draught of Korland beer on the table in front of Birger. Exotic and expensive stuff.

Sweetly Renate said, "Here you go."

"Thanks."

Birger lost himself in the sip as he drew the white foam head into his mouth. He enjoyed the hoppy bitterness; it was even better than he had imagined. A sweet aftertaste lingered. *Citrus fruit had been used in the making,* thought Birger.

Renate swept her dress aside so she could sit down.

Placing the drink back on the table, Birger asked, "Making friends?"

"Oh, yes," Renate flashed a smile at the confused nobleman by the bar. "What a pleasant gentleman, buying a lady and her friend a drink like that."

The man returned her smile, and one of his bodyguards stomped towards Birger and Renate.

"Yes, stand-up fellow. I'm not so sure about the company he keeps, though."

The bodyguard was young, broad-shouldered, and tall, maybe a head taller than Birger, it was hard to tell from sitting. The man's clean-shaven jaw was twice as wide as his shiny cranium and flowed almost seamlessly into his shoulders with no neck to speak of. His silver chest plate shone brightly over his burgundy and white outfit. Birger knew they were Roviere colours. A longsword dangled menacingly at his side.

The oaf slammed a leather enclosed fist onto the table, and growled, "It ain't polite to take a man's coin and give nothing in return." There was a youthful quality in his voice.

"Oh my," said Renate, surprised. "My apologies, sir. Here. Give your master this."

She extracted a white handkerchief embroidered with a bright pink flying serpent.

The man snatched it and said, "That ain't what I was meaning, and you know it."

His two friends came to stand behind him, and both looked like typical guards with nothing interesting about them.

Birger cleared his throat. "Listen, no-neck. You don't look too bright, so I'll keep it simple. The lady isn't like your mum. She doesn't do that kind of thing."

The gears turned slowly as the man's brow knitted into a confused expression, and Birger doubted they would click all the way over.

After a few seconds, the bodyguard finally said, "I think you're insulting me."

72

"Sorry, shiny, look, let me make it even simpler for you." Birger subtly leaned forward, his right hand slipping under the table. "I'm saying you're dumb. Your mum's a lady of the night, and you should leave my friend alone."

Renate's eyes stretched wide with an amused smile as she took a sip of her drink.

"You'll die for that!" the man snapped, raising a fist.

12

BODYGUARDS

The Barrel Side Inn was packed to the gunnels with patrons. At the far end of the room, a couple of bards sat on the stage playing a jolly tune while a few people danced. The left wall of the room was the curve of a giant barrel, and the attached bar served customers freshly poured steins.

Birger and Renate each had a delicious, foamy drink in front of them. Renate leaned comfortably forward, cupping her tankard, while Birger's hands rested under the table.

Three men, dressed in the burgundy and white of Roviere, menaced the pair, and the tallest one was barrelling towards Birger. The man pulled up short as cold steel threaded through the linen cloth of his trousers and pricked at his groin.

Birger's rapier nestled strategically in place. Any further forward, and the oaf would become less of a man, while sudden moves would leave him bleeding out on the floor.

With a wolfish grin, Birger said, "Oh, don't be like that. I'm trying to help you." He was enjoying the moment more than he should be. "Let me point out the obvious… Sorry… I keep using big words. What I mean is that I'll explain what's happening," Birger drawled the words as if speaking to a simpleton. "You're picking a fight you can't win, so stop barking orders like a captain at sea and walk away."

"I ain't no captain. I'm Sergeant Pat, and you're crossing the wrong man." Pat moved cautiously despite his boasting. "And there are three of us and one of you."

"Nice to meet you, Pat. And no," Birger shook his head, "besides your horrible counting," Birger pointed to Renate as if to say, there are at least two of us. "Look around. You're standing in a whole tavern of us."

Pat chanced a glance, and he turned sheet white. His friends shuffled uneasily behind him as they realised that the din in the place had gone gravely quiet and a half-circle had formed around them.

75

"Next time your lord wants to go slumming, I suggest picking a different drinking hole." Birger smirked with satisfaction.

He didn't need to know the people, because they were Magpies, and the Code was the same everywhere. They looked out for people that needed it, especially if the one creating the need had more than their share.

Pat backed off, and Birger let him, "We got other business anyhow."

"Well, look at you," said Birger in faux pride, "Not so dumb after all."

"This isn't over, scum..." Pat bared his teeth. "You'd better watch your back. You can't hide in here forever."

Birger didn't like the way Pat glowered at him.

Pat led the other two thugs away, and they joined their master at the bar. The crowd parted to let them through, but the atmosphere remained tense, making the retreat anything but comfortable.

Pat and his boss hurried to the door. The moment it swung shut behind them, the common room resumed as if nothing had happened. It felt familiar. A little security in the chaos of the last few weeks.

A pang of spiteful pleasure at sticking it to the wealthy caused Birger to flex his jaw. The same feeling he got when he burgled a rich mark and could see them discover the theft. It was a vice he didn't indulge often due to the inherent danger, but when he did, it was sheer bliss. Wealth needed redistributing. The rich had it, the poor didn't, and Birger was happy to be the active agent.

Renate grinned at him. He responded in kind, slipping his silver rapier back into its sheath. It was no longer needed, since he knew for certain that they were amidst fellow Magpies.

"Wow, you have quite the mouth on you," said Renate.

"Was it a bit much?" asked Birger in jest.

"Maybe you went a little hard on the dumb stuff, but the rest was pretty good."

"Eh," Birger shrugged.

"Now, tell me," Renate's eyes shifted to concern, "how are you?"

The question made Birger uncomfortable. The illusion of familiarity was dispelled, and he was reminded that this wasn't home. His fear for Wynn's safety and guilt over Benny's fate were renewed. He looked at Renate with a flat expression.

... Empty eyes staring...

76

She doesn't even know me, thought Birger, *and she's asking such a personal question?*

Unsure how to respond, he said, "I'm just fine."

"Come now, you can't be over eighteen or nineteen years old; you just lost a friend who must've been dear to you if he trusted you enough to send you to see the Shade." Renate gave Birger a knowing look.

As she continued, emotion showed in her eyes, "Benny was a kind soul who often took in strays, and he was beloved by many. I'll miss him next time I go to the Guilds of Anthir. During my first visit, he spent a week guiding me through the local customs and that cold nature you northerners are so proud of."

She smiled. "I'm well aware that you Anthirians don't show your feelings like we West Haven folk do, but a bottled-up loss has a way of breaking free. Be honest with me. How are you doing?"

"It's not the first fish in my school to get caught," Birger intended the words to be dismissive, but the compounding loss of Sten and Benny crackled in his voice. *Lot damn the mutts for all of that.* "Fins like me have to fend for themselves, and nothing has changed. Life is tough, so toughen up."

He steeled himself and straightened his posture.

Anger seethed in Birger's belly like a threatened serpent as he thought, *How dare she probe at what isn't her business?*

"I see. Not ready to talk yet. I'm sorry for prying," Renate smiled warmly and raised her mug. "To good friends lost. May they drink sweet ale in the halls of the All-Mother."

"May Anchorhall receive them with a song, and may their merry-making annoy Cos into casting them back to the world." Birger used the toast to let his anger subside.

Anchorhall was the afterlife for worthy souls. The Cult of the Weave believed that a life that disrupted the balance of the world led to a weakened soul, and Lot would freeze it in her icy prison to preserve it.

However, if you lived to maintain balance, you would have a powerful soul and be given access to Anchorhall. Birger found it somewhat reassuring to think of Benny and Sten sharing a table in the grand halls of the afterlife. They had both been brave and spent their time dedicated to bringing balance. Without question, the Valkyries collected them both.

Birger took another long pull from his stein, when the creak of the main entrance door swinging open drew his attention. A chilly breeze cut through the hearth-warmed atmosphere of the common room, and a slender man stepped in.

His eyes were dark, sharp and spoke of hard-won experience. Birger noted his angular nose and gaunt cheeks with an olive complexion, that were uncommon traits in Rendin, suggesting he might be foreign born. The collar of his green jerkin flared out from under his cedar brown leather coat like a bird stretching its wings to take flight. His jacket had silver floral patterns that connected evenly spaced brass buttons.

The layered sheets of leather framing the man's shoulders and the coat's decorated deep cuffs gave him a sophisticated silhouette which Birger experienced as quite intimidating. His gray trousers ended in polished boots. Several straps crisscrossed over his body, connecting to his belt, each bearing a variety of pouches or fine mechanical tools.

A slender sword sat on the man's hip, and his left hand rested on its black hilt. The weapon's guard was adorned with a floral theme, and if it had been ivory and gold, Birger would've assumed it to be a ceremonial sword, but the black gave it a more sinister look.

The man was heading for their table, and his presence became more intense with each step. Purpose and determination radiated from him as if he were death itself, here to claim a life.

"Lorenzo!" Renate's loud welcome startled Birger, "How wonderful of you to join us!" She stepped up to Lorenzo and gave him a kiss on each cheek, which he returned.

The show of friendliness threw Birger's first impression in stark contrast, and he wondered, *Did I imagine the air of danger?*

In an unfamiliar accent, Lorenzo said, "Good to see you too, Renate."

Birger wondered where the man was from. His skin was more bronze than Rendinians typically were, but not as dark as the brown of Korland.

The kissing made Birger uncomfortable. He wondered if he should stand in greeting…in the end he did, awkwardly waiting for the display to end. After a long hug that grew uncomfortable for Birger, Renate broke away.

With a motion of her hand, she said, "I must introduce my new friend, Birger from Anthir." She smiled. "He's a *verified* guild member, and he brought important news."

The emphasis on verified, was referring to the Dagger and Bird tattoo she checked when they first met.

"So your messenger mentioned." Lorenzo nodded as he took Birger in. "My name is Lorenzo Soto, originally from Itavia, now West Haven. Some refer to me as the Shade, and Benny's told me much about you." Lorenzo stretched his right hand to Birger with the palm facing up.

A hand greeting? How do these work again? Birger tried to remember what he had read. *At least he isn't trying to kiss me.*

Birger put his hand forward, trying to match Lorenzo as best he could. They rotated their palms down and back to a middle position before clasping them together in a shake.

"Funny that," said Birger as he retracted his hand, "he told me almost nothing about you. Could we find some privacy?" He took care to scan the room for curious eyes, but he couldn't see anyone paying attention to them.

Lorenzo smiled and nodded. "Follow me."

Birger got up and followed Lorenzo to the bar. Keeping his hand near his rapier and watching the man's movements for any sign of betrayal. He wasn't sure if the Shade was also a Magpie, and taking chances seemed stupid.

Lorenzo signalled to the well-muscled bartender with three fingers held to his heart. Birger could imagine the woman doubling as a bouncer with those arms, and he wondered if she, like Noxolu, was the local Guild Leader.

He heard that was quite common in most cities. Innkeepers were well known, so it was easy for them to get a lot of votes. The woman nodded at Lorenzo and jerked a thumb towards the door on the right side of the bar.

They followed the woman's instructions, and Lorenzo entered first. Birger saw that the giant barrel continued into the hall beyond the door.

When Birger shut the door, Lorenzo poked one of the metal studs laid into the steel ring of the giant barrel. It gave under the pressure and with a clink, several planks swung inwards to reveal stairs that dropped to lower levels.

Lorenzo stepped inside, and the other two followed. Behind Birger, the door swung shut by itself and he marvelled at the mechanisms at work.

"Lucinda," said Renate over her shoulder.

"What?" asked Birger, confused.

"Lucinda closed the door. The innkeeper, her name is Lucinda. You looked up at the door, so I'm explaining."

"Oh." Birger blushed at his lack of comprehension. "Of course, thanks."

They took three more turns on the spiral stairs that ran along the inside of the giant barrel. Each time passing a closed door, until finally, they reached the bottom. Lorenzo opened the door and led them into a small room beyond.

A table filled three-quarters of the space, benches lined the walls for seating, and above hung a lamp.

"We have absolute privacy here," said Lorenzo, as he invited everyone to be seated.

13

THE SHADE

Birger, Renate, and Lorenzo sat in a cosy, well-lit, highly claustrophobic room with a faint musty smell. Birger experienced a sense of dread, like he might get buried alive at any moment.

Knowing they were several feet underground, even under the water table, made Birger long for a window with fresh air, but he wasn't going to get one, so he had to suck it up. At least, the plush red cushion of the bench was comfortable.

Lorenzo rested his elbows on the tabletop and steepled his hands. "I've been following your exploits with some interest, Birger Light Foot. Your theft of the painting Mangelo Ire by Marco Petty was impressive. How long was it before they realised you had swapped it for a forgery?"

"Realise?" Birger smiled mischievously. "Last I heard, the fake was still hanging in Lord Bjornson's main hall. And it was the Eave El' Grande."

Lorenzo returned the smile and nodded. "Oh, that's right. It was, wasn't it? And your acquisition of the Viridian Dragon was an impressive display of patience. I doubt any guards expected someone to hide in a barrel for over eight hours to get into Duke Fordson's keep."

Birger raised an eyebrow at that. Benny must've reported much more than Birger expected back to the Shade. No one else knew how Birger got into Ferdinand Keep.

"Thank you. I pride myself in showing the nobility that their treasure is no safer behind their high walls than us mackerel living in the Squat."

Birger paused, considering what Lorenzo was doing. "Now, we've confirmed each other's identities. Can we get straight to the point?"

Lorenzo inclined his head. "Indeed. Well, what would you like to discuss?"

"Stopping West Rendin from starting a war with Anthir," said Birger. "One moment."

He reached into his satchel to produce the four scrolls and placed them on the table. Stroking each scroll flat as he unrolled them.

Lorenzo watched him work, and asked, "How's Benny?"

"As well as anyone else in Anchorhall," said Birger, with a grim glance up. "Ulfhild murdered him in cold blood."

"What, Benny's dead?" asked Lorenzo, surprised. His face darkened. He bowed his head and pursed his lips. "We honour his life and his pursuit of balance. We'll carry his legacy from here."

Lorenzo drew his black sword and sliced his own finger. The cut welled with blood, and he smeared it across the blade. Putting the weapon back, he held his hand over his heart, moving it in a spiral. Birger didn't recognise the ritual, but it seemed linked with Lot from the spiralling motion.

Lorenzo closed his eyes. "As he was murdered for the ambition of the Blood Queen, I shall deny her what she seeks. I swear it."

A blood oath? That was unexpected, thought Birger. He could admire a culture with such deep and meaningful displays of honour for the dead. "I second that. And Lot have mercy on Ulfhild when my vengeance catches up to her."

"Tell me what happened," said Lorenzo.

Birger explained everything as he remembered it. The other two were silent for a while after he finished.

Lorenzo broke the silence by saying, "Benny was a good man. He died bravely."

"I'm so sorry, Birger," added Renate, and she put a hand on his shoulder. "No one should have to go through that."

Birger didn't like being touched, but found Renate's hand comforting. "I'm not the one that got lanced like a puss filled wound."

... Sucked dry like a waterskin...

After that, there was a quiet moment where it looked like no one knew how to respond. Renate let go of Birger's shoulder, and Lorenzo's eyes dropped to the documents on the table.

Birger felt awkward, knowing what he said was inappropriate. *Press into the work. Maybe everyone will forget you're an insensitive loudmouth.*

"These three are crab scratch." Birger pointed at the document. "And this one," Birger put a finger on the page furthest away, "is the Queen bee sending her drones to fetch a sword dressed in Anthir's colours. The target is a knight by the name of Sir Kallen du la Rent. Oh, and she says to kill him if he gets in the way."

He paused as Lorenzo looked more closely at the one pointed out.

"Makes no sense, really," continued Birger. "Why would that scum Fordson and the Blood Queen collude like this? I mean, they sent a small army looking for these. The Duke hasn't given a gullshite about the city in years. Anthir isn't the happiest place at the best of times, but I'm pretty sure he risked a revolt. And why would he want to pick a fight with West Rendin like this, anyway?"

"Let's see here," Lorenzo nodded thoughtfully.

He produced a complex, gear-covered device from his pocket that resembled a pince-nez. Lorenzo clicked through the switches on the device as he pored through the pages.

Renate cleared her throat and asked, "Birger? Do you really want vengeance?"

There was apparent concern in her voice, and her eyes were soft.

Birger tried not to look at her as he replied, "Ulfhild and her mutts deserve worse."

"You know what they say about revenge. When one seeks it, dig two graves. When pursuing it against the likes of Ulfhild, you only need one."

"What would you do?" snapped Birger, his eyes flashing with anger. "Should I sit back and do nothing?!"

"Peace, Birger. I'm not the enemy. Would Benny want you to throw your life away for revenge?"

Birger dropped his head. He could still hear Benny telling him to slow down so he could deal with Sten's death. The old man was never about revenge. Even if he had been, Renate was right. Ulfhild was absolutely terrifying. The image of Benny's last moments came to life in Birger's mind again, and the claustrophobic nature of the room redoubled.

... empty eyes ...

Birger's chest tightened; his heart pounded so loudly in his ears that he couldn't hear what Renate was saying.

Focus Birger, he told himself as he fought for control over his breathing. *I need to use the conversation to occupy my mind.*

"What did you say?" Birger rubbed his temples.

"I asked if you were alright?" said Renate, as if repeating herself.

"Yeah, I'm fine," lied Birger. "Look, I don't know if I want to kill Ulfhild or that scum Bo that helped her murder Benny. All I know is that this thing, whatever they're doing, is bigger than Benny and me, and I want to help stop it. I have people in Anthir that I care about, people I swore I would look after and keep safe. I won't let anything block me from doing that, and if that means going toe to toe with a monster like Ulfhild, count me in."

Birger realised that Lorenzo had stopped reading and was now staring at him. "I hear your passion and bluster. But I wonder, are you sure you want to lead a life like that?"

Birger surged to his feet, his dagger in hand, and snarled, "If you think I'm all talk, come, and I'll show you what I'm made of!"

Lorenzo removed the gear-covered pince-nez from his eye and placed it on the table.

With an amused smile, he said, "I don't doubt that you're someone that dives headfirst into the jaws of a shark. I asked, are you sure this is the life you want to lead?" Then he tilted his head to the side and locked his gaze on Birger. "I know that road well. It's paved with the bones of my friends and slick with their blood, and one day mine will join them there."

Birger felt foolish standing in such an aggressive pose when the other man was at ease. He put his dagger away and sat back down. It took a lot of control to restrain the defensiveness that had raced to the surface.

"I believe in the Magpies' Code," Birger said. "It says that you should always help those who cannot help themselves, if you are able. I am able, and no one can prove otherwise. I won't let anyone else control my destiny but me. So, here I am, ready to add my bones too."

There was a long silence until Lorenzo said, "You want to protect your people, and you want to control your destiny." Lorenzo stroked his chin absently. "I want to make you an offer. Will you hear it?"

Birger nodded yes.

"I make you no promises about your safety or the outcome of our mission."

Birger nodded again.

"I offer you a life dedicated to unraveling conspiracies, like this one that Ulfhild has cooked up, and any other threat to the peace of the region. Think of it as the Magpies Code to maintain the balance, but instead of balancing coin, it's balancing blood."

Birger regarded Lorenzo with a strange mixture of scepticism and borrowed trust. Without Benny's word, Birger would've told him and his grandiose ideas to take a walk off a short plank.

Maybe I still should, thought Birger. It sounded like this man wanted him to become a killer or something. *I don't kill people for money.*

Birger leaned back on the bench and asked, "What, are you trying to turn me into...an assassin?"

"No. Think of it more like interference. Stealing knowledge from those that would use it to harm others. Money can buy armies, and power can control them, but knowledge can undo them. It's the only defence against people like Ulfhild who have more power than you."

As Birger considered it, the memory of helplessly watching Ulfhild murder Benny choked him. Cos, he still felt powerless knowing that Wynn could be in trouble, and he wouldn't even know–and there it was.

Birger could do nothing, not because he wasn't there, but because he didn't know. He didn't know if she was in trouble, didn't know what the mutts or the Cos-damned Duke wanted. If he knew more, he could be in the right place at the right time. He could be where he was needed and do what was required.

He came to see the Shade for knowledge in the first place. Now, he was being invited to become a thief of that same knowledge.

Birger narrowed his eyes, processing Lorenzo's words. "So, what you are saying is...you want to turn me into a book thief? I know your intel has been reliable in the past, so you must know what you're doing, but say, who would pay for this knowledge?"

Lorenzo smiled. "Like I said. I would bring balance by channelling it to where it needed to go."

Birger looked at Lorenzo, scepticism plain on his face. "That sounds like a load of gullshite."

Renate cut in, "Birger, Lorenzo isn't just a Magpie. He's the Shade, an agent for Queen Armandine."

A chill ran down Birger's spine as the implications hit him. His heart started pounding loudly in his ears again. His chest constricted with a familiar sensation of being squeezed by a giant hand.

Birger shot to his feet and raised his voice, "You're the Queen's man!" He looked at Renate, "You brought me to a man who can destroy Anthir in the fires of war?!"

14

DESTINY OR DISASTER

Birger stood, fixing Lorenzo with a harsh stare across the table. Four scrolls were neatly arranged on its surface. Renate leaned away from Birger's sudden movement, but looked more concerned than scared. The table and benches left barely enough space for two people to stand next to each other, never mind have a fight.

"Calm down," said Lorenzo as he stood up, looking Birger in the eye.

Lorenzo showed no signs of strain, anger, or intimidation. Instead, his posture was relaxed. His gaze met Birger's evenly, his voice drawled at a sleepy cadence. Birger's hand rested on the hilt of his sword while Lorenzo let his arms hang loose at his sides.

All the outstanding fighters Birger had met in his time had one thing in common. Something about their experience gave them the confidence to relax when others would be tense. Lorenzo looked just like one of them. This didn't bode well for Birger's chances, and running wasn't an option in these tight confines.

Lorenzo smiled calmly. His tone pleasant, as if talking to a dear old friend about the weather when he said, "I *am* a Queen's man. The Queen has no desire for war with Sawra. I exist to unravel the ambitions of those who want to plunge the continent into another disastrous conflict. The Civil War wasn't good for anyone, and there would be no benefit in repeating it."

Renate placed her hand on Birger's shoulder, its warmth unexpected, yet offering reassuring comfort to his weary body. "Lorenzo is telling the truth, Birger. Benny had his reasons for sending you to us. You knew him well, right? Do you think he would ever do something that could put Anthir in danger?"

"No. Benny was a true Magpie who lived by the Code and cared about Anthir more than most." The admission in light of his outburst made Birger's cheeks burn.

Lorenzo said, "Based on your attitude in our conversation today, I'm inclined to send you on your way. However, I'll cut you some slack since you're dealing with the death of a friend, and Benny sent you here for a good reason. He and I have been preparing you to become a knowledge broker for years."

"Years?"

"You're good, and now more than ever, I need good people," said Lorenzo simply. "Your encounter with the Black Wolves isn't the only one like it in Azrea. Benny joins a long list of shades to fall in the last couple of months."

"Also," Lorenzo pointed at the scrolls, "this is what I needed to fight against the Black Wolves and whatever they're planning. With my network strained by losses, I need new capable shades to prevent this looming disaster."

Lorenzo placed both hands on the table's surface, spread his fingers wide, and lowered himself back into his seat.

He locked eyes with Birger, his gaze severe, and said, "The real question isn't if you're in, because you're already in. The question is, do you want to continue?"

Lorenzo paused.

"On the Code, I swear I'll never ask you to be part of any action that I know would lead to harm for Anthir. So, do you want to take control, get the knowledge you need to fight back, and strike at the people that mean to harm your friends?"

As Birger considered his options, the dry smell of dusty parchment filled his nose. *Was this an opportunity to claim? A challenge that would take me to new heights? Or would I be selling my soul to demons beyond the Darkveil?*

Regardless, Birger was aware of a simple truth. He had nothing to go on without Lorenzo. His only other option was to go after Ulfhild directly, which was suicide. If he walked away now, Lorenzo would take control, leaving Birger with no role in what came next for his people. Knowledge would give him agency; he wanted it; he needed it.

No way, he thought. *Walking out isn't an option.*

Birger clenched his jaw, and shaking his head, he sighed. "I think this is the bit where I tell you, 'no, I can't,' mope around aimlessly for a while, realise I have no choice, and come back ready to join. Instead, how about we skip all that and you just tell me, what's my cut?"

Birger's face shifted into a self-satisfied grin. "If I steal diamonds, I get my fair share after selling them off. Most of the information we'll get won't be sold but used. I don't work for free."

Lorenzo's grin became strained. "I thought you might say that. Five silver coins a day until you're trained, then you move up to two gold coins. All travel and gear are handled as long as you get them from a crown quartermaster."

"I don't need training," said Birger with a raised eyebrow.

"You're a fine thief. But the job is more complicated than breaking in and stealing things. You need to learn decorum and how to be part of a team."

"Fine, but I want one gold a day and three after I show you I don't need the training." Birger cleared his throat and, narrowing his eyes. "I don't know you well, but Benny told me I could trust you. Regardless, I want to be as clear as the Everwinter Sea after a high slack tide. If something smells off, these documents and I are gone."

Birger had never encountered Itavians because of their rivalry with Korland, who controlled trade in the waters around Sawra. However, he had read about their customs. They concluded deals with a handshake, so Birger offered his hand in the same way they greeted earlier.

With a smile and a nod, Lorenzo clasped Birger's arm to the elbow, squeezing their forearms together. Renate added her hand on top, gripping them both.

"I bind you to your word until you're released from it by the other. Should either of you renege on the agreement, Mag, the Great Spider, will curse you to your death."

Surprised, Birger turned to Renate. Only then did he notice what she was doing around their forearms with her free hand. There was a loud pop that ripped a tear in reality, pulsing with bright purple and teal light. Stinging cold radiated from the opening that looked like a miniature weavestorm dancing in her palm.

She released her grip on them, and reached inside the hole, coming out with a thin translucent thread. Renate wrapped it around their clasped arms and bound the string into a slipknot. She stroked her fingers over the material and set it to glow with a pink hue that throbbed for three heartbeats and then sank into Birger and Lorenzo's arms.

"What was that?" Birger asked. "Are you some kind of priestess?"

Renate smiled. "Something like that. If either of you break your word, the spell will release necrotic venom that starts with your arm and ends in your death unless the deed is reversed. I wouldn't recommend testing it. It's an unpleasant way to go."

Lorenzo let go of Birger's arm and said, "We're bound by the goddess of magic now. With that behind us, I've decrypted most of this message, but I need a key for the rest." Lorenzo placed his index finger on a paper leaf. "What I can read describes an item to be retrieved from the temple of Lot in the Holy City."

Renate gasped. "Would they dare steal from the goddesses?"

Feeling foolish for still standing, Birger sat down on the bench. He caught the pillow at an odd angle and shifted himself until he found a more comfortable spot.

With a hopeful grin, Birger said, "Well, maybe the divine ladies will take care of the problem for us. And from what I've been told, Lot white knuckles a grudge like a fisher with a marlin on the line."

"They would be stealing from the clergy," Lorenzo said. "I must admit, it's more ambitious than I would've expected."

Birger pointed at the other scrolls. "And the rest?" His patience was wearing thin. After weeks of waiting to know what the scrolls contained, he'd hoped for more than just 'they plan to steal something'.

"I don't know. Each requires a different code. I only found a partial key, piecing things together from the legible orders. There must be another key that the receiver has to unlock the rest. Using brute force to crack the code could take months, maybe years."

"So that's it?" asked Birger, "and after I promised you my firstborn and sold my soul and everything?"

Renate burst out laughing. Lorenzo's lips didn't move, but his eyes beamed with humour.

Once Renate had regained her composure, Lorenzo said, "You can rest assured, I'll put your firstborn and soul to good use. For now, I'm more concerned with the original orders, anyway."

Lorenzo leaned back. "Sir Kallen and his father, Lord Caoimhín, arrived at the palace to see the Queen this week. Sir Kallen carries a sword that looks rather exotic, and it appears magical. As I understand it, Ulfhild has already attempted to capture it once, so that must be their target. Thanks to Birger's immediate action and swift travel, we have the initiative, but we don't know how much lead time there is, so we'll have to act quickly."

With a sly smile, Birger asked, "Can we set a trap?"

Lorenzo seemed to consider the option, and Birger found it hard to read what the man was thinking. He didn't show much emotion.

Renate pointed to Birger's Onyx wristband. "Where did you get that?"

"Oh, this?" He looked at the bracelet, twisting it around his arm to display the engraved dragon's head. "I found it with the scrolls. Normally, I would've liquidated any assets I snatch from a mark by now, but my usual fence wasn't available." Saying it sent a pang of sadness for Benny down the back of Birger's throat.

"Interesting, may I?"

He nodded, and Renate moved closer to investigate.

"When I crafted the bonding between you two, this wristband did something to my crafting. Like it was checking and approving my spell. At first, I thought it was a talisman of protection, but it allowed my magic, so this can't be the case. Those things reject any magic that the holder doesn't explicitly allow."

With his curiosity piqued once again, Birger looked at the band. "So, what is it?"

Renate squinted, her mouth moving quietly, as if reading.

Finally she said, "The inscription resembles stillari writing. But it's not close enough for me to decipher it. Could be a dialect?"

"Stillari?" Birger raised his eyebrows.

"Tall, long ears, pretty eyes, live in Stillendam."

Birger gave her a level look. "I know what they are...I was surprised that you thought it looked like their writing."

Renate turned and asked, "Lorenzo, you said that Caoimhín recently arrived at the palace?"

"Yes." Lorenzo nodded.

"Caoimhín's the best archaeologist and linguist of our age. I would love to hear what he had to say about the artefact. If anyone can figure it out, it's him."

"Agreed." Lorenzo sank deeper into the bench. "But before we do that, we must see the Queen of West Rendin to stop a war and potential murder."

15

THE GRAND PALACE

Could Lorenzo actually convince the Queen not to attack Anthir? Birger worried.

There was a faint, annoying hum in his ears, and his eyes burned from tiredness. Despite going to bed early, catching sleep was like fishing for eels with his bare hands. Every time he closed his eyes, his mind obsessively tried to sort this whole mess out.

How do I tell my brain to stop thinking? he wondered. *It's like watching the same play on repeat, and when sleep finally does come, it brings nightmares.*

Something plucked him from the mire of his own mind. He flinched, seeing no-neck Pat and covered his face.

The brute's burgundy and white uniform stood out like a sore thumb. He approached alongside a pair of palace guards dressed in navy blue, enjoying a bout of inter-court banter.

Renate stood next to Birger on a vast terrace with her back to the crowd. He shifted uncomfortably, careful not to show his face as the group passed, but it wasn't necessary. They weren't paying attention.

When their voices receded into the crowd, Birger looked up to make sure the coast was clear. The thudding of his heart eased, and he looked up at the awe-inspiring Grand Palace in front of him.

Appreciating something beautiful always calmed his nerves.

It was one of the tallest buildings he had ever seen, some mountains capped out at lower altitudes. The emerald rooftops of the two highest towers had clouds circling them, and Birger wondered about the poor soul who had to climb the stairs to clean up there. Between them, the core of the building curved in a crescent moon shape.

It wasn't the building's height alone that made the sight hard to process; it was more that the building's footprint seemed too small to support it. The architecture comprised thousands of archways that were symmetrically spaced in all dimensions.

Birger saw well kept greenery sprouting from the many patios that decorated it and he wondered, *Who're all the people that live up there? Surely the Queen alone didn't need that much space?*

He once read that the Grand Palace had been the ancestral home of the Rendinian Kings and Queens for the last three-hundred years. A war had literally been waged over who got to call it home, and if the books were to be believed, it was as deadly a place as any ocean storm. Birger surely didn't want to get caught up in the court intrigue.

Come to think of it, he pondered, *I'm here to stop a war, a theft, and a potential murder. Gullshite, I'm already caught up in the web... aren't I?*

A cold knot twisting in Birger's stomach made him wrestle his mind away. Looking for Pat, who had vanished into the crowd, didn't help him feel much more at ease, but searching was a distraction. And his heart couldn't handle thinking about Anthir anymore.

He caught the smell of lavender drifting up from the gorgeous palace garden. Drawing it in, he turned to lean his elbows on the rail. Birger guessed that the highest treetops were about three stories below him. Wondering how much of his weight the delicate-looking rail could take, he tested it and found it solid.

It was always good to know what you could climb in any given area.

Being so high above the city meant Birger had a magnificent view. He could see everything from the West Keep down by the harbour to the well-kept gardens in the east. West Haven was a place of vast riches. The buildings around Parliament Hill made Anthir's best look average.

Birger licked his lips and thought, *This would be the perfect place to scout targets for a caper.*

Pivoting, Birger rested his lower back against the rail, eyes wandering over the courtyard to the west side of the terrace. Servants were bustling everywhere, while to the east of the platform, he saw visitors race up and down a cream staircase that connected to the gates. Directly south of Birger, were the giant double doors that led to the Minister's Court. That was where Lorenzo had been for the last ten minutes.

Renate turned towards him, her smile expectant. "Impressive, isn't it?"

Birger shrugged. "I've seen better."

Renate's smile broadened to show her teeth. For the first time, he noticed her canines were long and sharp.

"Oh, you have? I wonder where? Ferdinand Keep, while impressive by Sawran standards, would be small compared to any of this." Renate put a finger to her lips. She was wearing another blue dress which had a collar that reached up to her chin. She regarded Birger for a moment and asked, "Is it possible you're more widely travelled than I thought?"

Caught in his lie, Birger quickly changed the subject. "How's this place even possible?" He gestured at the tall towers. "They look like they might topple in a stiff breeze."

"Magic."

Thank Cos she let it go, thought Birger. "What do you mean?"

"You're fairly well read, do you know about the Age of Horror?" Renate asked.

"The scary tales parents tell their children, so they'll behave?" asked Birger sarcastically. "Sure I have."

"You think they're just stories?" The humour evaporated from Renate's smile.

"What? Are you saying it was real?"

"Have you ever been to Lonstad?"

"No," Birger shook his head. "But I've read about the Knights of Alba, who supposedly fight nightmarish creatures there."

"Not supposedly. They're still fighting the same enemy that took the combined might of the entire continent to stop. The will that controlled them during the Age of Horror might be gone, but the dead things that dwell there aren't. The Knights of Alba spend their lives keeping the monsters on the far side of the Jorman Rise. Unfortunately, most people in the west want to believe that they're only fanciful tales."

"Sure," Birger shrugged non-committally, "and what does that have to do with a palace in West Haven?"

"The Age of Horror ended thanks to a few heroes. Among them was a powerful wizard named Vernum Salja, who set up a society of wizards called The Isle. They were sworn to defend Azrea if anything like that ever happens again. However, for them to exist independently from the political whims of any one country, they needed to be considered a sovereign power."

She cast her hands wide. "For that, the surrounding nations had to acknowledge their sovereignty, which brings us to the Grand Palace of West Haven. The King of Rendin asked for it as a tribute to recognise The Isle as an independent state. Before this was here, the King lived in West Keep, and this was the market."

Birger felt his shoulders tighten with irritation at being lectured, and an urge to show that he knew all about the story of Vernum Salja rose from his belly.

He eyed Renate sceptically down his nose. "Alexander Epicoch has a more critical opinion about The Isle. In his Treatise on the use of Magic, The Power to Dominate a People, he argues that if the wizards of The Isle really used magic, weavestorms would've destroyed the place ages ago. According to him, they're an isolationist cult conning nations into paying tributes."

Renate's jaw tightened with annoyance. "The Murians consider all magic an affront to their god Sarghus and Epicoch is nothing but a politician. He writes from the comfort of his desk in Mura, and has never even left his city."

I hit a nerve there, thought Birger.

He cocked his head to the side and said, "When you spoke about the city before the palace, it sounded like you were recalling a memory."

"Did it now?" Renate smiled. "Must've been a slip of the tongue. Come on, let's check out the guest quarters." She pointed west. "Those statues were imported from the Stillari of Stillendam."

Birger scoffed, still feeling rather obstinate. "Another bunch of elitists who isolate themselves from the rest of the world. I don't see why I should be interested in anything they make?"

Renate's face went red, and her voice was high-pitched as she said, "You ignorant, child. Sometimes I forget how closed-minded humans can be!"

Renate clenched her jaw and then closed her eyes. Birger heard her take a deliberate breath, and when she opened her eyes, she appeared calm.

"I can see you like to read, and that you're smart. Use that intelligence to look beyond what's written and find the truth for yourself. You're judging other races purely from the perspective of bigoted authors with political agendas. Not all you read is truth. You should consider all the perspectives. Knowledge is power, but misinformation is too."

Heat flushed Birger's cheeks, a scowl twisting his brow and setting his jaw. *High and mighty snob,* thought Birger. *Who was she to call me ignorant and make herself out to be some all-knowing entity?*

Renate took another deep breath. "I'm sorry, Birger."

Her face softened into a kind smile. "Sometimes, I let my past cloud my judgement. I feel angry when you refer to the stillari as elitists because I have a need for more understanding in the world. It's easy to judge those who are different. But remember, others always have their own reasons, and their own context that you can't understand if you haven't lived their life."

Birger blushed. Feeling like an idiot, he grappled with his words in silence. To her credit, there was a notable lack of accusation in Renate's eyes. Still, it was uncomfortable, and Birger started looking around to break away from the confrontation.

He rubbed at his tired eyes; stifling a yawn, he thought, *I need to lighten up. Lack of sleep is making me cranky.* He could've sworn that his onyx bracelet tugged him slightly west. *Maybe I should go look at the statues. They seem important to her.*

That was when Birger noticed a blond man wearing a navy-blue shirt over brown trousers leaving the Minister's Court. The man towered above the stream of people flowing around him. An oversized sword strapped to his back marked him as being some sort of soldier.

Birger pointed at the tall man and asked, "Who's that?"

Renate followed his finger. "Oh, that's Sir Kallen. Well spotted. He's heading to the guest living quarters. Let's go introduce ourselves."

Renate didn't wait for a response; she simply started walking and left Birger staring at her back.

Cos, the woman does whatever she pleases with no regard for what I want, Birger thought. *Then she suddenly warms up and engages me on an emotional level that feels intrusive. She's... she's... infuriating!* He sighed. *But now isn't the time to start another argument.* Birger shoved the annoyance down and hurried after her. *Be nice.*

Sir Kallen stopped to talk to a servant – a man dressed in a delicate pink outfit that must've cost a fortune. All the servants in the palace wore more expensive clothes than most Anthirian merchants. After handing the servant something, Sir Kallen proceeded towards the west courtyard.

Thanks to the brief delay, Birger and Renate had gained significant ground on Sir Kallen. They were still outside conversational distance. Birger would rather not shout like an uncouth fisher and draw attention to himself, so he started to jog, dodging courtiers as he went. Running reminded him that his knee was still bothering him, but he ignored it.

Sir Kallen reached a door and put his hand on the handle.

He opened it.

"Sir Kallen!" Renate shouted.

The volume of her voice echoing off the palace walls made Birger's head hurt.

The tall knight whirled around. A throwing knife zipped past his neck, missing his carotid artery by less than an inch.

Had Sir Kallen not turned, Birger would've found himself rushing towards a dead man.

The weapon skidded across the marble square, coming to rest a short distance from Birger's feet. A greenish-black substance glistened on the blade in the bright morning sun.

Is that poison?

16

OUT OF SIGHT

Sir Kallen was a big man, both tall and broad. Under his plain navy-blue shirt, Birger could see thick slabs of muscle, and the Knight wore brown trousers with simple sandals. He had the most striking blue eyes Birger had ever seen; they looked like crystals complete with a sparkle.

His blond hair seemed to defy gravity as the front playfully swept skywards, and the ornate hilt of a giant sword poked up from his left shoulder. To Birger, the man's handsome face screamed epic hero, but his choice of clothing argued dockworker.

Birger stood at the entrance to the courtyard opposite Sir Kallen. The space contained various potted plants, pillars, benches and statues of humanoid women posed in dancer's forms. He thought of them as humanoid because they sure weren't human.

Their almond eyes had a feline quality, and long knife-blade ears fanned wide from their heads. If anything, the goddesses looked more like the illustrations of the stillari that Birger had seen in Sten's books.

It made sense to Birger. The humans of Azrea inherited the Cult of the Weave from the stillari when they settled here, after all.

A sinister throwing dagger lay on the ivory tiles about fifty feet from him. The Knight's eyes flicked to the dagger and hardened. He snapped around while stepping clear of the doorframe. His massive weapon came forward into a middle guard, ready to deflect any further attacks.

Without thinking, Birger shot forward, drawing his rapier. He *was* here to stop a potential murder.

"Keep your distance," said Birger, glancing over his shoulder to find Renate wasn't there. "Or disappear altogether." He rolled his eyes.

How did she do that? he wondered. *Well, I guess I won't have to worry about her getting in the way.*

The spacious courtyard allowed Sir Kallen plenty of movement, but before he could step clear, two more throwing knives whizzed out from the room. The Knight deflected them effortlessly.

It required considerable dexterity and speed to catch those blades so cleanly at that range, especially considering the size of his weapon; in fact, Birger was pretty sure it was nearly inhuman.

Birger raised his hand, blocking the sun from his eyes to see inside the room. With a reflexive jerk, he caught a whizzing knife on his onyx wristband, deflecting it away from his face.

Aeg! thought Birger. *That was too close.*

Three figures in black emerged from the room with their faces covered in hoods and scarves. Two circled Sir Kallen, and one darted towards Birger. Each of the stalkers had a short sword parallel to one arm, and a dagger held surreptitiously behind their backs.

In jest, Birger asked, "So...you're not the cleaners then?"

The sinister character didn't respond.

"Not much of a talker? That's disappointing. I find a bit of banter takes the edge off in a fight. You probably don't have a name either?"

Again, no response, but their eyes narrowed.

Birger heard a servant shouting in alarm, calling for the guards. He realised he looked like an armed intruder himself and certainly didn't fit with the palace decor. His eyes darted around, instinctively scouting for escape routes.

As the assassin closed the distance between them, pre-battle fear made Birger's heart thump in his ears and his limbs went cold. He shifted into a prime guard, aiming to keep the incoming attacker at a distance by pointing his rapier straight ahead. Steel flashed. Birger parried and fell back, barely evading the relentless assault. His opponent was far too fast for any kind of counterattack.

His knee protested–a month of travel, mostly on foot, hadn't done it any favours. He could feel his opponent manoeuvre him around. That wasn't good, and the full reality of how bad only landed when Birger cracked his sword off a sculpture to his right. He tried to back away and found a pillar behind him. He was in a trap, and he couldn't do a thing to get out.

Aeg blind me! thought Birger in a panic. *I have to move, or I'm dead.*

He changed to a quinte guard, a stance designed to protect against attacks from the left, hoping it would help him step out of the nook, but his opponent was ready. And several quick cuts forced Birger back in place.

Nothing drains your energy or lathers you in sweat faster than fighting, and this dance was taking its toll. He was scared, tired, and his muscles ached.

You failed them, thought Birger's cynic.

Guilt washed over Birger. Mistakes from the past months flashed through his mind. The image of Wynn, in particular, stung – he wished he could've seen her one last time.

Stop that, Birger scolded. *I'm not dead yet, and I never give up. If this stinker's going to kill me, I'll make them work for it.*

The assassin's eyes were smug. They had closed the net on Birger and clearly thought the fight was theirs for the taking.

"You've got some fancy footwork clam-face," said Birger. "I'll give you that... but hold the celebration. You haven't won yet."

He summoned all his strength, beat the short sword to create an opening, then flicked his blade and followed with a thrust to exploit it. But instead of forcing his opponent back, Birger felt several cuts glance off his armour, and narrowly dodged a lunge.

During the evasion, the black onyx band on Birger's wrist plucked him to his right, causing him to trip on his lagging left foot. He tumbled into the statue, and a surge of pain shot through his knee.

Then something improbable happened. Birger's weight toppled the heavy stonework over. It crashed down on the edge of a nearby wooden bench, flipping it into the air. For a brief moment, Birger caught sight of the assassin's eyes stretching wide in grim realisation. The bench struck the assassin on the head, knocking them down in a crumpled mess.

"See?" Birger asked the fallen enemy. "Told ya. It's not only skill that counts, but luck too."

Birger lay back to consider the series of unlikely events that had conspired to leave him breathing and the more skilled combatant dead. He said a quick prayer, thanking Aeg, and then rolled onto his side. Clutching his painful knee, he climbed to his feet.

The guards were approaching from all directions, albeit still a distance for them to cover. Birger had a little more time. If he moved fast enough, he might get out before they arrived. Things happen quickly in a fight, and not much time had passed since the first dagger flew through Sir Kallen's door.

That thought brought Birger to the more critical concern of how Sir Kallen fared, and the answer was, clearly, a lot better than he had with his opponent. Two dismembered and beheaded bodies lay sprawled at the Knight's feet in a pool of blood.

Sir Kallen faced Birger with a faint blue light emanating from his sword. He held it to his hips with one hand on the hilt and the other on the base near the pommel. The sword's point raised only a few inches off the ground. Birger had read about the stance. He thought it was called Boar-tusk or tooth or something like that.

Sir Kallen asked, "Who are you?" his voice a deep bassoon sound.

"Uh, I'm Birger," he said, imagining his own voice a crackly soprano by comparison, and he held a hand up for peace.

His armour and choice of weapon, he realised, made him an easy suspect as a fourth assassin. But surely the Knight had seen him...well, perhaps defeat was too strong, so Birger went with foiling one attacker.

He sheathed his rapier with a nervous smile. "I was helping."

Sir Kallen opened his mouth to speak, but his eyes rolled back in his head. With a dull thud, followed by a clatter of steel, he toppled over like an old oak tree felled by a forester's axe.

Birger tried to run. However, on the first step, a searing pain shot through his knee, making a convincing argument against it. All he could manage was a quick shuffle.

Gullshite! he thought. *If the big man dies, I'll look like the Cos-damned assassin.*

Birger bent over the body to check for signs of life and sighed with relief when he saw the Knight labour for breath. The man was sweating and shivering with fever.

Damn, thought Birger, *he must've gotten nicked.*

Birger searched him for injuries and found a bloodstained tear in the Knight's shirt along his ribs. Next, he checked the nearby short sword, and while the blade was battle-scarred, there was nothing else to see. On the dagger, he found the dark green substance gleaming on its edge.

Definitely poison, thought Birger.

A pair of hard-soled boots drumming on the stone behind Birger drew his attention, and he stood up. The time for finding clues was over.

Maybe if I explain, they'll listen, hoped Birger.

102

"Hey you, hold it right there!" came a voice that made Birger feel sick, and he turned to verify his suspicion.

Running towards him, well ahead of the palace guard, was Pat – the no-neck, bald bully from the Barrel Side Inn, wearing his Roviere burgundy and white uniform.

"Gullshite," muttered Birger, and on instinct, he hobbled away as quickly as his injuries would allow.

His only option was the open apartment door. In half a heartbeat, he was through it. The room large was decorated with crystals, paintings and tapestries that looked worth stealing under different circumstances. A fire crackled in the hearth. Three overstuffed chairs made up a comfortable sitting area, and on the opposite side of the room there was a large double bed with a sturdy chest parked at its foot.

The windows were thin slits with no space to climb through, and there was nowhere to hide.

"Double Gullshite!"

He had to find another way to evade Pat.

Birger turned back to the door, and stars flashed in front of his eyes before something hard smacked him on the bottom. The last thing he saw before everything turned black was Pat's self-indulgent smile bearing down on him, with the butt of his spear raised high above his head.

"Told you I'd get ya, scum," said Pat.

Thwack.

17

CELLMATES

Birger shook awake in panic. *The assassins! Anthir! War! I need to do something!*

But the pain thundering in his head made him regret the sudden movement. It felt like someone had used his cranium and jaw as a pestle and mortar.

He rubbed at the angry welt on his forehead and thought, *That no-neck bastard didn't have to go so hard.*

After what you did to him at the Barrel Side, you're lucky he didn't kill you.

Maybe I went too far with the insults, agreed Birger, and forced his eyes open. *I haven't been in the best mood lately, and I guess this is what you get when you lash out at the people around you.*

Birger spat trying to clear the metallic taste of blood from his mouth, but it didn't help. A droplet tapped on his skull, and reflex almost made him shake his head again, but he stopped himself.

"Agh," Birger groaned in a croaky voice.

All his equipment was missing, and he wore a rough linen sack. His body hurt all over, but the highlights were definitely the head, followed by his right knee. While it was less painful than his head, it graduated to the top of the list when he tried to move.

Birger sat in a cell the size of an Anthir shack. A fat rat chewed on the bones of the former occupant. The steel bars ran from floor to ceiling on two sides. Birger's cozy little dungeon home was one of a set of four, and thankfully, the others were empty. The place was dark, damp, grimy, and above all, smelly.

"Oh great. They gave me a corner apartment, but I can't afford to stay. I have friends in Anthir that need me."

But what would you do if you escaped? thought his cynic doubtfully.

I'd think of something.

Birger's cellmate, the rat, took a break from its meal to give him a side-eye.

"What're you looking at?"

The rat didn't respond, it only returned to its food.

"That's right, mind your own business."

If the Knight died Birger was likely to get blamed. Lorenzo had asked him to wait outside, stay out of trouble, and be ready when the man returned. Instead, Birger had done precisely none of those things.

He had to find a way out, but his head hurt too much to think straight and he couldn't see a way to bend the bars or pick the lock.

Frustrated, he picked up a loose rock on the floor and threw it into the metal bars. With a clang, the stone caught the rod at a bad angle and somehow bounced straight back, hitting him on the eyebrow.

He sucked air through his teeth and rubbed at the sore spot. The rat got a fright and scurried into the gloom of the other cells.

"Run, you coward! You're a terrible conversationalist, anyway..."

Giving up wouldn't do. Birger looked around, sifting through his thoughts for options. *Why had those thieves locked themselves up in a room with only one way in or out? Cos, I only survived by pure dumb luck, but Sir Kallen, by Aeg, he was a scary man. Not Ulfhild scary, with all her dark mojo and whatnot. But, if that's what the knights of West Rendin are like, I don't see how Sawra ever stood a chance of winning a war against them.*

Birger longed for the onyx armband that had sat on his wrist for the last month, and he realised he hadn't removed it since the day he put it on, not even to wash. Now he felt naked without it. He was sure the thing had saved him on at least two occasions.

Birger rubbed his wrist and found it chafed. *Those came from iron cuffs.* While he had never spent time in a dungeon before, Sten made him practice escaping manacles as part of his apprenticeship.

Plan for the worst, and hope for the best. Considering escape, Birger thought, *I should look for a way out of this mess.*

Birger tried to stand, but his everything hurt too much, and he sat back down.

He reconsidered the whole escape thing and put his hands on his head to stop the world from spinning. "Maybe later."

From out of nowhere, a furry white creature the size of a hedgehog appeared on top of the corpse in Birger's cell. It had large pink eyes and eight long legs. It wasn't a spider, but that was the only thing Birger could think of to compare it to. The spider-like creature had two feathered sweeps extending parallel to its mandibles that carefully tasted the air. One of it's front legs pawing around, as if to check for traps.

Birger watched it for a moment. "Wow, you're a big one."

He was used to spiders. Sten had a pet spider kept in the house, but it passed away a couple of months after Sten.

At least I can think about Sten's death without pretending it didn't happen now, thought Birger. *Benny would be proud.*

Thin, emaciated face being sucked dry like a waterskin, hollow eyes staring.

Birger shook his head and accepted the pain because it cleared the awful image, even if it replaced it with stars and too-bright-light.

He slumped forward to inspect the peculiar creature. "What're you in for?"

The spider stared back at him without responding, but Birger felt like the creature gave off a sense of curiosity.

"Nothing to say for yourself, then? Well, I don't blame you. You're probably innocent like me, right? My crime was coming to the aid of some blighter that didn't need any support."

Birger thought of how Sir Kallen had toppled over and reconsidered, "Or maybe I didn't do enough. I imagine the Knight would've told the guards I was helping him if he could."

He stretched his legs out in front of him and leaned back against the hard stone wall.

"Well, Snow, you look like a Snow. Is it okay if I call you Snow?"

Snow didn't seem to mind the name. Birger wasn't sure if it was a male or female spider. Thinking still hurt so he decided to go with male and would stand to be corrected.

Birger studied the pair of bright pink eyes, but he glimpsed something scurrying towards them. On pure instinct, he grabbed a nearby pewter plate and threw it at the blur. It turned out to be the lunging shape of the rat returning from the adjacent cell to pounce on Snow. There was a brief tussle between the two creatures before the plate made contact and sent the vermin slewing across the stone floor.

The force of the throw made him crack his arm into the stone wall. The point of impact was right on his funny bone and nerve shock shot into his fingers. Birger winced and nursed the lame arm while he watched the rat screech back into the shadows.

"And stay out!" Birger yelled after the rodent. "You alright, Snow?"

Birger examined Snow for injuries, and the arachnid allowed it. None of the bites penetrated the strange spider's exoskeleton.

"Wow, you're a tough one, aren't you?"

He gave Snow a tentative pat and, seeing that the spider seemed receptive, opened his hand to offer as a platform. Snow tested the surface before he got on. The pads of the creature's feet were silky, and he was heavy.

"Your world is so much simpler than mine," said Birger as he held Snow up with both hands. "I came here from a great city in Sawra not that long ago. Maybe I could show you someday. I think you would like it. We have the best fish you would ever taste...Don't tell anyone, but I've been terrified since the day I left."

Birger looked up and considered what he had just said. "Benny was right when he said I was trying to hide from the truth by taking risks, and come to think of it, I didn't stop hiding from the pain after Benny died. When I finally accepted it, I felt angry, you know, at everything, at life. Maybe that's why I've been so Cos-damned irritable," Birger looked at Snow, and with a frown added, "I guess it's a bit late for regrets now."

Birger set the spider on his lap, and Snow tucked his legs under himself before preening his fur.

"Ever since I climbed out of Foss' window with the onyx bracelet on my arm, I've felt some kind of strange force intervening in my life. Like a compulsion to do certain things I wouldn't usually do. And look where that got me...."

Birger smiled at Snow. "Looks like I might've lost my mind already. Here I am, talking to a spider as if you understand me."

Birger frowned and then burst out laughing, but his jolly moment got cut short when he heard heavy soles thumping on the stone stairs.

He sighed, "Oh no, is it time for the headsman already? I thought I would at least have till sunrise tomorrow. I hear breakfast is to die for."

Snow eyed the noise and then scuttled up Birger's shoulder. A moment later, two pairs of leather boots appeared on the staircase opposite the cell door. Navy-blue hose ballooned from the boots, collecting at the base of their silver breastplates.

The two guards entered the corridor outside Birger's cell. One was skinny as a pole, and the other broad as a bull. They each held a halberd in their right hand, and the big one carried a box in the other.

The skinny guard gave him a big smile that showed off yellowed teeth and said, "Good afternoon, my young guest. I hope you've enjoyed your stay in our fine establishment. My name's Mick, and this handsome mountain of a man is Gunther. We'll prepare you for an audience with Her Majesty, so let's get you cleaned up."

Birger shot Mick a confused look. Gunther placed the box in his hand on the floor, rested his halberd against the wall, and snapped up a bucket. Before Birger could react, the big man swung the bucket. Water flowed through the bars, splashing across Birger's face. He sputtered, trying to recover from the sudden ice-cold bath.

"Now, now," said Mick in a failed attempt to reassure. "It's just water. You'll be fine. Here," he tossed a rough sponge at Birger, "use this."

The sponge bounced off his chest and landed on his lap.

Still spluttering, he swiped the water out of his eyes and stared daggers at Gunther. "I would just as happily face my judgement dirty."

"Dramatic, aren't we?" Mick laughed. "Your preference isn't my concern. We've got orders to bring you to the Queen, and we don't bring unwashed, mangy mutts to see Her Majesty. So you use the sponge, or Gunther will do it for you."

"Watch your mouth Jack Tar. I'm no mutt."

"Jack Tar?" Mick burst out laughing again. "Are you fresh off a fishing boat or something?"

Birger's temper boiled at being the butt of the joke. "Shut up!"

"Cool your flanks, boy." Mick wiped tears out of his eyes as he spoke, and Birger's cheeks burned bright red. "Get yourself clean. We don't have all day, and you had best be thorough about it."

Mick gestured to Gunther.

Gunther stepped forward. Birger considered being stubborn, but was deterred by the image of the big fellow forcibly scrubbing him clean. Reluctantly, he picked up the sponge and saw Snow sitting on the skeleton. Not a drop of water on him, and Birger wondered again if he was losing his mind and only imagined the spider sitting on his shoulder.

As Birger scrubbed himself, he had to admit that the cold water was somewhat refreshing. Having all the grime and dried blood cleaned off his cheeks felt so good. His head still hurt, but the cold water helped.

"Good lad," said Mick, as he stepped forward to unlock the cell with a rattle of bronze keys.

Mick threw the door wide, and Gunther produced a neat collection of folded items from the box he brought. Birger recognised them as his own gear, and the mountainous guard put them neatly in the cell before stepping back.

"Here are your goodies. Get dressed quickly now. The Queen of Rendin waits for no man."

"West Rendin," said Birger as he eyed Mick and stalked to the gear. "Why're you giving my stuff back?"

"Just doing as ordered. Hurry, before Gunther and I lock you back up and say we couldn't find you."

Birger didn't need any more encouragement and started getting dressed. He picked up his grey linen doublet, the shirt that went under his leather jerkin, and the onyx wristband rolled free. Snow skittered over to the item and started sweeping his feathered appendages over it.

Curious, thought Birger as he continued getting the rest of his gear on.

When he was done, Birger offered Snow his hand and the arachnid climbed aboard. Birger placed Snow on his shoulder and slipped the onyx band back onto his wrist. He felt a thrill ripple through his body. A sensation similar to making a dangerous jump.

Even more curious, thought Birger. *I really need to take a closer look at the thing later. Right now, I've got to figure out what's happening here.*

Mistaking the look in Birger's eye for suspicion, Mick said, "It's all there. Except for your weapons. Only the Queen's-own may carry those in her chambers."

Birger nodded at Mick and realised it was true. Everything was there except for the weapons, even his money.

"Follow us then." Mick started up the spiral stairs again, but Gunther waited.

Birger was startled when Snow scurried down his arm and climbed into his satchel. "Sure, you can come if you like." In a whisper, he added, "You better stay out of sight while we see the Queen."

18

THE QUEEN

Though stepping out of the cell felt good, Birger couldn't shake his suspicion entirely. Aside from that, climbing the stairs was painful, with his knee sending fresh agony surging up his leg with every step.

That's not good, thought Birger. *And did the palace really need so many Cos-damned steps!?* But the pain was minor compared to the icy fear that he might mess up with the Queen and condemn Anthir to war.

With Mick leading and Gunther following behind, they escorted him through the dungeon to a heavy wooden door. Mick knocked, and an eye peeked through a thin slit at head height.

There was a rustle of keys, and the door swung open, allowing them to enter. The guard, letting Birger and his escort out, locked the dungeon door again, and then opened a second door to the palace proper. A squad of four guards occupied the antechamber. They were all dressed in navy blue uniforms with accents of white, and three sat around a square table playing a game of dice.

Birger nodded at the guards, and with a smile, he said, "Thanks for the hospitality, fellas."

One replied, "Any time," but Birger couldn't tell which one had spoken as they never looked up from the table.

In an appreciative tone and a hint of mockery, Mick said, "Ah, ain't that nice. I think they'll miss you. Not to worry, I'm sure you'll find your way back in no time."

Birger sneered at the back of Mick's head. They entered the marble halls with its high vaulted ceilings in the palace proper. For the first time, Birger realised it was already dark outside; he had no way of telling the time from inside his cell.

The hallway was lit by candles housed in golden holders that lined the wall. The palace interior was breathtaking, sporting a range of interlaced arches.

Every surface was either gold trimmed or covered in fine purple silk. On instinct, Birger started casing the place for some fanciful future burglary.

111

"Don't worry," said a gentle voice from behind, and Birger was surprised to see it was coming from Gunther. "Mick's just pulling your leg. We know you're with the Shade, and so are we."

Gunther gave Birger a gap-toothed grin and elbowed him playfully in the arm.

"Oh," was all Birger could manage.

Mick scoffed and said, "Close your mouth, boy." To Gunther he added, "What did you tell him that for?"

"You've had your fun, Mick." Gunther eyed him sternly. "The kid is scared. He needs to know he's safe."

"Whatever, be like that."

A rotund man with thinning grey hair and a swirling moustache approached them from the far side of the hall. He wore a fancy teal doublet embroidered with silver waves.

"Oh, Cos," cursed Mick. "Not this wanker."

"Evening, guards," said the man in a cultured voice. "Is this our hero? The one that saved Sir Kallen?"

"Evening, Lord Irthan," said Mick. "We're on our way to see Her Majesty. I'm afraid we can't chat right now."

"How rude," Lord Irthan narrowed his dark eyes at Mick, and for a moment, Birger thought he saw pent up violence in the short, round man. "What's your name, guard? I would like to have a conversation with your captain."

"The name's Mick Jenkins, sir." Sarcasm dripped from Mick's words. "I look forward to hearing all about your report, sir."

For a moment, an oppressive authoritarian air surrounded the Lord. But then he smiled pleasantly and looked at Birger.

In a conspiratorial tone, Lord Irthan said, "I should like to have a word with you in private. Once you're free of these oafs and have concluded your business with the Queen, come see me. I assure you, the House of Irthan takes better care of heroes than the House of du la Rent. Good evening...for now."

The round man winked at Birger, ignoring Mick and Gunther as he walked past, and a moment later, he vanished down the hall.

"That man is slimier than an angry toad," said Gunther.

Mick snorted. "Yup, top-shelf backstabber."

Birger kept quiet and wondered, A *web of intrigue thing?*

They turned two more corners before Mick stopped at a large double door depicting hand-carved scenes from an epic battle. The detailed expressions of soldiers and terrified horses were incredibly

112

lifelike. Birger inspected the scene briefly before Mick whipped the door open for them to enter.

A young male servant, dressed in formal light pink attire and carrying a white and blue ceramic teapot on a silver platter, exited the ornate doors. He bowed to them and left. Gunther acknowledged the servant.

Mick stepped into the room and announced formally, "Your Majesty, I present Birger of Anthir."

Birger felt his chest tighten in panicked anticipation.

Gunther prodded Birger from behind and said, "Go on. You'll be fine."

Birger nodded and made his way into the vast room. Two large crystal chandeliers hung from the high ceiling. Shelves filled with books lined the walls, and other sections were decorated with large maps or paintings.

To Birger's left, the room stretched past a beautiful burgundy tapestry that stopped near a solid, dark wood desk. Behind it sat a middle-aged woman who radiated confidence. Everything about her was tasteful and measured.

When Birger looked into the woman's bright green eyes, he felt weak under the weight of her gaze. He had to will his sore legs to continue putting one foot in front of the other.

Her complexion was darker than Birger's but lighter than Lorenzo's, and not a single strand of her chestnut brown hair was out of place. A platinum crown rested on her head, and she wore a bright purple silk dress lined with golden angular patterns.

The painting behind her gave Birger a surge of confidence. It depicted a woman in a red gown backdropped by the evening skyline of Mura. He knew it as the Eave El' Grande, and on the desk in front of the woman sat the Viridian Dragon he liberated from Duke Fordson. That meant she had been Birger's patron via proxy at least twice.

Lorenzo stood on the woman's right, with his black rapier at his side. To the woman's left, Sir Kallen was dressed in formal navy-blue court clothing with his giant sword strapped to his back. The large knight fidgeted with a tiny teacup on the desk, trying, and failing, to fit his large fingers into the ear.

Birger was surprised to see the Knight on his feet just a few hours after being poisoned. *What kind of constitution must that man have?* he wondered.

Next to Sir Kallen was a man with similar sky-blue eyes and slightly tussled short blond hair that was streaked with grey. He sat in an overstuffed leather armchair.

The man wore a red waistcoat over a white shirt and neat tan pants that ran down to pale leather shoes with silk laces. He stopped his gold-rimmed glasses from sliding down his slender nose as he read from the book that rested in his lap.

Seated in a similar chair sat a gaunt man with wispy white hair and deep worry lines on his forehead. He had crooked, liver-spotted hands resting in his lap, and his neck hunched forward.

The old man wore a bright red gabardine adorned with gold vines and a white collar flared out from under his chin, making it look like it was propping up his head. A cane carved from pure ivory and topped with a decorated gold handle rested against the man's leg.

Birger, his stomach tight with anxiety, stopped halfway to the desk. He felt like a cod in a school of hammerheads.

"My Lady," he said, bowing, as Mick snickered behind him.

Birger's cheeks turned hot with anger. Mick was making him feel like a fool, and he had to restrain himself from saying something rude to the mollusc. Gunther elbowed Mick and shot a hot scowl at the skinny man.

"That'll be all, Mick," Lorenzo said. "Thank you both for escorting our guest."

Birger noted that Lorenzo, rather than the Queen, dismissed the two men. With a formal greeting, Mick and Gunther left and closed the door, leaving Birger unsure of what to do next.

"Your Royal Highness," said the crooked old man, his voice hoarse with age. "I must object to a peasant attending a discussion of state."

Lorenzo's voice held an edge of frustration as he said, "We've already discussed this, Duke Londel. Birger has vital information to add."

"Well, Lord Soto," said the Duke, "in the courts of East Rendin, when we need information from a peasant, we write it down." Under his breath the Duke added, "And we never let vulgar thugs into the palace."

"My Lords," the Queen interjected, her melodic voice silencing both men.

She turned her attention to Birger. "It's a pleasure to meet you, Birger of Anthir. I'm Armandine du la Rent, the Queen of West Rendin. I apologise for your treatment within my home. I trust you

114

understand my guards had to err on the side of caution. It's hard to distinguish potential assassins from friends in these situations."

Duke Londel rolled his eyes, causing Birger's stomach to flutter nervously. Then Birger experienced something that had never happened before; he couldn't speak. It wasn't that he had something to say that the audience wouldn't approve of; rather, his brain was simply blank.

So Birger nodded, and the Queen gave him a wintry smile.

Queen Armandine turned to the room. "Thank you for joining me, gentlemen. I couldn't let this issue wait until morning. The invasion of my palace is a serious matter and must be dealt with immediately."

Sir Kallen, having given up trying to lift his cup by the ear, had his hand awkwardly wrapped around it. "Yes, Your Majesty," said Sir Kallen and gave her a brief bow. The movement caused his grip on the teacup to jerk. A loud crack reverberated through the room, followed by a hiss of pain from the Knight and a splash as tea spilt onto the floor.

Duke Londel's face reddened, but everyone else in the room feigned ignorance as Sir Kallen began cleaning the mess with the hem of his tunic. At least Birger wasn't alone in feeling awkward and displaced.

"Lord Soto has investigated the situation," the Queen said, motioning to Lorenzo. "He's finished analysing the scene. Lord Soto, would you share your findings with us, please?"

Every gaze in the room shifted towards Lorenzo, who bowed low and said, "Of course, Your Majesty. First, I know this to be a foiled robbery rather than an explicit assassination. Birger, please provide the documents you found in Anthir?"

Lorenzo looked at Birger, who felt small under the sudden attention of all assembled. It took him a moment to realise what Lorenzo was asking and then panic followed as he considered that it might implicate Anthir. The attackers hadn't been wearing Anthir's colours as the orders said they should, but the documents would make the connection.

Lorenzo gave Birger a wink. Could he trust the man that much? Did he have any other choice?

Finally, Birger gave in. Realising that everyone was watching him, he rushed to comply. On his way to the large hardwood desk, he stumbled over himself to extract the correct document from his satchel. An awkward pause later, Birger slapped the scroll on the table with a loud bang, and he winced.

Catching the Duke's sneer in the corner of his eye, Birger thought, *Rich jerk, you're the reason I love my job.*

Lorenzo ignored the fumble, and began, "Their weapons were coated with a deadly poison made from aconite, which should've killed Sir Kallen easily. If I hadn't been aware of this document, I would've concluded that the good Knight was their primary target. However, thanks to young Birger, we know their orders were to recover your sword, Sir Kallen."

Lorenzo pointed at the weapon strapped to the large man's back. "And, according to the palace servants, you refused to be separated from it for any length of time."

Lorenzo waited for a nod from the Knight before continuing, "Further, the documents reveal a plot to *frame* Anthir for the deed."

Birger sighed with relief as Lorenzo's play became clear. *Thank Cos,* thought Birger. *At least I can trust him in all this.*

"I hypothesise the robbers found no opportunity to steal the sword," Lorenzo continued. "As per their orders, they resorted to assassination. According to Miss Couture, she called out to Sir Kallen as he opened the door of his apartment, leading to a missed surprise attack."

"That's true," said Sir Kallen, holding pieces of tea cup, and looking for a place to put them.

"I think their plans changed," mumbled Birger.

He froze with his eyes wide. *Did I say that aloud?*

Duke Londel barked, "You dare speak without permission in the presence of the Queen!"

"Your Grace!" said Queen Armandine, casting a stern glare at the Duke. "Please, speak freely, Birger."

The duke scoffed at that, and Birger fought against the blankness in his head, willing his mouth to form words if only to spite the puffed-up Duke.

In the end, stubborn resolve defeated fear, and Birger managed, "I said, I think their plans or orders had changed."

116

19

STATE OF PLAY

Birger's heart was pounding in his ears, his cheeks burned with embarrassment, and he desperately wanted to shove his head out of a window for fresh air. The vast room felt overbearingly hot, even though it was only being heated by eight braziers evenly spaced along the decorated walls.

He tried to avoid looking towards the reading man in the overstuffed leather chair, and most of all, to ignore the hateful Duke Londel. Queen Armandine looked beautiful in her purple dress. She stared at Birger with her enchanting green eyes, which didn't make speaking any easier. So he tried to find his courage at his feet, inspecting the soft, white bearskin rug.

With a clink, Sir Kallen put half a broken porcelain teacup on the Queen's desk, giving her an apologetic grimace. She nodded in reply, as if to say, don't worry about it, and looked pointedly back towards Birger.

Calmly, Lorenzo asked, "Changed? What do you mean by changed?"

Birger's voice crackled when he said, "They had no escape plan."

Lorenzo encouraged Birger while everyone else remained silent. "No escape plan? Tell me more…"

"Well, that's how I got cau…I mean, I…you know, I—"

"Yes, yes," interrupted the Duke. "We know you got caught running from the scene like a common criminal."

"Your Grace, please," said Queen Armandine. "Allow the boy to speak."

Birger swallowed hard, but the Queen standing up for him made him feel better.

And by Cos, I really don't like that man. The best way to stick it to him would be to show that I'm more than he thinks, figured Birger, and he took a deep breath.

"I went into Sir Kallen's chambers before the guards came," he said. "And there was no way to exit the palace from there. The windows are narrow slits that wouldn't fit an adult. Their only viable escape route would've been to slay every palace guard on their way to the gate. And that would be suicide. If it was a robbery, a safe escape route would've been the primary concern."

Lorenzo looked at Birger, beaming with a proud smile, and even the older gentleman, who hadn't spoken so far, looked up from his reading.

Londel didn't say anything.

Take that, you strutting puffin, thought Birger.

Sir Kallen asked, "But why would anyone want to assassinate me? I'm not of any significance."

"I don't know," said Lorenzo. "However, what Birger says is accurate enough. Perhaps knowing their plans were exposed led them to take more extreme steps? What might be important about your sword? Or might it be revenge?"

The older blond man sat up and asked with concern, "What about the particular woman you fought in Heaven's Peak? She called herself Ulfhild, didn't she?"

"That's right, Lord Caoimhín mentioned you fought Ulfhild in Heaven's Peak," said Lorenzo in a tone that invited the Knight to elaborate.

Sir Kallen opened his mouth to speak, but closed it again in the face of all the other people already talking. Birger could see that the Knight wasn't the sort to force his perspective into a conversation.

"Who's Ulfhild?" the Queen asked, her face rigid as she spoke.

Birger noted she didn't show any emotion outside of chastising Londel, not even an inflexion in her questions.

"Ulfhild, the Blood Queen of the Black Wolf gang," said Lorenzo, pointing at the papers on the desk. "She issued these orders."

"A murderous witch!" blurted Birger, hearing the words and the emotion before registering that they came from his own mouth. He felt the incredible weight of self-consciousness flood over him.

"Birger here knows her too well." Lorenzo looked at him with concern. "She's a resident of his home city and caused the death of a mutual friend."

...Empty eyes staring...

Birger ground his teeth and refocused on the conversation.

"She took over the gang fifteen years ago," said Lorenzo. "She earned her moniker by slaughtering all twenty previous captains and the old gang leader. Her origins before that point are vague, and it isn't clear how much is fabricated for intimidation value. Most

118

believe that she was an escaped slave from Voeterland, where she worked as a butcher. Which paints a rather grim picture if you consider that the tribes of Voeterland are mainly cannibalistic raiders who like their food fresh."

"So she is a piece of work," said the Queen. "Do we need to be concerned about Anthir?"

Duke Londel interjected, "Your Royal Highness, I don't buy for a second that Anthir was framed. As I've been saying since I arrived. The East and West must stand together to take action against Sawra before they can mobilise against us."

"It's unclear, Your Majesty," said Lorenzo after the Duke stopped talking. "I don't think war is what Anthir is after. These documents *prove* that the objective was to frame Anthir for the attack."

Birger tried to harbour in Lorenzo's aura of calm to navigate the overwhelming situation. *This prick of a duke wants to go to war with Sawra. If Lorenzo told them what Fordson did, teaming up with Ulfhild, that might be the evidence needed to give him what he wants.*

Lorenzo said, "The assassins were professionals, didn't carry anything to identify them, and looked southern by ethnicity. I would also remind you, Duke Londel, that you aren't liable for the criminal elements in your land—"

The Duke scoffed. "You would have us wait until Fordson sticks his sword in our collective faces before you act? This is just like with Mura. You're all cowards!"

Lorenzo shrugged and continued calmly, "Your Grace... we don't know what Ulfhild is planning. I would have us collect evidence and respond when we had enough to know we aren't making a terrible mistake. We know Sir Kallen was in danger and that they were after his sword.... Birger, if you could produce the other scrolls, please."

Birger extracted and unrolled the other scrolls onto the Queen's desktop. He felt relieved that Lorenzo had kept Fordson and Ulfhild's relationship out of the conversation. Londel was a jerk, but he might be onto something, even if Birger didn't want to admit it.

The Queen said, "I agree. Evidence first, then conclusions." Inspecting the new documents, she asked, "They're encrypted?"

Lord Caoimhín perked up with the word 'encrypted'. He got to his feet with a simple black cane and shuffled to the desk, his eyes sparkling with excitement. The older gentleman swapped his glasses for goggles adorned with whirling gears and switches similar to the one Lorenzo used at the Barrel Side.

"They *are*, Your Majesty," said Lorenzo. "I've been able to decipher enough to infer that the document contains orders to gain an item from the temple of Lot in the Holy City. I need a key to decrypt the rest."

Caoimhín nodded as he scanned. "That's correct. I see the same. These quintri devices can only calculate up to eight letters. I believe they have used a phrase which is twenty-seven characters long." He scratched his head and then said, "Death co."

"Death co?" asked Lorenzo.

"The first eight characters must be 'Death co'. You can tell by how it translates and the number of shifts applied to each character."

Lorenzo smiled as he said, "Lord Caoimhín, your great mind is an asset, as always. Your Majesty, with your permission, might I petition Lord Caoimhín for help with the matter I originally came to ask about?"

The Queen nodded. "You may, Master of Spies. Lord Caoimhín, if you help Lorenzo, I would take it as a personal favour."

Lord Caoimhín bowed his head in agreement.

Birger's eyebrow lifted at the official title, and he wondered, *Does that make me a spy for West Rendin? If it did, would that mean I'm a traitor to Sawra? Lorenzo never said he was the Queen's Master of Spies, but I guess now I understand what Renate meant. The Shade must be the name of West Rendin's Master of Spies.*

Sharp as a razor, aren't you? thought Birger's cynic sarcastically.

Shut up, you.

"Lord Caoimhín," said Lorenzo, "please look at the bracelet that Birger is wearing. I can't make out the inscription, and I was hoping it may be a clue to finding the rest of the key. Birger recovered it from the same location where he found these documents."

Lord Caoimhín's eyes glinted with curiosity as he said, "Of course, show me."

Birger found it interesting that Lord Caoimhín was so emotive, while the Queen was so stoic she almost seemed Sawran. Birger stretched his arm forward to show the armband, and Lord Caoimhín examined it, turning his arm this way and that, reading the words aloud. Birger didn't understand any of it, and from time to time, Lord Caoimhín would click over gears or flick a switch on his goggles.

120

Finally, Lorenzo asked, "What are you seeing, Lord Caoimhín?"

"I don't see anything that helps with the key." Lord Caoimhín looked up at Lorenzo and then Birger. "And it's not a bracelet. This is a ring."

Confusion must've radiated from Birger because Lord Caoimhín smiled and explained, "It comes from my excavation. It belonged to one of the Titans, the world makers. It's hard to know if you're interpreting a dead language correctly because there is no one to ask. However, I believe this is the ring of the High Priestess of Aeg named Chancebringer. It's supposed to have been made from a scorched scale from Aeg's dragon hide. The stories say that it's both blessed and cursed."

"Excuse me, My Lord," said Birger, "but even if Sir Kallen there stuck his finger in a pod of jellyfish, it still wouldn't fit. How can this be a ring?" again allowing his mouth to run without the filter of his brain.

You're in the company of royalty and you use fisher's slang?

Duke Londel blurted, "Peasant...Really, Your Royal Highness. Your Master of Ceremonies would be appalled to know you allow this kind of thing in your chambers."

"Thank you, Duke Londel." Queen Armandine sternly eyed the man. "If you could refrain from telling me how to run my conference, I would appreciate it. And Uncle, one more outburst, and I *will* ask you to leave."

Birger grinned, which earned him more ire from the Duke.

"Titans were enormous," said Lord Caoimhín with a smile, putting a reassuring hand on Birger's shoulder. "And you can call me Caoimhín. I don't care for all this formal title stuff."

Caoimhín cast a reproving eye at Londel and then a conspiratorial one to Birger. The man had a grandfatherly way about him.

"So Birger," said Caoimhín, "I assume you were stripped of this while in the dungeon? Tell me, in your cell, did you notice anything strange? Something like abysmal luck?"

"I had a few odd moments."

"I wouldn't recommend taking it off for long." Caoimhín looked down at the armband again as if to double-check. "It says that it grants luck to those who wear it and that this luck would be for the greater good, whatever that means. However, it warns that the Weave would reclaim that luck after the ring was removed."

"Reclaim?" Birger considered the life-saving luck he had enjoyed over the last month, a coldness spreading into his fingers and toes.

"But if it gave me luck, it can't be working. The guards captured me easily."

"Captured, not killed," said Lorenzo. "You said the room you entered had no way out. If you had tried to run, you wouldn't have made it far before a longbowman from the towers pinned you to the ground."

Incredulous, Birger asked, "But couldn't it have made the arrows, miss?"

"For the greater good," said Caoimhín, "by whatever logic, it must've decided that your capture would better serve the greater good."

"I would agree with that," said Queen Armandine. "Your escape would've made this conversation impossible. The information you hold wouldn't have reached those that needed it. Give me a moment to think…"

Everyone waited patiently while the Queen reflected. Eventually, she looked at Sir Kallen and Caoimhín, saying, "Thank you for your service, gentlemen. Lorenzo and Birger will continue investigating this situation. Lord Caoimhín, you and Sir Kallen have pressing business to see to. It can't wait for this investigation to conclude, so Sir Kallen, I'll send a full regiment under your command to defend the City of the Titans. I trust you'll be able to keep yourself safe with such a force."

Sir Kallen bowed to the Queen.

The Queen looked directly at the Duke. "Your Grace, for the moment, I don't see enough evidence that Sawra was directly involved. I can't back your petition to muster a declaration of war."

Londel barked, "Queen Armandine, you must reconsider! If we wait for them to attack first, it will be too late, and must I remind you, West Rendin would be first in their path. I'm looking out for you, my niece."

Coldly, the Queen said, "I appreciate your concern, uncle, but I have made my decision. *Goodnight to you*, sir."

More nimbly than Birger was expecting, the crooked old Duke popped up from his chair. Clearly fuming, he snatched up his cane, and then, as if remembering that he had a limp, started shuffling out of the room.

Sir Kallen and Lord Caoimhín waited patiently for the puffin to leave. When they could hear his footsteps receding in the distance, Caoimhín said, "Your Majesty, a moment more if I may?"

"Of course, Lord Caoimhín."

"I apologise for the delay in offering this. I didn't want the Duke to be present for it. However, I think it must be part of your consideration in the future, as it cannot be a coincidence."

"Go ahead."

"Thank you, Your Majesty. This sword," Caoimhín pointed to the large blade on Sir Kallen's back. "Its name is Belmung. During the attack on Heaven's Peak, Ulfhild took the daggers of Kazamung."

"I'm sorry, Lord Caoimhín, I'm not familiar with either of those names. Could you explain?"

"Naturally, Your Majesty. It's not commonly known, because this happened in a time when the stillari society was still considered young. Before the five Ladies were the five, there were eight."

"Eight goddesses?"

"No, Your Majesty. The other three were male gods. Belmung the destroyer, Kazamung the creator, and Hazmothane the first son."

"So, Belmung, which is connected to Kallen's sword, was an evil god?" asked Birger.

"A fair observation, but also no. The stillari histories tell us that at some point Belmung, with the support of the five ladies, refused to act as the destroyer. For whatever reason, this caused strife with Kazamung and Hazmothane. It ended in Hazmothane being locked in the realm of shadows, and the Darkveil being closed behind them."

"And you say that these weapons belonged to them?" asked Armandine.

"Yes, and more. Belmung and Kazamung nearly destroyed one another in combat. All that remains of each of them is locked within those weapons. They, like Chancebringer, are considered pieces of divinity."

Lorenzo asked, "Lord Caoimhín, what uses could these 'pieces of divinity' be put to?"

"Any number, really. They're each powerful in their own right. I cannot be certain what they have in mind. I'm simply noting that Ulfhild has pursued three of them, and so it might be logically assumed that she may seek another in Kindra as well."

"We appreciate you sharing this information with us, Lord Caoimhín." The Queen inclined her head towards him.

"Any time, Your Majesty," said Caoimhín with a deep bow.

"Thank you, Your Majesty," said Sir Kallen. "We'll retire for the evening. We have a long way to travel come dawn." Then he looked at Lorenzo. "If you find those behind this, please let me know."

Lorenzo nodded to Sir Kallen and bowed to Lord Caoimhín as the two left the chamber in the wake of polite greetings.

Birger found the Queen's presence increased with the others gone. She was a high-powered woman, beautiful beyond anything he had ever seen, and he wondered if that was causing him to feel so strange in her company.

When the door was secure, Queen Armandine turned to Birger. "Lorenzo informed me you've accepted the offer to become his charge. Considering your service to me so far, I'll grant you leave to keep the artefact. As long as you serve the crown, it's yours."

Grant me leave to keep it? thought Birger. *Who in the Darkveil did she think she was?*

The Queen of the palace you're standing in, you moron. If she wanted your Cos-damned britches, she could take them, and you wouldn't be able to stop her.

By Aeg, Birger shuddered. *What would've happened if she said I had to give the armband up? Ring,* he corrected. *No, screw that, it's an armband. It might've been a ring to some giant being, but it's an armband to me.*

Then the Queen turned to Lorenzo and said, "What are you thinking?"

20

THE PLAN

Queen Armandine turned in her pale-wood chair to look at Lorenzo. Birger wondered if all monarchs gave off such an aura of absolute order and control. She carried herself as confidently as a galley sailing through shallows, and Birger felt a great deal of respect for the woman.

On her desk lay documents he brought, along with an inkwell and a quill pen resting in a gold-veined-marble holder. It had a shelf built into it, and Birger wondered what other stationery it contained.

Lorenzo leaned back against one of the ivory walls, and a couple of feet above his head, there was a tall lead-glass window. Despite the Queen's attention, he appeared relaxed and stood in silent contemplation. The woman wasn't even watching Birger, but he felt the seconds of silence drag and wondered how Lorenzo could stand it.

Finally, Lorenzo said, "He's up to something."

Queen Armandine asked in a dismissive tone, "Isn't he always? But what?"

"Who?" asked Birger bewildered.

"Duke Londel," said Lorenzo. "I know you were under pressure to bring him into this conversation, My Queen, but I think we might have let him hear too much."

The Queen asked, "You think he might be behind this?"

"I don't know yet, but he was pushing the angle harder than was reasonable for the evidence." Lorenzo put his index finger to his nose and grimaced in thought.

"Would it be helpful to review what we know?" asked the Queen.

"Yes, let's do... So, Ulfhild and the Black Wolf gang attacked Lord Caoimhín's excavation at the City of the Titans, where they stole multiple powerful artefacts. Considering the band on Birger's wrist as an example of what they might have, we should expect a few surprises. A rigid plan won't do. Our best option is to approach this experimentally."

The Queen nodded in agreement and added, "Then we have the orders, along with Chancebringer."

"Here are a few open questions," said Lorenzo. "Who were the messages meant to reach? Who was the ring meant to help?"

"For the assassins attempting to kill Sir Kallen?" Birger asked, feeling like he spotted something Lorenzo missed, and his chest puffed up.

"A good thought," said Lorenzo. "However, given their actions, they couldn't have been the final destination. As you said, they had no intention of surviving their attempt to kill Sir Kallen. Even if their orders changed, their reckless approach suggests that their actions were one gambit in a larger game. I would bet someone in West Rendin, possibly even West Haven, orchestrated it, and we're dealing with fanatics."

Birger wanted to kick himself for opening his fat mouth. It was so obvious now that Lorenzo said it.

I should've seen it myself.

Birger yearned to leave Lorenzo and the Queen with a good impression of him, but he felt that hope slipping away.

"And why didn't they wear Anthir's colours?" asked Lorenzo, waving his hand. "Finally, we know they're after an item, presumably an artefact, at the temple of Lot. But the document still isn't fully decrypted."

"So the Holy City is our next best lead?" asked the Queen, tapping her finger on the desk.

"Correct, Your Majesty. Other options would be to pursue Ulfhild directly, seeking an agent in the city, whom we have no way of identifying, or doing nothing to see what happens next."

With more outrage in his voice than intended, Birger demanded, "How could we do nothing?!"

"Lorenzo is merely laying out the possibilities, Birger." Queen Armandine almost sounded empathetic. However, it was fleeting, and soon the Queen's features were cold once more.

It left Birger desperate to find a way back to that warmth, like a man stuck in the winter cold. He blushed when he realised he was staring and dropped his eyes to the floor.

Lorenzo ignored the interruption. "I must go to Kindra myself. This is too sensitive to leave with anyone else."

"I need you here, Lorenzo," argued the Queen.

Birger found it strange that the Queen didn't order it. Instead, there was a note of pleading in her voice.

Lorenzo smiled, his friendliness suggesting a deep familiarity between them. "I know the situation with Earl Irthan is sensitive. Becka Black returned from Larsea this afternoon, and there's no better spy in the kingdom, Your Majesty. She can monitor the Earl and alert you to his plans even better than I could."

Queen Armandine gave Lorenzo a warning look that suggested there was something she wasn't saying, but Lorenzo didn't flinch.

In the end, the Queen said, "I understand. Whom will you be taking with you?"

"I'll take Renate as our team's mindweaver. Mick and Gunther for reliable hands, and maybe Eric for muscle." Lorenzo tapped his index finger on his lips.

"What's a mindweaver?" Birger asked.

"Someone that knows how to help others sort through their thoughts," said Lorenzo. "She helps me build the team."

"Oh." Birger didn't really understand what that meant, but he felt too self-conscious to ask again.

Lorenzo stepped up to Birger, put a hand on his shoulder, and said, "I think it's best you stay here and help Becka with her work, Birger."

The statement struck him like a loose yardarm. "What?! You want me to stay here? In West Haven?"

The Queen looked at Birger and Lorenzo, a small smile cracking her marble facade.

"You're a dedicated, resourceful, athletic, agile, and streetwise young man," said Lorenzo. Birger found the compliments reassuring. Still, he couldn't help looking for the but at the end. "You're also injured and fatigued. With your potential, you could become a master spy. We need dedicated time for me to train you. I don't want your death on my conscience when I know you aren't ready."

Outrage pushed the words up Birger's throat and past his teeth before he could even think, "I'm here to protect Anthir, not to play court games."

Lorenzo gave him a stern look, and Birger's chest constricted under anxiety's tight grip. He had overstepped speaking to Lorenzo like that in front of the Queen.

Lorenzo's expression softened, and he spoke his next words kindly, "I admire your passion, Birger, and letting it rule you reaffirm what I'm saying. Besides, playing 'the game' could be the best way to maintain peace with Anthir. You heard Londel. He wants war with Sawra, with West Haven's backing, and you know what I didn't say to him. Irthan is part of the situation playing out here, too."

Lorenzo turned back to the Queen. "I'll take Birger to brief Becka and leave by morning."

21

SUPPORT

Birger sat brooding on a dark wood bench, his back to the east wall. Candlelight played like stars on the stained-glass windows overhead. A bookshelf stretched across the west, from the door to the desk in the southern corner.

There was a feeling of wrongness about every room in the palace. Like there was something missing, and Birger realised what it was. He couldn't smell any dust. Not even on the books, and he found it disconcerting.

Snow, Birger's new arachnid friend, groomed in a cozy nook he made for himself on the bookshelf. The creature had done well to stay out of sight during their conference with the queen earlier that night.

Mick and Gunther were waiting for him when he left the Queen's chambers. Mick, the loud-mouthed mollusc, made a snide remark about Birger being left behind, but it was hardly the biggest thing on his mind.

He fiddled with his rapier's hand guard as he thought, *I can't believe I tripped over my own feet in front of the Queen! And for Cos-sakes! Can my mind stop playing the same scene over and over? I can't change what happened. Just stop!* The frustration made Birger's head ache.

Someone's got to make sure you see how stupid you were.

In response, he sneered uselessly at his cynic.

A quiet knock at the door plucked Birger out of his downward spiral. He shot to his feet, thoughts racing, *What do I do? I'm dressed like a thief, and it's late at night—what if a guard thinks I'm breaking into Lorenzo's office?* Birger really didn't fancy another stint in the dungeon.

The door cracked open, and he slipped into the shadow behind it. "Birger?" called a woman's voice.

Relieved, he stepped back into the light and saw her, "Renate?"

"There you are!" Renate's voice echoed off the walls.

129

Snow shifted from preening to preparing a pounce, but he must've decided against it because he simply watched.

Birger felt his own honed criminal instincts ring out with alarm. Being in the fancy building filled with expensive things already made him feel constantly on the brink of being caught.

He suppressed the urge to shush her and impatiently asked, "What're you doing here?"

Renate still wore her blue dress and carried a black leather case in her hand. She pushed the door closed behind her and turned her fading grin on him.

"Oh, wow. Well…I came to check that you were alright."

Birger scowled. "I'm fine, despite your *help*. You abandoned me in a fight and left me adrift in deep waters."

"I did no such thing."

Birger gave her a questioning look. "Really? Explain how vanishing without a trace moments after a poisoned knife got thrown at us can be anything else."

Renate furrowed her brow. "Birger, when I hear your tone of voice, I feel annoyed. I'm no good in combat, whereas you've told me stories of your prowess. And you leapt into the conflict by choice." Birger found Renate's neutral phrasing of events strange, but he couldn't argue. It was all true. "I left to go get Lorenzo–"

"Much help that did."

"If you would allow me to finish?"

Renate paused until Birger agreed with a nod. Snow had settled back down and was grooming himself again.

"When Lorenzo and I arrived, we saw the big fellow from the Barrel Side dragging you off to the holding cells. He had the palace guard with him, and Lorenzo couldn't intervene without the Queen's permission because you tried to run." Renate let her explanation settle, then said, "Now, I understand you felt betrayed?"

"That's right," said Birger, a little less agitated.

"Could you sit down on the bench?" asked Renate. She pointed to the seat behind him. "Then I can work while we talk."

"Work on what?"

"Your knee, Lorenzo mentioned you were limping on it."

She lifted the black leather case in her hand, and Birger realised it must be a medical kit. He complied. As he sat down, she knelt before him and got to work undoing the straps of his greaves.

Renate asked, "Now tell me, what do you need to know so you can feel more secure here?"

130

Something about that question struck Birger in the gut. He felt fear, anger, and anxiety mixing. "I don't know. This place is...is overwhelming, Renate. I don't belong here. I get into a place like this knowing I don't belong, and I get out with anything I can carry as soon as possible. Now Lorenzo has me cooped up here, waiting to find out what to do next. I don't do well being locked up."

Renate pressed gently at the swelling on Birger's knee, and he hissed with pain.

Renate acknowledged, "I hear you, Birger, and I see your heavy feelings about it... You're going through a lot at the moment. What...would you like...to have...happen?"

"I want to do something. Sitting here is driving me insane. I need to put my hands to work and feel like I'm finding a way forward. Cos, Renate, this whole thing is beyond anything I've ever done, and I don't know what to do next, but I have to do something."

Birger sighed, his stiff muscles easing a smidge.

Renate let the silence sit between them while she motioned with her hand, and a small tear formed in reality right above Birger's knee. Surrounding the shimmer of teal and purple light, ice crystals rapidly grew on his bare skin.

On the bookshelf, Snow stopped his grooming to watch her work. She brushed the ice away and reached into the hole to pull a translucent white thread from the other side. Renate kept pulling until she had ten feet of the material. She snapped her fingers, closing the tear, and the chilling cold vanished along with it.

"You know, it's strange," Birger said. "I can be patient on a job. I once sat in a bush from sun up to sun down, studying the movements of a mark, but I can't sit here waiting for Lorenzo. I think I just want to feel useful."

Renate gave him a warm smile and started wrapping the thread around Birger's knee. "I understand. So let me see if I heard you correctly. You know you can be patient, and you want to feel useful. Great. Birger, can I offer something?"

Birger looked at her and wondered, *Offer something? That's a weird thing to ask. People usually just tell you what they think. This must be the mindweaver thing that Lorenzo was talking about.* "Sure."

"You saw a friend die in a pretty horrible way, you have more friends in danger, and you have been in multiple life-threatening situations recently. Any of those could leave someone emotionally crippled, yet here you are, still going and still wanting to be helpful."

"I guess."

Renate extracted a small pair of scissors from the case next to her. She continued to strap the magical thread around Birger's knee, snipping at it from time to time. As she went, Birger could feel the tension build until the joint couldn't move at all.

"Perhaps you can give yourself a little grace." Renate looked up at him, still smiling. "You're in the right place, doing the right things to make a difference."

They were quiet for a moment as Renate worked, and then she added, "I'll talk to Lorenzo and see if we can find grounds to bring you along to Kindra."

"Really?! Would you do that for me?"

"Yes, I will, because I think you need support while you deal with your emotions, and the palace won't give you that. But I can't promise anything. Lorenzo will ultimately decide."

Renate used both hands and started rubbing down the knee strapping. It turned the material from translucent white into a glowing pink, and the threads bled together into a solid form.

"Thank you, Renate." Birger dropped his eyes to his knee. "It means a lot to me you would try. I know I've been a handful since I arrived. I'm sorry."

"Apology accepted." Renate beamed, her eyes sparkling despite the late hour.

"But I reserve the right to be a bonehead again in the future," said Birger, pulling a silly face.

"I would expect nothing less from you!"

The two of them burst out laughing. After a moment of joy that Birger hadn't felt since Anthir, Renate returned to her work on his knee. She kept rubbing the surface, and after a few minutes, the glowing pink faded until it vanished.

"What's happening to it?" Birger asked, stroking his fingers over the area. He could still feel the ridges where the spell material lay.

"I've immobilised your knee. You pulled the ligaments, and they'll need time to recover. My spell should take the pain away, but remember that just because you don't feel it doesn't mean it isn't hurt. So take it easy."

"Healing that doesn't heal?" asked Birger with a big grin. "What kind of priestess are you?"

"I never said I was a priestess." Renate gave him a skew smile. "And even if I were, that isn't how healing spells work. They can only support the body to do its own healing more effectively. It can

132

keep the body alive and speed up the process, but it can't heal what the body isn't able to do for itself. With this, your knee will recover in a few days instead of weeks."

"Not a priestess?" Birger asked, worried. "So, you're a wizard?"

"What, you think I'll bring a weavestorm down on you?" asked Renate with a knowing look.

"Well, isn't that how it works?"

"No." Renate laughed. "I know what I'm doing, and I'm well trained. Only amateurs dabbling in magic without training are likely to cause a weavestorm. A skilled crafter is as safe as any priest."

"Well, if you were going to blow me up, you probably would've done so by now."

Renate gave him a faux exasperated huff.

Birger shook his head and said, "Thank you for doing this, Renate, but will I still be able to run, climb and jump with my knee like this? I think I'll need it given the circumstances."

"Sure, but not as well as usual. Your movement will be limited, and you can re-injure it, so be careful."

"Okay."

Renate stood up and put a reassuring hand on Birger's shoulder as she said, "You're among friends, Birger. For now, I have to go, but don't worry. Whatever happens, we'll stop, Ulfhild."

Birger nodded and smiled again.

As they said goodnight and Renate left, Snow jumped in place when the door closed behind her.

Hope kindled in Birger's belly. He really wanted to go to Kindra; being useful would allow him to feel complete.

What's the point of a clue if you aren't going to follow it? If Renate can't convince Lorenzo to bring me along, I'll go solo. I've slipped out of tighter spots, and can solo the journey to the Holy City if needed.

Birger looked down at Chancebringer on his arm. While in the dungeon, he longed for it and, having it back, he resented it.

How much of what happened was this thing's doing? Birger wondered. *Shaping my destiny as it saw fit. Sure, I had a few impossible jumps go my way. I travelled a long distance with no problems and arrived in time to see the assassins attacking Sir Kallen. However, what about getting discovered on the rooftops, Benny's death, and the dead-end room? The Cos-damned thing feels like it brings more bad luck than good.*

133

The blackness of the armband filled Birger's vision as his eyes lingered on it. With a sudden flurry of movement that caused Snow to jump and scurry down the bookcase, Birger pulled Chancebringer from his arm and threw it at the wall.

In hindsight, Birger realised he should've known better.

22

TOWER OF LIGHT

Chancebringer bounced back off the ivory wall, striking Birger with a heavy smack to the forehead. He yelped in pain as the onyx armband clinked on the bench, rolled to the wall, and stopped there. Mocking faces seemed to stare at him from the lead glass windows of the office, igniting a desire to hurl something at them next.

Snow pounced playfully on Chancebringer and began examining it with his sweepers.

"Ouch!" Birger rubbed the sore spot. There was no blood, but a bump grew under his hand. "I just wish it wasn't so painful to let it go. Maybe I can shake off this bad luck by gambling."

The arachnid diligently swept the artefact for a few seconds. Satisfied, he stopped. Snow circled it twice, got a firm grip on it with his mandibles, and pulled Chancebringer over to Birger.

"Oh, no, Snow, I'm okay," said Birger, but Snow wasn't deterred. The large spider lifted the ornate wristband into Birger's satchel, bundling in after it.

Birger laughed as he looked down. "So you wanna keep it, do you? Fine, the Queen probably wouldn't be too impressed with me throwing the thing away after she gave it to me." He considered that for a moment. "And it might still be an important piece to the overall puzzle."

Birger checked his old pocket watch. It was late, and as the night dragged on, he found himself yawning, but the door swung open, interrupting him. Lorenzo entered, walking with a confident swagger. He was still in his dark leather coat and, despite the hour, he didn't look tired.

Following behind him was a petite, dark-haired woman. Birger found her piercing green eyes and the unique Y-shaped scar on her left cheek intriguing.

A clean, woody scent with a light citrusy note followed her, a perfume Birger had never encountered before. She was dressed in a functional green leather jerkin over a white lace shirt. On her chest, a grey neck tie lay in an upside-down 'V' and slim brown boots were fit snugly around her calves.

Gesturing with his head, Lorenzo said, "Birger, Becka Black. Becka, Birger Light Foot."

"Oh, hi," Birger responded. "With a name like 'Black', I thought you would be wearing something else?"

Becka cupped her cheek with her hand, fluttering her lashes; she asked in a playful tone, "Were you expecting a little girl in a white dress wearing a pink bow? Well, with a name like Light Foot, I would've expected your feet to be on fire."

Becka walked further into the office. She moved like a younger sister barging in on her older sibling's party, complete with an aloof skip in her step.

Birger wiggled his feet. "Ah, they usually are, but I got too many complaints about soot on the carpet." He tried to get up, but slipped and landed back on the seat with a thump.

"I see," said Becka with a girlish giggle, "clearly, the name isn't based on your sure footing either."

Lorenzo smiled at that.

"Ha ha ha," said Birger in a mock laugh.

You're such a fool, thought Birger's cynic.

Thanks, I really needed you to say that, he replied sarcastically.

He tried again and made it to his feet.

Flashing a smile, Lorenzo said, "Glad to see you two are getting on. Becka, Birger's been a great help to me."

In a dry tone, Birger interrupted, "Helpful enough that I'm getting taken out of rotation."

Lorenzo continued, undeterred, "I think he can help you with Earl Isaac Irthan. He's an excellent thief and can retrieve the contract with Roviere that the Earl intercepted."

Becka looked at Birger and smiled. "A good thief, hey? That's all good, but I have some gossip from Larsea that you need to hear."

"Go ahead," acknowledged Lorenzo.

"Word has it that the Wild Lands are on the warpath."

Birger frowned. "How does that change anything? Aren't the greenskins always at war?"

Lorenzo turned to Birger and said, "The greenskins prefer to be called ukthuun. The Wild Lands aren't what we would consider civilised. But they're not as devoid of order as you might think. They, along with many human tribes, have proper settlements. That

136

means trade and agriculture or animal husbandry. It's been years since they sent any organised attacks south."

Birger's eyes widened as he listened. He couldn't imagine the greenskins in an organised military force.

Lorenzo continued, "So, despite the raids Anthir faces from time to time, we consider them at peace. At least concerning their impact on us, because they have plenty of wars between themselves."

Becka nodded. "If the Wulfher scouts are right, and I would never bet against one, the Wild Lands are gathering a force like nothing we've seen. They're taking aim at all the southlands."

Becka rested an elbow on her hip and put her finger on the scar below her eye. "Kings Fort worked with the Nobork clan's witch-doctor Oraana to broker a peaceful trade deal. They were on the verge when Ulfhild, the Black Wolf gang's Blood Queen, showed up. That was three weeks ago."

Lorenzo bared his teeth. "I've been hearing Ulfhild's name more often than I would like recently."

Becka gave him a grim look. "That woman is bad news. She met with Krunak, a hothead with delusions of grandeur, and while their leader might be deluded, the Rotog clan is a significant power in the Wild Lands. Afterwards, Krunak called all the other clans together. He used an old prophecy of Frost Wild dominance to rally a Wartide under his banner. Here, look. I had it translated."

Birger read about the Frost Wild once. It was the shamanistic religion of the northern tribes. Lots of hunting, fighting, and surviving in a harsh climate.

Becka flipped open her notebook and showed it to Lorenzo. Birger peeked over his shoulder to see,

When the blue star collides with the red
And the king of the Dwan lies dead.
The Wild legions will regain their height
and again control the south with might.
But beware, the blue tower of light
It brings down a holy blight,
And summons destruction with a ready blade
That will cause the Wartide to fade.

"Blue tower of light," said Birger. "That has to be Sir Kallen?"

Lorenzo raised an eyebrow. "What led you to that conclusion?"

"I don't know." Birger wondered why he said it. "Something about the man screams Blue Tower of Light. When he was fighting, I saw an actual blue glow coming off him, and also Ulfhild tried to

137

assassinate him. Besides, did you see the guy? He is like some kind of perfect man."

Lorenzo looked at Birger with an entertained smirk while Becka chuckled.

Pleased with their friendly reactions, Birger continued, "If I were writing an epic legend, he would be the hero I picked. He's good-looking royalty. He wields a sword like he was born with it, and the weapon contains the essence of a god. It's like he fell out of the 'perfect hero' tree and hit every branch coming down. If he isn't the Tower of Light, I'm a sea slug's aunt."

Her voice still laced with mirth, Becka said, "Dock slang. How quaint. I have to admit, you're right about Sir Kallen being the perfect man." She pursed her lips in a pleased grin and wiggled her eyebrows. "Regardless, the Wartide is already on the way to attack the dwan and kill King Duncan Anvilhart."

Birger had read about the Wartide, but he was sure those accounts must be exaggerated. According to the authors, the human population on the continent halved, and many towns were completely wiped off the map during the last invasion.

"We should send a warning to the Tower," said Lorenzo.

"Already done." Becka nodded. "I sent a pigeon before leaving Larsea. I tried to reach you too, which I have to assume you didn't get?"

Lorenzo shook his head. "I've been busy, and someone has been killing off shades, so we are a little short staffed at the moment."

Becka's smile faded as her brow furrowed in alarm. "That sounds serious."

"Yes. Don't worry, your sister is safe. Petra's still working in Lorilla. Can I ask you to look into it after this Irthan business is done?"

Relief filled Becka's eyes before once again turning playful and she said, "You got it, boss." She gave Lorenzo a mock salute.

Lorenzo lifted a disapproving eyebrow, and Becka grinned at him.

"Why would Ulfhild work with those monsters?" asked Birger. "This could bring them right to Anthir."

"It seems a reckless play, even for her," agreed Lorenzo. "But who knows what she arranged? Maybe she asked them to stay away from Sawra?"

Becka shook her head. "Don't think that would matter much anyway regarding peace in Anthir. The city is in full revolt…"

"What?!" gasped Birger, his shoulders slumped in defeat. His thoughts turning dark, *Has all of this been for nothing? Instead of saving the city from war, I abandoned it on the eve of war. Oh, Cos, I hope Wynn is safe.*

Becka nodded and said, "That's the other thing I learned. It would seem Duke Fordson pressed the population too hard and then fled the city. Noxolu, the local Magpies Guild Leader, is heading up the rebels. The trigger was the killing of someone dear to the Anthirian Magpies. Sorry, Birger. I don't mean to be the bearer of bad news twice over, but you might have known him. His name was Benjamin Bolton."

"Birger was there when Benny died," said Lorenzo, placing a gentle hand on Birger's shoulder. "And it was Ulfhild that did the killing. I can't say I'm surprised at the response, but I'm surprised Fordson would abandon his Duchy so easily."

Lorenzo gave Birger a concerned look and said, "Anthir has taken its own path now, and if Fordson abandoned his Duchy so quickly, fighting would be minimal. Noxolu is smart, and she isn't one to allow unchecked violence, so the odds are that your people will remain safe. For now."

"Lorenzo, you can't ask me to sit here in West Haven while you go to Kindra," pleaded Birger. "Please, man, I'll lose my mind. I can't do anything about a revolt, but I have to stop Ulfhild."

Lorenzo remained quiet for a time, eyes locked on Birger.

Breaking the silence, Becka said, "Hey, I don't need a thief on call for the next week. I only really need one thing stolen."

"What if I stole it tonight?" Birger asked. "I could have it done by morning and still come along?"

"You haven't studied the target, mapped out guard routes, or created opportunities," challenged Lorenzo. "How sure are you that you can do it with so little preparation?"

"You said Irthan, right? So I met the guy on my way to the Queen. He invited me to come to see him. I could take that way in."

Becka said, "No, making a house call at midnight would set off all kinds of alarms for him and his guards. But that isn't needed right now. I already had my people scout the Irthan estate. He only uses it for Parliamentary visits, so it's not as secure as the nobles that live in West Haven permanently. I can give you what I have."

"Renate thinks I should bring you along to Kindra as well," considered Lorenzo. "Right, well, I would be a fool to ignore the council of my team, and it seems like a plan is possible. But, Birger,

139

if things go wrong, please get out of there. It's not worth unnecessary risks. You can always come back in a couple of days to finish the job. You won't be going to Kindra if you're dead or captured."

They spent the next hour laying out the plan. When Birger finally left, he hoped that taking off Chancebringer wouldn't be the end of him.

23

A THIEF IN THE NIGHT

Winter was rolling into town, and Birger had a feeling that it wouldn't be any worse than the average day in Anthir. Cold was like a rat living in your shack to Anthirians, so familiar that it blended into the background and could even be thought of fondly.

There was a pang of regret as Birger realised that he would miss the mid-winter festival of Lot. It was one of his favourite, mainly because of the food. He loved roasted bream, especially as it was prepared for the end-of-year celebration. Ever since he left Anthir, he had been sorely disappointed with the quality of food. The cuisine of West Rendin lacked flavour, and they ruined bream by boiling it.

A chilling bite in the wind plucked him out of his pleasant daydream. The snowflakes came down in a swirl, reducing visibility, and the moon lay hidden behind the clouds.

Thank Aeg for that little blessing, thought Birger as he prepared for his break-in.

The Irthan manor was on Patton Street, with its back flush with the Royal Canal. Birger approached by boat because it was the least likely to be guarded. No one could climb up that side of the building.

Almost no one. Birger smiled to himself.

He moored his boat to a large rock in the canal, opposite Manor Hill. That was where the real wealth of Rendin kept their estates. Though most of their extravagance wasn't visible from his boat because of a dense forest covered in a fine sheet of snow. Only the occasional tower poked out above the foliage.

As much as Birger would've loved to try his hand at burgling those particular targets, he had work to do. He could earn his spot on the team by concluding the work Becka needed before morning, and he was going to succeed convincingly.

Birger had even spent an hour at the Barrel Side, losing every dime he had left in a game of dice. Hopefully, it would be enough to pay off his luck debt, because he was determined to do this without Chancebringer.

This job will be all me.

Along with his usual gear, he brought a couple of extra goodies for tonight: a grappling hook dangled from his belt next to a hooded lantern. The hook was in case he needed to run along the rooftops, since buildings here were spaced further apart than in Anthir. Also, with the weather being overcast, he would need the lantern to find the right documents. Ambient city lighting alone wouldn't be enough.

Birger stomped his soft leather boots on the wood bench of the boat to loosen his leg muscles. True to Renate's word, the pain in his knee was gone, but the leg was stiff, and he needed to limber it up.

Birger reached into his climbing pouch, grabbed a handful of chalk, and rubbed it into his fingers. The fine white powder was his trade secret. It allowed him to rise rapidly in notoriety among the Magpies, and to take on routes others would consider too dangerous – like this one.

He first discovered the substance while posing as a dockworker and casing a ship for a job, only to get pulled into unloading a marble delivery. During the heavy labour, Birger noticed that the dust kept his hands dry and improved his grip. On a hunch, he collected the powder to try climbing with it, and the results markedly improved his livelihood.

He stretched his shoulders and started his ascent up the rough brick surface. Climbing was fun. He enjoyed solving the wall puzzle, and he spent several minutes mapping the best route in his head. He thoroughly tested every handhold and checked every foothold. Solid holds were sparse. There would be no room for error.

Birger looked down at his boat and saw that his mooring line had come undone.

Damn, he cursed in his head. *I won't be getting out that way.* His hand slipped, and he caught himself just in time. A sigh of relief escaped his lips. Plunging into the canal would mean hypothermia and failure. Neither was an acceptable outcome tonight.

Birger was playing with the big kids now, and people were depending on him. Not to mention that dying from cold exposure in West Rendin would be highly embarrassing for a Sawran.

He felt a weight shifting in his satchel and scurry up his back. He jerked his head to the left and saw Snow on his shoulder. "Did you get bigger since I last saw you? Sorry buddy, I don't have time to play."

The spider just looked curiously at Birger, then scuttled onto the wall. Snow climbed effortlessly, and Birger noted the weight on his grip lighten as Snow stepped off.

"Show off."

Snow hovered over the next handhold that Birger was planning to grab. After a moment, the spider skittered forward to the next one Birger had mapped and then the next.

"What are you up to?" he asked, but Snow didn't stop to explain.

Puzzled and amused, Birger put his hand on the first hold and found the edge lined with a solid, sticky web that gave him a firmer grip.

Snow is helping me climb!

From there, the ascent was almost effortless. So much for his trade secret. It would seem he had a new, more powerful one. Snow's webbing was so strong that Birger could hang off the fibres in complete security. Soon he reached the first-story window, about twenty-five feet above the water. He leaned over to peek through the glass pane and found a dark, empty dining room.

Snow sat on the windowsill, watching Birger. Hoping Snow would understand, he pointed to the second story, where a light glowed in the window. Snow got straight to work, building another handy path for Birger, and it brought a big smile to his face.

A stroke of luck, Birger thought. *My trip to the tavern was expensive, but it looks like it paid off. Or perhaps earning Snow's friendship had nothing to do with luck?*

He heard the murmur of voices before reaching the lit window and slowed his pace near the ledge. He was careful not to expose himself as he peered inside.

Birger squinted, seeing Earl Irthan in his bright green doublet, seated behind the desk. He spoke to someone Birger couldn't see. Based on where Irthan was looking, the other person must've been seated next to the window, so Birger moved to peek from the other side. He wanted to leave no doubt in his competence – every detail mattered.

An old man's voice croaked from nearby, "She's a nuisance, but she'll have to do. I can see no other way to reach him. This must be tied up by the end of the week."

"Certainly, Your Grace..." said Irthan. "But I was counting on West Rendin marching to war with Sawra to crater this deal with

Roviere. Without it, taking the paperwork is only stalling the proceedings, and I need the leverage on Ethrium."

The old man sighed, clearly frustrated. "Fordson didn't mark his assassins, so the Queen didn't believe they came from him. I was sure Soto would've been told of Fordson and Ulfhild colluding, but if he had, he played the cards close to his chest."

Is that Londel? Birger wondered.

"I'm afraid they weren't Fordson's people," explained Irthan. "We found his safe-house in Little Sawra this evening. All of them were there, dead, with signs of aconite poisoning."

"So the Murians sent assassins from the Hand of Sarghus to intervene? They must know what we're up to."

"It seems a fair guess, Your Grace. It won't be long before the Feet of Sarghus follow."

Hand of Sarghus? Feet of Sarghus? Birger wracked his brain to remember. Sarghus was the god on the continent of Apour and, famously, Murapii. But this talk of hands and feet made no sense to him.

"Cos-damn them! I thought we had more time. Did Ulfhild at least mobilise the savages in the north?"

"I believe she did, Your Grace," replied Irthan meekly.

"At least one thing is going our way," said Maybe-Londel. "Then it doesn't matter if the West goes to war with Sawra. We need to convince the Queen to support the dwan. It's not as good as having them divided into two fronts, but it'll do. When we have all the artefacts, they'll be too pre-occupied to stop us."

"Your Grace..." Irthan cleared his throat nervously.

"Out with it Irthan," snapped Maybe-Londel.

"Well... Your Grace, it's just...considering Muria is already moving in on us..."

"Are you faltering in your resolve Isaac?" Maybe-Londel's tone took on a dangerous edge.

"No, no," Irthan back pedaled, "I'm not. You know, I was just thinking we should be careful, Your Grace. Not to worry. I'll find another way to pressure Duke Roviere."

"Good," Maybe-Londel's tone didn't change. "Leave the planning to your betters Isaac. I'll tell you when I want to hear your concerns."

After a pause, Irthan spoke with more composure, "One more issue, Your Grace, is that of Bo."

"I'm done talking about him," Maybe-Londel said with clipped words. "Tell him we'll end his contract if he doesn't get the job done right now. Ulfhild needs to get her people in line. The Black Wolf gang are a bother to work with."

"As you say, Your Grace."

"Rendin needs us to act now and speed is of the essence. If Murapii strike before we're ready...It doesn't bear thinking about. I regret the need to do it this way, but those fools won't listen."

"It won't come to that, Your Grace. And you did all you could. The King of the East and the Queen of the West are both weary. The civil war hit them hard, and neither wants to believe conflict with Mura is unavoidable."

"And in the name of peace, they'll allow an empire to rule them. They've chosen their path, and when the weak do nothing, it's up to the strong to take charge."

Irthan nodded. "Our assets are on the move. We already have much more power than we could've hoped for. The last pieces will fall into place, Your Grace. No one can stop us now."

"For order," said Maybe-Londel.

Irthan echoed the statement and stood up.

A crooked, liver-spotted hand smacked down on the inside of the windowsill. A bent older man wearing a bright red gabardine adorned with gold floral patterns appeared. Birger's suspicion was right.

It was that half-dead old bastard, Londel.

He picked up his cane but walked to the door without using it, stepping as lightly as a much younger man. There was no sign of the limp he had in the Queen's study.

What in Aeg's oceans? Birger wondered. Anger swelled in his gut as the old duke's involvement in the situation became clear. *It's like this puffed up old fool and Ulfhild are trying to get Anthir wiped off the map. How would the destruction of my city help to hold back the Murians?*

Birger slipped away from the window to avoid being seen. Meanwhile, Snow crawled over Birger's hand, hurried up his arm, and returned to the comfortable satchel. The increased weight made the strap sit awkwardly on his neck, and Birger adjusted it.

"Thanks for the help, buddy," whispered Birger, and he got a distinct sense of acknowledgement from Snow.

Come to think of it, how did Snow know where I was planning to go? he shelved the question, *This isn't the time.*

The footsteps receded, and Birger heard the thunk of a door closing. When he peeked over the ledge, the lamplights had been snuffed, leaving the room dark, which meant they weren't coming back soon.

Birger found secure footing and climbed onto the ledge to test the window. The latching mechanism was of an older, simple design, which put a smile on Birger's face.

They hadn't expected any burglars to come from this side of the house and so failed to upgrade the latches to the latest secure variety. A mistake that he was more than happy to exploit. He dug his fingertips under the jamb, wiggled the frame, and after a moment of effort, the latch popped open.

Moving aside, Birger carefully opened the window with a faint creak. With practiced grace, he slipped through and onto the plush carpet, closing the window silently behind him. In the dim light, he scanned the room for anything unexpected and was relieved to find nothing of the sort. Everything was exactly as Becka had told him it would be.

Either Irthan was a neater man than Birger sized him up to be, or he had an excellent housekeeper. The desk was bare. He made a beeline straight to its drawers. The room was too dim for him to see clearly, so he clipped his bullseye lantern off his belt and struck the wick with his flint and steel.

Now that he could see, he pored over the paperwork. After several minutes, Birger found a single stalk of wheat stamped into a wax seal that held a bundle of documents together. He had found it.

The sleeve that held them also contained another document, stamped with an anchor. They all looked like contracts of some kind, but the one Birger wanted was outlining trade terms between Roviere and Moriant. More grain for more steel. Again wanting to ensure he didn't miss anything, he took the whole bundle.

Birger killed the flame in his lantern and put the desk back in order. Moving towards his entry point, he extracted a long string from his thieves' tools and tied one end of the line to the sturdy chair Londel had used. A 'slipped buntline hitch' would give him what he wanted.

Birger ran the string across the window latch to keep it open. The line had to remain tight, so the latch didn't slip down at an inconvenient time. When Birger was outside again, he closed the window and pulled hard on the string, which released the knot and allowed the latch to click back in place. The job was done without a trace of evidence, and Birger took a self-indulgent moment to appreciate his own genius.

Too easy.

As expected, Birger's rowboat was making its way downstream in a leisurely tour of Manor Hill. He secured his footing on the ledge so he could look up, readied himself, and then jumped.

24

NEAR MISS

Struggling against the biting snow, Birger heaved himself onto the slate-gray rooftop of Earl Irthan's manor. A gust of icy wind hit him in the face.

He squinted to catch a glimpse of Manor Hill's grand buildings North of the canal. In contrast, Parliament Hill consisted of drab, nearly identical structures neatly arrayed in the early morning gloom. At least the Grand Palace, the Parliament building to the northwest, and the temples added some character.

That was when Birger noticed someone sitting on the far side of the roof overlooking Patton Street.

A guard? They don't seem aware of me.

Birger moved along the roof with all the stealth his stiff right leg would allow and kept a close eye on the lookout. From his vantage point, he could see the figure's profile. It was a young woman with reddish brown hair hanging over her face, dressed in leather armour almost identical to his own.

It can't be her! Despite the grave risks, he moved closer.

What are you doing, you idiot? You have to get back and report.

Fine, Birger turned towards the royal bridge to leave, but his stiff leg didn't like the idea and, in protest, shifted a tile underfoot.

"Gullshite," breathed Birger.

A familiar voice asked, "Who's there?"

"Wynn?"

"Birger?"

Confusion turned to excitement as Birger asked, "What're you doing here?"

"Looking for you!" Wynn spoke in a voice that was far too loud for his liking.

Nothing's changed, he thought, mildly annoyed but happy to be dealing with it.

The sound of boots pounding and doors slamming open echoed from below, announcing imminent trouble.

"This place is about to become a rip at high tide. We need to leave," said Birger.

Wynn jumped up from her seat on the ledge. There was nowhere to hide on the shallow incline of the manor's roof. They needed a bit more distance between them and Irthan's place to avoid getting caught.

The next house was a long jump, too far for Wynn and perhaps too far for Birger. The Earl's house guards would be upon them in a matter of moments, and Birger couldn't afford to get caught.

He bent down on one knee at the edge and beckoned Wynn to come. She nodded and then broke into a full sprint. Birger braced himself, holding his cupped hands ready, and propelled Wynn to the roof across the gap with a spring. She rolled into the fall as she landed, just as Birger had taught her. Perhaps there was hope for her yet.

With the other side clear, Birger grabbed his grappling hook from his belt, made space for a runup, and went for it. He came up short; but the hook bit into the eaves on the other side.

There was a loud crack, and a shower of splinters or ceramic fragments rained down on Birger while he smacked bodily into the brick wall below. He sagged as the catch tore from the roof, and he braced himself for a drop that never came. He looked up to see Wynn straining to hold on. She had caught the grappling hook by the two free prongs before it could tear away completely.

"Hurry, I can't hold it much longer," said Wynn.

Birger could see sweat beads form on her brow from the effort, and he climbed. He toppled over the edge and collapsed onto his back, wincing as he nursed his blistered and bruised palms.

"Thanks!" Birger panted. "Cos, it feels good to be working with you again."

"Except this time, it's me pulling you out of the fire. I could get used to this," said Wynn with a prideful grin.

"Me too."

Birger smiled back. He took Wynn's hand to pull himself up, and they ended in a near hug. Wynn didn't recoil, and Birger held on to her hand as he brushed her hair out of her face to get a better look at her. True to their luck, the moment was cut short when alarmed shouts called for them to halt.

"We have to move, come!" Birger shouted, and he broke into a run, pulling Wynn along by the hand.

He didn't know the rooftops of West Haven and didn't feel like repeating their last move every time he crossed between buildings. They needed a way down, and moving along the edge of the roof, Birger found it. The pair jumped on top of a carriage parked next to the building and hopped down to the cobbles.

A lantern shone from the Irthan manor's roof, and Birger sprinted towards the shadows of the nearest alley, heading roughly towards the palace.

The rest of Parliament Hill was dreary. The cobbled streets were lines of uniform buildings that looked like administration offices. To say it lacked character would be to say water was wet. At least that meant the streets were fairly predictable. As long as they chose alleys that headed westward, Birger knew they would end up near where he wanted to go.

"Here," Birger said, pulling Wynn in behind a stack of barrels.

A handful of guards from Earl Irthan's estate rushed by, but two of them stayed to search the area. Sweat chilled Birger's neck in the night breeze as the two heavily armoured guards walked into the alleys. One whirling their wicked-looking mace by the strap.

"They went down here," said the rounder guard that lead the way. He held a spear out in front of him, as if expecting Birger to jump on him at any second. "Bring that light so we can see what's going on here."

"You're jumping at shadows again, Ippen," said the taller one with the mace in a woman's voice. She hefted the lantern from her belt and shone it into the shadows near Birger and Wynn.

Birger leaned back, reaching for Wynn to draw her deeper into the shadows, but she handed him off. He felt something clipped off his belt and turned to see her holding his extinguished lantern in her hand. With a whirling windup, she lobbed it onto the building, and it clattered loudly on the roof tiles.

"Rats!" shouted the woman, whipping around and mercifully taking her light with her. "They're on the roof!"

The spearman seemed more reluctant to believe the diversion. However, with his light source quickly receding into the distance, he was forced to accept defeat and follow.

Birger sighed with relief, and turned to Wynn, giving her a nod of approval. They waited for a moment to make sure the guards had turned the corner and then dashed along the alley. At the next crossing, they darted into another alley. Birger braced his back to a wall while he listened for any further sign of pursuit.

There was none. *It's almost too good to be true,* thought Birger. *I missed Wynn so much more than I expected, and having her back is like seeing the sun after a long, dark winter. What were the odds?*

There were only a few guards and lots of city, so losing the remaining pursuit was simple enough, but Birger kept them moving in the shadows to be safe.

Besides, thought Birger. *Being dressed in dark leather with burgling equipment dangling from your belt didn't look great when you were striding down Royal Avenue.*

Interrupting his thoughts, Wynn asked, "Where are we going?"

"Back to the palace," said Birger.

"Wait, what do you mean by 'back'?" Wynn grabbed Birger by the shoulder and tugged him to a halt.

The moon chose that moment to peek out and line the curve of her cheek. He felt her warm breath on his neck. Maybe it was the adrenaline, but he wanted to kiss her right there.

"Oh, right, I'm sorry." Birger realised they hadn't talked yet, and she didn't know what he was doing. "Let's get somewhere safer and I'll explain."

Birger found a safe, dark nook between two buildings and tucked into it. He looked at Wynn, the joy of their reunion bubbling in his throat. He knew he had a goofy grin on his face and didn't care.

"You have no idea how relieved I am to see you," Birger admitted.

A sheepish smile form on Wynn's lips. "I'm happy to see you, too."

Taking Wynn's hand, Birger said, "I thought you were staying in Anthir?"

Her smile widened, and suddenly, he found himself in a tight hug. "I had no choice," Wynn murmured. "Anthir got dangerous after you left."

Time froze as Birger enjoyed that closeness and breathed the familiar scent of the stolen perfume she wore. All the doubt, fear and chaos of the last month vanished, and he wanted that moment to last forever. He knew it couldn't and forced himself to break away.

"Did you leave because of the revolt?" he asked.

"Yeah, the revolt. Birger, it was…" her eyes turned dark and her lip quivered with pent up emotion.

Birger gathered her back to him in a reassuring hug and held her for a second. She shook with sobs that she didn't fully voice, and they simply stood there for a little while.

Finally, Birger reminded himself, *I still have a job to do. I can't let this keep me from getting back to the palace, no matter how much I would rather stay here.*

"There's something I need to tell you." Birger stepped back, firmly holding Wynn by her shoulders and locking eyes with her. "That night in Anthir, we stumbled onto something big. Ulfhild is up to something terrible, and she's bringing war, not just to Anthir, but everyone."

Tears streaked down Wynn's face as she looked at Birger with confusion in her eyes. "War? What are you talking about? What do you mean, Anthir is already in a war?"

"It's complicated. The revolt's bad, but it's not nearly the worst she's done. Anthir's in more danger than some civil unrest. I can't explain it all here and now, but trust me on this. I'm going to do everything I can to stop her. Not just for Anthir's sake, but for Azrea, for Benny."

Wynn winced at the mention of Benny. "What did you do with the scrolls you found?"

An oddly specific question? thought Birger's cynic. *Too good to be true?*

"Why?"

Hush, you paranoid rat-arse, thought Birger. *It's Wynn, and she just travelled six-hundred miles to be with me.*

In a reassuring tone, Wynn said, "That must've been how you figured these things out, right? What did they say?"

See, she's just curious, thought Birger. He didn't remember telling her about the documents, but he was tired and might have forgotten it.

"That's right. One was about stealing something from a knight named Sir Kallen, and the other was to steal a thing from the Temple of Lot. Hey, you could come with me to Kindra! It would be so great seeing the Holy City together, and I'll introduce you to Lorenzo and Renate. I'm sure they would let you come with us if I asked."

"I don't know." Wynn looked away. "I don't have my stuff with me."

"Can I go get it with you? Or could we pick it up on our way out? We're leaving in the morning if I can get this back to Lorenzo before sunrise." Birger tapped his satchel and grinned broadly. Maybe it

153

was the adrenaline from the chase or the lack of sleep, but he hadn't been this happy in a long while.

"I stored my things in Little Sawra, which is all the way on the other side of the city. It would take too long to get there and back before dawn." Wynn looked up at the brightening sky and then added, "What about if I wait for you at the West Gate?"

"That makes sense," agreed Birger.

Assuming Lorenzo relented and let me come... It didn't matter. If Lorenzo says no, I'll get Wynn and follow anyway.

The track north was long, and he was already lamenting the precious little sleep he would be allowed before they left. In his tired state, it seemed as good a plan as any, even though he didn't want Wynn to leave.

Finally, Birger said, "Okay, that's the plan. I'll see you at the gate in four hours. Then I can tell you all about what's happened."

Birger hugged Wynn tight, breathing in the smell of her cherry-sweet perfume. Her skin felt soft against his, and he wished he didn't have to let her go.

25

STAY OR GO

Birger yawned. His extremities tingled as he stumbled up the marble stairs. The guards at the gate accepted his codeword but insisted that he remove his grey hood while on the palace grounds.

A hole in the clouds allowed the early morning sun to shine in all of its glory, and with nothing to shield them, it burned his tired eyes like salt in an open wound. Squinting didn't help because those dastardly clouds held the sun at just the right angle to ensure that blocking it would also blind him.

All the running had soaked his doublet with sweat, and, thanks to the chafing of his jerkin, a blister had formed in his armpit. While shifting his armour to stop it hurting him, he nearly stumbled into a statue in the guest quarters. A couple of passing servants stifled a laugh and Birger pretended not to notice.

Man, I'm tired. His thoughts seeped out of his foggy mind like molasses.

Birger noticed that the statue he had damaged the previous day during his fight with the assassins was gone. Fading blood stains marked where Sir Kallen had dealt with his opponents.

The guards told him that Lorenzo's quarters were down a corridor connected to the courtyard. However, it took Birger longer than it should've to find them. He would be lost in the palace without directions. The place was ten times bigger than any reasonable person would ever need it to be.

I miss Anthir, things there are much more conservative and sensible, with no magically enhanced architecture at all.

Thinking of Anthir, Birger touched the place on his arm where Wynn's hand had been. His shoulder still carried the scent of her perfume from where she had rested her head.

His whole body ached to hold her again, and he thought, *Did all that actually happen or was my sleep-deprived brain playing a trick on me? No, it was real.*

He probed at the angry blisters on his hands that testified to the near miss on the roof.

Too good to be true. With Chancebringer in your pocket, your luck isn't that good. Something's wrong here.

No way. She came to help me, replied Birger. *Can't you just let me have this one?*

Birger's cynic didn't answer.

The palace halls were lavishly decorated as always, with intricate tapestries, and Birger recognised a few of the stories they told.

He allowed himself a moment – or perhaps his tired mind couldn't resist – to absorb the vast history depicted along the walls. He always loved reading about it, and his inner historian gushed at the fantastic display. He attempted to correlate each artwork with events from his memory.

Birger stopped when he found his favourite story. It had creatures of stone and bark looming over desperate-looking soldiers in front of a flat-topped mountain. Leading the men with a shining bright warhammer in hand was King Louis Grengarbane.

According to the tale, Azrea belonged to an extensive grengar empire. This scene depicted the final battle against them at Kindra, where King Louis took their capital.

Speaking of Kindra, you have a job to do, remember? thought Birger, and he pushed himself along. His mission succeeded, so he would get to see that mountain for himself.

A few more turns brought him to a dark wood double door, which he was fairly certain belonged to Lorenzo.

Birger knocked.

There was no answer, so he rapped on it again.

Still no answer.

Again, and nothing.

What do I do now? Birger questioned. *Where should I go?*

He lifted his hand to knock again.

"Birger," called a woman's voice from behind him.

He whipped around, startled, despite recognising Becka's voice.

With cocked eyebrows, Becka Black said, "You're easily surprised."

The raven-haired woman's keen green eyes held Birger. He smiled at the fact that she was entirely dressed in matt black. Becka wore tight tactical trousers, matching boots, and a shineless chest plate. She had a pair of daggers on her hips, and a short cloak draped over her shoulders. Dark circles under her eyes suggested she hadn't slept either.

156

Birger ignored the comment and tapped his satchel where Irthan's documents lay. "I got it."

"Wonderful." Becka smiled. "Mind if we step inside? This isn't a good place to talk shop."

Despite how tired she looked, Becka moved with a playful elegance as she pushed past Birger. She opened the door to reveal a room larger than most merchant apartments in Anthir.

A mantle decorated with floral patterns housed a fireplace stocked with fresh-cut wood. Facing it was a half-circle of overstuffed chairs separated by a sturdy table holding two pitchers of wine and six cups.

Multiple doors led off to other rooms on both the left and right, while the far side glowed colourfully with a row of mosaic windows.

For Birger, the most notable by absence was Lorenzo.

They entered the room, and Becka showed Birger to the seating area, where she made herself comfortable on one of the massive chairs.

Where is he? Birger wondered. *Didn't the man sleep? I have to tell him about Wynn before I forget.*

Becka wriggled deeper into the seat and said, "Aaaah, Lorenzo has the best couches. Come, sit, try it out," she pointed at the overstuffed chair opposite hers. "He imports them from Kurhan, you know. I told him they're mine if anything ever happened to him." Becka smiled. "Now, tell me what you found before you collapse."

Birger opened his satchel. Inside, Snow's pink eyes sparkled with mischief. Birger petted his furry white head. Reaching past the curious arachnid, he extracted the document he found at the Irthan manor.

Did Snow get even bigger? Birger wondered. *Nah, it couldn't be. Probably the lack of sleep was doing things to my perception.*

He held the bundle out to Becka and sat down while she paged through it.

He found the seat lived up to the promise as he sank into its comfort. "Oh, yeah, that hits the spot." He fought to keep his eyes open and straightened up to avoid the sleep from overwhelming him. "And, the job went smooth as a baby's bottom,"

Becka looked at him with a skew smile. "It was like that, hey? Funny, though, that's not what I heard. Maybe we know different babies?"

Birger blushed.

157

You should've known better than to lie to a spy.

"It sounded more like you and Earl Irthan's house guards had a bit of a foot race around Parliament Hill."

"Okay, maybe that bottom was attached to an old beggar with leprosy. But that was mostly in the escape department. Which reminds me, I need to speak with Lorenzo. Where is he?"

Snow chose that moment to slip out of Birger's satchel and nestled on his lap. He realised Snow was approaching the size of a small rabbit and thought, *Cos, he really is growing fast.*

"Oh, cute!" Becka squealed with child-like excitement and shot forward to pat Snow.

The spider nuzzled Becka's hand and swept his feathered appendages over the rings on her fingers. Birger enjoyed the woman's excitement and realised for the first time that she couldn't be that much older than he was.

"What is it?" asked Becka. She cooed while Snow curled his legs under himself and made quiet chirping sounds.

"Oh, him?" Birger watched the display unfolding in his lap. "This is Snow. He's a friend."

"Oh, hi Snow, you're so cute! Oh yes, you are," said Becka. "I've never seen anything like him."

Birger also started absently petting Snow's soft fur. "Lorenzo?"

"Out. He'll be back when you're ready to leave. Tell me what else you saw."

Becka went down on her haunches and continued petting Snow as Birger spoke. "The Earl was talking to Duke Londel."

"Oh, my! Are you sure it was Londel?" asked Becka, her voice ladened with scepticism.

"Yep. I don't think I could forget that liver-spotted prancing puffin if I tried. But I need to talk to Lorenzo urgently. Where can I find him?"

"Prancing puffin!" Becka laughed. "That's so good. I'm going to remember that one. Sorry, but Lorenzo isn't available." She leaned her face down to Snow and pouted. "What's the third-in-line to the East Rendinian throne doing in a private conference with Earl Irthan...?"

"I don't think Snow knows either."

"No, probably not. I guess I'll have to rely on your account then. Tell me everything they discussed."

Birger recounted the conversation between Londel and Irthan in as much detail as possible, and when he was done, Becka stroked at the scar on her cheek.

He cleared his throat. "So it looks like our issues are connected, like Lorenzo said it would be."

"What do you mean?" asked Becka, her eyes widening. "Other than the obvious Anthir, Ulfhild stuff."

"Bo, he's sort of my nemesis. It's possible that they're talking about a different Bo. However, I reckon there can't be so many people with a dumb name like that running around working for the Black Wolf gang. Or," he sighed, "maybe I just hope it's him. I owe that man some payback."

Becka's eyes squinted as she smiled kindly at Birger. "Is there anything else I should know?"

She stopped petting Snow and stood up. Snow wasn't happy with that and got up to nuzzle her hip with one leg pawing at her fingers.

"Just that I need to speak to Lorenzo."

"I'm afraid you can't." Becka gave Birger a sympathetic look.

Birger grunted in frustration, and Snow looked up at Birger with a sense of concern.

"You get used to it," Becka said. "I'm satisfied. Lorenzo will be at the stables in one hour. Be there if you still want to go to Kindra. Good job Mr Light Foot."

Her words washed over him in a wave of relief. He grinned like a fool.

She stood up and walked to the door with that girlish skip in her step.

Becka looked back, already halfway through the threshold.

"I'll need to take a closer look at this business with Mura," she said. "I don't like them killing people in my city, even if the victims were thugs. Thanks for your help, and have a safe trip. I hope we work together again soon."

26

PREPARING TO LEAVE

Birger yawned as he trekked across the palace grounds towards the stables. It felt like a night after Noxolu sponsored rounds at the Rusty Tankard. Even thinking of the ever-angry innkeeper stirred a flicker of longing in his heart.

I hope she's safe, thought Birger. *What I wouldn't give to have her shout threats at me while I break plates in the commons with an over-the-top gymnastic display. I miss them, all of them. Aeg, please look after the Anthirians.*

Despite the fatigue, thinking about home didn't summon flashing images of Benny's final moments. *Could Renate's magic have done something to me? I don't know if that's even possible. Was that how mindweaving worked?*

Bone weariness made Birger's limbs heavy, his right knee still stiff, and a popped blister on his left hand stung every time he flexed it. He only had time to splash cold water on his face, devour the food that somehow appeared in Lorenzo's room and run.

Birger entered the palace's stables, situated below the grand reception platform. A small assembly congregated in the vast expanse. Stable hands laboured in the horse stalls along the west wall and neatly arranged tack hung along the east.

Lorenzo stood at the centre of the group, and he was dressed in his signature green leather. Birger recognised most of the other people too. Renate wore a turquoise riding outfit with her blond hair tied back in a bundle.

Renate, standing to Lorenzo's left, gave Birger a warm smile. To his right stood Mick and Gunther. Gunther was scowling at Mick as if the loud mouth had just said something rude. Both wore light brown leathers, complemented by silver breastplates and halberds.

The strangest member of the group stood next to Gunther, and was a full head taller. Cords of thick muscle wrapped his frame and they writhed like snakes under the surface of his skin when he shifted his weight. A laurel of purple-grey hair circled the man's head and jut out on the sides like extended ears. Bright yellow lupine eyes gleamed with a predators intensity. A short beard framed his face, flaring out from the corners of his jaw.

On his right shoulder was a bear-pelt guard, and the animal's head, still intact, rested on his chest. His forearms and legs were wrapped in the same fur, and despite his exceptional height, the man looked stocky.

Around his neck hung a loose bone necklace nested in a rugged bed of chest hair. On each of his feet he wore an iron-shod bear's paw boot. Birger saw a gleaming double-bladed axe clipped to his back by a giant bone handle, strapped with red leather.

All in all, it was the most intimidating human being Birger had ever seen, and he gave the new face a wide berth as he approached.

"Finally crawled out of your hole in the ground, fisherman?" Mick taunted.

Gunther's scowl redoubled, and he smacked Mick on the shoulder.

"Hey!" Mick snapped back.

Birger shot Mick a wry smile. "I need my beauty sleep. I don't want to end up looking like you." Despite the retort, the comment stung. At least it seemed Gunther had his back.

Gunther waved and said, "Ignore Mick. He's as gracious as a warty toad this morning. Good to see you again."

Mick glared sullenly at Gunther.

"Good morning, Birger. Glad you could make it," Renate said.

Birger grinned, first at Gunther, then at Renate. "Becka let me know I was on the team."

Sighing, Lorenzo said, "Between Renate, Becka, and your persistence, I could hardly refuse."

Mick broke away from Gunther's stare and with a forced smile, he said to Lorenzo, "Letting this bunch push you around, boss? You going soft on us?"

"Soft as a razor's edge, Mick." Lorenzo winked.

Renate hugged Birger. He felt a bit uncomfortable but didn't pull away, touched by her genuine delight. Renate had already proven herself as a friend, and Birger was becoming more at ease with her way of doing things.

Yet, when she fussed over him, fixing his hair and straightening his armour, it elicited a few snickers from Mick. The self-consciousness became too much for him, and he politely disengaged, feeling Snow's weight shift in his satchel.

"Oh, hello there," said Renate, looking down. "Who're you?"

Birger found two large pink eyes peering up at them. Snow shrugged off the canvas flap and shook out his fur.

Renate's eyes stretched wide, along with her grin. "Wow! Aren't you the cutest little weavespider I've ever seen?!"

Gunther nearly jumped into Mick's arms. "What in the Darkveil!? Is that thing a spider!?"

Everyone looked at him in surprised shock when they heard the high-pitched noise that burst out of him.

"Oh," said Mick as he half held Gunther up, "now I'm suddenly husband enough for you?"

Gunther let go and stepped back while shooting ice daggers at Mick.

Mick grinned. "If you really need a hug, I'm sure the spider wouldn't mind."

"Enough, Mick!" Gunther retorted, stepping back defensively. "You know I don't do spiders."

"It's okay," said Birger. "Snow's a sweetheart. The worst I've seen him do is shamelessly beg for pats."

"Oh, he's just a baby," said Renate. "Where did you get him?"

Renate stroked Snow's head gently, and he made the high pitched chirping noise that meant he was happy.

The mysterious big man didn't budge or react at all.

"We did time together in the dungeon," said Birger.

"What?" barked Gunther. "Are you saying this was the same white spider sitting on you in the dungeon?"

"Yeah, the same. I must admit, I wasn't expecting him to grow up this fast."

"Grow up fast?!" Mick cocked his head to the side. "I swear the thing tripled in size since yesterday."

Lorenzo cleared his throat. "Gentlemen, lady, shall we begin?" his tone carried a gravity that silenced the room. Renate continued to massage Snow's head. "Birger, Becka told me all about your performance last night. Congratulations. Now, let me introduce you to the team. You already know, Renate. You met Mick and Gunther yesterday. They're handy in a tight spot, and I trust them implicitly."

He pointed to the scary man. "This is Eric Wolfanger. Eric is a Wulfher from Kings Fort. There's no one I would rather have next to me in battle." Lorenzo turned to the group. "This is Birger of Anthir, where they call him 'Light Foot' for his exceptional ability to move unseen."

Each group member nodded to Birger.

Wulfher, hey?

Birger had read about them. They were an elite core of soldiers that operated out of Kings Fort. They kept the grengar of the Darkveil Forest away from civilisation.

There were many stories about them, and some seemed far-fetched, but what had to be true was that they were some of the fiercest warriors around. When you earned your first stripes in a battle against creatures made of stone and bark, as tall as a three-story house and as broad as two carriages, you had to be. It took more than strength to survive there.

"Here is the situation as it stands," Lorenzo continued. "The Black Wolf gang are conspiring with elements in the court to create conflict, and we don't know precisely why. They've already riled up the ukthuun of the Wild Lands and are working to cause strife between West Rendin and Sawra. A play to destabilise the kingdom and split our focus so they can do something else."

"Ukthuun?" asked Mick, puzzled.

"Big, green killing machines," said Gunther.

"Oh, greenskins."

"We must do what we can to avoid war." Lorenzo ignored the interruption. "Where we can't avoid it, we ensure the kingdom stays strong to defend itself. Something to be wary of is that there are powerful magical artefacts in play that could be used for a wide range of mischief."

Lorenzo scanned the group. Making sure they all acknowledged that point before he continued, "The implications of war with the wild north stretch beyond West Rendin. When the Wild Lands bring a Wartide south, everyone's at risk. So this threat can't be ignored, and whatever Ulfhild and her allies plan, we need to stop that too."

Lorenzo let his words settle, then asked, "It's up to us to change the course of history and save lives. Are you ready?"

"Yeah!" shouted Birger, Mick, and Gunther.

Renate nodded, and Eric shrugged.

With a friendly grin, Gunther gave Birger a meaty thumbs up.

Gunther seems like a decent man to me, Birger thought. *Did Mick say they were married?*

"Good. Our intelligence says the enemy seeks an artefact at the Temple of Lot in Kindra. The plan is to stop them, but whatever happens, we must let West Haven know all we learn. Take prisoners if you can. It's hard to question the dead." Lorenzo looked at Eric.

Eric just folded his arms and shrugged his hill-like shoulders.

The clip-clop of hooves pulled Birger's attention to a stable-hand leading seven horses from the far side of the building. Four were powerful-looking chargers, two of them were regular travel mounts, and one was a packhorse.

They were all tan with long fur and well-stocked saddle bags. Birger almost failed to recognise that they were Sawran Highlanders because he had seen none so well groomed. Usually, their long fur was matted and dull, but these had flowing, shiny coats, and their manes were clipped around the eyes.

Birger and Renate took the two smaller horses while the others mounted the chargers, and Mick grabbed the reins of the packhorse. Exploring his saddle pack, Birger found it filled with food, camping gear, and a bow with a quiver of arrows.

He had never shot a bow. It wasn't something you could easily practice in the Squat, and Sten focused more on sword play or daggers during their training.

About Anthir, am I forgetting something? Birger wondered, but his addled mind gave him nothing meaningful. *Oh... I hope someone is still taking food to old Hamish. Revolts can be distracting. I guess the children would help him. At least I gave him plenty of money.*

Everyone mounted up. Lorenzo led them from the stables, and through the lush green lawns next to a small lake that rounded out the picturesque palace grounds.

As they rode, he saw a large exotic succulent with bright pink leaves. *A short time ago, I could never have imagined a place like this. And yet here I am, riding to stop bandits from stealing an artefact from a temple, and saving the continent from being overrun by uks.*

What happened to my simple life of plotting new ways to torment my dad?

They left by the palace gate onto Du la Rent Avenue, which led them through the drab Parliament Hill and would take them to the Marked Ward. It was a monument of Rendinian culture, containing almost anything anyone could want to spend money on.

It would take about an hour to wind through the city and slums to reach the West Gate. Too weary to pay attention, Birger let his horse follow the others, resting his eyes as they travelled. He was aware of Renate speaking to Mick.

It sounded like she was using her mindweaving on him, asking her strangely phrased questions. But Birger couldn't be bothered to eavesdrop.

Eventually, he nodded off.

Startled awake, Birger heard Wynn call his name.

Gullshite! thought Birger. *I completely forgot to speak to Lorenzo about her!*

"Birger!" came the call again.

The slums of Little Sawra, north of the West Gate, were a ramshackle collection of huts and cottages. Despite the name, they looked like luxury living compared to the Squat of Anthir. The cobblestone roads were covered in sludge from melted snow. Birger noted Wynn had somehow kept her boots clean as she came running from that direction. She was forced to dodge a couple of carts in the modest traffic.

Lorenzo pulled up short of the gate to look back at Birger, with the rest of the party following his lead. Birger felt small under their gaze. He waved at Wynn as he dismounted and tried not to overthink the awkward discussion that was coming.

"Hi, Wynn," Birger called back to her.

Lorenzo was looking at Wynn like a hawk stalking a field mouse, and Birger gulped nervously.

"She's a friend from Anthir," said Birger, hoping to ease the tension.

"I already know all about her," responded Lorenzo.

That sent apprehension crawling up Birger's spine, and he thought, *What does he mean he knows about her?*

"What?" asked Birger, "I mean, how?"

"Becka," said Lorenzo with a glance at Birger. He turned to the others. "She'll be coming with us. Renate, Mick, don't let her out of your sight for a second."

Birger sputtered and asked, "Wait, what do you mean?" Not knowing what was going made him feel agitated.

"We'll talk later," said Lorenzo, to end the exchange.

Neither his tone nor his words were harsh, but Birger felt kicked in the gut and thought, *What's going on? What did Becka say? Why isn't it harder to bring her along?*

Wynn reached Birger, wrapping him in a warm hug. Her reddish brown hair flopped in his face, with the familiar cherry-sweet smell of stolen perfume wafting into his nostrils.

Wynn pulled away and said, "Thank Aeg. I was afraid I missed you."

Birger was stumped, so he simply smiled in reply. He looked up at the rest of the group, unsure of what to do next.

Renate said, "Don't be rude, Birger. Introduce your friend."

"Right," Birger recalibrated. "Everyone, this is Wynn. She is my apprentice from Anthir. Wynn, meet Renate, Lorenzo, Mick, Gunther and Eric."

Wynn elbowed Birger in the ribs and said, "Hey, who's your apprentice? I was the one saving your butt last night."

"Yeah, right," replied Birger, "*was* my apprentice, I guess."

Mick stifled a laugh.

Lorenzo smiled at her and said, "Pleased to meet you, Wynn. I see you're ready to travel, so I assume Birger invited you on our journey."

"He did."

"We wouldn't dream of turning Birger's saviour away. You may ride the packhorse alongside Mick."

Wynn bowed awkwardly. Renate dismounted and hugged her. The friendly contact clearly caught Wynn off guard. She inhaled, and her eyes stretched.

Birger grinned, recognising the discomfort of a fellow Anthirian caught in a hug.

Breaking away, Renate said, "Enough with the introductions. Come, child, I'll help you get set."

Lorenzo got down from his horse and, turning to Birger, said, "With me, please. I need to talk to the guards at the gate."

That added weight to the ominous feeling in the pit of Birger's stomach.

I don't like this, thought Birger, but he followed.

27

OVERWHELMED

How am I going to justify this? concern roiled in Birger's gut as he and Lorenzo approached the city wall. *He'll say I should've already told him about Wynn. What if he sends her away? Cos, what if he sends me away...*

You brought this on yourself by not telling him earlier.

Not helping, Birger retorted.

The West Haven city wall towered over the buildings nestled against it, and its gatehouse stood open during peacetime, giving free passage to all. If war were to come down from the north, that would change.

The smell of mud and horse droppings wafted through the air. The guards scrutinised Birger from the battlements as they marched up and down. Their polished silver helmets complemented their navy-blue uniforms, which had a flare of white in the britches.

They look well-trained, thought Birger. *If I bolt straight towards Little Sawra, I could lose them in there.* He distracted himself by indulging in the familiar activity of assessing his escape options.

Lorenzo stopped and looked around to ensure no one was within hearing range before turning to Birger. "First, I want to say I'm sorry."

The words stunned Birger. He was expecting a fight, instead, he got an apology. *What's going on?*

"I should've already spoken to you about this." Lorenzo smiled reassuringly. "Becka and her agents were shadowing you all night. She told me about your briefing, and as you probably guessed, she relayed it all to me."

Where is he going with this? Birger wondered.

"What reason does Wynn have to come to West Haven?" Lorenzo asked.

"She said she followed me because I asked her to."

"That was what she said," Lorenzo pursed his lips, "and what do you believe?"

169

"She cares about me and would want to keep the people of Anthir safe." Irritated by the implications of the question, Birger scowled. "Stop beating around the bush. What's this all about?"

Lorenzo paused, letting the moment linger before saying, "Wynn's appearance on that rooftop was no coincidence. After she left you, she returned to the Irthan manor and left through the front door two hours ago."

That set Birger's mind racing, and a pit formed in his stomach. *How could this be? What did it mean?*

"I can see this news didn't land well, and the next part likely won't land any better, either. I offer you only the truth, Birger. Building this team requires trust. Since I need you to trust me, I'll layout the full truth here and now." Lorenzo locked eyes with Birger. "I want her to come along because I plan to use her for counter-espionage."

"What's that supposed to mean?"

"Willingly or not, she's a spy for the enemy. Allowing her to stay with us means I can feed her false information so that we can mislead the wolves about our plans."

I told you so, thought Birger's cynic.

Not now.

His mouth dropped open. "That'll put her in danger! If they find out, they might kill her."

Lorenzo shook his head. "I don't think so. They're more likely to twist it to their advantage the same way we are."

Deflected, Birger continued searching for an excuse. Wynn's betrayal twisted his guts. He couldn't fathom travelling alongside her knowing what she had done, and desperately wanted to block Lorenzo's idea. "We can send her away, can't we? She hasn't earned her spot as I did."

You coward.

Lorenzo looked at Birger with gentleness in his eyes and put a hand on Birger's shoulder. "We know little about what's happening here...I understand you may not feel comfortable with this, and I know what I'm asking is hard for you. We've been a step behind this whole time, and this could let us level the field. On a scale from one to five, how willing are you to follow?"

Birger went quiet. Could he follow? Well, he wasn't sure. Inside him, love, kindness and disgust wrestled, pushing the mission into the background, but in the end, Lorenzo was right. They needed this.

"A four I guess," Birger replied.

"And what's behind that four?"

"I don't know what to tell her? I'm not a good liar."

"Lying rarely works." Lorenzo smiled. "Omitting facts differs from lying. What you discussed with the Queen is confidential. Tell Wynn you aren't at liberty to speak about it. This also includes ongoing investigations she's not involved in, such as the Irthan estate. We can discuss Kindra and our current investigation. You don't have to lie to keep the enemy in the dark."

Lorenzo paused as Birger processed what he had said. "Being authentic is the only way to lead. If those around us can't trust our word, the team unravels, and when the job robs you of who you are, the enemy wins the same as if you failed the mission."

"Lead?!" Birger was taken aback.

"You'll lead this team in time. Each of us must lead when the time comes. Leadership is an ability I expect from all my agents. In your case, the time to lead will be when we need stealth."

Birger gave Lorenzo a doubtful look.

You're a terrible leader. He's going to be disappointed.

Lorenzo said, "Each of us has a unique skill set. Who better than the expert in that area to lead the team when those skills are needed?"

"I know how to pick pockets or move around unnoticed. I don't know anything about leading people." Birger shook his head.

"I told you there would be training." Lorenzo cocked his head to the side and shrugged. "Here, give me the original scrolls and put these five in their place."

Lorenzo handed him the documents. Four of them looked like copies of the scrolls Birger had already, and the fifth was new. "She'll try to steal this from you at some point, let her. Now, return to the others. I need to speak with the guards."

"Wait. How isn't this lying?"

Lorenzo smiled, but it didn't reach his eyes. "We never said this information was true. We are simply taking precautions, and should she decide to act deceitfully, well then, as they say in Anthir, what you cast to sea, comes back to shore."

Birger nodded, feeling his shoulders slump.

Returning the nod, Lorenzo said, "So, where are you on that scale now?"

"Five. But tell me, what would've happened if I said no?"

"I would've put her under house arrest and departed without her. As I said, this team is built on trust, and I need you to be with me entirely. I appreciate your willingness to put your personal feelings aside for the sake of our mission."

Birger grimaced and shifted uncomfortably.

Lorenzo grinned. "Well, Mr Light Foot, let's get this done. Welcome to the team."

Lorenzo continued on towards the guardhouse, and Birger walked back to the others. Although he was satisfied with the ethics of planting the documents, this leadership talk didn't sit well with him. He nearly killed Wynn as his apprentice, who was now working for his enemies. Maybe his terrible teaching even forced her to join the mutts.

Renate had aided Wynn in moving the supplies around on the large packhorse so they could saddle it. While Wynn appeared tiny on the giant animal's back, she looked at home as if she had ridden a beast like it before. Birger wondered where the saddle came from. Then he realised they had brought it, knowing that Wynn would join them.

Had Lorenzo known all along?

Birger awkwardly mounted his horse. Unlike Wynn, he wasn't comfortable on top of the animal, having only ridden a few times in his life. To punctuate the point, Wynn pulled up next to Birger with the elegance of an experienced rider. His heart was thudding in his ears.

I can't do this, he thought as his anxiety built. *I can't keep myself from confronting her.*

"Good morning. Get much sleep?" Wynn asked with a playful smile.

"Me?" Birger surrendered some resistance, and half smiled in return. "A couple of hours, you?"

"Same."

Birger disengaged, and when Wynn didn't press him to speak more, he felt relieved, but it was short-lived as a surge of fury rose in him. Outrage pushed against his temples, making his head throb.

How could she betray me? He ruminated as the anger boiled, the building pressure urged him to say something.

You're going to mess this up, thought Birger's cynic.

This isn't good, he thought. *How could I stay calm?*

He looked around. He needed a distraction, something, anything.

"Are we going back to having a little nap now that your girlfriend is all travel-ready?" teased Mick, leaning leisurely in the saddle of his charger.

172

"What did you say?" demanded Birger, anger spilling over like a full fishing net plopped on a skip's deck.

"What's gotten into you, son?"

Birger's cheeks flushed red and his fist clenched at Mick's quip. It was like Mick embodied every snarky bully Birger had ever met. Benny's death, Wynn's betrayal, Sten, it all came crashing in, and he had enough.

Seething, Birger grabbed Mick by the shirt. "Shut your mouth, gutter scum!"

Their horses bumped against each other. Birger's horse shuffled at an inopportune moment. When Mick deflected his grab, Birger tumbled into the dust with a puff. He pounded the ground in frustration, climbed back onto his horse and set off through the gates.

A big part of Birger desperately wanted to keep riding. The weight of embarrassment pressed down on his shoulders like that dreadful armour knights wore on victory marches.

With an effort, he convinced himself to halt his Sawran Highlander outside the city gate, huffing in frustration.

28

A FRIEND

It was mid-morning. The sun climbed the sky unhindered by clouds, and a salty gust of chilly wind rushed over Birger from the nearby coast.

He took in the built-up strip of land known as the outskirts that continued beyond the walls — wooden houses with thatch roofs and large labour yards. Birger saw a fishers-pier down the wall where the morning catch was being offloaded, and everywhere, townsfolk bustled with chores.

A meaty block of a man that must've been a farmer bringing his cart to market greeted Birger with a warm smile. The gesture contrasted Birger's dark mood rather sharply, causing him to feel self-conscious, and he forced a polite nod as the man passed by.

He was exhausted and couldn't think straight anymore. His chest felt tight, and he was panting.

How could I let myself act like that? he thought.

A reassuring hand touched down on his shoulder. Relaxation spread through his muscles like a tree taking root, and the sensation drew him back, his breath steady once more. Birger glanced back and found Renate smiling kindly at him from the back of her horse.

In a soothing tone, she said, "Mick doesn't mean any harm with his remarks."

"What? Oh Mick, yeah, it's not really him." Birger drew in a deep breath. "It's all just too much, Renate."

"Tell me more…"

"My life's been turned on its head, and I feel like I'm drowning. I can't stop all these bad things from happening, and now I must betray a friend who betrayed me. Why can't it be simpler?" Birger squeezed his reins and picked at the leather bulge.

"Thank you for entrusting your thoughts to me, Birger. I can hear this is weighing on you." Renate stroked his back, and the calming sensation spread deeper into Birger's core. "You want to feel in control. And I sense you want to figure things out… What would you like to do with this?"

"Trust Wynn? I want to think she's a good person trying to do the right thing." Birger looked up and sighed. He closed his eyes and allowed the icy wind to cool his hot cheeks.

Renate let Birger bask in that sigh for a moment, and then she said, "You want to trust that Wynn is trying to do the right thing. Could I ask you to step into her shoes for a moment and tell me, if she were trying to do the right thing, what could lead her to act as she did?"

"I don't know," responded Birger, going quiet.

Renate let the silence sit between them and rubbed his tense shoulders with one hand while controlling her horse with the other. His muscles were much more relaxed than they had been a moment ago.

Birger looked down to where he was picking at his reins and said, "I guess I assumed it was because she got a better opportunity with Ulfhild. Maybe the mutts pay well?" Birger's answer seemed glib even to himself.

"So you see that as an assumption. I wonder, how true is that assumption?"

Birger looked at her. "It's an assumption, so it's not true."

He contemplated for a second.

His face fell, and he gasped, "Neffily!"

"What do you mean?" Renate tilted her head curiously.

"The only reason she would do what the mutts wanted would be if they took Neffily."

He looked down at his hands, noticing that Snow had climbed out of his satchel and rested his forelegs over the saddle's horn. The large weavespider shook the dust out of his white fur coat and looked at Birger with concern. Birger knew it was concern because he could somehow feel it radiating from Snow.

Birger put his hand over his face. "What have I done, Renate? I dragged Neffily and Wynn into an impossible situation."

"Not you," Renate shook her head, "Ulfhild dragged them into an impossible situation. You couldn't have known what she would do. You're a hero, Birger. Without you, we wouldn't have this chance to stop her now. Sir Kallen might be dead...Heroes don't have it easy. They face trials so that others can have peace. You're destined for greatness if you can tame your emotions and accept that you can't control all things."

"What do you mean? I usually feel as emotionally barren as a hammerhead."

"Not showing emotions isn't the same as not having them. When you bottle them up inside, they have a way of erupting." Renate smiled her signature kind-smile and stopped rubbing Birger's shoulder to jerk a finger back at the gate. "How do you feel that served you today?"

Birger already missed the pleasant massage, Renate's hands were magic. He shook his head. "I look like a fool. I don't know how I can face the group now."

Renate's eyes turned stern yet were filled with compassion. "You had a moment of weakness. Your team is still getting to know you. How you handle this moment will define how they see you. So what... would you like... to do... with that?"

Birger weighed his options. He wished he could shove his head in a pile of sand and pretend it never happened. That was the coward's way, and Birger didn't want to be a coward. He resolved to face this situation like any deadly trap and dangerous jump. He gripped his reins with one hand and stroked Snow's fluffy head with the other.

Finally, Birger broke the silence and said, "I'll show them I know when I'm wrong, and I'll find a way to keep Wynn and Neffily safe."

Renate smiled. "Yes, you will. You have a heart of gold, Birger 'Light Foot'. You're going to do great things on this team."

Birger circled his mare around to face the city and saw the others pass through the imposing gatehouse. Wynn eagerly led the way, and Mick lingered at the back.

Birger looked at Renate and said, "Thank you."

Renate inclined her head graciously. She was an impressive woman. Something about how she spoke to him made Birger feel safe. Not the I-want-you-at-my-side-in-battle kind of safe. He knew she was no good there. It was something else. She just kind of held a space for him to think. Maybe there was something to this mindweaver business?

When Wynn reached them, Birger smiled weakly and said, "I'm sorry, Wynn."

"You didn't do anything to me?" deflected Wynn.

"I did, I really did... I'm sorry for all of this. We should be back in Anthir, running on the rooftops of the Apartments."

The guilty smile she returned wasn't lost on Birger as Wynn said, "Yes, we should."

Birger glanced at Mick, who gave him a sheepish eye from behind Gunther. "I'm sorry, Mick."

"That's alright, mate. I don't fancy running around rooftops in Anthir, anyway."

29

BREAKING DOWN WALLS

"A mind that knows is inferior to a mind that understands, but in the wisdom to enact that understanding lies true enlightenment"
Jing Mindweaver Rilu Assat

The ride to Stella was tense. Birger avoided Wynn like she was a leper, Mick's jokes continued to land as well as a drunken sailor's quips at a noblewoman's wake, and Eric scared everyone half to death by saying absolutely nothing.

As a small mercy, Lot made it almost impossible for them to talk, with dense flurries of snow that slowed their progress, and the party didn't reach Stella until nightfall.

Birger's furry companion, Snow, revelled in everyone turning fluffy white. Not to mention how much the weavespider enjoyed Wynn and Renate's company, where head scratches or belly rubs were available on demand. Birger grumbled something about also wanting that kind of attention. Fortunately, it went unheard, allowing his stoic Anthirian facade to remain intact.

The clip-clop of horseshoes on cobblestone echoed between Stella's tidy buildings. Being near the capital on a main road, the small town enjoyed padded municipal budgets. Lit streetlamps lined all the roads, and a few teamsters on carts took advantage by making after-hour deliveries.

Sometime ago, Anthir added lamps in rich areas too, claiming that they would make the roads safer at night. *Yet,* Birger thought with a smirk, *they didn't do much to keep third-story windows secure.* While they allowed pedestrians to spot ambushers, the light didn't reach the rooftops. It also robbed people of their night vision so Birger could safely escape with their valuables. *I guess Roar did do something for me, after all.*

Stella was more charming than most of West Haven. Her pristine streets spoke of a carefully crafted image, designed to portray West Rendin's prosperity to land traders from the East and Quan.

A single cathedral perched on the east hill overlooking the market square. In places like this, the goddesses had to cram for space like paupers in a single building, and sometimes they would even have to share a priest.

Birger liked to imagine them drawing straws to see who would get the comfy bunk, like he and his fellow fins did in the fin house. Except in the fin house, it was about who got the least lice-ridden bunk. *Oh no,* Birger corrected himself, *naturally I'm not including Lot in that bit of imagination theatre.* That made him wonder if the goddesses could read minds and ultimately decided it was best to assume they could.

Apart from the thin layer of ice, the streets were clean and scarcely populated. During Birger's last visit, the harvest festival had been in full swing, with people filling the streets. Carved potatoes adorned every corner, each of them sculpted, and some were modified with other vegetables to add a horse's tail here or a crooked nose there. Given how much of it was around at the time, Birger was astonished to see it all cleared away.

The town's sole inn, the Yellow Yeoman, was a squat building on the market square's southwestern corner. A thick snow blanket spread across the roof, with yellow walls embracing a wide oak door that sat on top of seven limestone steps.

A smoke plume above a red stone chimney hinted at warmth, and Birger glimpsed the fire's glow in the common room through a small glass window. Over the door hung a sign depicting a man in yellow court garments bowed over a pitchfork.

Birger checked his pocket-watch, and said, "It seems unusually quiet for this time of night."

"It's mid-week and snowing," Gunther explained, "meaning few travellers and the locals can't afford tavern drinks every night."

A young stableboy with a mop of black hair and plain yellow work clothes took their horses. Eric and Lorenzo followed him to the stalls, and it sounded like Lorenzo was tapping the boy for information.

Snow leapt out of Birger's satchel and scampered down his leg.

"Oh, Cos!" Gunther jumped as he saw Snow scuttle after the horses. "Is that thing bigger again?"

"Maybe," said Birger. Snow did look bigger. Soon, the weavespider wouldn't be able to fit into the satchel.

Gunther shuddered. "I can't believe you all touch it. I feel ill just thinking about it."

182

"Snow's harmless," said Birger.

"Besides," said Wynn, "he's so cute!"

"Ugh!" Gunther groaned, and Mick heckled him with a laugh.

Gunther rolled his eyes at Mick.

"Where's he off to anyway?" asked Wynn.

With a shrug, Birger said, "To go hunt albatross? Honestly, that weavespider is on his own mission most of the time. If he wasn't so adorable, I might've ditched him by now."

"You couldn't!" Wynn gasped.

"I'm not saying I will. Like I said, he is adorable."

Gunther's shoulders trembled, his face twisted with disgust, resembling a man gutting a hagfish. Birger found the big man's fear of tiny old Snow amusing, but he wasn't going to poke fun at him. Mick had done enough teasing already.

As the levity passed, everyone remembered the cold and hastily headed for the inn door, shedding layers of ice from their clothes along the way.

"Last time I came through here," said Birger, "they were so full I had to stay in the stables. Let me tell you, there's nothing, quite like ten horses passing gas to lull you into a deep sleep."

"Ugh!" Wynn grimaced at him. "That's disgusting, Birger."

"Seriously, you should try it. You'll sleep like a baby."

"Only someone that has never had a baby would say that they sleep well." Renate winked at Birger.

Mick and Gunther chuckled, pushing the door open, and hearth warmth welcomed them in. A rotund woman stood behind the counter with a jolly smile spread across her round cheeks.

She wore a green scarf that morphed into a blouse tucked into a long yellow skirt. Gertrude exuded welcoming kindness with every gesture. During Birger's stay in the stables, she brought him leftovers and an extra blanket at no charge, even with her inn overflowing with guests.

Besides the innkeeper, two dark-skinned women, possibly travelling merchants from Korland, were seated at a table. They glanced up at the opening door and then returned to their quiet conversation.

Gertrude noticed the newcomers right away and said, "Birger! Back so soon?" He was surprised she remembered him. "And you brought friends! I love company. Come in! Come in! It's far too cold out there to dally. Come on, sit down. I'll get you something hot on a plate to take the edge off. I have rooms available, and you're welcome to have them."

"Nice to see you again too, Gertrude," said Birger.

"Thank you, madam," said Renate as she approached the counter to discuss the terms of their stay.

Mick and Gunther followed in search of some refreshments, Mick put his hand on Gunther's back to say something. Gunther tilted his head to the side and his jaw tensed. Mick spoke again and Gunther's face softened, his lips turning up in a pleased smile.

What's that about? Birger wondered.

Gertrude gave Renate a kiss on the cheek as if they were old friends. Birger smiled at the warmth that radiated from the innkeeper. It reminded him of his mother.

Mum, too, had been a kind soul like that, always bringing home strays and cooking them meals, thought Birger, a pang of loss followed the memory. He hadn't known her long, she passed when he was only five, but he cherished the many splendid memories of her.

Birger caught himself and realised how exhausted he was. His mind tended to wander when he was tired. At that moment, all he wanted was an ale and his feet up next to a warm fire – two of three comforts were within reach.

He slumped onto the bench by the east wall, and Wynn settled across the table. Burning wood crackled in a broad fireplace on the opposite wall, and an illustration of two ships at sea sat on the mantle. Three more six-seater tables with benches occupied the room, illuminated by a central chandelier. The table's surface was slightly sticky and had the yeasty tang that came from years of spilt drinks. Birger felt at home.

With Wynn across from him and the sense of familiarity, he allowed himself to pretend they were back in Anthir at the Rusty Tankard after a long night's work. The fiction eased the tension in his shoulders and reminded him Wynn's actions were driven by the predicament he put on her. He sighed and tried to hold on to that perspective.

Birger closed his eyes, rubbing the painful bruise on his forehead. This train of thought made him feel guilty, and he worried for Neffily. He longed to ask Wynn about it directly. *Not knowing is always worse,* thought Birger.

What if it isn't about Neffily at all?

"Renate will have rooms ready for us soon," said Wynn, noticing his slouch and taking it for exhaustion, which wasn't wrong.

"I need a drink first." Birger opened his eyes. "It's been a long day."

A large, sweet-smelling stein plopped onto the table in front of Birger and Wynn each.

Birger looked up into Mick's crooked smile, and the man said, "To show you that there ain't no ill intent between us, hey?"

"Micky here has a big mouth on him," said Gunther, standing next to Wynn. "But he has a good heart, too. You get used to accepting the one for the benefit of the other."

Mick noncommittally tilted his head. Gunther gave Birger a gap-toothed smile, shrugged his massive shoulders, and plonked down on the bench.

"Thanks," said Birger, ogling the stein.

It felt as though a desert's worth of sand coated Birger's tongue, making him desperate to taste the freshly poured brew, even if a petty part of him wanted to throw it in Mick's face. *But sometimes,* he thought, *you must set your moral high ground aside to quench your thirst,* and Birger's cynic agreed with him for once.

As Mick joined Birger on the bench, Birger took a full-mouthed sip from the ice-cold drink. A refreshing flush of golden fluid filled his mouth, and he smacked his lips.

Mick wiped the foam away. "A beauty, isn't she?"

"Best I've had since the Rusty Tankard," agreed Wynn.

The drink was a wonderful blend of hops and peaches that popped on Birger's tongue like quintri fireworks.

"One of the best things about winter is the cold drinks," said Birger.

With a face-splitting grin, Mick put his hand on Birger's shoulder and said, "Sub-basements can only do so much. Look, mate, we're a team now, and we've got to have each other's backs. So, like, I might still poke fun at you from time to time, but you know it's all meant in good fun, and if things go south, I'll be at your flank."

Gunther nodded slowly and warmly. There was something big brotherly about him. Birger had never had a big brother, but Benny had the same air about him.

It showed in little things, like looking out for him when no one else would or giving him straight talk when he needed it. Something that most people wouldn't do because they didn't care, or they were afraid you would stop talking to them if they did. Birger could imagine Gunther having a conversation with Mick like Benny had with him on that last night.

Man, I miss Benny, thought Birger, and asked, "Did Lorenzo tell you to make peace with me?"

Mick shook his head. "Lorenzo don't tell anyone anything. He suggests. He advises, but should you say no, he finds another way. That's just Lorenzo."

"A strange way to lead," said Birger, and he took another sip from his brew. "I thought leaders gave orders and shouted at you for not following them."

"Lorenzo ain't that kind of man," Mick smiled, "and I sure wouldn't follow him if he were. He says trust makes teams. If he must do it in a way that breaks your trust, then it's not the way. I don't know if I buy it fully, but I would kill for the man, so maybe it works."

Gunther nodded. "Saved our bacon more than once, too. Lorenzo is a good man to know if you find yourself in a tight spot."

The door swung open with a thump that rattled the windows, and a large group of armoured men dressed in burgundy and white poured into the building. They were laughing and joking as they sidled over to the bar.

"Oh no," said Birger and sank low in his seat. "It's that no-neck prick and his pals from the Barrel Side."

The other three craned their necks to see what Birger meant. There were ten of them standing by the bar, all armed, armoured, and travel-weary. They looked like veterans, and Pat looked like he was in charge.

As Renate passed by the Roviere guardsmen, Birger overheard one making an inappropriate comment. Despite his desire to be invisible, Birger shot up to his feet again and was about to say something.

Renate waved him off and warned, "Ignore them. We don't want any attention."

Birger prepared to sit again when no-neck Pat turned around and made eye contact. They looked like sweethearts bumping into each other at the tavern with other dates. Pat's face contorted into a sneer, probably looking at the nasty purple bruise on Birger's forehead. Birger childishly stuck his tongue out at Pat.

Top shelf master thief persona there, thought Birger's cynic.

Yeah, well, you're dumb, thought Birger.

I'm you, you idiot.

186

As Birger sat on the bench at war with his inner self, he heard the shift of wood on wood, and he realised Gunther had followed his lead. Ready to start something if Renate hadn't said otherwise.

So, the whole having my back thing wasn't just talk.

No-neck Pat was now talking to Gertrude, and after a moment, he smashed his fist on the countertop. Pat looked over at Birger in outrage, ready to kick things off.

"We took all the rooms," said Renate as she sipped on fine red wine. "I expect he's just found out."

Pat stomped to the table near Birger, his entourage in tow, and fell into the bench, making the wood scream as it skidded across the floor. He looked at Birger with murder in his eyes, and Birger stared right back.

Pat was the first to break eye contact, but not in defeat as Birger first thought. He was leering at Wynn. The man's neckless form straightened, and he advanced on her, his cronies flocking behind him like he was the scouter after a morsel.

Here it comes, thought Birger.

In the most obnoxious way possible, Pat said, "Oi love, you look like some fun. Why don't you leave this boring lot and come join us boys for a little while? We got plenty of gold," he glanced at Renate and added, "and you still owe us, so we got room for two."

Birger's anger hoisted him to his feet before his mind could do anything about it, and the sudden movement flung the bench into the wall with a crack.

Weird, thought Birger, *wasn't Mick sitting on the bench too?*

Birger glanced around and saw everyone standing, with Wynn glaring up at Pat as if she were glaring down at him.

"Say that again, you swine," snarled Wynn, pointing her finger in his face.

30

BRAWL

The Yellow Yeoman's common room was cosy and filled with the scent of beef stewing on an open fire. Gertrude, the innkeeper, watched the unfolding conflict wearily from the bar, with her usual joy fading in the face of the building tempest.

No-neck Pat loomed over Wynn, her finger pressed against the tip of his nose. Anthirian women were known for their ferocity, and Pat bought himself a front-row seat to a demonstration. Even with his crew behind him, it wouldn't make a difference.

Pat leered down her finger and said, "No need to be like that, love. We're just having some fun."

Birger counted ten versus his four, not adding Renate because she was useless in a fight, and he tried to calculate their odds. He had seen Wynn in these situations before, and the likelihood of a peaceful resolution dwindled with every word spilling from the moron's mouth.

"You're the reason we have to sleep in the barn tonight. Least you can do is provide us with some entertainment." Pat hammered another nail into his own coffin, and his eyes flickered to Birger to see if the comments were landing.

The dolt didn't know what was coming, but the two women across the room figured it out, because they were making their escape up the stairs.

Good thinking, ladies, thought Birger. *This isn't going to be pretty. I might as well help things along.*

He said, "Don't worry, Pat, you'll love it in the barn. No better place to be a horse's ass."

Pat's face turned a shade of red that almost looked purple. "Shut it!" he yelled. "This time you're the one that's outnumbered."

Renate asked, "What would Duke Ethrium Roviere say about you acting like this?"

It's gone too far already, thought Birger. *I don't think even you can talk things down now.*

"His Grace ain't here, is he?"

One of the duller-looking gulls at Pat's back said, "I'm worried about what the Duke might say too, Sergeant."

Pat gave the man a grim look. "Shut it you. They ain't talking to the Duke anyhow. They're just bluffing."

"Sorry, Sergeant," responded the other man, retreating to the safety of his fellows.

"Listen, big fella," said Mick, "We don't have time to flirt with you. Apologise to my lady friends now, and we won't feed you and your little troop of jesters your boots before planting you in the snow outside."

One of Pat's gaggle chose that ill-timed moment to knock the lovely illustration above the hearth over. It hit the ground with a crash and a tinkle of broken glass.

No-neck Pat acted first, lunging at Mick, only to find Wynn's stiff elbow planted square on his nose. The stocky man's head snapped back from the blow, with a small fountain of blood trailing along the arch. Pat staggered and caught himself, but Wynn hit him like a ramming ship, unleashing a flurry of punches as she rode him to the floor.

Birger didn't know how, but Renate had vanished again. He watched Gunther take two big steps around the table and hit an incoming guardsman so hard that tooth fragments burst from his mouth. Mick threw his ale in one man's face and smacked another with the tankard.

Birger needed room to move, and he needed to stop the rest of the guards from flanking Mick, who was covering Wynn. In two steps, Birger climbed the table, his stiff right knee slowing him down, but not enough to be a problem.

With a runup, he jumped with his left knee extended in front of him, and bodily cracked a guard in the chest. Breath burst from the man, and sharp pain exploded in Birger's kneecap. They both collapsed in a heap on the floor, with Birger on top.

Aeg blind me! thought Birger. *They have studded leather under their surcoats.*

He got up and tested his knee, which was numb, but he didn't think it was broken. The man he hit gasped for air like a beached fish, and Birger scanned for his next target. They were outnumbered, but it was a close fight. Gunther was handling four on his own.

Mick, Birger, and Wynn had each landed telling blows, but as the initial surprise faded, the tide turned. The guardsmen were used to working as a team and they used their numbers well. Birger could see them regrouping, preparing to encircle Gunther, while the rest kept Birger, Wynn and Mick occupied.

Lorenzo's voice cut through the noise, followed by a booming thunderclap and a flash that disorientated Birger. Through hazy vision, he glimpsed the imposing seven-foot-tall wall of muscle that was Eric step forward and grab two Rovians. He lifted them off the ground and held them there like naughty children.

Next to him, Lorenzo waited for everyone to recover. Birger spotted Renate snapping a weave tear shut and Snow peeked out from behind her leg.

Right, magic, thought Birger, rubbing his eyes, and wishing whoever was blowing on that shrill whistle would stop.

"Cease this!" ordered Lorenzo and walked up to Pat. "We don't want any further tensions with you, Sergeant. If you leave now, I'll neglect to mention this incident to His Grace, Duke Ethrium Roviere, next time I see him."

There was a deep gash on Pat's eyebrow and another on the bridge of his nose. Elbows were prone to cutting the tender skin on someone's face, and Wynn hadn't held back. As a result, Pat was a bloody mess as he eyed Lorenzo wearily.

Lorenzo flashed a ring to no-neck, making the stocky soldier blanch sheet-white. The rest of Pat's flock took a step away from Lorenzo, and Eric dropped the two he held. They landed with a clatter and scattered out of the room with their friends.

"I'm sorry, Your Grace," pleaded no-neck Pat with his eyes downcast as he too made for the door, "I didn't know, Your Grace. My apologies. We's leaving, Your Grace."

Pat didn't even look at Birger as he slinked out the door.

That's a bad sign, he thought. *Pat's been humiliated, and shame has a way of festering into new levels of hate. If I run into him again, I'll need to be ready for a dagger in my back.*

Also, what is this, Your Grace business? Now Lorenzo was a Duke, too, thought Birger. *Next, I'll find out the man is the Emperor of Murapii or something.*

"Ah, we had'em, boss," grumbled Mick, who was nursing a fat lip. "It was just a bit of fun."

Renate scowled at him. "We're on an important mission, Mick. We aren't here to have fun."

A string of curses fluttered in Gertrude's wake as she approached them. The reddish-purple veins bulging on the round woman's forehead showed she wasn't impressed with Mick's idea of fun, either.

Renate huffed in frustration. "I'll deal with this. At least clean up the mess while I try to keep us from getting kicked out in the snow." Her expression calmed as she turned to face the distraught innkeeper, and Snow trailed behind as she went.

Lorenzo approached Birger and the rest with a grim expression. Eric folded his arms in the way tectonic plates shift to cause earthquakes. Gunther straightened his breastplate, Wynn timidly tucked a broken chair under half a table, and Birger nudged at the clay shards of a stein with his toe.

Lorenzo said, "We need stealth and speed... Now I've revealed my movements to anyone smart enough to pay attention, and considering that, I feel angry." He looked at Wynn. "I understand you want to defend your honour," he looked at Mick, "and you want to back up your team. What will we change to safeguard the sanctity of our mission from here?"

Despite there being zero aggression in Lorenzo's tone or accusations in his words, Birger's cheeks turned ruby red with shame, and he wasn't alone. All four of them looked like children caught with their hands in the pantry. Lorenzo had a way with words that made you feel like you should've known better.

"Sorry, boss," said Mick, and the others echoed him with sheepish nods. "We'll clean up the mess and stay out of trouble from here."

The lot of them got to cleaning. Eric and Lorenzo walked back outside. Renate continued to speak with Gertrude. Birger noticed a substantial amount of gold pass between them.

Mick smiled at Wynn and said, "How about that opening, Miss Elbows? Did you see how his head whipped back?"

Mick imitated the head movement, showing the blood spray with his fingers, and chuckled. Wynn and Birger both smiled despite themselves.

Gunther added, "And you, Mr Flying-kick? I've never seen anything like it in a tavern brawl!" He laughed with a deep belly sound that shook the windows.

The laughter was contagious. Soon, they were all chuckling like sailors on deck scrubbing duty after a prank on the ship's cook. Birger hadn't felt so connected to a group of people in a month. He was enjoying it even though laughing hurt his ribs.

I must've bruised them in the fall, thought Birger as he probed at them. He strained to pick up a piece of the table that lay cracked in two on the floor, and asked, "What's Eric's deal? What kind of man lifts two fully armoured soldiers by the scruff of their necks and holds them there?"

Gunther shrugged, kicking the broken wood aside to salvage the metal cutlery in its debris, and said, "All I can say is that I'm glad he's on our side."

31

THE FEET OF SARGHUS

"Halt!" commanded a tinny androgynes voice with an accent that made it seem like their tongue was trying to dance out of the speaker's mouth.

The voice came from a soldier who stepped onto the dirt road, and in the dusky gloom, Birger couldn't make out much more than a silhouette. To the right of the causeway, a half-dozen figures stood wearing navy-blue surcoats and red cloaks draped over their shoulders.

They wore vulture-beaked helmets, resembling birds with kite shields on their left arms and pikes in their right hands. What terrified Birger about the tin-birds squadron was the coiled golden serpent on their wind-rippled banners. The emblem of the religious fanatics from Murapii, the Feet of Sarghus.

The hulking behemoth that was Eric either didn't hear the order or, more likely, didn't care, and hr rode his horse right past the soldier. The tin-bird lowered their spear towards the bear-like man, who idly pawed the leaf blade aside with less effort than Birger would use to swat a fly. This sent the tin-bird stumbling into their comrades, who weren't happy. They clattered into ready positions, their weapons extending like porcupine quills.

Plate armour, Birger mused. *They would be slow in a chase, especially give we're on horses, but nearly impossible to kill with a rapier.* He was about to remark about them being tin cans and what he would like to stuff inside, but stopped himself.

Maybe this was what getting old and wise felt like, he thought.

"No need for that, friend," said Renate gently, raising her hands in the way people do when they hope to avoid imminent violence. "My companion is a little slow in the head." She shot a frustrated looked at Eric, and he countered with a scowl. "We're on official crown business, and I can speak on behalf of my party."

The same hostile voice scolded, "Your crown holds no authority over us."

The tin-bird had regained their footing, and although Birger couldn't see their face, the armour had a distinct air of embarrassment. Humiliating a soldier was a terrible way to start a conversation; it was likely to make them more irrational than usual, and these fanatics had a reputation for being unreasonable.

The tin-bird continued, "The Feet of Sarghus answer to none but His Head. Call your mercenary back to submit to our authority, or we'll take it as heresy."

And there it was, thought Birger. *Heresy. The word that sent the feet marching to war.*

Renate bowed her head. "Clearly, you are important among those who walk the path. I'm sure a devout walker of the way can see the wisdom in staying his blade for a simpleton who doesn't know any better."

"You know the Book of One?" The tin-bird's helmet tilted sceptically to the side.

Lorenzo joined Renate, with Gunther and Mick on the flanks, while Birger and Wynn hung back.

Turning this into a fight would be a horrible idea. Even if they took down seven fanatics here, Birger could see a camp for twenty, bustling with activity a few hundred yards away. Backup would arrive quickly, but Birger's group would be tired, maybe even injured, and easily overwhelmed.

"None shall have, where others of the faith have not, or all shall give what they can," recited Renate deftly.

It was a quote from the Book of One, thought Birger. He had never properly read the religious texts of Murapii, but Sten had a copy in his collection, and Birger had skimmed through it once.

Thank Aeg, Renate was handling the conversation, though surely she could crack at least one joke at their expense. The outfits were practically begging for it.

"I'm fond of 'Let none abide the darkness, for in darkness grows the end of us all.' Tell me, has darkness touched you and your companions?" asked the tin-bird, its voice reverberating with accusation.

Renate smiled disarmingly. "I assure you, we are of the light."

"Lies!" barked the tin-bird, and metal scraped on metal as its cohort took an aggressive step forward. "Your gods are slaves of the darkness. How can any of you Azreans hope to see the light without the hand of Sarghus to guide you?"

Renate eyed the line of pikes pointing at them, and Birger wondered what they were hoping to get out of this situation. A wicked-looking stone talon was visible beyond the cliff face backing the camp, meaning Thornhall was very close. Murdering travellers on such a busy road near town would draw its Lord's attention, and with that would come their men-at-arms. Could it be bluster?

Renate responded to the accusation with silence. She was simply watching the tin-bird while they scanned back and forth from Mick to Gunther. Birger thought he sensed a nervousness in their movement.

After several moments of awkward silence, the tin-bird said, "If we didn't already have a witch for the stake, I would've introduced you to the purifying fire of Sarghus." There was a pause like the tin-bird wanted to get some reaction from Renate, but she refused to give them the satisfaction. "Get out of here before I change my mind and convince the inquisitor to make space for another."

The squadron of tin-birds raised their weapons and stepped back in a unified fashion that told Birger a fight would've been a really bad idea. These were disciplined and well-trained soldiers that knew how to work together. Even though they were no longer in their aggressive stance, Birger could feel hatred radiating from them. The eerie eyeholes in their helmets intensified the effect.

Renate said nothing as she and Lorenzo turned to lead the way past, up the mountain path towards Eric. Mick and Gunther kept their eyes locked on the hostile squadron as they followed. Wynn seemed ready to burst out of her skin with pent-up emotions.

Birger's satchel stirred, and two furry white legs stretched out in a lazy yawn as Snow slipped past the cover. The big weavespider casually pulled himself out of what Birger had started to think of as Snow's nest. With all the cobwebs spun in there, Birger didn't really want to stick his hand in it anymore.

Under Lorenzo's guidance, Birger had taken a new leather satchel suitable for documents in Stella. Where he also bought himself a new grey outfit with hints of blue. So, Chancebringer was the only thing, other than Snow, in the nest.

"Good timing, Snow," said Birger, "you managed to avoid the tension entirely."

Snow tilted his head to the side as if grinning, and then nuzzled Birger's hand for a back scratch. Birger shook his head and obliged the small furry creature. Gunther shuddered and hastened his horse to the front of the queue as Mick pulled up next to Lorenzo.

"Who were those soldiers?" asked Wynn.

"The feet of Sarghus," said Lorenzo. "They're the militant division of the Cult of Sarghus: The Divine, which is the religion of the empire of Murapii. I must check in on my local informant. Let's get to the Iron Caster and stable our horses. Then we can investigate this some more."

"But what are they doing here?"

"That, dear Wynn, is an excellent question and one that disturbs me greatly. I should've been notified the moment they entered the kingdom."

"And what in Jor's name did they mean, they already have a witch for the stake?" Mick asked.

"In Murian society," Renate explained, "only priests may use magic, and they consider all other magic users to be pure evil. If they caught one, or someone they elected to be one, they would bind them to a stake, soak them in oil, and set them on fire. They call it purification."

"So that tin-bird was saying they have a woman they plan to burn alive?" Birger gasped in shock. "We can't let that happen!"

"Yeah," agreed Wynn. "No way. We must help. It's the Code."

Gunther grunted in agreement, and Mick nodded as well.

"These are the Feet of Sarghus, not some random group of bandits," Renate said. "They're elite and efficient professional soldiers that are renowned for their brutality. Not to mention their camp would be a fort with a wooden palisade, earthworks, and ditches that would be hard for an army to assault. And even if the Lord of Thornhall could supply the force needed, it would take at least a couple of days to reach him, and by that would be too late."

"I don't think there is a castra nearby," said Lorenzo, using the Murian name for a military camp. "There isn't enough foliage to hide one here, and judging by this camp, they look like exploratores, scouts, and if they have a prisoner, it has to be here. Nonetheless, as Renate says, force isn't an option. We don't need to give the Head of Sarghus an excuse to call a divine march on West Rendin. And I'll remind you we're on a mission that we can't delay. We'll have to do what we can tonight, but in the morning, we leave, one way or another."

"What's a divine march?" asked Wynn.

With a shudder, Renate said, "The followers of Sarghus see themselves as a serpent with many legs, like a reptilian centipede. His followers call it a divine march when they send his feet to 'cleanse the land of heretics.' In other words, mass murder and land grabbing in the name of a god."

Despite the icy air and Birger's nose already tingling with early frostbite, he felt his limbs go cold with fear. They had enough going on without a group of armed crazies, who believed they had the divine right to kill, running around.

"The last thing we need is another potential war to worry about," said Lorenzo, rubbing at his temples.

Birger looked back at the grey and red tents nestled into an outcrop along the cliff. His fear redoubled for whoever found themselves in the clutches of those faceless monsters. There was something in the anonymity of a covered face that made people inhumane.

He had seen it before in Anthir, at the masquerade parties hosted by Golden Tree Hill's wealthy residents. Servants and abducted strays were abused so badly that the victims were lucky if they were only beaten to death.

"Take my horse with you. I'll stay and spy on this lot of vulture-faced looneys," said Birger. "Maybe I can find a way that won't involve kicking the whole one-eyed serpent in the face."

Mick burst out laughing at Birger's comment, and even Gunther had a chuckle. But Lorenzo and Renate didn't look amused.

"I'm going too," said Wynn. "I'm good at moving silently in the woods; besides, two pairs of eyes are better than one." The way she looked at Birger told him she wouldn't take no for an answer.

Without thinking it through, Birger nodded, and Wynn gave him a thankful smile.

"It's too dangerous." Lorenzo shook his head. "I don't think we should risk it."

The words burst out of Birger as he said, "My sailor's brown eye, it's too risky. As Wynn says, the Magpies Code dictates we must help if we're able, and I'm able. There is no way I'm letting these tin-birds burn someone alive."

He was surprised at how strongly he felt about it. "You slip away from the Code, one little compromise at a time, and I'm not starting here."

"You tell it like it is," urged Mick.

Gunther came up next to Birger and put a supportive hand on his shoulder.

"Birger's right," agreed Gunther. "That's how the world falls to evil, when the able stand by to let the defenceless suffer. Besides, I don't like bullies."

"Yep," said Mick. "What they said."

Even Eric had a glimmer in his eye that Birger hadn't seen in him before. It didn't make him less scary; in fact, it did quite the opposite, but he was clearly ready to join the ad hoc mission.

A sense of conviction settled on the party, and Birger knew he was among like-minded people. He realised why Lorenzo picked Magpies to work for the shade. They all believed in the Code and lived by it. They share a vision of the world for which each of them was willing to risk their lives. This group – or rather team – had motivation beyond simple payment. They shared purpose and it would carry them through almost anything.

Despite knowing nothing about the captive woman, they were all ready to risk everything to help her. Besides, a little sneaking around couldn't hurt.

But then again, Wynn had a knack for revealing their presence at the worst possible moments. Maybe this wasn't such a great idea after all.

32

BURN THE WITCH

"Alright," said Lorenzo. "We'll secure Birger and Wynn's horses in town while we investigate. Meet us on the ridge over there with your report, but please be careful not to give our presence away. We act as a team. The rest of us will return in two hours."

Well, I'm committed now, thought Birger.

He nodded despite the doubts lurking in the back of his mind. When dusk turned into night, visibility would be limited to campfires. They had to move fast.

Birger's six companions had drawn their horses into a circle for the conversation, each wearing a mask of grim determination. Snow jumped down from Birger's horse and landed lightly on a tuft of grass.

Birger fastened his saddlebags. Once Gunther was also on the ground, he offered him a reassuring smile and took Birger's reins, tying them to his halberd, which rested in a saddle scabbard.

"You're doing a good thing, Birger," said the big man. "I'll rush back to help as soon as I can. Until then, stay safe."

Birger smiled. "Thanks Gunther. Just don't be late."

Gunther's face contorted with anger as he glared at the camp and growled. Birger could tell that the large man wanted to come with him, but three was a crowd, and crowds were harder to hide. Dismounted, Wynn passed her reins to Mick. She bunched her dark hair into a short ponytail and tied it off with a leather thong.

Mick winked at Birger. "Hey, fisher boy, don't go snatching their night knickers and riling them up before we get back. We'll want them docile and unsuspecting for a rescue mission." Mick's tone was reassuring, even if his remarks were cheeky.

Birger chose to smile, recalling Gunther saying that Mick had a good heart beneath his unbearable mouth. Like they said they would, the pair was ready to stand by him to face this challenge. Perhaps it was time Birger gave this teamwork business a real try. He had been in partnerships before. How different could this be, really?

He untied his old cloak from the horse, flipped it to the brown side because it would be harder to spot in the wilderness, and donned it over his nice new outfit. He tested his soft boots on the red dirt, which felt very different from the city streets and roof tiles he was used to. Snow brushed against his ankles like a cat, making a soft purring sound to ensure Birger noticed.

"You're coming with us then?" he asked Snow.

Snow dropped into a ready crouch.

"If you can't keep up, find someplace to hide, okay?"

The way Snow looked at Birger gave him the sense that Snow thought he had said something monumentally dumb, and Birger grinned.

"All the same, buddy," he said. "We must stay out of sight and move fast, so we can't wait if you fall behind."

Lorenzo got the others back on the road, and Birger waved to them as they pulled away. When they were out of sight, he turned to Wynn. The twilight was darkening, and she was a silhouette against a grey sky backdrop.

"No shouting this time," Birger warned Wynn, and she blushed.

"I know, I know!" Wynn grimaced and shook her head.

"Stay low. Follow my lead."

Birger became aware of how directive he was with Wynn, in stark contrast to Lorenzo's way. *Lorenzo never told me what to do,* thought Birger. *He only asked questions and gave suggestions, letting things happen as they would. Is it worth trying it that way?*

But what if she messes up? retorted Birger's cynic.

He paused on that thought and then said, "No, I have a different idea. You grew up on a farm, sneaking around the bush, right? Why don't you lead?"

Wynn was taken aback. "Me?"

"Sure, you said it yourself. You're a lot better in the woods. I barely spend any time outside the city. You take the lead."

Wynn brightened up and grinned from ear to ear. She briskly turned, crouched low, and began moving alongside the ridge that backed onto the camp. Snow darted ahead of her, silently scurrying across the dirt between the tufts of grass. Birger observed Wynn's quiet movement and felt relieved no one was watching him.

Each step crunched on the hard dirt or rustled a bush against his legs. The Cos-damned things were everywhere, making it impossible to find clear footing. To make matters worse, his right leg was still stiff from Renate's healing magic.

Birger studied Wynn in the dim light, noticing her swerving gait that allowed her to glide between the knee-high brush. She aimed for clumps of shorter, softer foliage or dirt, running on the balls of her feet. Birger tried to mimic her, and though it helped, his movements remained much more clunky.

Wow, how foolish would I have looked if I took the lead? thought Birger. *Wynn would've been laughing at me while I had no idea what an amateur I was.*

Perhaps this was why Lorenzo took the approach that he did. The man accepted that he didn't know everything and that others, even ones with less broad experience, might have skills or knowledge that he didn't.

Is life actually more complicated than we think? wondered Birger. *Maybe we couldn't see it because we're too caught up in what we 'know' to ask what others saw. That would be how the Feet of Sarghus became fanatics. They have a different way of seeing the world, and they're willing to use force to make people see it their way. But wasn't that exactly the same as the Magpies Code? You're just another hypocrite fighting a hypocrite.*

No, thought Birger in response, *you're wrong. The Magpies Code is different. It's about helping those that can't help themselves; it isn't about forcing a viewpoint on someone else.*

Justify all you want, replied his cynic. *In the end, you harm someone to serve what you think is right, like these tin-birds.*

Birger pushed the inner dialogue aside and tried to focus on the act of stepping deliberately. He didn't want to keep arguing with himself. The Code was an important cornerstone in his life, and he didn't need to pick holes in his beliefs right now. The facts were that someone's life was in danger, and he was going to do something about it.

As they closed in on the campsite from above, Birger saw most of the tin-birds were sitting around campfires eating. Their beaks lifted enough to allow them to put a spoon to their mouth but not such as to reveal their faces. Two guards patrolled the ridge, and it looked like another two were patrolling the lower perimeter.

Birger, Wynn and Snow settled behind a low shrub to watch the ridge patrol. They observed for over an hour. There was no sense in rushing these things, and they had to be sure of every fact. Birger checked his beat-up pocket watch again. After four cycles, he was sure it took the pair about fifteen minutes from one end of their route to the other.

Wynn was surveying the camp. The night had moved in by the time they were both satisfied.

She pointed at something, and Birger followed her finger to a tent that looked more extravagant than the others. Still grey, it had red frills lining its edges and was much taller than the rest. *A command tent, perhaps?* Birger wondered.

A distinctly female scream tore through the night, and Birger's heart raced. Without sparing a thought for the patrol, he, Wynn and Snow shot towards the bluff edge to take cover between two sizeable bushes.

Birger tried to identify where the scream came from. Snow was already staring at the larger central tent when another agonising cry made Birger shudder. What was more disturbing was that the soldiers in the camp continued about their evening routine, completely unfazed by the sound of another human being in pain.

Among the fifteen smaller tents, faceless figures ate quietly around three campfires, cleaned cooking pots, oiled weapons and engaged in evening prayer. To the west, one tin-bird tossed a fresh hay bale into the horse corral while another made use of the latrine trench.

Birger saw a storage area surrounded by carts loaded with barrels and crates directly below them. An oil barrel stood open from recent use, and beside it, on a cart bed, lay wooden stakes with a bundle of linen strips. It didn't take long for Birger to find a torchbearer moving around the camp, planting freshly assembled torches into the ground and igniting them.

"We've got to do something," urged Wynn. Her voice wavering with concern as she fixed Birger with an intensity in her eyes that he hadn't seen before.

"I know, but what?" Birger scanned the camp again, hoping for potential options, and he glanced west towards the ridge patrol. "Those two will turn back any minute, and if we try sneaking down there, we might as well put an apple in our mouths and shout, 'We're here to join the roast.' The others are probably on their way back."

Birger flinched as more piercing cries clawed at his heart. Wynn scratched in the dirt on the ground. He squinted against the darkness to figure out what she was up to.

"What're you doing?" asked Birger.

"Looking for a big rock."

Snow looked up at Birger and Wynn, then at the camp, before taking off at a run.

"And where are you going?" Birger asked, expecting no response from the arachnid. "Look, we're supposed to be working as a team here. Let's try using our words and communicating."

"I have an idea, but I need a fist-sized rock."

Birger joined Wynn in her search and asked, "What's the idea?"

The screaming continued, but now sounding hoarse and exhausted. Birger's heart ached for the victim as he sensed the resigned acceptance in the voice. Inwardly, he cursed the vulture-faced slugs and their self-righteous cruelty.

Birger stood up, but his right knee throbbed and made a popping sound. *That was odd,* he thought. *Wasn't Renate's magic supposed to stop that from happening? I guess she also told me not to push it too far. I must've undone too much of her crafting.*

Regardless, he couldn't waste time worrying about his injury, so he ignored the pain and tried to spot the patrol. His heart skipped a beat when he saw they had turned and were heading straight towards Wynn and Birger.

"Gullshite!" Birger hissed. "The patrol is coming."

Wynn echoed the sentiment and excitedly exclaimed, "Found one!" as she held up a rock.

"Shhhh."

Wynn shrank away from Birger's rebuke, but only for a moment. She aimed and hurled the rock, hitting a torch near the open barrel. With a resounding smack, the torch toppled onto a cart and started rolling.

The linen, evidently soaked in oil, went up like a hovel's thatch roof. The torch rolling, bounced off the open barrel and dropped to the ground. The torch maker's carelessness did the rest, as the fire leapt on spilt oil, racing up the barrel where it found a near-endless fuel supply.

"What in Aeg's deep blue sea was that?" demanded Birger in shock.

"A distraction!"

"We're supposed to keep them docile. This will make them awake and focused–"

"On a fire eating their camp," interrupted Wynn. She looked sternly at Birger. "I had to do something. Now they'll be too busy trying to put out the fire to notice us."

Wynn had a point. Alarmed shouts echoed off the cliff and from the ridge patrol. The sound of metal scraping and clanging, resembling someone running with a backpack full of pots, approached Birger and Wynn.

"Gullshite," Birger whispered, dropping lower, "someone is coming."

"We've got to move."

"Well, don't just sit there…"

"Ugh." Wynn rolled her eyes at Birger, broke into a run heading north, and he limped after her.

"Halt!" The tinny sound of the command sent a chill down Birger's spine, but he refused to obey.

The noise of rattling cookware intensified as they pursued them. Birger glanced back in time to see one tin-bird chasing them, with no sign of the second.

Suddenly, the tin-bird stumbled. It tried to take flight, but its armoured limbs were ill-suited for the task. Unable to lift off, it clattered into the dirt, its pike vanishing into the night.

Despite the pain in his knee, Birger smirked as the tin-bird plucked and pulled, evidently stuck to something in the grass. But his amusement was cut short when, thanks to inattention, he tripped over a large rock, and found the ground rushing up to knock the wind out of him.

"Birger!" Wynn called out.

"Go!" He coughed up sand.

Birger stole a look at the tin-bird and saw that the soldier had already recovered. He tried to get back up, but his knee buckled, and he found himself face-first in the dirt. A heavy metal hand clasped over his shoulder, and soon after, stars burst in front of his eyes.

"Saboteur!" Birger heard the words as if they echoed from the other end of a metal pipe. The forceful hand hoisting his body up felt distant, like the pain belonged to someone else.

Birger's body spun around as another steel gauntlet hurtled towards him, dodging on pure reflex, it wasn't enough, and the glancing blow cut his left cheek. The wound stung, and his face went numb.

A flying dark shape struck the tin-bird, but the soldier shrugged it off with ease, and Birger heard Wynn cry out in pain. When the gauntlet drew back for another attack, Birger fought the urge to scream in anticipation.

A white blur appeared on the tin-bird's helmet, causing the soldier to recoil before landing the punch. Through the fog of his head injury, Birger realised Snow had leapt onto the tin-bird's face

206

and was pawing through the tiny black peeping holes at the eyes inside.

Smart little fella, thought Birger.

The tin-bird caught Snow and flung him aside, yet it gave Birger room to buck, and along with the recoiling momentum, he wriggled free. His aching knee made standing hard, but he did manage to draw his rapier.

But what now? wondered Birger.

Rapiers couldn't compete with full plate armour, and finding a weak spot in the darkness would be nearly impossible. Fortunately, the camp was noisy, and they were far enough away that no one would come to help the tin-bird anytime soon.

Thank Aeg we get to die without an audience, thought Birger with an inward shrug.

The tin-bird was already up, lumbering at Birger. "None can stand against the Feet of Sarghus. Surrender, and you'll face swift justice."

"I would really rather not," replied Birger. "Besides, I can't stand sweaty foot smell."

The comment went ignored by the tall soldier, who simply charged ahead with outstretched hands. Birger lashed out with his sword, to no effect. The tin-bird didn't even attempt to defend themself from the attack. Hopping back on his left leg, unable to stand on his right, panic welled up in Birger's throat.

Wynn crashed bodily into the tin-bird's knees, causing them to buckle, and the enemy stumbled. However, the soldier backhanded her, sending her sprawling onto the ground with a pained grunt.

Birger tried to target an eyehole, but his aim was off, and the tip of his rapier skidded uselessly across the solid steel helmet.

"Cos damn you," cursed Birger.

"Your evil goddesses are impotent in the face of Sarghus," laughed the tin-bird, and they shot forward more quickly than someone so big should be able.

What was it with big people outside of Anthir? wondered Birger. *It felt like they all simply defied physics. Big things are supposed to be slow. Be slow!*

A steel gauntlet wrapped around Birger's right wrist, unbalancing him. The soldier didn't even bother to disarm him before tossing Birger over a hip, planting him in a cloud of dust beside Wynn.

Gasping for breath, Birger said, "Oh good," he sucked for more air, "I was getting tired of standing up."

The tin-bird didn't look amused. It drew a steel-covered boot up for a stomp that never landed. A high-pitched squeal of metal scraping on metal caused the soldier to stiffen. They craned their neck back, and Birger's eyes traced their line of sight.

"Stop that," said Gunther from behind the tin-bird.

The long shaft of a halberd stretched from the tin soldier's back, held firmly in Gunther's hands. The tin-bird whirled around in a lurch, attempting to escape the weapon's bite, and in a sudden rush of motion, lunged towards Gunther.

Gunther was good, but the tin-bird was inhuman. They pummelled Gunther's defences with relentless force. Gunther parried a strike, but the tin-bird caught his weapon in one hand while slamming the other into his face. Gunther didn't make a sound, but blood gushed down from an open wound across the bridge of his nose and trickled from each of his nostrils.

Birger looked over at Wynn and saw she wasn't moving. Panic seized him, and he checked her pulse. It was faint but still there. He sighed with relief and searched for Snow, but it was too dark. Birger picked up his rapier and pushed through the pain to get to his feet.

Every part of him hurt, but he kept going.

Gunther took hit after hit without landing anything significant. The plate armour was too hard to breach, and the tin-bird was incredibly strong.

"Hey, vulture-face!" Birger shouted, drawing the tin-bird's attention for a split second.

Gunther capitalised on the opening, striking the soldier's right upper arm with the axe blade of his halberd. The edge bit into the armour, but it was a shallow wound. Instantly, the tin-bird retaliated with a thundering blow to Gunther's jaw, forcing the large man to one knee.

Just one knee? thought Birger. *That punch would've killed me.*

Snow darted out of the darkness, weaving between the tin-bird's feet and wrapped around them once. *What are you up to?* wondered Birger, but he didn't wait to see.

The soldier was already pulling back to strike Gunther again, and Birger had to help. He stumbled forward, aiming his rapier for the wound Gunther left in the tin-bird's back, and the long thin blade snuck home. Birger felt the resistance of flesh, then the hard stop of the metal plate at the front, and the tin-bird flinched away from the pain.

With the sword still lodged in the wound and Birger less nimble than usual, the tin soldier yanked the rapier from Birger's grasp as they turned to face him. Another explosion of stars filled his eyes as the ground jumped up, knocking the wind out of Birger with a full-body impact.

Birger decided it was no longer worth considering which part of his body hurt most; instead, he thought the world was just pain. For a while, he couldn't see anything but honeycombed spots, and his ears rang with a high-pitched buzz. He was vaguely aware of the tin-bird crashing down on top of him.

That's odd, Birger thought, as his vision partly returned. Gunther was still down on his knee so he couldn't have hit the tin-bird. My rapier attack was deep, but it was low and off-centre, so it couldn't have been crippling or lethal.

Birger glanced down at the tin-bird's feet, seeing they were bound by some type of sticky thread. Gunther stood up, raising his halberd high, and for a moment, Birger thought the big man was aiming at him. As the heavy blow came down, the sound of screaming metal filled the air, and Birger's vision turned black.

33

RESCUE

Birger tried to open his eyes, but they refused. Someone touched his head. He couldn't tell who it was or what they were doing.

"Easy," soothed Renate's voice. "Just rest and let me help."

Birger had no choice. His body was as unresponsive as if submerged in thick, viscous fluid. His mind began drifting off in the currents of emotion. Wynn featured prominently as his mind circled around his desire to help her. It hurt that she hid things from him; he felt overwhelmed by his own weight of responsibility and worried about what else could be behind it.

He had to admit, he hoped her reason for spying on them was because of Neffily, and that only intensified his guilt. Birger didn't want to believe that Wynn could betray him for anything less.

If only he could ask her, clear the air, they could work on a plan to save Neffily together. But what if he was wrong? What if she had nefarious reasons? Had she been playing him all along?

A hand stroked his cheek, sucking him back to the present. He tried opening his eyes again, and this time they did respond. It was dark and his vision blurry, but he could see orange light dancing on Wynn's bruised face as she looked at him, concern in her eyes.

Aeg, she's beautiful, thought Birger.

"He's waking up," said Wynn.

"Oh, good." Renate appeared above him. "How're you feeling?"

"Better than I should be," said Birger with a drawl. The left side of his face was stiff and his head ached.

"Your injuries were quite extensive. I had to immobilise your leg and seal the wound on your cheek. Would you answer a few questions so I can check on your head injury?"

"Sure," said Birger as he tried to sit up, but Renate pushed him back down with a firm hand.

"Don't get up yet." She smiled gently. "What's my name?"

"Renate."

"Great, thank you. And what is your name?"

211

"We've done this already in the Barrel Side Inn, you know." Birger grinned at Renate. "Birger 'Light Foot' of Anthir."

"I know," Renate said with a wink and smoothed his hair. "You seem as good as can be expected."

Sarcastically, Birger added, "You mean, considering I got beaten up by a tin-bird."

Renate shook her head and turned to Wynn. "He'll be fine. Keep him company for a minute and give him some of this water before you let him up. I need to go see Lorenzo."

Renate handed Wynn a waterskin and then got up to walk away.

"Did we win?" asked Birger, rubbing at his painful temples.

Assessing himself, he discovered: his head ached, check; his neck was stiff, check; his ribs throbbed, check; his knee was... locked, yet not sore, so magic, check. Something heavy rested on his stomach, and he peeked down to see. It was a furry lump of legs bundled up in a ball, and Wynn stroked Snow's head.

"Gunther got her," answered Wynn. "I wasn't awake at the time, so I didn't see exactly what happened."

"Is everyone else alright?"

"Bumps, bruises, and cuts." Wynn helped Birger drink some water. "Better than we would've been if she held on to her pike."

"She?" Birger gave her a perplexed look.

"The Feet of Sarghus soldier. We took her helmet off and saw that it was a woman."

"Oh."

"Gunther has a broken nose, and Snow lost a leg, but Renate took care of them both." Wynn dropped her voice to a conspiratorial register, and murmured, "Renate was using magic. Do you think that's safe?"

Birger realised that he had grown to accept Renate's abilities, and had forgotten that Wynn didn't know about them. Most people, like Wynn, believed that magic users caused weavestorms. He used to believe the same until Renate explained that wasn't how it worked.

He smirked. "Oh, she seems to know what she's doing. I guess if she were going to bring a weavestorm down on us, she would've by now."

Wynn looked worried, but she nodded. "Well, I'm glad you're alive. When I woke up, you weren't moving, and I thought the tin-bird had killed you."

Birger propped himself up to look around. He wanted to see what the tin-bird looked like, especially since she could demolish the three of them so easily. Lorenzo stood on the lip of the ridge, watching the fiery spectacle tinting the landscape. He had a Quintri tele-magnification scope held to his eye, and Gunther stood next to him.

Renate passed by a skinny young man with light brown hair, wearing plain linen farmer's clothing, and sat quivering on a rock. Eric stomped into the long shadows to the west of the camp, and Birger caught Mick's lanky frame slinking towards Birger and Wynn.

A lump shimmered with a metal sheen a short distance away, but it was hard to see much of the de-shelled tin-bird in the darkness.

"By the five, I thought I told you to keep them docile," scolded Mick, "and you go and burn down their Cos-damned camp?"

"I didn't think you would mind some grilled bird." Birger smiled and gently put Snow on top of a pile of rags that turned out to be his old cloak.

Awkwardly, he climbed to his feet. Renate had left zero room for movement when she addressed his knee this time, forcing him to swing his leg out like a yardarm.

Birger rubbed his sore head. "You would've done the same if you were there; they were torturing her."

"Stop protecting me, Birger!" Wynn snapped and put her hands on her slender hips, a strand of red-brown hair dropping in front of her face. "*I* did it, and *I* can explain it myself."

Wynn's anger nearly toppled Birger back to the ground, and he had to steady himself with his right hand on the dirt. A short struggle later, he stood looking at Wynn. Her eyes still smouldered with fury, and Mick had an annoying smirk on his lips. In the face of rising shock, anger, and embarrassment, Birger had to resist smacking the taller man.

"I wasn't protecting you." Birger jut his jaw forward in anger. "I was just answering a question."

"You were answering as if you decided to do it." Wynn scowled at him.

"Whatever." Birger rolled his eyes. "Suit yourself. Tell it the way you want to tell it, then."

Wynn folded her arms, her jaw tight, and her mouth drawn into a thin line.

"Look," said Mick. "I'm not here to cause a tiff between you. It doesn't matter who did what. It's done, and all that's left for us now is to work with what's there."

Mick pointed at the frail-looking farmer and said, "Peter over there needs us to save his sister's life, and fighting with each other doesn't make that happen." Mick turned back to them. "Why don't the two of you park this argument until we finish what you started?"

Birger's cheeks burned with shame. *How did Mick become the sensible peacemaker?*

Since you started acting like a child again.

Considering the situation, Birger had to agree. He looked at Wynn and saw her scowl evaporate, her cheeks turning a couple of shades pinker.

Birger cleared his throat and said, "Sorry Wynn. I didn't mean to take credit from you. I think you did the right thing, is all."

Wynn nodded. "Yeah, sorry, I overreacted. Let's go save this girl?"

Birger sensed Snow was keen to help too, and he hunched to look at his furry friend. Seven legs didn't look much different from eight; one of his front legs was a short stump. Birger stroked Snow's head. The weavespider let out the high-pitched purring sound to show his appreciation for attention, but their was a quiver of pain too.

"Thanks for saving me, buddy," said Birger. "I saw you tied up her legs with webbing when she came for me. You fought bravely, but your fight for tonight is done, okay?"

Snow gave Birger a sad look; he wasn't happy with being left behind.

"I know," Birger pulled his mouth tight and added, "you already gave one leg to save this girl. You've done your part. We can handle it from here. Besides, someone must look after that scared farm boy over there."

Birger smiled as he sensed the tension in Snow ease a little. Birger pulled himself up to his full height and walked over to the dead tin-bird on the ground a few paces away. The vulture-like helmet lay discarded next to the body.

The woman's face was harsh and crisscrossed with scars; she had short dark hair, a broad nose and skin that looked like glowing coals in the firelight. She had been the most formidable opponent Birger had ever fought in direct combat, that was certain, and she seemed as strong as two men.

He looked up to see Lorenzo, Renate, and Gunther approached.

"Good to see you on your feet again, Birger. We need to hurry," said Lorenzo. "The enemy is preoccupied with the fire, and beating it with sacks will take most of their night. The wind is rising and there is a real chance it could consume their entire camp."

Lorenzo turned to the young man trailing behind him. "Sadly, Peter, there's not much you can do here, and I give you my word that we will save your sister if possible."

Peter dropped his head despondently.

"The brother?" asked Birger.

"Yes, he was in the town square petitioning people to help him rescue his sister when we found him," said Renate.

"I want to help, sirs and ladies," said Peter. "I must help my little sister. She didn't do anything wrong, and those monsters dragged her off like a criminal."

"What's your sister's name?" asked Birger.

"Emily, sir, she's only seventeen," said Peter, "we were selling healing herbs in the square; it was only Cat's claw, and while I went to the baker for bread, those knights decided that treating pain with herbs was witchcraft, and they nabbed her. I tried to stop them, but they were so strong."

Peter hung his head in shame, and Birger spotted a purple welt on the young man's cheek, causing his own puckered wound to throb.

"Don't worry, Peter," said Mick, "we won't let the tin-birds hurt your sis."

"Yes, stay here, out of sight. Let us do our work," said Lorenzo firmly, then he turned to the others. "Birger and Wynn, could you draw us a map of the camp as it was before the fire?"

"Sure," Wynn answered before Birger had a chance, and she grabbed a stick to draw boxes in the sand.

Birger crouched next to her to see if he could add anything, and while he offered a few adjustments for scale and perspective, she had it pretty much dead on. Lorenzo inspected the drawing for a moment.

"What do you see?" asked Lorenzo.

Birger took a rock, placed it on the larger central tent, and said, "The screams came from here." Peter whimpered but otherwise remained quiet, and Birger continued, "The fire is to the east. To the west are the horses and latrines. They were relying on patrols to keep the perimeter safe because there is no trench or palisade."

Gunther walked over to Peter and gave the skinny youngster a big hug that made everyone chuckle. Peter looked like a doll in the large man's arms. After a moment, Gunther put him down and pulled away to say, "We'll get her back. One way or another, she'll be coming home with you tonight."

Peter's worries faded, or maybe he was so surprised by the hug that he forgot about them all together. The skinny farmer sat down in the dirt, accepting the sense of helplessness he likely felt.

"Renate and I will ensure that the Feet have their focus locked on the fire in the east, and Eric is already in place to cover your escape. Mick, you're in charge of the extraction. What do you think?"

"Sure thing," said Mick. "I reckon we find a way in from the west. How does that sound to the rest of you?"

"We'll want to avoid the horses," said Wynn. "They've been spooked already with the fire, but someone might be checking on them."

Birger scratched at the drawing with his stick. "We could come round the latrine side. It's closer to the cliff face anyway, so it'll give us more cover."

"Agreed," said Gunther. "But how will we get up and down the cliff?"

Wynn tapped a coil of rope that hung over her shoulder. "We can climb. A few hundred paces further west of the latrines, it looked like there was a landslide with a sturdy tree above it."

"That's an excellent suggestion." Renate gave Wynn a supportive squeeze of the shoulder. "You have a keen eye for spotting opportunities in the wild."

Wynn blushed.

"Yeah, excellent suggestion," agreed Mick, "though, if the girl is hurt, how will we get her up?"

"I can strap her to me," said Gunther. "I have leather straps in my gear. I can make some quick modifications to secure her to my chest."

"Right," said Lorenzo, with everyone nodding in agreement. "It appears we have a plan. I recommend you remain unseen. Since one is already dead, we're beyond diplomacy, but if we don't get caught, they might think a desperate local did it."

"Right, boss," Mick agreed, "let's get it done."

A sense of purpose filled the group as they split into their respective units, and no one spoke as they moved. Birger surveyed the area, searching for any sign of the second guard returning, but found none.

Curious, he thought. *It was weird for the tin-birds not to check on their missing comrade, even while fighting the fire.* Birger

216

flipped his grey hood over his dark hair, attempting to move silently. His mast-straight leg made it nearly impossible, and he wished Renate had left him slightly more room to move.

Wynn carried the rope, while Gunther worked on the improvised leather harnesses he mentioned. It only took a moment for them to reach the tree near the cliff's edge, and Wynn spared no time getting to work. Her rope work was exceptional; Birger was sure he hadn't taught her how to tie a figure of eight on a bight, but it was the ideal knot for the situation.

In no time, the other three slipped down the rope, using the landslide to make the trip simpler. Birger grabbed onto the bristly fibres. It prickled at his scabbed-over hand, and he started his descent with his busted knee frequently getting in the way.

The ache radiating from his ribs was a surprise. Renate's magic could dull pain but not take it away entirely, and over the last week, he had been accumulating many injuries.

Tonight's fun with the tin-bird had left his ribs tender, but thankfully not broken, or he wouldn't have made it this far. He endured the pain and continued with caution.

Within moments, they reached the latrines, the foul odour of exposed sewage and smoke assaulting their nostrils. To the south, Birger could see the horses anxiously pacing in their corral.

Surely, someone should be tending to them. This is all too easy.

Mick drew his longsword. He and Gunther had left their halberds behind for obvious reasons. Birger also unsheathed his rapier, though he wasn't sure why, considering how useless it had been earlier that evening.

He decided that it made him feel safer as he guided the group towards the command tent. In the distance, Birger noted the soldiers beating at the fire while two commanders barked orders. Thankfully, the tin-birds paid no attention to the camp, and even if they did, their night blindness would make it hard to tell friends from foes at a distance.

Taking a deep, soot-tainted breath, Birger gripped his hilt tight, swept the tent flap aside, and then gasped in shock.

34

TERROR

A young girl lay on a wooden rack, thick leather straps binding her hands and bare feet. She was dressed in a plain grey robe; her tousled red hair framed a face too young to be marred by so many cuts and bruises. Dangling over the table's edge, her feet were raw with recent burns. Her toes were bent at odd angles with blood-filled holes where toenails should've been.

Thank merciful Lot, she was unconscious, thought Birger and spiralled his heart.

Next to the torture rack, he saw a table holding a pot filled with smouldering coals heating various metal implements. Beside that, lay bloody pliers on a tray. A shiver of revulsion ran through him.

The inhumanity of the scene surpassed anything he had ever seen before, and a part of him wanted to murder every tin-bird he could find. Behind him, Wynn retched; there was a splash, and a stomach-churning odour followed. Birger managed a last minute turn to avoid vomiting on the unconscious girl himself, and instead soaked the simple grey rugs that covered the tent floor.

Wynn gasped. "By the All-Mother, how could they?"

"Rat piss and crow farts, the lot of them," hissed Mick through clenched teeth, his lanky form quivering like a branch in a violent wind. "Maybe we should stick around and ask them how they like to lie on that rack themselves."

Birger wiped at his mouth with his sleeve and gasped for air, trying to regain his composure. The rest of the tent was spartan, with four braziers, a single bedroll, a chest at its foot and a table in the middle that contained a map of Southern-Azrea.

The only ornate feature in the space was the prayer altar, with the serpent of Sarghus boldly on display. It stood on the far side from the entrance. A single candle burned next to an open copy of the Book of One. It appeared well-worn from frequent use.

Gunther pushed Birger aside and rushed to check the girl's breathing. "She's alive, but barely. She'll need Renate's help, or she might die from shock."

Gunther's face was contorted in a mask of anger, and he efficiently undid the leather straps. Wynn wiped her own mouth clean, grabbed a knife from the table and started cutting lengths of linen strips from her undershirt.

"Here," she said, handing them to Gunther, "wrap her feet and hands with these."

Gunther accepted them and started dressing the wounds, "Thanks."

"We don't have time to play doctor," urged Mick, "one of those buzzards could come back at any moment."

As if summoned, a Murian voice came from the tent entrance, and Birger whipped around to look. A vulture-faced tin-bird, bearing a serpent of Sarghus on each of its pauldrons, stood there holding the door flap. A moment of shock froze everyone in place, their minds failing to comprehend the scene.

The tinny voice crackled to life but was cut short when a large hand emerged from behind to seize the tin-bird by the windpipe. With a sudden pluck and a ripple of the tent flap, the soldier vanished into the night.

"What the frozen witch tit was that?!" exclaimed Mick. His longsword hung suspended in the air for a moment before he lowered it. Mick hurried to the entrance, peeked outside, and pulled his head back in. "They're gone."

"What do you mean, gone?" demanded Birger, his heart racing and his breath shallow.

"I mean, they're just gone, vanished without a trace..."

"That's not possible. That was a Cos-forsaken tin-bird. How can something just grab them and make them vanish?"

"Look for yourself if you don't believe me." Mick gestured at the flap. "They're gone. And how's it going with that girl? We need to leave now."

"Got it." Gunther finished strapping the unconscious girl to his broad chest. The girl looked tiny as her head rested on his shoulder. He wrapped her legs around his waist. The harness would suffice, but Gunther needed to hold on to her to prevent her from flopping around like a beached fish.

"I'm not going out there!" Wynn protested. "What if whatever took that soldier is still lurking around?"

"It probably is," said Mick, "but what choice do we have? We can't stay here."

"We're leaving," said Gunther and walked out of the tent with the limp girl in his arms.

"Ugh!" grunted Wynn in frustration, and hurried after Gunther, clutching the knife as if it was her only cork-float on a sinking ship.

Birger's injuries suddenly felt like a looming death sentence. He couldn't run or fight, and his mind was still too hazy to think clearly. In fact, he had exactly zero survival tools other than sheer pig-headedness.

Mick looked at him like he knew what the younger man was thinking and shrugged. "You coming?"

The question was simple, but answering it was tough, and Birger felt unsteady with fear. His breath came in short rapid bursts, and he felt faint.

His plump cheeks drawing gaunt like a waterskin being drained.

"Hey," Mick's voice seemed distant, "hey mate, are you alright?"

Birger tried to answer, but his mouth felt slack, and his vision swam with intrusive images of Benny dying. At that moment, all he wanted was to hide under the table, praying for all the terrible things in the world to disappear.

"Hey, Birger." Mick was shaking him, but it was hard to focus on the voice. "Come back to me, kid. This isn't the time to pass out. We've got saving to do, and our team needs us. That girl needs us."

The girl needs my help; the words brought Birger back. *Wynn needs my help. I must help Wynn and Neffily.*

"There we go," Mick's voice was steady, reassuring, "you're alright kid. Come, let's get out of here."

"Sorry, Mick," said Birger and shook his head. It hurt. "I don't know what happened there."

"Could be Soldier's Heart, but don't worry about it now. We've got to go."

Birger grunted. Mick was referring to the way soldiers came home changed after the war. *Could it be?* he wondered.

The two turned to leave. Outside, the fire raged more aggressively than before. As the wind picked up, the tin-birds struggled to hold their ground. A few were lying on the dirt, with others kneeling over them, possibly treating injuries.

Good, thought Birger, *they deserve to be devoured by that fire.*

"Let's go back past the horses," said Mick, glancing over his shoulder. "I want to leave these vultures a farewell gift. You stay with me, okay?"

Birger didn't answer, concentrating on putting one foot in front of the other, not dwelling on what might lurk nearby, for fear of succumbing to panic again. He stole a look at the cliff, spotting the silhouettes of Gunther and Wynn ascending the rope.

Thank goodness, they made it, he thought with relief.

Mick stopped by the unattended horses, kicking the wooden gate of their enclosure open. Startled, the animals backed away; and one bolted past Mick, triggering a stampede, as they all charged through the gap, disappearing into the night.

"Okay," said Mick, "now we can go."

Birger stumbled as he tried to follow Mick, but with his stiff leg offered no support, and he toppled onto something metallic.

"Are you okay?" Mick asked urgently.

Birger nodded and pushed back to see what he had landed on. A tin-bird with its throat ripped out lay sprawled in a near black shadow. Its surcoat was drenched in blood, and the wound revealed a grisly mess of exposed larynx, shredded muscle, and limp arteries.

Mick came over to investigate. Birger felt sick again. He lifted himself off the dead soldier and barely took a step before dry heaving his empty stomach.

Mick grimaced. "After what they did to that girl, they deserve worse. But this is crazy. Do you know the kind of strength needed to do this to a human? Skin doesn't tear easily, you know."

"Could this be the tin-bird from the tent?" Birger wondered. But he recalled seeing a hand grabbing that one, and this appeared more like an animal attack.

"Could be, but I don't think so. It doesn't have the officer's pauldrons like the one in the tent. I think this one was looking after the horses. I suppose that's why it was so easy to get into the camp. Something's been hunting them. We can't be sure it's a friendly, so let's get out of here before we lose our throats too."

The fear was already so intense for Birger that the idea of dying this way barely added any more weight. A part of him thought dying might not be so bad, it would put an end to all the pain.

Mick started towards the rope, and Birger forced his body to follow. Climbing back up was tough going. The scabs on his hands tore, and they stung. He nearly reached the top when his right leg gave out, causing him to fall and knock his already tender ribs.

"Come on, mate," said Mick, bending down to grab Birger's wrist. "You're almost there. Don't give up now."

"I'm not giving up; I just need a moment to rest."

Mick pulled, and Birger's feet scraped against the gravel of the slope for traction. At the top, they collapsed in a lump, and both men gasped like a fresh catch on deck.

"You're too damned heavy," complained Mick.

"And you smell like a wet dog."

Mick looked at Birger, then burst out laughing, and Birger joined in. The fear, the horror and the pain suddenly seemed comical, as if they were all some big practical joke. Laughing caused his ribs to throb, making him laugh even more.

"Why did I even come on this rescue mission?" asked Birger. "I can barely stand."

"You're part of the team, mate. No way we would leave you out."

"That's dumb. I was dead weight, and you had to carry my hobbled ass."

"And next time you'll carry me." Mick grinned from ear to ear, giving Birger an awkward slap on the chest as they lay on the ground. "Come on, we've still got a distance to cover."

And that was when a large, dark figure soared up the cliff-side, landing a few paces away.

35

UNWANTED

The silhouette loomed on the fire-lit horizon. Birger realised that he and Mick were both holding their breath, as if the shadowy figure might miss them if they remained still. It turned its gaze towards the burning camp, and Mick hurriedly helped Birger to his feet.

Birger's injured leg made standing up awkward, but adrenalin numbed the pain. They broke into a quasi-run. After taking a few panicked steps, he glanced over his shoulder.

"Gullshite!" cursed Birger and jerked to avoid tripping on a clump of grass.

"What?" asked Mick.

"It's gone!"

"What do you mean, gone?" Mick craned his neck to see.

Again, Birger turned back towards the tree, and his heart skipped a beat when he found someone standing right behind them.

"Eric!" Birger barked with surprise, and Mick swung around so fast he nearly toppled them both over.

"What in the Weave are you doing here?" snapped Mick, his words clipped and his eyes wide.

The large man grunted at them as he coiled the climbing rope around his arm and strolled past without a word. Birger noticed something dark glistening on Eric's hands. It was blood. Fear made bile rise in Birger's throat, observing the bear of a man sauntering on.

"He scares the rat piss out of me," said Birger.

"I know, mate. He scares Lot's ice out of me too."

Birger raised an eyebrow at the curse and made a spiralling gesture over his heart to ward off Lot's wrath. *Did I imagine Eric leaping up the side of the cliff?* he wondered. *It must've been a trick of the light – But could he have ...*

"Do you think Eric killed the tin-birds?" there was a tremor of fear in Birger's voice.

"I hope not." Mick's apprehensive expression hinted at similar thoughts. "Frankly, I would rather not think about it. Let's move.

The sooner we get those kids home and get back on the road, the better."

The cold steel of Mick's chest plate eased the rope burns on Birger's palms. He realised how much he genuinely appreciated Mick at that moment. The man didn't have to help him, and doing so put him at risk, but he did it anyway.

Birger and Mick trailed Eric at a safe distance, about a hundred paces behind, taking care to avoid the low bushes hidden in the darkness. Birger saw Wynn and Gunther had made it to Peter, with the girl still secured to Gunther's chest. She was now awake and evidently in pain. They stood on a ridge by a couple of trees, not far from the road.

As Birger arrived, Peter gave his sister something to eat, possibly cat's claw to ease her pain, and helped her take a sip from his waterskin.

"Hey," Wynn greeted them as they arrived.

"Is she okay?" asked Birger.

"Considering that someone broke all her toes, tore out her nails, and seared her feet with hot coals…sure." Wynn's voice trembled with disgust and anger.

Mick and Birger both nodded, their faces grim. Without a word, Mick broke off and moved towards Gunther, giving his husband a side hug to avoid crushing the girl. The two exchanged concerned looks, ensuring each were both still whole.

Birger steadied himself, blowing on the hot wounds in his palms as he inspected the damage.

"Looks painful," said Wynn, scrunching up her nose.

"It is." Birger grimaced.

Wynn let out a long sigh.

"Are you alright?" Birger asked when Mick was out of earshot.

"Yes…" Wynn hesitated. Her mouth opened as if she desperately wanted to say something and closed it abruptly. At last, she said, "I'm fine. It was hard to watch."

"For me too," Birger said hesitantly, wondering if he should say more. A gaping hole formed in his stomach as he prepared himself to speak up. "Listen, Wynn. We haven't had a chance to talk properly since that night in West Haven, and I feel a few things need to be said."

Wynn nodded wearily. He longed to hug her, kiss her, and reassure her that everything would work out. But first, he needed to get things off his chest.

He saw her hesitate, and before Birger could speak, Wynn suddenly leaned forward and pressed her lips to his. A thrill of pleasure and shock ran down Birger's spine. *That was unexpected,* he thought. In the back of his mind, he wished he had time to freshened up, but his primal instincts took control, and they didn't care.

The soft, warm sensation overwhelmed him. All the pain and stress of the evening vanished amid this blissful feeling. *Who needed magic when they could have passion-fuelled euphoria?* Birger felt emotions surging that he struggled to label. *Was it love, exhilaration, infatuation... lust? Could it be all of them at the same time? Did it matter?*

Wynn pressed against his sore ribs but he didn't care, in fact, he wanted to get even closer. Amidst the acrid smell of smoke and the musky aroma of sweat, Birger picked out the sweet scent of her stolen perfume. The one he kept telling her not to wear, and she kept ignoring him anyway. That was the impression of Wynn that came to him each time he missed being close to her. He had wanted this for so long, he could scarcely believe it was finally happening.

The kiss seemed to last forever as they explored each other's mouths. *Who could keep track during times like these? And who would bother?* Birger thought. The desire burned in his stomach, he struggled to contain his eagerness, and things were heating–

"Oi, you two. We best get moving before the vultures realise this girl is gone," shouted Mick.

Wynn broke away and Birger thought, *Gullshite! Can't Mick leave us alone for a little longer?*

Wynn turned to face Mick and asked, "Shouldn't we wait for Renate and Lorenzo?"

Peter stood by Mick's side, while Gunther gently rocked the girl strapped to his chest and hummed a lullaby.

"They know how to get to the inn," Mick shook his head. "We need to get these two home. We're not out of the woods until then."

"Oh, thank you, sir," Peter choked through relentless sobs, his face streaked with muddy tear tracks. "I don't know what we would've done if you hadn't come."

"Don't thank me," said Mick. He jerked a thumb at Birger, "Thank this fella who insisted we help your sister."

"Oh, I can't thank you enough, sir!" Peter sobbed and pushed Wynn aside, wrapping Birger in a tear-soaked hug. The man smelled of sweat, and the pressure caused Birger's ribs to ache.

"Oh, damn," said Mick, "If I knew you would do that, I would've told you Eric was the hero."

That drew a chuckle from the crowd, except for Eric, who only glowered.

Birger wanted to rewind time, erase Mick and Peter from the scene, and relive his moment with Wynn.

"That's alright, Peter," Birger gently disengaged from the hug. "We did what was right."

"You saved my little sister's life, sir!" Peter said, his voice cracking, as he moved in for another hug, but Birger blocked him. He disliked being hugged and didn't want his already aching ribs hurting more. "You're a hero. I don't have much, but here, take this." Peter held out two silver coins.

Wynn gave Birger a knowing smile and winked as she moved away. She walked towards Gunther. He longed to call her back, but he had to deal with this first. *Damn*, thought Birger. *There is no way I can easily recreate that moment; what if it never happens again?*

"I can't take your money," Birger rejected the offer. He wasn't in the habit of taking money from the poor. The Code was quite literally about doing the opposite. *You don't take from those that have nothing to give.*

"Please, sir, I can't begin to express how much this means to me," Peter insisted.

"It's a grave insult to refuse a gift from a Thornhaller," said Mick helpfully. "You had better take it."

Birger sighed as he looked at the coins. "I can't take the only coins you have."

Peter dropped his head. "Please, sir, don't refuse me, or I'll owe you a life debt."

Birger felt annoyed and frustrated at that, but he knew it would be disrespectful to ignore the man's custom. Taking a deep breath, Birger pushed his desire-filled impatience aside. *It's over, and I need to refocus myself.*

As he calmed himself, a plan formed in his mind. Birger reached into his pocket to fish for a gold coin.

He snatched Peter's silver, while at the same time depositing the gold into Peter's pocket.

"Thank you." Peter bowed his head.

"Consider your debt paid."

"Thank you, sir. I insist you join us at our farm for dinner tonight. It's the least we can do to show our gratitude."

228

With that, Mick jumped in and said, "No, no, you've already paid your debt, and we have more to do tonight."

The young girl let out a yelp, startled by a bat flying overhead, and she pulled into Gunther, who said, "Hush, you're safe."

"Is your name Emily?" asked Wynn in a gentle tone.

"Yes," confirmed the young girl with a whimper. She looked scared and exhausted.

"Alright, Emily, we'll take you home now, where you'll be safe." Wynn gave her a warm smile.

The girl nodded, nestling deeper into Gunther's arms. The burly man hugged Emily tightly as she closed her eyes and rested on his shoulder. Birger approached Snow, who curiously peeked out from inside his cloak bed, and he stroked the weavespider's head.

"How're you holding up, buddy?"

Snow shuddered and pushed his head into Birger's palm.

"Hop into your nest so we can get moving," he said, opening his satchel for Snow to climb in. The weavespider moved gingerly, the missing limb causing him pain, and Birger winced in sympathy.

As Renate approached, she said, "I'm glad to see you're safe."

Renate's face was drawn and eyes sunken with exhaustion. Lorenzo supported her with his right arm, his coat flecked with soot and sprinkles of blood on his cheek.

"We're just about to leave," said Wynn.

"Excellent plan. Renate bought us some time, but there is no point in tempting Aeg, so let's move," agreed Lorenzo, and they started towards Thornhall.

"Lead the way, mate," said Mick, putting his hand on Peter's shoulder.

Wynn, Peter, Mick, and Gunther, who was still bearing Emily, walked in the front. Birger saw a weary look flash across Wynn's face, but she forced a smile and started chatting with Emily about farm life. With comical hand gestures and a light tone, she proceeded to distract the girl from her recent ordeal.

Despite all they had been through, Wynn put the needs of another before her own. She was a strong woman, and Birger felt his attraction surge. It was clear to him that she had grown beyond the clumsy apprentice he had in Anthir. Maybe he could stop thinking of her as that girl and allow something more.

Or maybe your libido is clouding your judgement, and you're being conned.

Renate came closer, stepping away from Lorenzo's support to examine the girl's wounds. With Eric holding the rear, Birger hobbled along in the middle, his stiff leg making it hard to keep pace. Lorenzo pulled up next to him.

"Was it worth it?" asked Lorenzo.

"What?" asked Birger.

Lorenzo smiled with his eyes as he said, "Rescuing the girl."

"Ah," Birger finally understood. "I think so. She's only seventeen, and what they did to her will haunt her for the rest of her life, but she'll have a life to live because we chose to help."

"And how does it feel to have saved her life?"

"It hurts a lot." Birger laughed. "Still, it feels good to have it behind us. I couldn't have lived knowing I didn't do everything I could."

"You have a kind heart, young Birger, you put yourself at risk for others, you can turn a problem into a challenge, and you have a sharp mind." Lorenzo gave Birger a pleased smile. "Can I give you some feedback?"

"Sure," said Birger tentatively.

"In West Haven, when you spoke to the Queen, you hesitated. I'm not saying this because of appearances. It's about how well you can apply your mind among people with power. I understand it's a new kind of situation for you. In this line of work, you'll need to build a perspective that lets you feel at ease with that sort of individual."

Birger shrugged. "I suppose you have plenty of experience with that kind of thing."

"Yes," agreed Lorenzo, "and that wasn't always the case."

"So, how did you learn to deal with it?" asked Birger curiously.

"Let me show you. I notice my emotional state. Then I use my breathing to focus my mind. I count to ten inhaling and exhale quickly five times. Start again from one if you lose count." Lorenzo demonstrated. "The key is to let your mind observe your thoughts without judgement. There are no good or bad thoughts, only thoughts. Watch them fly overhead like birds passing. Would you like to give it a go?"

Birger followed the instructions. He furrowed his brow in contemplation as he realised he hadn't become defensive with Lorenzo's feedback, even though he was tired and hurt. *What was behind that?* he wondered. *Must have something to do with the way Lorenzo spoke. Hold on, I was meant to be observing, not judging my thoughts. What does observing your thoughts even look like, anyway?*

Birger asked, "How do you prevent yourself from judging your thoughts?"

"Focus on the feeling of the breath moving into your lungs and how your body changes. Then notice your feet pounding on the dirt as you walk and allow yourself to be," guided Lorenzo. "Thought, pain, and emotions are energy vibrating without meaning until you assign it. Choose to let them remain meaningless for a time and rest in that space."

Birger focused on his feet, feeling the grit grind under his soft soles. His limp gave him an uneven gait, and his knee ached with each step despite the magical healing. He felt the subtle chafe of his britches against his thighs and noticed the shuffle of his glossy new leather jerkin over his grey linen doublet.

The numbness around the cut on his cheek made him stretch his jaw as the cold air brushed over his face. Birger focused on each sensation, acknowledging it, and moving to the next. A subtle sense of tranquillity soothed the nearly debilitating terror that lurked behind a thin veneer of bravado. The embarrassing memory of Mick witnessing him being overwhelmed by fear heated his ears and threatened to shatter his newfound peace.

Birger refocused on his steps and the small bursts of pain that came with each. *When you stop seeing pain as a bad thing, it can almost have a grounding quality that anchors you to the here and now.*

"Do you notice how the world slows down?" asked Lorenzo in a calming voice.

Birger nodded. He could feel the chaos of the burning camp, his injuries, and the anticipation of the soreness they would bring in the morning. The girl's suffering and the image of her on the torture rack. He thought about the thing hunting the tin-birds, killing them as easily as picking strawberries. Even his tiredness faded into a void of peaceful presence.

"Next time you find yourself in a situation that wants to overwhelm you, remember that you grow only by going through pain with an open and curious mind. Your mind is a powerful tool that can create or destroy, and putting you at risk when misused. So don't borrow trouble from the past or the future. Create space for your mind to operate in the present by focusing on the reality of the present moment. You can be mindful of the future without letting it create problems in the present."

"Thanks," said Birger, looking over to Lorenzo, "So you're a mindweaver too?"

"I'm still learning."

"Right, but are you able to live in the present all the time?" Birger asked.

Lorenzo laughed, "No, no one can, but I come back to it when I need to or if I end up drifting too far away."

Birger smiled back and said, "Okay, but heavy breathing aside, can I ask you something?"

"Go ahead."

"You have a bunch of gadgets, right? Can you show me how they work?" Birger pointed at the pouches strapped across Lorenzo's body.

"Which one?" clarified Lorenzo.

"What about the one you used to decode the documents?" Birger chose tentatively.

"Ah." Lorenzo produced the pince-nez from his pouch and handed it to Birger. "Look," Birger took it and held it up to his eyes, "there are gears on the top. One changes the letter of the current slot you are decoding, the next gear lets you shift the slot, and the last increases the number of slots you have."

Birger inspected the thing, noticed the gears, and tested clicking them over. He handed it back to Lorenzo, then asked, "You have to look at a coded document for it to work?"

"You need something with letters for it to do anything at all. When we get back to Thornhall, you can try it out." Lorenzo placed the device back in his pouch. "If the document isn't coded, using this will make it illegible."

As Birger settled into his new role as a spy, his identity as a thief was receding. Balancing power felt more permanent than giving a poor man money. It wasn't simply an issue of economics. Economics were simply a manifestation of the laws of power, and money expressed that. Lorenzo was working at the root of the evil that shaped the world.

Roar loomed in Birger's mind, and an old hate smouldered in his chest. A kind of hate reserved for those closest to you. Only they could inflict enough pain to elicit it, and the rejection of a father was chief among them in Birger's mind.

Perhaps Roar was the reason Birger felt so strongly about balancing power and would risk his life for it. He took Lorenzo's advice, deciding not to dwell on the past or future. Roar had caused him enough pain, and he didn't need to open up old wounds when he had plenty of fresh ones.

Birger glanced at the front of the party ahead of them. Gunther carried the girl without complaint and showed no sign of fatigue. They would be off in the morning, and hopefully, the tin-birds would leave the people of Thornhall alone for a while.

"Why do Mick and Gunther work with you?" Birger asked Lorenzo.

Lorenzo smiled at Birger. "Mick is a resourceful man and a decisive leader. Besides being streetwise, he and Gunther fought for the crown in the civil war and earned the royal loral of honour three times each."

"But why do they trust you?" asked Birger.

Lorenzo looked ahead, his eyes softening with a sadness that Birger hadn't noticed before. "There are many reasons that someone might trust another. I do my best to be a fair and honourable man, and I hope that, combined with our shared purpose, they work with me because they believe in what I stand for."

Once Peter and Emily were safely home, the team returned to the inn and Birger collapsed boneless to his bed. In the morning, they would be back on the road. There was no time to spare.

233

36

NORD FOREST

Birger pulled his oilskin further over his head to keep the sleet off his face. The crown stable-master had thought of everything when he filled the saddlebags. A good thing because, without those supplies, Birger and his companions would be facing severe hypothermia, frostbite or even death in this weather.

At the head of the column, Eric was speaking to Lorenzo and pointed to the westward trees. Lorenzo replied, and Eric shot off in that direction, evidently unaffected by the awful cold.

"There's a dry place to camp up ahead," Lorenzo called back over the downpour's deafening noise. "The horses can't handle this for much longer; let's move quickly!"

The party started moving again, and Birger yearned for a warm, dry place to eat a cooked meal. The day's travel had been the hardest so far; with his injuries stiffening, even breathing was painful. The only pleasant thing was the memory of kissing Wynn and the hopes of repeating the previous night's event once in camp.

"You alright there, Birger?" asked Gunther, pulling his Sawran Highlander up, next to his.

"Yeah, fine," replied Birger.

"Okay," Gunther nodded, "It's just you don't seem your usual energetic self. I've barely heard a witty retort from you all day."

That made Birger smile, causing his cheek to ache, "Do you have something against a bit of post-battle brooding?"

"Not at all. I've been known to indulge in a bit of brooding myself. It's a West Haven ex-soldier tradition, but I don't usually need to protect my ribs so much, nor side-eye young ladies with such a longing smile," said Gunther, tilting his head over to where Renate and Wynn rode behind Lorenzo.

Birger was thankful for the heavy downpour. He would've hated for Wynn to hear Gunther's comment.

"Not sure what you mean," lied Birger.

"Hey, if you don't want to talk about it, that's fine with me. But we all saw what happened between you two last night."

Birger blushed, "It's nothing."

"Maybe," Gunther gave Birger an empathetic look. "You're both young and in a tense situation. It's completely normal to feel awkward about it. How long have you known each other?"

"I don't know, half a year?" Birger was finding it hard to keep track of time through all the recent craziness. It was hard to imagine that they only left West Haven three days ago.

"I see, and how long have you been holding a candle for her?"

"Since I met her, but then she became my apprentice and I had to put that on hold," Birger admitted. "You and Mick?"

Gunther smiled. "He drives me up the wall sometimes, but yes. Married going on fifteen years," Gunther smiled broadly and his dark eyes twinkled under his heavy brow. "You know, Mick and I have been together since childhood. His folks were drunks, always beating on him, and one day my dad went into his house and broke his old man's jaw–"

"What!?" Birger's eyes stretched and his mouth hung open. "Just like that? Your dad walks into some bloke's home and smacks him one?"

"Yup. He didn't brook bullies. After that, Mick came to stay with us. My mum always wanted a big family, but she couldn't have any more kids after me, so she happily welcomed Mick into the Harper family."

"Your childhood sounds a far shot better than mine."

"It was pretty good, for a time. Until my dad passed away a couple of years later when the mines got attacked by nikkuni raiders. Thank Lot, I had Mick, he was there for me while I grieved. Despite his exceptional talent for making people angry, he's a good man."

Nikkuni raiders? Birger's eyebrows popped, surprised the small greenskins from the north would attack so far south.

"Yeah," Birger looked at Mick, who was talking to Lorenzo and remembered his moment of terror in the tin-bird camp. "Mick saved my life last night. I froze up, and Mick talked me down. He could have left me behind, but he carried me through, so I can see what you mean."

"Mick has saved my life more times than I can count, and he would die before he let a friend down."

"What about Lorenzo?"

"What about him?" Gunther looked over at Birger quizzically.

"Why do you stick with him?" asked Birger. "You two are smart and tough; you could be making good money running your own crews. Why have you chosen to throw your lot in with him?"

"Deep question," Gunther contemplated for a moment, then said, "to be honest, the thought of doing anything else had never even occurred to me."

"Why is that?"

"Because of Lorenzo himself."

Birger tilted his head to the side for a better look at Gunther's face, and with a frown, he said, "What do you mean?"

Gunther smiled, "It's a long story."

"I'm not in a hurry." Birger pointed at his general injuries.

"Well, after my dad died, times got tough, but, thankfully, the Magpies kept our family from starving. My mum never let us see how bad it got, but we knew, and still she treated Mick like he was her own." Gunther gently put his big hand on Birger's shoulder and said, "I say that so you can understand how hard we took it when she came down with leprosy a few years ago."

Birger's face dropped, and he put his hand to his mouth. "By the All-Mother, I'm so sorry!"

Gunther's smile remained in place, and he said, "Think nothing of it, because by then Lorenzo had drafted Mick and me to work for the Shade. When he heard about mum, he had his personal healer take care of her, and she made a full recovery."

"Really?" Birger asked in surprise. "But the cure for leprosy costs a fortune!"

Gunther looked up at the slowing rain and opened his mouth to catch a few drops on his tongue. "That's right, and Lorenzo covered the cost without ever telling us about it."

Birger saw parallels between his own experiences with Benny and Gunther's story. The old fence always asked for what was due in their regular business, but the man gave Birger everything he had in their personal relationship.

"I think I understand. I had a friend like that once." Birger's mouth tugged at the corner, and emotions welled up in the back of his throat.

"Had?"

"He died a little over a month ago." The weight of Birger's emotion was still there, but he was thankful there was no flashback.

"Sorry to hear it," said Gunther, pursing his lips, sadness in his eyes.

"That's why I'm here. To make sure that his death means something."

The sleet stopped, but the noise of people trying to talk over the previously thunderous downpour continued. Wynn laughed, and Mick stopped mid-sentence as everyone realised they didn't need to shout any more. Beyond the trees, Birger saw a cliff shaped like a giant tidal wave curling over a dry island where Eric stood by a stack of wood. He worked his flint and steel, casting sputtering sparks on it.

"Thank Aeg," breathed Gunther. "I thought we would have to test our tents against this weather tonight, but this is perfect."

Birger had to agree, the place was a sight for sore eyes, and the idea of an inviting, warm fire lifted his mood.

"Come by when you're set up," said Gunther with a broad grin. "I'll make the classic Harper stew tonight. It's legendary for taking the edge off any cold."

Birger found the broad man's gap-toothed smile infectious. Gunther hurried off and Birger sidled up next to Wynn, riding on her large packhorse.

"How's Snow?" Wynn asked when she noticed him.

"Still hiding in his nest," replied Birger. "He hasn't wanted to come out all day."

"The poor thing lost a leg," Wynn grimaced, "how would you feel if it were you?"

Birger felt as though he had lost a leg himself and flexed his stiff knee; it still ached. "I wish there was something I could do for him."

"No need to worry," said Renate. "He's in there with Chancebringer, right?"

"Yes, so?" asked Birger.

"Snow is a weavespider. He eats the enigmites that live on it, helping him regain his strength."

"Enigwhats?" asked Wynn with a quizzical look.

"Enigmites," Renate chuckled, "are tiny creatures that feed on magic. You can barely see them, but that's what weavespiders eat."

"Really?" Wynn's voice was high pitched with curiosity.

"Of course, let me explain." Renate's eyes twinkled with excitement. "I love talking about this stuff! So you heard of the magical realm known as the Weave? That's where weavestorms come from. It's inhabited by living creatures like Snow."

"Creatures plural?" asked Birger.

"Yes, there are a lot of different species, but it's a fairly surreal place, and while some of it mirrors our world, there are a lot of differences."

"Like what?" Wynn pulled in close, her eyes wide and her mouth hanging slightly open.

She looked very cute, and Birger found himself smiling wistfully at her, but she didn't notice.

"Well, like here, most life revolves around the sun, which feeds the plants, and animals eat the plants, and we eat both. In the Weave, the cycle starts with energy flowing through the threads."

"Flowing how? Like water?" Birger tried to imagine what it would look like if there was water running all over the place. *Would it be like the sea?* he wondered.

"Yes, kind of like water running through millions of rivers, with enigmites feeding from the magic."

Snow peeked out of the satchel. Maybe because he heard his name being thrown around so much.

"Is that what Snow eats too?" Wynn ruffled the fur on Snow's head.

"Sort of; weavespiders can't digest the magic directly from the threads, they eat the enigmites," explained Renate.

"Oh, like deer eating grass?" clarified Birger.

Renate nodded, and said, "Yes, just like that."

"But what do the enigthingies feed on in our world?" asked Wynn.

"Enigmites," corrected Renate, "they gather on magical artefacts or enchantments, and with enough time, they can drain all the power from it. Something as powerful as the Chancebringer has likely attracted an endless buffet of them over the millennia while it lay hidden in the city of the Titans."

"But wouldn't the ring have lost all of its power over that time from them eating it?" asked Wynn, perplexed.

"Powerful artefacts like Chancebringer are not self-contained; they continuously draw energy from the Weave. Think of it like a spigot. The enigmites can clog it up but can't cut it off from the source."

"Are weavespiders dangerous?" asked Birger, wishing he had asked before he started touching Snow.

"Yes, very," said Renate seriously, and Birger cringed. "Their bite effectively creates a small, controlled weavestorm. Not to mention that an adult weavespider's head is around six feet off the ground."

"What?" Birger coughed.

"Snow is only a baby?" Wynn asked, scrunching up her face for emphasis.

"Yes, and growing fast," noted Renate, "I think that the amount of food he gets from Chancebringer is speeding up his life cycle."

"No wonder this damned satchel feels like a galleon's anchor," said Birger.

Renate laughed loudly and said, "Oh, that reminds me. You had better make sure nothing ever crushes Chancebringer while it's on you."

"Why's that?" asked Birger.

"Because, it has a rift to the Weave inside of it," she explained. "If it broke, the rift would destabilise and explode into a weavestorm."

Birger's face went pale, and he felt the weight of the onyx band redouble in his satchel.

"But don't worry, that's very unlikely to happen." Renate grinned. "When we've set up camp, bring Snow to me. I'll look at his leg and see if I can make him more comfortable."

Birger acknowledged her with a grunt, his mind still fixed on the new dangers he didn't know he was bringing along.

As the group dismounted at the dry campsite, a fire already danced pleasantly on a few logs laid out in a stone circle. Eric obviously took the initiative to ensure food could be prepared as quickly as possible. He was always ravenous by the time the party stopped for the day.

Birger longed to sit by the flames and warm his hands, but he knew duty came first. Everyone busied themselves with brushing down their horses, making sure they were still dry under the blankets, and attaching feeding bags to their heads. Then moved on to set tents beneath the natural stone roof.

Birger removed his chaffing armour and placed it alongside his rapier in his tent.

"Birger," Wynn asked, "Do you have a moment?"

37

TEAMING

Wynn looked beautiful where she stood next to him, backlit by the campfire, and Birger longed to kiss her again. Her reddish-brown hair was still mussed from removing her oilskin, and she had a dust smudge on her chin that made Birger smile.

The shelter under the outcrop bustled with activity as the team set up camp, and Birger's tan tent was barely standing on its own. Even without his injuries, he wasn't particularly good at bushcraft.

Gunther settled next to the fire with his cooking pot and a cask of water, leaving Mick to pitch their tent on his own, and Birger saw Eric heading into the darkness.

Wynn's tent was set up, and it looked way better than Birger's attempt.

"How can I help?" Birger's eyes twinkled with hope.

"I noticed you had a long bow on your horse," Wynn pointed to Birger's Sawran Highlander. "Can I borrow it for some hunting?" Her head tilted slightly to the right with a skew smile and those big blue eyes. Similar to an expression that Snow often used to request belly rubs.

Birger felt a wave of disappointment, his cheeks warming, and he hoped the blush wasn't visible in the dim light. "Sure, I guess." He shrugged. "You can keep it. I don't even know how to string the thing."

"Thanks!" Wynn bounced with excitement before running to the horse. She had the weapon strung in short order, and slung a quiver of arrows over her shoulder.

Gullshite, thought Birger. *I was hoping she would ask to share a tent. And it's time we had that talk we've been putting off.*

Renate walked alongside Lorenzo as the pair approached him, and Lorenzo asked, "Do you have a moment?"

Birger took a deep breath to clear his head, and said, "Sure, what is it?"

They were both well dressed and looked more like a couple on holiday in the country than people who spent the day travelling through the Nord Forest. Lorenzo held a small leather pouch and Renate, her healer's case.

"While you boys chat, is it alright if I check on Snow's leg?" asked Renate.

"Of course." Birger nodded, and she knelt to open the canvas satchel lying on Birger's bedroll. Snow made an annoyed sound, and Birger's heart twinged with pity for his friend.

Lorenzo guided Birger to the campfire. "We'll be in Kindra tomorrow. Would you please help me make sense of a few things?"

"What would that be?"

"For a moment, imagine you were going to steal an artefact from a temple. What would be your approach?" asked Lorenzo, his eyes narrowing and his right ear turning subtly towards Birger.

"Easy, I would case the place. You wouldn't want to stumble into a trap or miss a potential opportunity because you failed to take the time to learn the layout and security measures."

"And what would you do to get that information?"

They reached the fire, and Birger took a moment to enjoy the warmth. It was almost too hot on his chilled hands, his fingers tingling as his circulation improved. He hadn't realised how cold he still was until that moment. Pushing his greaves forward, he let them bake and spread the heat more evenly over his injured knee. He wouldn't be forgetting that fight with the tin-bird any time soon.

"A source, someone on the inside that can tell me what to expect." Birger tapped his finger to his chin. "Though that might be complicated with a temple. It's easy to turn a servant on an abusive rich ass, but people can take their religions seriously. I guess, with enough time, finding a disillusioned source would be possible, but if speed was key, I would try an indirect or even more direct way."

"Tell me more?"

"For the indirect way, you could find someone that works in the temple, make them drunk and ask them questions, or more directly; you can visit the mark as a patron and take notes as you go. For the latter, I would probably pose as a noble coming to visit an ancestor's grave."

Birger rubbed his hands together and blew into them, feeling the warm breath flow between his fingers. His palms were covered in stiff scabs that ached when he squeezed them.

"Interesting. Your experience in this matter is evident. Thank you for sharing it with me. I don't imagine it would be easy to find someone that was tapped for information indirectly, but someone posing as a noble would stand out."

Gunther looked up from where he stirred the water in the cooking pot and said, "Hey boss, did you bring the salt and spices?"

"Here," Lorenzo replied, handing Gunther the pouch he was holding.

Gunther put the pouch on a wooden board in front of him. Mick walked up to the trio, dragging several large stumps in his wake, and arranged them around the fire for seating.

"Thank you, Mick," said Lorenzo as he took a seat. "Anything I can carve for you, Gunther?"

"Not yet," replied Gunther, "But that will change shortly."

"What's the plan for tomorrow?" asked Mick as he, too, settled on a log seat.

Birger parked on another stump, and his leather greaves burned pleasantly as they tightened over his thighs. Due to the lack of flexibility in his knee, he kept his right leg straight.

"I'll go over what we have once everyone is back, and we all get something to eat," replied Lorenzo, "for now, I'm not exactly sure. We have many unknowns to account for, and it would be helpful to get everyone's perspective. Birger, are the documents I gave you at West Haven still secure?"

He knew Lorenzo was asking if Wynn had taken the documents, and the reminder that she was a double agent made him frown. Birger hesitated for a moment before saying, "As secure as a pirate's wooden leg, at least when I checked this morning."

"Alright, let me know if that changes." Lorenzo looked deep in thought. "We need to know what the opposition has in play and what they know."

"Who exactly are the opposition?" asked Gunther absently as he extracted some carrots from a sack.

"I can't be sure. A pigeon was waiting for me this morning in Thornhall, and it was from Becka. There were three new developments outlined in it. The Wartide has reached the Tower and laid siege to the dwan."

"What?" interrupted Mick. "That's close to here. We had better keep our guard tight tonight."

"Less than fifty miles, in fact. I'm not yet sure how that comes into play for us, but Ulfhild set them in motion for a reason." Lorenzo glanced over at Birger and said, "It also appears that events in Anthir have developed. The Magpies' leader, Noxolu, overcame the Duke's forces in the revolt. She established the city as a new merchant's republic, and all but expelled the Black Wolves from the city."

"A merchant's republic aye, like the Korlanders have?" asked Birger, trying to make sense of what that meant.

"Sort of, yes," said Lorenzo. "And finally, Becka confirmed that someone you know has been operating in Kindra."

Birger looked at Lorenzo with a quizzical tilt of his head. "Who?"

"A Black Wolf Captain, known as Bo."

"Right." Birger's cheeks burned, and his blood rose as he thought of the scrunch-faced bully.

The memory of Bo's red stained face looking on as Benny was murdered, only marginally more provocative than the desire to question the brute about Sten's death. Bo had a lot to answer for.

"Is she sure it's him?" Birger's voice came out in growl. All that pent up anger clawing at his guts in search of an escape.

"Settle down there, mate," said Mick. "No need to kill the messenger's messenger."

"You don't understand," Birger snorted, and in his mind, Bo loomed like a storm ready to break loose. "He's a monster that deserves to die."

Mick opened his mouth to say something, but Gunther put a hand on Mick's knee, prompting him to close it again.

"Bo was involved in the death of Birger's friend," explained Lorenzo. "If he's here and behind this theft, we'll stop him."

There was a confidence in Lorenzo's statement that made Birger feel calmer.

The conversation died as Mick and Gunther traded chastising glances while Lorenzo let things settle. Birger's thoughts darkened, and he struggled to pinpoint the specific reason. Based on what he had learned from the Irthan Manor, he already knew Bo was involved in this.

Maybe I'm upset because it's another reminder that Wynn isn't being honest with me. Birger turned his feelings over in his mind, trying to see what might be behind them.

He realised the kiss was messing with his head. He wanted everything to be okay. He and Wynn could work together, save the day, and continue to explore the exciting, unfamiliar territory of being together. Instead, he had to face the fact that they were on opposite sides of a game, destined to take an ugly turn.

Eric emerged from the darkness with a bag, tossing it to Gunther, who fumbled to catch it, but dropped his carving knife in the process.

"Hey!" Gunther snapped, evidently annoyed, "what was that?"

Eric pointed at the bag while shrugging, and Lorenzo indicated that the big man should sit down. Begrudgingly, Eric complied as Gunther investigated the sack. He extracted several turnips, mushrooms, and wild tomatoes.

"Oh my," said Gunther as his scowl morphed into a smile. "Fine, you made your point. Thank you."

Gunther gave Lorenzo the turnips and Mick the mushrooms, instructing them to get carving and cast the result into the cooking pot. When the first carvings hit the water, Wynn arrived with seven fresh rabbits dangling from her belt.

"Rabbits?" asked Wynn, exaggerated humility in her stance as she held up her prize.

"Wonderful!" celebrated Gunther with a big smile. "That's just what I need. Could you skin them and add them to the pot, please? Birger, make yourself useful and stir the stew." Gunther handed the ladle over while Wynn got to work.

It was nice to have a job; it kept his mind off what he had to do. Renate joined them with Snow curled up on her chest, and she settled next to Birger, stroking the weavespider's head. Snow leaned right, his mandibles askew, he looked at Birger with wide eyes. Birger sighed before giving the weavespider a belly rub, prompting Gunther to shudder and shift to the far side of the fire.

"Glad to see you're looking more like yourself there, Snow," said Birger with a warm grin as he ruffled the spider's fur. "Thanks for taking care of him, Renate."

"Don't mention it," she stroked Snow's back and said. "If you don't mind, I would like to take some of the webbings in Snow's nest. It's practically identical to magic-weave and would save me a bit of effort in reaching between dimensions each time I craft a spell."

"Really?" asked Birger.

"Yes. You can mould it into different shapes and imbue it with the essence of something to charge it, which is what any magic user would do. It wouldn't be as powerful, but it would work well enough for most spells. And crafting a spell isn't the exhausting part of doing magic; it's spending your life energy to create the rift between realms that drain you."

"You spend your life energy to craft spells!" exclaimed Wynn from the side. "That sounds horrible."

"The crafting is no different from what any artisan does; it requires tools, skill, understanding and patience," explained Renate. "Your soul is connected to all the other realms, and you can access them through that connection if you know how, but it drains your soul to do it. Don't worry though, it grows back with enough time."

"Oh right," said Wynn, "it still sounds dangerous to me."

She finished preparing the meat and took a spot next to Renate. The pot was simmering nicely as more ingredients plopped into the broth. Gunther opened the pouch of spices and started crafting his Harper stew. Birger's stomach rumbled, but the others were too focused on the food to notice.

Once dished out into bowls, Birger eagerly tasted it. The stew was savoury with a sharp spicy burn that didn't last long before being replaced with a sweetness that lingered on the tongue. Mick and Birger made everyone laugh as they recounted what had happened when they first met in the dungeon.

Afterward, Lorenzo asked the group for their thoughts about the upcoming situation in Kindra.

Wynn was the first to get up and said, "I think I'll retire for the night."

Birger quickly stood and chimed in, "Me too."

Everyone else seemed inclined to enjoy the fire for a little while longer, and Snow appeared quite happy with the perch he found on Renate's lap.

When they were out of earshot, Birger cleared his throat, "Wynn, can we go for a walk and talk about a few things?"

38

MATTERS OF THE HEART

Birger was keenly aware of Wynn by his side as they strolled into the chilly, moonless night. She shivered. Birger directed the light of his lantern onto the snow at her feet, helping her see. Then he invitingly opened his fur cloak. Wynn pulled in under it, and her clothes were icy where they touched his skin, but he didn't care; instead, he allowed himself to revel in her closeness.

The Nord Forest was dense, with pines poking for the sky, underbrush covering the ground, and massive water-smoothed rocks strewn about.

Nearby, Birger spotted a cryll bounding towards a tree. It was a small, furry creature with a shock of hair on its head and a long, bushy tail. They only came out of hibernation during winter when the snow was thick on the land. The nimble critter scurried up the rough bark of the tree and vanished into the powder packed on its branches.

Birger and Wynn headed towards the main road, but his injuries made walking uncomfortable. Birger began thinking that it might've been better to find a spot near the camp to sit down.

Wynn sighed heavily, prompting Birger to speak first, "Anything on your mind?"

"Me?" Wynn nudged Birger, "I'm pretty sure you asked me to come out here in the dark." She winked at him.

Birger fumbled for his next words. "I did. A lot's happened since we left Anthir." He turned to look at her, and she pulled away from him with a curious frown. "Wynn, when you kissed me..." Birger paused, searching for the right words. He noticed her take a deep breath and hold it; *Was that excitement? Or nerves?* "I was about to talk to you about something important, and then, that happened."

Wynn nodded, but her eyes flickered like a spooked animal, before she said, "Look, Birger, about what happened. You know we were in danger, we survived, and there was all that excitement...."

Birger held up his hand for her to stop. While thinking what to do next, he felt his heart sink when he decided how to move forward.

"It's not about the kiss, Wynn. Look, back in Anthir you said you didn't want to come with me because of Neffily. I need to know what changed."

"I wanted to come with you," Wynn reeled back like a fish biting into hooked bait, "but I realised it too late."

"Yeah, so you said," confirmed Birger, his eyes grim and his jaw set. "Only I don't buy that it was your only reason."

"So what is my reason then, Birger?" Wynn's shout startled him.

"I don't know." Birger felt his blood rise, his cheeks flush, and anger boil in his guts. When he spoke, it was as if someone else had taken the helm, and, evidently, they were drunk, "You tell me! What are you hiding, Wynn?"

Oh, Cos, you went there, Birger's cynic thought. *Stop this now; you're being an idiot. You can't possibly think this is going to help in any way.*

But Birger's rage set his jaw in stone, and his mind locked up on the betrayal he knew was there. Her reaction to the question confirmed it. Yet, his rational mind knew this was a mistake. He could see the ship heading into the shallows, but he was powerless to do anything about it.

A bird call echoed through the dark forest. Birger had never heard the peculiar sound before, but his mind was locked on the argument.

"You arrogant prick," Wynn spat the last word at him and crossed her arms, "you think everything is about you, don't you? I've had it with your condescending tones, explanations that assume I'm an idiot and your constant brooding. Do you think you are the only person in pain? Can't you see beyond yourself for a second and realise that Benny wasn't only your friend? That you aren't the only one with a right to avenge his death?"

Birger sputtered as he tried to find a response to the unexpected onslaughts, but his tired, weather-beaten mind failed him.

All he could do was lash back, "You ungrateful wretch! I took you in, trained you, gave you my gear and brought you on a caper that you had no business being in; one that got my best friend killed, just for you to turn around and throw it all in my face!"

Wynn huffed out a breath of defiant air and turned her back on Birger. Her shoulders slumped, and a glint of tears ran down her cheek.

He felt like a horrible human being as he realised what he had said. It was too harsh and unfair, and worse, he didn't even actually believe it. He was the one that chose the caper, he was the one that brought her, and he was the one to blame.

Wynn's body convulsed with a shudder of emotion. He reached out to touch her shoulder, but she shook it off. "Look, Wynn... that wasn't fair." Birger sighed deeply, his hand still hanging aimlessly in the air as if putting it down would mean defeat. "Listen, I shouldn't have-"

"Shouldn't have what?" Wynn turned tear-filled angry eyes on him and continued, "Shouldn't have brought me here?"

Her defiant eyes cut Birger to the bone; he felt overwhelmed by the intensity of the situation. He tried to think of something to stop her anger, but he came up short.

"Well, I'm here, and you can't do anything about it now. We're stuck in this forest, but don't worry; you won't have to put up with me for much longer. I'll make sure I stop being a burden."

"Wynn..." Birger tried, but she turned back to camp and stomped off, leaving Birger alone.

That couldn't have gone any worse, he thought, frustration escalating.

Really... is that all you have to say for yourself? Birger's cynic sounded frustrated too. *I told you to stop. Now, look what you've done. Not only did you ruin the night for both of you, but you may have lost a friend.*

Birger rubbed the scab on his cheek, which burned in the cold, and his hand came away wet with blood. He must've agitated the wound in his anger.

Dumb, he thought. Birger dropped to the snow-covered forest floor, set his lantern beside him, and slumped forward, resting his head in his hands.

He scooped a handful of snow and threw it into the darkness, hearing it impact a tree with a satisfying crunch. He looked up when he heard a distant, high-pitched, animalistic laugh. He listened for the sound again while scanning the area, but all he found was an eerie silence. *Must've been from the camp,* he thought. *Probably Mick cracking jokes again.*

Gullshite, Birger thought. *There's no way I'll be able to sleep after this.*

He was right, but not for the reasons he thought.

39

NO REST

A sinister whoop of joy echoed through the dark forest, making Birger's heart leap into his throat. He tried to scramble to his feet, but his rigid right leg caused him to stumble, and he crashed back into the snow.

Birger rolled over, attempting to stand again. He heard the snow crunch with several rapid footsteps, and before he could react, a painful kick exploded in his right side. It sent him flipping through the air, he came to a stop against a boulder. Birger gasped. His ears rang like he stuck his head in a bell tower. He blinked, trying to clear his blurred vision.

A menacing figure appeared, hefting a battle-axe and looming over him. In the faint lantern-light, Birger made out dark green skin covered in red war paint beneath heavy hide armour. He reached for his rapier, only to realise it was still in his tent. Driven by survival instincts, he clenched his teeth against the pain of his injuries and dove into an evasive roll. The descending weapon narrowly missed.

The fur cloak draped on Birger's back tightened around his throat. He let out a panicked squeal as he got plucked several feet back.

Birger looked up in time to see the axe descending again, and he squirmed, struggling to free himself from the garment. The blade seared through his shirt and grazed his chest, drawing blood as he managed to unclasp the cloak in the nick of time. It threw Birger's assailant off balance, giving him a gap to scramble awkwardly to his feet.

Grabbing a collection of rocks from the ground, Birger flung a fist-sized one at the figure. He shouted, "Get away!" hoping the stone would land if the enemy hesitated.

The creature swatted the rock deftly out of the air. It stepped back into the lantern light, and Birger felt fear take hold. It towered at seven feet tall, its green skin pulled tight over broad slabs of lean muscle. Its ears were pointed, and its jaw wide, but what scared Birger most was the predatory look in its yellow eyes. It was an ukthuun warrior, fully armoured, ready for battle, and here Birger stood with nothing to defend himself but a few rocks and far from help.

The ukthuun said something in a language that Birger didn't understand. He heard echoes of child-like laughter respond.

A score of small, green-skinned creatures stepped into the light. Their eyes glimmered with bloodlust. Their hands and feet were disproportionately large for their small bodies. Huge ears poked out of their heads that resembled lionfish fins, and their mouths were filled with sharp fangs. They were nikkuni.

"How sweet." Birger looked at the ukthuun, and, gesturing at the nikkuni, he said, "You brought your kids."

The uk only glared at him in reply.

Birger glanced behind him for an escape route, only to find more nikkuni; they had encircled him while he had been sulking in the snow.

"Serves me right for being a whiny little fin," muttered Birger, a pang of panic stabbing him in the gut.

The greenskins stalked forward with hungry eyes as they closed the net on him. He was, in no uncertain terms, facing imminent death, and he had no way out.

What a way to end things, thought Birger. *My last interaction with Wynn would be a fight, and I never even got close to stopping Bo.*

With a surge of adrenaline, Birger turned away from the ukthuun, his survival instincts kicking in. He hurled three stones in quick succession, desperate to create an opening. Each one nailed a nikkuni in the head to create a small gap for him to dart through. His ribs ached, and there was a sharp stab in his gut as he darted off, but, he ignored it.

A series of heavy thuds and a crunch of snow drew everyone's attention to the new threat, and Birger squinted into the black to see what they were looking at. A blur of vicious teeth and fur landed on a group of nikkuni, crushing them under its weight and ripping several more to shreds.

"Oh, good," said Birger, "now we can all die together."

It was hard to see in the gloom, and as the ukthuun moved to strike at the beast with his axe, he kicked the lantern over, killing the light altogether. Birger was used to the dark, and usually, it would be like a comfortable blanket pulled over him—but not tonight. The sounds of death were everywhere. Muscles were tearing, tendons snapping, bones crunching, and something wet splattered on Birger's face that smelled awful.

With his heart pounding in fear, Birger did the only thing he could. He chose a bearing roughly in the direction of the camp and ran for his life.

Fallen logs and rocks slapped at his feet, and he stumbled into a bramble bush that tore his shirt and cut up his arms. He cussed and resumed his flight; the pain meant nothing if he got himself killed. He realised that his right leg moved more than it should, and with each step, he felt an unnerving clack in his knee.

Renate isn't going to be happy with that, thought Birger, and he felt hopeful that he might get a chance to receive that lecture.

Birger pushed himself harder than ever, and to his relief, caught a glimpse of firelight flickering to his right; he had veered off course, but luckily the forest didn't allow him to stray too far, and now he could correct his mistake.

"Uks!" shouted Birger as he burst out of the trees, more brambles catching his neck and ripping the skin open.

The others were already armed and armoured. Gunther and Mick stood side by side with halberds in hand. Wynn was behind them, with an array of arrows sticking out of the ground and her long bow at the ready. Lorenzo held his slender black sword in one hand and Birger's rapier in the other, while right at the back, Snow crouched on the ground next to Renate.

Birger gratefully accepted his rapier from Lorenzo.

"Join the line." Lorenzo swung his sword in a figure-eight motion to limber up his muscles.

Birger complied with the order, unsheathed his weapon and absently rubbed at the bloodied scratches burning his skin. Snow scuttled up to Birger and pushed against his legs. The weavespider was getting stronger, or perhaps Birger's injuries had weakened him; the action almost bowled him over.

Gasping desperately for air, Birger warned Snow, "Hey buddy, this is…going to be dangerous. Find…somewhere safe to hide."

The weavespider shook himself and stared at the dark trees with grim determination.

"There are tons of them out there," said Birger looking at Lorenzo, "and there was something else as well; it was big, some kind of beast. It attacked them, and I barely got away."

"Bugger," said Mick, "just what we need."

"Easy, Mick," said Lorenzo, "focus on the task at hand."

"Where's Eric?" asked Birger.

Whoops and crazed giggles advanced on them from the darkness. Gunther nodded at Birger, explaining, "We heard shouting, so he went to find you."

Gunther had barely finished his sentence when the greenskins broke the treeline in a charge. They were primarily nikkuni, but there were at least a few of the big ukthuun among them. Wynn loosed several arrows, each landing with pinpoint accuracy. Birger's mouth dropped open, impressed.

As the first wave of nikkuni arrived, Mick and Gunther showcased their teamwork, wielding the two halberds in practiced unity. Lorenzo danced along their flank, his slender blade flicking at the enemy like a painter's brushstrokes on a canvas. He whirled and turned, deathly calm, and six more greenskins, including two ukthuun, died.

Birger struggled to hold off two nikkuni coming after him, wincing with pain from his leg and ribs. The injuries threw him off balance, and he barely kept himself alive. He lashed out with his rapier, nicking one of the tiny creatures on the neck, but it shrugged it off. Despite the blood squirting from the wound, it kept coming until one of Wynn's arrows sprouted from its chest.

Their brief respite was interrupted by a massive ukthuun, its hide armour so thickly layered that only the skin on its nose was visible. It pushed the second nikkuni out of the way. Barrelling into Birger and Mick, it bowled them over.

The brute rolled onto Birger, crushing his legs. Its weight made his bones creak, sending debilitating pain radiating from his knee. He screamed, and the ukthuun scraped against Birger's shins as it turned to punch him in the ribs. Birger took the blow as well as he could, but there was a loud popping sound and the impact left him doubled over.

Birger watched as Snow leapt and latched onto the ukthuun's face. Snow sank his fangs into its exposed nose, and a burst of bright purple and teal light erupted from the wound. Ice crystals rapidly grew over the ukthuun's head, and Birger felt a biting cold radiating from Snow.

Suddenly, multiple events unfolded simultaneously. The weight of the ukthuun on Birger's legs vanished as it was sucked into what Birger thought of as a whirlpool in the air. Lorenzo whipped around and opened the throats of the four remaining ukthuun warriors in one fluid motion.

Renate gathered something glowing in her hands, hurling it into the wave of greenskins. It exploded and knocked several to the ground. Gunther hauled Mick away from the vanishing ukthuun. Wynn dove over Birger to protect him as the miniature weavestorm exploded to cover the entire area in fresh ice.

There was a moment where no one moved, and even the titters of the nikkuni fell so silent that Birger could hear the wheezing in his chest with each breath.

A blood-curdling howl shattered the stillness. A terror with a massive, fanged maw and grey fur loped onto the remaining nikkuni from behind. Even hunched over, the creature was eight-foot tall. It tore savagely into the enemy, making the ukthuun attack seem like child's play. Birger couldn't see the animal well, but he recognised its bearskin armour and a massive bone axe whirling in one claw.

The combination of events sent a ripple of panic through the greenskins, and their ranks broke into a chaotic retreat.

The beast flashed yellow lupine eyes directly at Birger and set off after the mob.

40

WHERE TO START

Wynn rolled off Birger's chest, shivering, ice crystals from the Weave implosion clinging to her hair. Sharp pain shot through Birger's chest and he gasped to get air into his lungs. With adrenaline still pulsing through his veins and the cold numbing his skin, he didn't even feel the fresh cuts.

The yips of *nikkuni* echoed between the trees in the darkness. *The greenskin raiders might have retreated*, thought Birger, *but our victory was a narrow one, and they're still out there.*

"Hurry, we need to warm up," Renate urged, pointing to the fire, where Mick was already warming his greaves.

She rushed to fetch a few blankets from the nearest tent, returning to hand one to each of them. Birger tried to take it, but his arms felt like lead.

Greenskin corpses lay strewn about, firelight dancing in the dark pools of blood spreading in the surrounding snow. Gunther cleaned his halberd with the trousers of an ukthuun warrior, then paced over to Mick. Lorenzo joined them.

After a moment of fidgeting, Mick blurted out, "What in the Darkveil was that... *thing!?*"

"That... that was Eric," Birger managed to say, finding it harder to breathe by the second.

Birger tried to stand but couldn't and Gunther stepped over to help.

"Thanks," said Birger.

Then Birger turned to Lorenzo and asked, his face twisted in anguish, "It was him, wasn't it?"

"Yes," said Lorenzo, clenching his teeth.

"There's no way that *thing* was human!" Mick's eyes stretched wide in disbelief. "It had a Cos-damned muzzle, complete with terrifying fangs..." His face paled with realisation. "Oh..."

"The legends about the Wulfher... are real?" Birger's voice quivered, reflecting a cocktail of agony and fear.

Wynn shivered, sat on a log by the fire, wrapped in her thick woollen blanket, following the conversation warily. Near her, Snow shook the ice off himself in a wide halo while Renate approached Birger to check his wounds.

"Be gentle with him," she warned Gunther. "He's white as a sheet and his lips are turning blue. Lay him down by the fire so I can take a better look at him."

Birger didn't feel well, but still wanted to take part in the discussion. He tried to wave her off. "I'm fine. I can handle it..."

"Humour me." Renate gave him a disarming smile.

She placed a blanket close to the fire, onto which Gunther gently set Birger down. Snow scuttled over to give Birger a nuzzle on the cheek, his fur tickling Birger's ear.

"I'll go check on the horses," said Gunther as he got up.

Lying down made it harder for Birger to keep track of what was happening. When Renate touched his ribs, pain exploded through him. His back arched in a spasm, his arms shook, and tears filled his eyes.

"Sorry," said Renate, continuing to work, "I need to see if anything is broken. Please lie still."

Ignoring the commotion around Birger, Mick asked, "Well, are the legends true, Lorenzo? Are we travelling with a monster, leaving a trail of destruction and terror as we go?"

"No," said Lorenzo, his words clipped with uncharacteristic harshness, "I will discuss *none* of my team without them present. If you want to know what or who Eric is, ask him yourself when he returns. We must move. I'm gathering my things and getting ready to leave. There is every chance the *ukthuun* and *nikkuni* were looking for us, and they might return with reinforcements."

"Why do you think the uks were after *us*?" asked Wynn, knitting her eyebrows together with concern.

Lorenzo took a long breath before explaining, "Ulfhild sent the Wartide south to the Tower, which isn't far from here. Laying siege requires supplies, which means foragers, but it's too soon for them to be venturing this far."

"You think Ulfhild knows we're going to Kindra?" asked Mick.

"Yes," confirmed Lorenzo, "it's likely she's sent them looking for us. We need to get out of here right now."

Renate fixed Lorenzo with a stern look. "Birger has a broken rib, internal bleeding and a torn knee ligament. We aren't going

258

anywhere until I stabilise him. He'll die before we reach the main road."

"Right," said Mick, conceding his point for now, "I'll pack the tents."

"I'll help," said Lorenzo and followed Mick.

Birger tried to push himself up, wincing and gasping for air, as he muttered, "Just brace my leg...like before...I'll manage."

"Birger, stop! You can't tough your way through this." Renate put a hand on Birger's shoulder. "I don't even know how you got back to the camp in this state. Maybe the cold and adrenalin numbed the pain, but you're in bad shape. So, keep quiet, lie still, and let me work."

"Fine," Birger conceded, feeling so drained made it hard to argue.

Renate took a pair of scissors out of her case and cut Birger's shirt, then unravelled a few lengths of Snow's webbing.

Snow purred soothingly as he raised his four front legs and placed them on Birger's shoulder. The white spider swept its feathery appendages over Birger's face, making him giggle, bringing another wave of pain.

With Renate kneeling on Birger's right side, Wynn settled on his left side and removed Snow from Birger's face.

Birger saw the concern in Wynn's eyes. He wanted to apologize for their earlier argument, but the mounting pressure in his lungs robbed him of speech.

"Is there anything I can do to help?" Wynn asked Renate.

"Keep him down and put this between his teeth." Renate gave Wynn a cloth-wrapped stick, which she placed into Birger's mouth.

Despite his best attempts, Birger couldn't see what Renate was doing, and Wynn held him firmly in place. He surrendered, lying back when he heard the hurried footsteps of Gunther returning.

"The horses are dead, they've been slaughtered..."

Unfazed by Gunther's news, Renate placed both hands on Birger's sternum. "It's going to hurt," she said and pressed.

Birger bit the stick so hard, his jaw creaked like a ship's mast. He lost consciousness while Renate wrapped the webbing around his chest. But the hot searing pain of something cutting the skin between Birger's ribs brought him back from oblivion, followed by relief, as air filled his lungs.

Renate worked frantically, and Birger felt her pressing something against his side. "This isn't working," said Renate, with a note of contained panic. "Wynn, keep pressure here. I'll be back in a moment."

"Okay." Wynn shifted forward to take over.

Still gasping, Birger managed to spit the stick out. "Wynn...I'm so sorry."

Wynn leaned down to kiss him, her tears dripping onto his forehead. "Please, don't talk," she murmured.

Snow scuttled to Wynn's side and brushed himself against her thigh to comfort her. Wynn smiled at him.

The pressure in Birger's lungs returned, with every second heaping more weight, making it harder to draw breath. He tried to reach out to Wynn's face, but he only made it to her elbow.

Renate sat down with Chancebringer in hand.

"No!" Birger tried to protest. "Not that."

"I have to," insisted Renate, "I can't save you without it. Entwining it with your soul will keep it from leaving your body and then I can draw on Chancebringer's connection to the Weave to power my healing."

"I don't want its luck. The cost is too high."

"Damn it, Birger, stop being so stubborn!" hissed Renate. "Fine, I'll isolate the luck factor. It won't affect you unless it slips onto your wrist, okay?"

Birger's ability to breathe shut off like a stoppered spigot, ending his protest, and Renate wasted no time getting to work. Wynn spoke, but her words sounded distant and distorted as he drifted into the pleasant warmth of unconsciousness.

Birger spluttered and gasped, the air once again flooding his lungs; Wynn's soft lips were pressed against his. The air burned. Wynn pulled back; her eyes were red from crying.

"That's it, Birger," said Renate calmly, "we've got you. Wynn, give him space."

Wynn pulled back. Birger shook his head to clear the haze and probed tentatively at his ribs. There was no more pain, and he could, once again, breathe comfortably, but his hands came to a narrow slit between his ribs. Birger looked at his wound and saw a cord passing through it. The line glowed with a pink hue that pulsed steadily.

"What did you do to me!?" exclaimed Birger.

"Saved your ungrateful hide," retorted Renate. She took a deep breath, visibly calming herself down. "I did what I said I would. The injuries were too severe to take all the pain away, but you should be able to walk now."

260

She held up Chancebringer, tied to a cord running between Birger's ribs. "This is attached to you. It'll let you heal quickly and keep the pain at bay, but you must take it slow. If this line breaks or you push yourself too hard before you recover, you could die."

Mick walked up to the fire, rubbed his hands together, collecting warmth, and blew on them. He had a thick fur cloak draped over his armour.

"The tents are packed," said Mick. "We'll be limited in what we take with us and we can't wait any longer. Can Birger keep up?"

"Yes," he said, *"Birger can."*

"What do I know?!" Renate exclaimed, frustrated she threw her hands up in the air.

"Don't worry, if I almost kill myself again, I promise to let you patch me up." Birger forced a smile. Though the pain was subdued, his body was rigid. Magical wrappings held his leg immobile and his ribs steady, but as he moved, he heard an unnerving click-clack.

"Thank you for saving my stubborn ass, Renate, and thank you too, Wynn."

Renate's eyes softened and she smiled. "Well, if you put it like that…" she said, helping Birger to his feet. Then Renate opened her arms wide pulling him into a long, comforting hug.

He didn't resist.

When she stepped back, Snow leapt onto Birger, ripping his already tattered clothes to climb to his shoulder, the weight making him sag to one side.

"I'm okay, buddy," said Birger to Snow.

Gunther and Lorenzo each carried a pair of saddlebags, adding them to the pile of belongings prepared for departure. Gunther shot a concerned look at Mick, who responded with a reassuring wink.

***

Wynn cleaned up the area while Renate collected the healer's kit. Birger joined them as they went to their tents to pack their belongings.

He moved carefully and started by checking his leather satchel. Finding it empty, he huffed in disappointment. A swell of emotion made him glance at Wynn, who was securing her bags.

After all we've been through, how could she still steal the documents? Birger thought, dismayed. *I wish Lorenzo had been wrong. This confirms without a doubt that she's working for Ulfhild.*

261

Disappointing as the truth may be, this was the plan. The misinformation she took back could create infighting among the enemy and give Birger's team an edge. He took a deep breath and told himself to focus on the imminent danger. The uks could come charging through the trees at any moment.

Checking his armour and rapier, Birger said, "I don't think I'll ever let myself get more than two paces away from you again."

"Pardon?" asked Lorenzo, as he hurried by.

"Can you teach me to fight? You moved through the greenskins as if you were Lot's reaper."

Lorenzo walked up to him and said with a smile, "Sure, maybe when we get a moment. Though Eric is a much better teacher, and besides, you already have the skill. You would fare much better if you fought to win."

"What do you mean?"

"You're always on the defensive because you have a kind heart. I suspect you've never killed another person."

Lorenzo was right. Birger hadn't killed anyone and didn't know if he could. He tried to pick up his jerkin, but the stiffness in his rib made him croak and he stopped.

"Hold on," Lorenzo said, stepping beside Birger, "may I?"

"Thanks," said Birger.

Snow hopped down as Lorenzo moved to help Birger take off his ripped, blood-soaked shirt. His actions were swift and efficient. They also hurt like a hook in the mouth, but Birger knew time was short, so he sucked it up without complaint. The brisk air made him shiver. Lorenzo retrieved a clean doublet from the bag and slipped it over Birger's head.

As he continued to work, Lorenzo said, "When you draw your sword, you do it to take a life." He looked at Birger with a coldness that shook the younger man to the core. "I would never unsheathe Kazania for any other reason."

They fell silent as Lorenzo helped Birger into the leather jerkin. Birger let out an involuntary grunt of pain as Lorenzo pulled the straps tight. Birger coughed to coverup his moment of weakness, but that just made the pain worse. He grimaced.

Lorenzo gave him a sympathetic look and a pat on the back, then turned to continue gathering the camp.

Eric emerged from the forest, once again in human form. His face and arms were a gory mess. The group fell silent, and Mick let his saddlebag drop to the ground with a thud that made Wynn jump.

262

"Okay, let's hear it," Mick demanded, staring at the bear-sized man. "What in the witch's frozen tit are you, huh? I can't go around terrified shitless of what's lurking behind me!"

"Calm down Mick," Lorenzo intervened.

"Calm down...!?" Mick looked exasperated. "This thing is out of control. Look at him! Besides, werewolves are killers. They *eat* people."

Eric stalked directly towards Mick.

Gunther winced and took a position nearby, gripping his halberd firmly.

Eric clenched his fists. Twisting his features into a snarl with his jaw jutting forward. "If you attack me, I'll show you what being terrified shitless feels like."

Lorenzo stepped between them, halting Eric with a stern look, then addressing Mick, "I've been working with him for years. Eric's in full control during his transformation."

Lorenzo looked at Eric, as if asking him to explain, and the tension in Eric eased. "Only our young lack control in their beruehrt state. I'm close to a thousand years old. I stopped losing control before Apour even knew what empires were."

"Beruehrt?" Mick sneered, pacing left and right, he said, "Is that your term for killing machine? Even if you *have* control, how are we meant to trust you won't murder us while we sleep?"

"Mick!" Lorenzo scowled.

"Gentlemen, keep it civilised." Renate interjected, stepping between Mick and Lorenzo. She looked at Mick and added, "I've known Eric for a long time. If he wanted us dead, we would be. You can trust him."

Eric growled at Mick, "Frankly, I don't care if you trust me. I'm here because Lorenzo and I have a deal. I'll keep you in whichever state he wishes you to be."

"Why hide what you are, then?" argued Mick.

"Ignorance is humanity's hallmark. You kill what you don't understand, and very few of you care to understand us."

Calmly, Gunther asked "What do you mean by 'us'?".

Eric looked reluctant to speak as he said, "I belong to the Wulfher of Schutzfort, or as you call it, Kings Fort, but..."

"Are you implying that everyone at Kings Fort is like you?" interrupted Mick, his voice laden with scepticism.

"No. Only a few of our young are born beruehrt. They undergo their first transformation at sixteen, during the full moon. It's rare, but some don't change until much older and…"

"And let me guess," Mick cut in again, "they wander off and one day they wake up to rampage through an unsuspecting village?"

"Yes." Eric's jaw tensed with annoyance. "That's likely the source of your werewolf legends. The point is, I'm no threat to you, unless you attack me first or, in your case, if you interrupt me again." A toothy grin spread wide across Eric's face.

Mick gulped, Wynn's mouth hung open in disbelief, and everyone stood frozen in shock at Eric's revelation.

Mick finally blurted through the silence, "You're a thousand-year-old werewolf…!?"

Eric pushed past Lorenzo and Renate, stopping inches from Mick. Birger saw Gunther tense, the axe-blade of his halberd wavering.

Eric leaned forward until his nose touched Mick's… "Grrr," he let out a comical growl and Eric threw his head back, bursting into a deep belly laugh. Mick joined in, followed by Gunther, Wynn, and soon the rest. Laughter hurt Birger's entire body so much he had to stop first.

With the argument over, the threat from the greenskins loomed over the group.

"We need to get moving," said Gunther. "Can we park this until we're in Kindra?"

Mick nodded at Eric, who responded in kind. The group broke off to gather the last of their things.

Birger took a deep breath, lowering himself to his good knee and grabbed his rapier from the floor. Snow jumped on his shoulder again, wrapping his thick, furry legs around Birger's neck. The weavespider's fur was soft and wrapped around him like a scarf in winter.

"Are you alright?" Birger overheard Renate murmuring to Lorenzo.

"Yeah," Lorenzo rubbed his temples, "just tired."

Renate put a hand on Lorenzo's shoulder, squeezing it. "We all get upset, let it go."

Birger looked at them separate. Seeing Lorenzo upset for the first time was unsettling.

Soon, exhaustion and the dull throb building around his injuries, conspired to distract him. *Why couldn't magic heal you completely like in the storybooks?* wondered Birger.

He picked up his bags with clenched teeth. A long night's travel lay ahead.

41

WEAVESTORM

Tittering laughter haunted their every step, but their pursuers didn't close in. Lorenzo led from the front, wearing quintri goggles that glowed with a faint purple-grey hue, while Eric brought up the rear. Birger was sure that the Wulfher warrior was why the nikkuni and ukthuun kept their distance.

Thanks to Renate's magic, Birger could walk under his own power. Being the slowest, he carried the lantern in the middle of the pack, keeping its light dim to avoid interfering with the others' night vision. He could tell that Wynn, drifting nearby, was at least as terrified as he was.

Mick and Gunther maintained opposite flanks in case an ambush went undetected, and a general air of alert weariness hung over everyone. Renate spent a while talking quietly to Mick as they marched. By his calm demeanor, Birger figured she was using that mindweaver thing of hers on him.

After some time, Renate dropped back, and Lorenzo moved to Mick's side. His hand still rested on Kazania and his eyes, illuminated in purple-grey, were alert.

"Mick," Birger heard Lorenzo say, a hint of embarrassment in his tone, "I need to apologize for earlier."

"No stress, boss," Mick winked playfully at Lorenzo. "I get it. You're looking out for each of us in your own way. Doesn't mean I like that you had me travelling with a Cos-damned werewolf without telling me...but I understand."

Lorenzo grinned.

"Besides," Mick shrugged, "You've done worse for me. And I'm sorry I didn't handle it too well. You know how I am; my mouth sometimes runs things for me."

"Imminent danger can do that," agreed Lorenzo. "I find it much more challenging to stay composed when someone is trying to kill my people."

Birger heard Mick snort in acknowledgement as Gunther fell in next to Eric on the other side of the group. Birger shifted the weight of the saddlebag over his right shoulder and tried to keep it from resting on Snow's fur. The seven-legged spider still curled around his neck like a winter scarf. Despite being near seven feet tall, Gunther looked like a man of average height compared to the bearskin-clad Wulfher.

Slapping a meaty hand on Eric's back, Gunther asked, "So, how does it feel to be a thousand-year-old werewolf?"

"Not as great as you might think," replied Eric. "The novelty wears off quickly; things you think are important lose meaning after a couple of centuries."

"Yeah, I guess it might," contemplated Gunther. "I wanted to say I'm glad you're on our side. I would rather fight *with* the big scary man than against him." Gunther had a joking quality in his voice, and Birger heard Eric bark a laugh.

"I'm just here for the food," replied Eric with a wolfish grin.

"I've known Eric for a long time," said Renate, "under that strong-silent-type front, he's just a cuddly pup."

Eric groaned disapprovingly, and the rest of the group laughed. Birger felt himself relax as the mirth cut through the tension.

Could the worst be behind us? Perhaps the greenskins stumbled upon us by accident? Maybe...

A glimmer of green light drew Birger's gaze to a spot between the trees on their right. He grabbed his ears to block a painfully high-pitched screech, and for a moment, Birger thought he would go deaf, but the sound ended with a pop.

Silence fell over the area for half a second before a huge implosion ripped trees from their roots and sucked them towards a purple and teal burst of light. Fresh ice crystals spawned on every exposed surface and a wicked cold bit into Birger's exposed skin. Snow jerked his legs up over Birger's face, stopping any further harm.

"Weavestorm!" yelled Mick, as the sucking power of the event threatened Birger's balance.

Wynn got plucked off her feet, and Lorenzo grabbed her hand, narrowly saving her from a quick flight to oblivion. Birger could tell by the straining on Lorenzo's face that he wasn't going to be able to haul her in on his own. Birger shot forward to help and found Mick right there with him. With effort, the three men finally managed to ground Wynn.

Birger felt the sucking power of the storm increase, and he heard Eric boom, "Run!"

Gripping Wynn tightly, Birger leaned against the immense pull of the storm, forcing his body forward in an awkward shuffle. Eric's big hand closed on Birger's right arm while Gunther's clasped onto Wynn's, and working together, the two hauled them along. The noise of the wind and splintering trees was all-enveloping, and Birger's heart raced with a primal terror. He pushed against his injuries, desperate to avoid slowing the others down.

It took them ten minutes of scrambling to escape the freezing gravity of the weavestorm. When they finally reached safety, Birger's lungs were searing with pain, his muscles knotted in agony.

"We have to keep going," thundered Eric, pulling him along.

Birger's body made a convincing argument to simply lie down and let death come, but he refused to listen. Instead, he put his mind to another task. "I saw a green light before the weavestorm. They usually don't do that, do they?"

"Nikkuni shaman!" Renate looked tired. "Their magic emits green light, but something went wrong."

"What?" asked Birger.

"Whoever caused that storm got swallowed by it." Renate glanced over her shoulder without stopping.

"Keep moving!" insisted Eric, quickening his pace. "Could be more. Next spell might hit."

"Be careful with Birger," Wynn gasped, her voice tinged with panic.

Her feet dragged, and she wheezed for air, still gripping Birger's other hand.

"Moving *might* kill him," Eric shot Wynn an annoyed look. "But the niks *will* if they catch up."

"I'm right here!" spat Birger in annoyance. "I'll be fine. Keep moving!"

Eric gave Birger an approving look that pumped a little pride energy into Birger's lame muscles.

"Chancebringer," said Renate. "You can't feel the pain. It speeds up the healing, but the damage is still there. If your rib snaps completely–"

"Stop borrowing trouble," interrupted Birger. "I can take care of myself!"

Birger plucked himself loose from Eric's grip, continuing to lumber as best as his stiff leg would permit.

The others won't die for me, thought Birger. *If it comes to that, I'll run myself into the ground. I'll run until death takes me.*

42

PAUSE FOR A SPELL

One small blessing was that the weavestorm's purple and teal light made navigation through the night forest easier. For a long time, no one spoke as they pressed on. The chuck-chuck-chuck of their feet landing on the snow sounded loud in Birger's ears. The occasional eerie screams, monstrous bellows, and creepy laughter punctuated his fear.

Eventually, the clouds permitted a sliver of light from the rising sun to fall on the trees. The noise of greenskin warriors was still echoing all around when they reached the point where the road joined to the Nord river's side. Everyone looked exhausted.

"We need rest," Lorenzo said, looking back wearily at the still-dark trees. "We can refill our water from the river, but let's stay in the clearing so we can see what's coming."

"They've been trailing us for a reason, boss," said Mick, his face determined. "It won't be long before they come at us, especially if we stop."

Lorenzo nodded in agreement, pushed back his goggles, to reveal dark circles under his eyes. Then he said, "You're right. Renate, is there anything you can do to give us an advantage from here?"

"I don't know," Renate considered it, "I could lay sticky lines across the road to slow them. However, I'm almost out of webbing and if I tear a hole to the weave, the nikkuni shaman will know. They could avoid my trap."

"It might catch a few!" Mick insisted, nervously pointing his halberd at the southern treeline.

Renate looked defeated when she said, "I haven't slept, and it's been a rough night. I may not have enough life energy to open the rift without causing a weavestorm."

A pang of guilt stabbed Birger in the gut as he thought, *She exhausted herself healing me.*

"Considering their numbers, wouldn't we need a lot of material?" wondered Wynn.

"Yeah, Wynn's probably right," agreed Renate, looking up in thought.

Eager to feel useful, Birger asked, "What about something to make it hard to see us?"

"I could use the river water to make mist? I should have enough webbing left over for that."

"Yes," said Lorenzo, completing a scan of the perimeter, "It's worth trying."

"They're out there," said Eric, his gaze hard as he pointed south, "waiting."

"Then let's be quick." Lorenzo looked withered when he turned to Birger and said, "Drink first. You need water to keep up. Everyone else, we need to keep Renate safe until her spell is done. I'll take first watch."

"With you," grunted Eric.

The rest of the party took turns to sip from the freezing water of the river. Renate wasted no time getting to work. Wynn finished filling up her waterskin and relieved Lorenzo from his watch, her longbow half drawn as she eyed the snow packed foliage.

Birger watched as Lorenzo sauntered over to where the others had discarded their saddlebags. With a smooth motion, he shrugged out of his left coat sleeve and rolled back his black shirt to expose the skin of his forearm.

Lorenzo shot an almost guilty glance over his shoulder, scanning the others, as if checking to see if he was being watched. His eyes lingering on Renate, causing him to miss Birger's curiosity. He reached into his saddlebag, rummaging around before extracting a small leather-bound box. Lorenzo flipped it opened and Birger saw something glittering.

A needle, attached to a small vial of luminous blue fluid. Lorenzo looked at it for a moment, before he pressed it firmly into his arm. Birger's heart sank as his mind leapt to all sorts of conclusions. Lorenzo visibly perked up. The slump in his shoulders vanishing and his exposed arm muscles bulged.

Birger's thoughts skidded to a halt. *Was Lorenzo using etherweave? Was that how he maintained his inhuman discipline and pace?*

When Lorenzo began gathering up the water-skins, he moved with more speed and determination. He turned back to the group and made eye contact with Birger. Guilt flashed in his eyes, but the dark circles were gone. Lorenzo looked like he just woke up from a long night's rest.

Birger broke gaze first. He heard Lorenzo walk towards the river and begin refilling his waterskin.

Etherweave, which came in a syringe, was the only thing Birger knew of that could give someone instant energy. Mercenaries and sailors often got hooked on it during wartimes. Birger had seen many die from overdoses in the Squat. He didn't want to believe that Lorenzo would use it.

What? You thought he did all this with no help? accused Birger's cynic.

No, it must be something else.

Don't be a gullible fool. Of course it's not.

Birger shuffled over to Renate, distracting himself from the inner turmoil. "Is there anything I can do to help?" he asked.

Renate, looking up from rifling through her black leather bag, pressed it into Birger's hands. "Bring this."

She walked over to the water and knelt while Birger held the healer's case open for her. Renate extracted a tool that looked like pincers with two long rollers on either side of the jaw. Lowering the case into the snow, he sat next to her.

Renate took the remaining webs out of her bag, pressing them through the rolling pin pliers. It squeezed the threads together into a thin sheet. Renate repeated the action over and over, allowing the crafting to grow wider.

Relieved from the watch by Gunther and Mick, Eric joined them at the river to wash the dried gore from his hands and face.

Not even looking up from her work for a second, Renate said, "Here, hold this." And handed Birger one corner of the growing sheet and moved away, working to enlarge the surface area.

Eric finished washing up, rose and returned to the watch.

Wynn took the opportunity, obviously curious to see what Renate was doing, to settle next to Birger. She leaned into him. She was a warm presence in the cold. For a moment, he let himself remember their kiss and wished he could kiss her now. Snow unwrapped himself from Birger's neck and climbed down onto Wynn, settling in the crook of her arm.

"Cos, Snow," cursed Wynn, "you're heavy."

The weavespider glanced at her apologetically, purring and rubbing himself against her.

"But you're too cute to put down," Wynn smiled.

"That's how he gets you," agreed Birger, and he felt a smile tug at the corners of his mouth.

Wynn grinned his way and then leaned forward to see what Renate was doing. The thin sheet of translucent material that she was making reached ten feet squared. She continued to work the roller, smoothing out every crease and bubble to ensure as even a spread as possible. To Birger, her work seemed similar to a baker kneeding dough and rolling it flat to make cookies, leading him to wonder how important the shape of it really was.

"Gunther, Mick!" Renate called. "Come, hold these corners for me."

Lorenzo set down the rest of the waterskins and joined Eric on the watch, relieving the other two so they could help Renate. Mick and Gunther lay their weapons down and, following Renate's instructions, each grabbed a corner. With Birger serving as an anchoring point, the other three stepped out to span the sheet between them.

"The niks are getting ready to push us," stated Eric as calmly as if he were ordering a stein at a bar.

"We ready to go?" Lorenzo asked Renate.

"It's not enough," Renate said with desperation. "I need to access the Weave to finish it."

Hundreds of raucous voices filled the trees as the greenskins drew nearer. Eric was right, they were coming.

"Meaning?" asked Lorenzo urgently.

"I need food, rest, sleep…a life source," said Renate with a stressed sigh.

"I'll buy us some time," Eric cast over his shoulder and disappeared into the trees.

"What about Chancebringer?" asked Birger, extracting it from his pouch.

Renate shook her head. "No, that could disrupt your connection with it and kill you."

"Staying here without cover could kill me," retorted Birger.

The voices in the trees turned into panicked shouts and the clashing of steel told Birger that Eric found them.

"Can you use mine?" Wynn stepped forward, her voice determined.

"If you give it freely," replied Renate, "but it's dangerous. If you have a single doubt about giving it at all, the spell could implode into a weavestorm."

"I'm sure," Wynn said with deadpan certainty.

Birger's mouth dropped open in surprised panic. "No, Wynn. I should do it."

Wynn gave Birger a stern look and asked, "And why is that?"

Birger couldn't find a good reason. He simply didn't want to see her get hurt.

"It's done," said Wynn, handing Snow back to Birger. "I'm doing it. What do you need, Renate?"

Grabbing Wynn's hand, Renate said, "Hold still, this is going to feel strange."

Bright pink light flared from the seam between their palms. When Renate let go of her, Wynn sagged. Birger stepped up to support her. The glowing light was still shining in Renate's hand when she slashed her finger through the air. A ripple of refracted purple and teal light ripped a way into the Weave.

Eric jogged from the trees, his axe, face, and arms coated in fresh blood. "Their reinforcements are here. We need to move before they regroup. Even I can't keep an army away from you."

Lorenzo nodded. He and Eric set to work, laying out the bags so the others could grab them at a moment's notice. Gunther, Mick and Birger still held on to their respective corners of Renate's crafting. With snow resuming his role as Birger's winter scarf.

Extracting thick translucent cords from the tear in reality, Renate swiftly incorporated them into the sheet. Birger figured the material drawn from the Weave must be much easier to work with because she doubled the sheet's size in a tenth of the time.

Renate coordinated the others to help her roll the sheet into a bolt of what seemed like translucent silk. Her hands danced over its surface, leaving trails of pink light that spread out like spilt ink.

Finally, the whole thing glowed.

Holding it by one end, she flicked to unfurl it over the river water, like a housekeeper sheeting a bed. The crafting stretched out and stiffened an inch above the river. Renate dropped to her knees, submerging it. When the water flowed over it, steam billowed up in enormous clouds.

"Get ready!" called Renate.

The cloud was thickening by the second. Swelling into a wall of fog that wrapped around them.

Lorenzo and Eric began passing out bags, while Gunther secured everyone a length of rope.

"How long do we have?" asked Lorenzo, now nearly invisible to Birger in the gloom.

"Several hours," said Renate.

"I'll take the lead," Eric volunteered, "I can follow the road by scent."

"Well," said Birger jokingly, "I guess being a thousand-year-old werewolf has its perks."

Eric grunted with the faintest hint of amusement.

"Your attention, please," Lorenzo's voice cut through the haze of exhaustion. "That rope is your lifeline. It'll be hard to find you if you get lost."

The group nodded in silent agreement, and each held tight to their bit of rope.

Birger put Wynn's arm over his shoulder, but Mick intervened, saying, "I got her. You'll be needing all you have to keep up."

Birger nodded appreciatively and the rope tugged him forward. The others were on the move.

Fatigue weighed on his eyelids, as the ground beckoned, promising to be the most comfortable bed he would ever know. Resisting was tough, but he wasn't going to give up now.

The best part of mortal danger is that it keeps you from doing much thinking, and Birger was grateful for that. He had a lot to contemplate that he would rather not...

As time dragged on, the mist did the job. Hours later, when they finally exited the fog, Birger saw the holy mountain jutting up from the horizon like a finger judging the sky.

"Look," said Birger, "is that Kindra?"

"We're nearly there," Gunther slurred. "Just a little more."

43

KINDRA

Kindra, the fabled home of the five goddesses, loomed over the frost-bitten forest. The bluff sat in a circle of lush green grass stencilled out of the snow and clouds, with the sun illuminating the five massive temples on the flat top.

"We're walking on King Louis Grengarbane's road." Despite his exhaustion, Birger couldn't help himself. He was a history fanatic, and this was hallowed ground. "The same one he took to liberate Kindra... Though, the road probably wasn't as good back then."

"And instead of uks nipping at his heels, grengar were throwing stones at his nose," added Eric, falling back from the lead position.

"Have you fought a grengar before?" Wynn asked Eric with overt curiosity. She had recovered enough to no longer need Mick's help to stand, but her longbow hung limp in her hand.

Birger stroked Snow, still posing as his scarf. The furry white creature kept watching the treeline behind the group.

Eric gave Wynn a flat look. "Fought them? The Wulfher are the keepers of the Darkveil Forest. I've been fighting them my whole life, even here. Louis was a good leader, albeit a little arrogant." Eric pointed to a mound with a large stone erected on it. "We broke their line there. Louis made a big deal of it. He likes a victory celebration, and the stillari have fussed over him ever since."

Birger noted Eric spoke about the long-dead King of Rendin in the present tense, but he dismissed it as a sign of age. *What a treasure trove of knowledge Eric must be. He would've lived through all of Rendin's history.*

"Really!" Wynn exclaimed with a loud whoop.

"Oi!" Mick snapped, shooting her a glare. "Those Cos-damned uks are still after us. Keep it down."

Wynn wilted from the rebuke. Birger gave her a sympathetic look, but Mick was right. Danger was near. Not that sound would matter much. They were on a road. He glanced back at the trees behind them. The greenskins knew exactly where they were.

Why hadn't they attacked?

Birger decided that he hadn't heard any greenskins in a while, and the conversation allowed everyone a break. The only sign of disturbance in the forest was the distant shake of trees, followed by birds screeching.

It wasn't worth worrying about. They couldn't move any faster. For now, all they could do was distract themselves as they walked on.

Looking to re-engage the group, he asked. "I read grengar are as large as a building and unkillable?"

Even Gunther drifted a little closer for the response.

Everyone seems to love a story about a great hero from the past, thought Birger—*more so when it's a story they already know.*

"Difficult to win a war against an unkillable enemy," Eric retorted sarcastically. "Nothing is truly unkillable. Even grengar burn. Louis' flaming hammer proved that, though Zolani, the Grengar King, is still an exception."

Renate had a knowing smirk on her lips. Despite her puffing breath, she still looked surprisingly fresh – a contrast Birger couldn't help but notice.

I thought she was too tired to access the Weave? Where are the bags under her eyes, the sweat from exertion?

"That battle must've been terrifying," speculated Wynn. "How were those soldiers so fearless, facing an enemy like that?"

"All battle is terrifying," said Lorenzo, warily watching the trees flanking the party's left. "The only people that don't feel fear in war are the dead. Fear keeps you alert and alive."

Eric snorted in agreement.

Snow made a high-pitched sound that startled Birger. Gunther shuddered and took two steps away from Snow. Birger whipped his head around to see what the weavespider was looking at, but found only empty road and pine trees.

"Birger," Lorenzo said, worried eyes turned towards him, "how mobile are you with your injuries?"

"I would rather not engage in any tight hugs, if that's why you're asking, but otherwise I'm good," quipped Birger, drawing an eye roll from Renate. "Why?"

Before Lorenzo could answer, there was a loud crack, followed by a tremor on the ground, and a pair of trees buckled.

"Cos!" Mick let out an alarmed curse. He and Gunther readied their halberts to defend the rear. "What was that?"

"Could the uks have a grengar?" asked Wynn, her voice crackling with fear.

"The greng would rather fight the uks than not," said Eric as he squinted his eyes towards the noise.

The tremor in the ground was subtle, but Birger realised that its intensity was increasing by the second.

"If we don't move faster, I think we're gonna find out," urged Birger.

Eric didn't move; he stared back longingly as another set of trees crumpled and more panicked bird cries echoed in the forest.

"This isn't a good time, Eric," warned Lorenzo, as if he knew something Birger didn't. "We need your help to get us safely to Kindra."

Eric turned a scowl at Lorenzo, and snapped, "You know what you're asking."

"Yes," Lorenzo's eyes were pleading, "and you know I wouldn't be asking if I had another choice."

"What?" Mick's eyes flicked between the two. "What are you asking?"

Birger followed Eric's gaze as the top of a horned head the size of a hay-cart punched out of the treetops with flowing red hair fluttering behind it in the wind.

With a longing growl rumbling in his throat, Eric said, "It's been a long time since I fought a bolgar."

"A what?" asked Wynn, her eyes stretched wide.

"A giant from the Wild Lands," explained Birger, grateful for all the reading Sten made him do during his apprenticeship. He was acutely aware that Wynn hadn't done the same during hers.

"What's going on with him?" Mick pointed at Eric impatiently.

"He wants to fight the bolgar," explained Lorenzo.

Eric's lip curled into a snarl and he said, "The possibility of an honorable death is hard to find for my kind."

Mick's mouth hung open as he stared at Eric.

Lorenzo, his voice calm despite the danger, reminded him, "You gave your oath to keep us safe."

That drew an angry grunt from Eric. "I know what I said."

"We don't have time for this!" urged Gunther. "It's coming!"

"I'm sorry to pull that card, my friend. We need you. If you die against that bolgar, the nikkuni will swarm us." Lorenzo's eyes looked pained.

Eric's teeth bared, and he looked on the brink of violence.

"Ermenrich," Renate's voice was soothing as she spoke, "This creature won't go far. You'll have another chance once everyone is safe."

Birger heard a tree splinter, and Snow swayed with the bobbing head advancing through the treetops.

"Less talking, more running," Birger squeaked, his voice laced with panic.

Eric looked back at the oncoming bolgar and roared in frustration. Resigned, he shouted, "Fine, go!"

As the group started jogging, Gunther grabbed Birger's saddlebag off his shoulder.

"I've got it," said Gunther, clutching the bag to his belly.

Birger grunted in thanks.

Wynn looked dazed. With her life force still depleted, she was slow to comprehend what was happening. Birger grabbed her hand, pulling her along and she trailed behind him. Eric jogged at Renate's side, and Birger wished he had werewolf stamina too. Instead, dull pain jolted through his body with every limping step.

Better an overworked crew than a ship pulled under by a kraken, he thought, finding strength in the old sailor's idiom.

He couldn't tell for how long they kept the pace. Time blurred in his fatigue-addled mind, and his muscles were cramping badly by the time he saw the Pilgrim's Mill waving at them on the horizon. Chest pain worsening, he sucked down air, and sweat poured off him. Birger sipped from his water skin to ease the burning in his throat.

"Small sips," reminded Lorenzo, still jogging steadily.

Birger didn't want to take small sips. He wanted to guzzle it down, but Lorenzo was right; the last thing he needed now was a stitch. He squeezed Wynn's hand. She was barely keeping up.

Snow, draped around Birger's neck, stiffened, his head swiveling like a predator tracking prey.

Huffing, Birger said, "We're almost there," as he looked over his shoulder to see what the spider had noticed.

Fallen trees splintered under rowboat-sized feet. They belonged to a figure with shins wrapped in thick fur.

He could've been mistaken for a heavily muscled man, standing among shoulder-high saplings. But in reality, those trees were fourteen-foot pines, and no man Birger knew of had glowing red eyes. The bolgar, with bull horns jutting from his head, wore thick metal gauntlets and a spiked plate pauldron over his right shoulder.

A thick red beard drooped down over his muscular stomach, touching a kind of armoured loincloth.

In a swift jerk, the giant hurled an uprooted pine towards them like a javelin.

Birger's shout cut through the cold air, "Down!"

ORPHANE HOOK

SAINT ARMAND BOROUGH

SAINT'S CAP

PILGRIM'S CROSS

PILGRIM'S CAUSE

DEVORE HILL

TOWN HALL

PILGRIM'S REST

LANDIOR MARKET

JOR BLESSED LAND

PILGRIM'S MILL

TEMPLE OF LOT

PILGRIM'S PATH

HOLY SPRING

TEMPLE OF MAG

TEMPLE OF COS

TEMPLE OF JOR

TEMPLE OF AEG

NORD HILL

NORD FOREST

KINDRA
THE HIGH CITY – WAR'S REPRIEVE
GOVERNANCE: MONARCHY
POPULATION: 34,600

44

REACH THE GATE

Birger pulled Wynn in tight, putting himself between her and the oncoming tree. It hit the road just behind the group, and the pine exploded. A large, sword-length splinter grazed Birger's shoulder plate, and he barely ducked to avoid another.

A quick glance told Birger the others had also taken superficial hits. Gunther, Mick and Eric had shielded them, their armour bearing the brunt of the impact. Gunther had a tear in his sleeve, blood welling in a ragged cut. Lorenzo sported a gash along his brow, while the rest had minor nicks and bruises.

"Move!" Birger shouted, ignoring the pain of his injuries; he pulled Wynn to her feet.

Leaping free of Birger's neck, Snow landed lightly on the ground.

"Snow!" Wynn called, reaching down to him.

Snow looked at Wynn and then Birger with worried eyes. He jittered on the spot, making low whistling sounds before darting in between the trees, headed towards the bolgar.

"Let him go," Birger told Wynn. "He can take care of himself. Come!"

"But..." Wynn began.

"We don't have time," snapped Birger, hauling her along. "Come, now!"

Although Wynn was hesitant, she didn't resist. Soon, the entire party resumed their desperate flight. Birger glanced over his shoulder to see Snow dart across the road, circling trees on both sides. *What's that weavespider up to?*

Birger didn't have time to take a closer look as the bolgar's gigantic steps greedily ate the distance between them.

Ahead of Birger, Mick yelled, "It's a lot faster than us!"

"Sure I can't fight it?" Eric glared at Lorenzo. "Could buy you time."

"I'm sure," replied Lorenzo with a wry smile.

"Ermenrich, no glory in a fight without an audience, right?" Renate shot back.

Eric looked unconvinced. "You think I should fight it right outside the city gate?"

"Have you noticed," gasped Birger, "that giant wants our bones for its bread?"

"That's a fairytale." Being so tall, Eric's long legs kept pace with the rest at a jog that looked almost leisurely. "He would use your bones to pick his teeth after the roast."

"Regardless," Birger gasped, "let's focus on getting out of here. Talk later!"

Eric shrugged.

Birger looked back. The bolgar stomped on the fragments of the shattered tree in the road. He was so close now that Birger could feel the earth-tremoring footfalls as he ran.

"Gullshite!" Birger cursed, "brace yourselves, he's coming!"

His mind reeled with imagined scenes of his friends' broken bodies lying on the road. Desperation dulled the pain in his ribs and stiff right knee; he didn't allow himself to slow. Birger readied himself to throw Wynn and himself into the trees. He stole a look, hoping to tell which way to dodge.

One moment, the bolgar looked like an unstoppable juggernaut and the next he tripped. Several trees on either side of the road buckled as the bolgar lurched forward, trying to find his feet. His massive bulk slapped down like a giant squid on deck. The earth shook and white-powder burst outward.

Wynn, Birger and Gunther slowed to look, while Eric, Lorenzo and Renate never hesitated.

Noticing the separation and grabbing Gunther by the sleeve, Mick cried, "Keep going!" he urged Birger to get Wynn moving too.

Birger pushed himself harder, despite his protesting ribs that were clicking and clacking with every step. For all his effort, however, his pace was failing. Wynn was overtaking him, still clutching his hand, soon she was hauling him along.

"Birger, are you alright?" asked Gunther, wheezing dulled the concern in his tone.

Birger puffed, "I'm fine." It was a lie. But, no way would he let his friends slow down to die on his account.

He saw Snow darting out of the trees. His long legs moving faster than seemed possible. He caught up in no time, and with a powerful leap, the seven-legged weavespider pounced on Birger's back, causing him to stumble.

"Hey!" gasped Birger, and looked at Snow hanging from his shoulder. "You tripped the bolgar... good boy."

Snow dropped his head to the side, then embraced Birger's neck to resume the winter-scarf position. Birger couldn't help but smile. He could feel Snow's exhaustion, and he tried to ignore his own.

Finally, the group broke past the snow-covered trees. The landscape opened into lush green grass spreading out for miles around the tall, blunt-top mountain ahead. In front of them lay Devout Hill, a bustling small village.

Birger saw its simple houses speckling the southern banks of the Holy Spring, which ran down from the temples. To the west, they had harvested the fields for winter, and shepherds tended their flock in the paddocks. Past the small town, across a wide stone bridge, stood the Pilgrim's Gate that connected to smooth ivory walls, stretching north.

Birger heard a slow, measured alarm bell ringing. It spurred people in the surrounding area into a panicked rush; they grabbed their children and ran for the bridge. Birger chanced a look over his shoulder to see the bolgar on his feet and running again. A furious scowl etched into his heavy brow.

"Gullshite! The bolgar is back up!" Birger exclaimed, trying to keep his eyes on the gate. *A little more,* Birger encouraged himself. *Hold out a little more.*

"Nearly there," Lorenzo said. "We only need to reach ballista range. The wall guard will cover us from there."

Despite the all-encompassing pain threatening to consume him, a spark of hope kindled in Birger's heart. He could hold on for just a little while longer. He was acutely aware that without the fine cord plucking at his skin, he would already be dead.

Chancebringer could save me, he thought. *I could slip it on, and something would happen that got me away from that bolgar.*

And what if Aeg decides everyone else should die to let you escape? questioned Birger's cynic.

That doubt landed in a sore spot. He still felt like Chancebringer was the reason for Benny's death. He couldn't live with these friends paying the same price.

Birger heard the panicked screams of women, seeing the monster coming. Broken out of his distracting thoughts, he became aware of his burning lungs and parched mouth. He fought to stay focused, eyes locked on the gate.

Just a little closer.

Atop the gatehouse, a massive weapon that resembled a crossbow was mounted on a belfry. Birger watched a soldier who sat in a chair attached to the weapon, cycling peddles that turned it, until the ballista aligned with the road. Four more soldiers worked as a team to load a bolt, and then the weapon's thick rope snapped forward, dispatching the projectile into the air.

Birger experienced a moment of panic as he watched the steel-tipped log barreling towards them. He followed it's arch, sailing overhead. Too late, the bolgar noticed the projectile and dove to the side. The missile cut through part of his unarmoured shoulder, a gout of fire-red blood painting the road.

Birger joined Mick, Gunther, and Wynn in a triumphant howl. Even Snow chimed in with a playful chirp. It felt like they had won, and relief made Birger's legs turn to jelly, causing him to stumble.

Then the giant stirred. Oversized slabs of muscle bulged as the bolgar pushed himself up. It ignored the open wound, blood running down its arm in a crimson sheet. Grim determination smoldering in its eyes. Birger watched as the wound started knitting itself back together. The blood flow soon stopped entirely, and the bolgar mopped away some of the gore.

"That's not even fair!" cried Wynn in despair.

"Bolgars have sped up healing?" asked Gunther, exasperated.

"They're not supposed to," answered Lorenzo.

A short distance behind the bolgar, a powerful white lion with thick fur and bushy mane trotted into view. On its back sat a small nikkuni wearing a black robe, its eyes glowing bright red to match the bolgar's. Its head spiked with a horned headdress. In its right hand, it held a crude doll while in the other dangled a lantern sputtering bright green flames.

"Hey," said Birger to Renate, "I thought you said magic didn't work like that?"

Renate shrugged, and Birger looked back at the display. The nikkuni said something that made the bolgar step away, out of range for the reloading siege engine.

"That's one," said Eric, limbering up his shoulders.

"What do you mean, 'one'?" asked Mick with a scowl.

"One of their war-leaders," replied Eric with a wicked smile curling his lips. "A Wild Lands war-party is led by a pair that work together. Each controls a flank. Most tribes rule with fear. So they don't operate well without their leaders. If you kill both war-leaders, the main body of the force loses coordination."

286

"Kill the shaman, we win?" Mick asked.

"Both of them," corrected Eric, "and it's not always a shaman. It's whoever controls the most dangerous thing on the battlefield. In this one's case, a speed healing bolgar."

"Right," Mick nodded sarcastically, "easy peasy."

"Okay," said Eric, turning to Lorenzo, "you're safe."

"Wait," pleaded Lorenzo, "we still need you."

Birger had never seen Lorenzo allow his eyes to widen so much. *Strange, I thought he would let any of us walk away uncontested if we wanted to. He seems genuinely disturbed at the idea of losing Eric.*

Eric scowled at Lorenzo. "I follow you because you promised me a good fight so I can find my honourable death. This bolgar and his pet shaman may be the most dangerous fight I've seen in centuries."

"I understand," Lorenzo nodded. "And I know what I'm asking is beyond any debt you owe me. I'm asking as a friend. I need you a little while longer. Please."

Eric looked back at the bolgar, which was muttering something, pacing up and down. The nikkuni on the lion lifted the green lantern and opened his mouth to shout; however, the sound that came out boomed far louder than should have been possible. The green lantern pulsed, and a shrill noise like the sound of a thin fog horn echoed in the valley.

The trees all around stirred with activity. An ocean of yipping green bodies flooded the grass plain, bursting forth like a dam unleashed, it filled the world with madness.

45

SIEGE

"I think the bolgar plans to come into town after us," panted Birger, scanning the writhing mass of violence teetering on the edge of weapons' range.

Eric didn't speak, but he had a wide grin on his chops and rubbed his hands together like a fisher with a full skip. His gaze stayed locked on the bolgar's sullen pacing. The shaman on the white lion cackled like a madman behind the giant, then kicked the animal in the flank to leap into the pine woods. More greenskins poured into view, the treeline bustled with bodies.

"Can you imagine a more heroic death than defending the Holy City from a Wartide?" Birger smiled through the pain and exhaustion. His legs buckled under him and he would've fallen to the ground if Wynn hadn't caught him.

"Hey Birger...take it easy, okay?" Wynn tucked under Birger's arm, supporting his weight. "You're looking very pale."

Birger's shoulders sagged, either from relief or from the warm touch of sunshine on his skin. The world swam in front of his eyes. As he stared into her eyes, he absorbed Wynn's fear, pain, and confusion. Birger wanted to take it all away. He wanted to save her. Most of all, he wanted her to be honest with him, to let him help her.

Birger realised then, with a sudden clarity, that he loved her. As if sensing his revelation, Wynn turned pensive eyes on him, her gaze softening as she absorbed his expression.

You're a moron, thought Birger's cynic. *She could be toying with your emotions to manipulate you.*

No way, he argued, *I know Wynn's character. I've seen her grow from a scared farm girl into a strong streetwise woman. A believer in the Code before she knew what the Code was. If she's misleading me, then she believes she has to.*

Or you're seeing what you want to see.

Renate interrupted his thoughts when she walked up, pulling his eyelids apart for a closer look. "Wynn's right. I'm not sure how much more strain your body can take."

"The bolgar is holding its position," noted Lorenzo from next to Eric. "We can take it slower from here, but we'll want to avoid being in range of the greenskin archers."

Mick and Gunther stood bent over double, their hands on their knees, facing Kindra. Sweat dripping from Gunther's broad forehead, he looked the worst off next to Birger. His bulk was anything but an advantage in a foot race, let alone such a prolonged one.

Gunther perked up and pushed himself upright. Pointing towards Kindra's gate, he said, "Riders."

The group craned their necks to see what Gunther meant. Birger saw a column of soldiers with gleaming breastplates pour out of the gates even as archers filed onto the walls.

"Paladins and battle clerics," Renate pointed out. "Capturing Kindra won't be child's play." She turned back to look at the green horde. "I wonder why they would try."

Lorenzo resumed moving towards the gates, and the rest followed as they spoke. All of them were weary after long hours of running for survival. Renate didn't look as bad, yet she still had a tangible sense of tiredness radiating from her.

"Same reason the greng took it?" Eric speculated. "The mountain's a centre of power."

"Right," agreed Renate. "You think they aim to disrupt the connection between the goddesses and their followers, creating space for their own gods to gain a foothold in the region."

"Sure," Eric nodded, "though I meant they wanted to piss in the goddesses' eyes."

The comment drew a few raised eyebrows, and Mick laughed before saying, "Sounds like gibberish. What do you mean, disrupt and hold?"

"A deities' power needs a way into the material world. Without it, priest's can't use magic," explained Renate. "King Louis converted the humans of Azrea to the Cult of the Weave from Sarghus, because Sarghus had no power here."

"Why didn't Grengarbane establish Sarghus instead?" Gunther asked.

"Louis could've, but that would've pitted the humans against the Wulfher, dwan, stillari, quintri, and more. All of whom were allies in driving the grengar back to the Darkveil Forest."

Gunther nodded his head slowly as if contemplating a puzzle. "So if the Wartide takes Kindra, they'll be able to draw on their gods for power, and we won't?"

"But that shaman was using magic, and what about that weavestorm?" asked Wynn while checking that Snow was alright around Birger's neck.

"Magic isn't exclusive to the gods," Renate corrected, calm as an experienced sailor instructing greenhorns in the rigging. "Deities make it easier to open a rift, craft spells, power them, encode them, and more. But if I had to guess, the shaman's lantern is a channel back to his gods."

"Let's get some food," suggested Lorenzo. "We can continue this discussion once we're safe."

No one argued with that idea. Birger was sure that food and safety were a prime concern for them all. Gunther came over to help Wynn support Birger as they began walking.

Birger turned his attention to scanning the soldiers approaching on the road ahead. His attention fell on a tall man with sharp features. The soldier had white hair and a teal-silver breastplate with a pentagram of Cos. A round shield strapped to his arm, he held a long spear, and rode a warhorse adorned in heavy armour.

Once the riders were beyond Devote Hill, they fanned out and took positions to guard the fleeing civilians. Here and there, an over eager greenskin clashed with a mounted soldier, but overall, the invaders simply held their ground.

With the effects of adrenaline fading, Birger leaned on Wynn and Gunther as they pressed on, each step a battle against the growing pain.

Birger's head lolled. It took all his will to fight back sleep. It was hard to keep track of the journey to the wall and he blacked out a few times. But the throbbing in his chest and leg woke him each time.

"Get to the Saint's Cup," instructed Renate as they passed under the elegant Pilgrim's Gate. "It's just beyond the grove; I know the owner. He'll make space for us."

Birger's vision went dark and when he next opened his eyes, Mick was bursting through a green door ahead of them. It belonged to a plastered building painted orange with darkwood beams crisscrossing the various sections. A steep brown roof capped the structure, and next to the door hung a sign painted with a golden chalice. The smell of beef roasting over an open fire made Birger's

291

mouth water. His stomach twisted and turned as if trying to consume itself.

The ear-piercing cry of a small child made him wince, their mother trying to soothe them as they walked by. Gunther and Wynn pressed through the refugees milling in the street with their meagre belongings. The air around them was thick with the scent of sweat and fear.

Despite this, Birger found his mind drawn to the monotonous drone of the nearby river. It played the bass to the high-pitched birdsongs coming from the Pilgrim's Grove, nature's bard, trying to bring calm to the chaotic crowd. However, the people were beyond consolation, and they took no notice.

Birger attempted to speak, but his mouth refused to open, and he thought, *oh, I know this feeling.* It should've bothered him more, yet he couldn't summon the energy to care. His body went limp as blackness enveloped him and this time even the pain failed to wake him.

***

For the next several hours, Birger passed in and out of consciousness as Renate worked on him. Wynn was there, feeding hot soup into his mouth, and he heard Mick check in on him at least once. It was like sitting outside a theatre, listening to a play, not being able to see the actors or interact with them.

When he finally opened his eyes again, the room was dark except for a single candle, and someone sat on a chair next to his bed. He strained to speak, but only a weak grunt escaped. Wynn shot forward in the chair. Her eyes were red rimmed from crying. She was fully armoured and clutched a sizeable pouch to her chest.

"Birger," Wynn's voice came out as a hoarse whisper, "don't try to speak. Renate had to immobilise your whole body to save you, and she said if you wake up, to keep you calm, and tell you not to worry. The effect will wear off by morning."

Birger tested his limbs and found that Wynn was right. He couldn't move except for his eyes. He looked around the room; it was small, with little more space than the bed required.

He closed his eyes, fighting to suppress the panic. The feeling of being paralysed was horrifying. Knowing that he couldn't move made him want it more than ever. Birger breathed in slowly, counting to ten as Lorenzo showed him, distancing himself from his thoughts. He took his time and let his heart rate slow.

Still counting, he thought, *at least, my brain is working fine.*

Fine is relative, noted Birger's cynic.

Yes, thanks for that.

"Snow's with Renate," provided Wynn, noticing Birger taking in the room. "He didn't want to leave your side, but Renate needed to look at his wounds, and there wasn't enough space here. You know, I think that weavespider's as smart as a person."

Birger blinked agreement.

"There's something I need to tell you..." Wynn leaned back in her chair, taking Birger's hand in hers. Her skin was warm and soft, except for a few callouses. "I haven't been fair to you, and I think I owe you more than that. You mean a lot to me. I think I might love you." She paused to look down. She squeezed his hand. A single tear dripped onto his skin.

Birger tried to open his mouth. He wanted to say he loved her too, to put his hand on her cheek and tell her they could work it out together, beat anything together. But his body didn't respond.

"Don't," Wynn put a hand on Birger's forehead, "straining against the spell can cause more damage. I don't understand everything yet; Renate has only shown me some basics. She said that you need uninterrupted time for your body to heal."

Wynn made a sniffling sound, wiping her nose with her grey cloak. She looked up at the roof for a long time, took a deep breath, and then let her eyes fall to Birger's again.

"I wish there were another way, but I can't see any. You should know that I didn't want any of this. They said that if I didn't..." her voice crackled and shook with emotion. "I don't want anyone to get hurt. Especially not you."

Wynn clutched the pouch in her other hand. *It's the right size for carrying documents,* thought Birger.

"I have to leave," Wynn voiced, her tone sombre, "and I won't be coming back. Ulfhild has Neffily, Birger. If I don't do what they say, they'll kill her," she hesitated, "or worse..."

Wynn looked like a ship whose captain couldn't decide to flee or charge, and Birger tried to open his mouth again; he wanted to tell her he knew, beg her to stay and let him help, but all he could manage was another faint grunt.

More tears ran down her cheek and pattered on his hand as she said, "Goodbye."

293

Wynn leaned in, placing a tender kiss on Birger's lips. Her warm breath washed over his skin, the line of tears on his face cooled abruptly, and he realised he was crying too.

The cherry sweet smell of her perfume lingered as she let go of his hand, rose to her feet, and walked to the door. She paused at the threshold. Birger strained, but his fight against the immobilising spell was futile. He ached to call her back.

With a hesitant hand on the doorknob, Wynn looked back and whispered, "I'm so sorry." She then stepped out, the door closing behind her with an echo of finality.

46

THE SAINT'S CUP

"Nothing, once directly observed, can stay unchanged. Leave no thought or feeling to stand without discovering what's behind it."
Jing Mindweaver Wakhi Illu

She was gone, and the room felt so lonely when Birger woke up. He spent most of the night in a fitful dance between heartbreak over Wynn, overwhelming anxiety about being paralysed and dreamless sleep.

There was a heavy weight on his legs, and he tried to lift his head to see what it was. With shock, he found that his neck worked, and he felt... fine, if a little sore.

By Aeg, thought Birger, checking his wrist. *No black armband.* He blew out a relieved sigh. *For a moment, I feared Renate had put Chancebringer on me.*

Realizing the paralysing spell had worn off, he slowly hoisted himself onto his elbows and cast his eyes down his body to find the source of the weight. Snow lay spread over of the bed, sweeping his feathered appendages over Chancebringer. The artefact rested on Birger's stomach, still attached to his ribs via a silvery cord. Snow had grown even more in the night and was huge, like a small shepherd's dog.

"Morning," said Birger and Snow stopped his feeding to look up with sunlight glinting in his big pink eyes.

A pang of glee, distinct and resounding like a ship's horn coming into the harbour, emanated from the huge seven-legged weavespider. It was followed by a loud purring that made the bed tremble.

"By the ladies," Birger's eyes stretched wide, "if you keep growing at this rate, we'll have to stable you with the horses."

Snow responded with a decidedly sceptical look. He leapt off the bed, loping closer to brush his sweepers over Birger's face. It tickled, and despite himself, Birger laughed.

"Okay, okay," he protested. "Enough of that."

Snow settled back to give Birger space and spun in a circle on the wood floor. Birger grinned at the display before testing the strength in his hands and feet. They flexed, and it felt good to move without overwhelming pain. Next, he bent his left knee; all good there. Birger took a deep breath, and he felt a spark, kindling fear to life in his chest.

What if my right leg is crippled forever? What if I couldn't use it properly ever again?

He pushed the doubts aside and summoned his courage; the knee bent, if a little awkwardly, and the fear that seemed so real a moment ago evaporated. Birger swung his legs off the bed and tested his weight on them, holding as he stood. He had never felt so good about standing under his own power before.

His armour lay neatly on the chair Wynn had sat in the previous night. Regret gripped his heart for a second, and he heard Snow whine. He looked at the spider, tilting his head to one side, and asked, "Can you read my mind?"

Snow shook his head, and Birger knew the arachnid was saying no.

"Then how do you know what I'm feeling?"

Snow gave Birger a skew look that communicated, are you daft? How do you think?

"You can feel my feelings," Birger lightly palmed off his forehead, "of course."

Snow acknowledged the statement, and then sadness radiated off the weavespider.

"Yeah," Birger shook his head, "she's gone. I couldn't stop her."

He slipped into his armour, tucking Chancebringer into a pouch near the wound on his side. Relieved that he could dress without help again, he proceeded. Finally, he belted his rapier to his left side, and he drew it from the sheath, studying the edge.

The blade had taken a few nicks and had dulled during his fight with the tin-bird. *I'll be needing this a lot in the coming days,* he thought. *I wish I had some oil to care for it.*

At the time, that battle with the Feet had felt like the greatest trial he would ever endure. Now, he had seen the extremes of what his endurance could handle, and the week was far from over. Still, neither compared to the pain of watching Wynn walk out of the door while utterly paralysed.

I have to get her back, thought Birger. *I have to help her save Neffily. It's my fault, it's all my fault. She loves me, and I let her down. Aeg, I tried so hard, but it wasn't good enough.*

Story of your life, replied Birger's cynic.

He shifted his weight to sheath the sword, and Lorenzo's words rang in his mind as clear as a bell. 'You would fare much better if you fought to win.' Birger was sick and tired of being on the defensive, always running at the first opportunity. The memory of the sea of aggression that seethed on the edge of the forest came to him unbidden.

There would be no avoiding this fight. It would be life or death, and in no uncertain terms, he would fight and kill or be killed. Besides, it wasn't as if defending and running had done much to help him in the recent past.

He ran his thumb along the still-sharp section of the sword near the guard, drawing blood, then sheathed the rapier. A large bead of blood gleamed on his thumb, and he said, "From now on, if I draw my sword, it will be to draw blood." He shoved his thumb into his mouth and sucked on it, tasting the coppery tang.

He hoped the symbolic gesture would mark a turning point. A small start. Besides Wynn leaving, Birger had another concern. *Was Lorenzo using etherweave? How do I feel about that? Would it be a danger to us if Lorenzo ran out? It wasn't like you could get it on any street corner. Was I being a hypocrite for caring? It's not like I have a flawless moral record.*

Snow trailed drearily behind as Birger headed to the door.

He noticed the sad feeling radiating off Snow and paused. *Now I'm making Snow sad,* thought Birger. *What a friend I am.*

They moved into a hallway lined with doors on either side, which ended at a descending stairwell. Near the bottom, a wall of pleasure struck him, the closest thing to Anchorhall he could imagine.

The sweet smell of grilled bream wafted over him, and he breathed it in. For a fleeting moment, his mind had tricked him into believing he was back in the Rusty Tankard with Wynn, Noxolu, and Benny waiting for him in their usual booth. The memory of Wynn's tears dripping onto his hand clipped the bout of fancy short. He remembered the soft, warm kiss and the finality of the door closing behind her.

Mums with children and the infirm filled the common room. An air of dread hung over them, accentuated by an unnatural stillness for having so many people in one place. In a round alcove on the far side of the spacious room, sat a large barrel tipped on its side. Fourteen tables surrounded the dance floor, which had been transformed into a play area for the kids. There was a small stage and a wide fireplace next to the bar counter.

Birger fell into the nearest empty seat, his appetite draining away his will to move. Snow settled next to him on the ground, his head in easy reach for a scratch, and Birger obliged him. A couple of children yipped with glee at the sight of Snow and rushed over to pet him, their mothers at once reluctant and yet not stopping the children.

A little girl in a grubby yellow dress and tousled red hair cried out, "Snow!" The weavespider responded with a playful wiggle as a small horde of children closed in.

"Made friends while I was sleeping, hey?" Birger gave the silly weavespider a skewed grin.

A short man approached Birger; he had slender shoulders with a round belly and wore suspenders over a white shirt that was tucked into black trousers. Though his hair was grey, it was still a full mane that swooped up like a bird's wing, and his moustache, Birger thought, looked like the billowing sails of a sloop.

"Good day, sir," said the man pleasantly, "my name is Henry Ollich, and this is my inn. Snow here has done us a great service entertaining the young ones yesterday. It was a welcome distraction from the chaos outside."

"Hello, Henry," Birger returned a thin smile, "I'm Birger. Snow enjoys being helpful."

"We met briefly last night, though I doubt you would remember," Henry nodded. "Lady Renate asked that I feed you and call for her once you came down."

"I'm not hungry," lied Birger, and he wondered why he would say such a thing.

"The Lady said you might say so," Henry's moustache smiled more than his mouth, "she said to bring you the bream, anyway. My question is, would you like anything to drink with your meal today?"

"Any ale would be fine." A flicker of annoyance stirred within Birger at Renate, deciding on his behalf, but his pride was insignificant compared to his hunger and thirst.

"Very well, sir." Henry bowed slightly and retreated to the bar.

As Snow chased the children, rolling playfully on the floor, Henry arrived with the food and a hoppy brew. Birger enjoyed the bream. It had been ages since he ate his favorite dish, and, remarkably, it was prepared in the Anthirian way. He savoured every bite, holding each for a time to allow the juices to fill his mouth.

As he emptied his tankard and polished off the last of his potatoes, he looked up to see the green front door of the inn open, and Renate walked through. She was in a silvery blue dress that ended near her ankles, showing off long slender boots with no heel, and her hair tied back in a ponytail.

Her facial expression was grim as she sat opposite Birger and said, "Good afternoon."

"Afternoon?" Birger raised one eyebrow. "Are you serious?"

"Yes," she nodded, "You slept for roughly twenty-four hours."

"Oh no," Birger grimaced and asked, "What have I missed?"

47

THE WALL

The stench of blood and carrion hit Birger like a wave of ice-cold water. Nausea bubbled up in his throat. Injured men and women lay in cots under tarps, stretching across the road between over-full buildings.

It bustled with people working on the wounded. Healers cast broken bones with sheets of mystic-weave in the same manner that Renate had treated Birger's knee. He recognised, in the stiff shuffle of the soldiers returning to their posts, the after-effects of that healing.

"The greenskins have been relentless," said Renate as they picked their way through the turmoil. "The first charge hit shortly after we arrived. It was a slaughter in our favour, but as we repelled one wave, another took its place, fresh and ready to fight. Since then, Lorenzo and Eric have been fighting on the wall."

"Are you serious?" Birger blurted out, unable to hide his disbelief.

It made sense that Eric, being a werewolf, could maintain that pace... but Lorenzo? Birger wondered. *He would be going on over fifty-six hours without sleep! Even etherweave couldn't sustain such a pace. Using the stimulant to stay awake for over two days would dampen your senses, and it could kill you if you kept it up for more than three.*

"Lorenzo is pushing himself too hard..." said Renate.

"You're worried about him," Birger said, knowing it was true.

She didn't respond; her gaze scanned the city as they walked. Birger followed her line of sight. Flaming boulders flew across the sky, crumbling buildings in the distance. More followed. As they ascended the stairs of the wall, he saw smoke billowing in several spots, his heart sinking in empathy for wrecked homes and businesses. People rushed around with buckets to douse the flames, but before they could save one, the enemy had struck another.

Above, on the battlements, Birger could hear the ring of steel on steel and the screams of people dying. Fear made his legs heavy, and he fought it to keep moving, drawing his rapier for courage. Snow zipped straight up the flawless ivory surface of the wall, one advantage of being a weavespider.

Also reaching the top of the wall, Birger found himself surrounded by green bodies pouring through the crenels. Majority of them were the child sized nikkuni, whooping and hacking at the defenders with glee. The bulk of the wall defenders were regular men and women, their faces contorted into masks of terror.

Among them, Birger saw a cleric with the wave of Aeg stencilled on her yellow cloak, throw a flickering bottle. It landed in a clump of nikkuni, shattering with crisp azure lightning exploding out. Through the sharp scent of ozone, the sweet smell of barbequed meat assaulted Birger's nose. A wave of nausea threatened to overpower him. He swallowed hard.

Arrows flew up the wall, and Birger kept his head low as he moved. Thankfully, the aim was poor and most of the arrows fell in the city. Ahead of Birger, a trio of paladins were being overpowered by a squadron of ukthuun bruisers, each at least the size of Gunther. The biggest one lifted its curved axe high before hammering it down on a pinned paladin. Birger watched as a loud explosion launched the ukthuun off the wall.

Birger clutched at his ears to stop the ringing and blinked his eyes clear. While painful on the ears, the shockwave seemed able to discern friend from foe. The force struck only the greenskins, leaving those that didn't plummet to their deaths stumbling around drunkenly.

Snow leapt into the fray without hesitation. The weavespider's bite closed on the first victim, a weave rift popping open inside their flesh. Terrified shrieks followed as the nikkuni warrior's comrades watched them get ripped out of this world. A couple tried to attack Snow, but the weavespider was too fast. He bounced back and then balled into them again, snapping out with his forelegs; Snow's chitinous armour deflected their attacks.

"Where are they?" shouted Birger, his heart thumping with fear and making him hyper-alert.

"They were to the south last I saw them," Renate pointed down the wall.

More writhing green bodies pressed against the defenders when an axe-blade ripped through the attackers in a broad swoop. A grim-faced, gore-covered Eric appeared beyond the carnage as he continued to commit violence on the enemy with unchecked brutality. Behind him, two halberds flashed in practiced coordination, killing a pair of ukthuun and knocking an assault ladder back off the wall.

Gunther pounded on his broad chest and roared with satisfaction. Mick's gaunt-faced grin, covered in, looked ghastly when he charged the next ladder. Nearby, Lorenzo slipped through the enemy, flicking Kazania this way and that. Dark red ribbons of blood trailed in the wake of his blade. The spymaster dodged between attacks as if performing a choreographed dance. If Birger hadn't seen him do it before, it would've been hard to tell that Lorenzo was sluggish, his steps heavier, his guard lower.

A shower of arrows made Birger duck. Nearby, two clerics, their skin like stone, wielding boulder-fists, bludgeoned the enemy to a pulp. A nikkuni zipped between them, darting towards Renate.

Blindly, Birger shot forward and caught the creature in the throat with his blade. The greenskin screeched in pain, air bubbles forming around the wound, and Birger hopped back before it could lash out with its serrated cutlass. He struck the small green creature again, whipping his blade across its neck. Blood squirted in rapid-fire bursts, and Birger had to dodge several more attacks before the nikkuni finally collapsed.

The smell of urine and blood filled his senses. Disgust and realisation made him feel sick to his stomach. Before he could stop himself, he vomited. There was no time to dwell on what he had done. He wiped his mouth with his sleeve and pressed onward.

Renate placed her hand on Birger's shoulder. She shouted over the din, "Thank you!"

Birger smiled weakly. He heard a loud creak, followed by an explosive snap. He dragged Renate down to duck as the streaks of flaming boulders arched through the sky, over the wall to land on the helpless town below.

"Come on!" yelled Birger as he pushed towards Lorenzo. Birger's sword thrust and flicked at attackers as they went, and with every kill, his stomach reacted a little less.

Another loud explosion told Birger that more paladins had fallen. On the tower ahead, Birger saw five clerics in teal-silver, bearing the golden pentagram of Cos. Collaborating to open a weave rift, they pulled out thick cords. With smooth, practiced motions, they began knotting it together. Working the spell crafting flat with their shields. It began to glow yellow.

Four of them stepped back and left the fifth to cast the spell over the wall. There was a bright explosion that stunned Birger. When his vision returned, tears blurring his sight, every greenskin in a hundred yards from the base of the tower lay in small charred heaps. The smell of cooking meat and burned hair hung thick in the air.

The carnage spurred terror in the remaining enemy, sending them into a scrambling retreat. Those remaining on the wall were mercilessly cut down and kicked through the crenels.

Birger doubled over, hands on knees, gasping for air. A moment later, Snow appeared, nuzzling him with concern.

"I'm alright, just tired," said Birger with a flat smile.

"You're close to recovering, but don't take it for granted." Renate checked Birger over. "If that web snaps and Chancebringer isn't on your wrist, your injuries could kill you."

"Don't worry, the cord is under my armour." Birger patted the leather jerkin under his grey surcoat.

Mick walked over and said, "Nice of you to join us, sleeping beauty." Sweat poured down his face, mussing his thinning brown hair. Mick's silver breastplate was dented and covered in dark red blood.

"You've been missing out on a great fight," added Eric, slapping Mick on the back.

Mick raised a skeptical eyebrow, retorting, "Great? Not everyone here is an immortal werewolf with a death wish, you know."

"The novelty wears off quickly." Eric had a toothy grin, like Birger had never seen. Clearly, the man was in his element.

"We were worried about you, Birger." Gunther looked worn, his skin covered in minor cuts. Grabbing Birger in a big bear hug, he said, "Thank Aeg, you look a lot better than yesterday. Good work, Renate."

"You look like a mess. How long have you been fighting?" asked Birger, protesting weakly, but smiling despite himself.

Gunther let him go, and blood rushed back into his limbs.

"They joined shortly after breakfast," Lorenzo's voice came, as he wiped Kazania on a rag before putting her away. He had dark circles around his eyes, his cheeks sunken, and, like the others, he was out of breath.

Birger gulped. *Time for a tough conversation...*

"Lorenzo...we need to talk," Birger tried to suppress the quiver of emotion in his voice.

"What is it?"

"Wynn took the documents and slinked off in the night," explained Birger with a wince, expecting the man to ask him why he hadn't stopped her.

Lorenzo nodded. "As planned. I figured she would make her move when we got here."

"There's more." Birger straightened himself and sighed. "She talked to me before she left. I couldn't move or speak, or I would've...."

"It's okay, Birger," Renate squeezed his shoulder, "it wasn't your fault. She knew you wouldn't be able to react. It's probably why she chose that moment."

It didn't make Birger feel any better. Things needed saying, and he would be damned before he let things go unsaid again. "Ulfhild has taken her best friend, Neffily, hostage. Wynn said they were blackmailing her. She didn't mean for any of this to happen."

The others stared back at him with blank faces.

"Don't you see?" asked Birger, frustrated. "She didn't mean for any of 'this' to happen, for people to get hurt. I think Wynn knew the uks were coming. You were right, Lorenzo. Ulfhild is behind this attack. A cover for whatever they're planning in the temple."

"Using the Wartide as cover for a robbery?" Mick scanned over the dead and dying. "It's brash."

"Even if it's true, they would be trapped, like us," said Lorenzo.

"Perhaps," agreed Birger. "But what's the worst that could happen? We head to the temple, find nothing, come back and help defend the wall... but if I'm right?"

Lorenzo looked at Birger, his face lined with worry. A brief flicker passed across his face before he clutched his belt pouch. The pouch collapsed, empty.

"By the five," Renate cursed, her eyes on the distant treeline. "There! To the north."

Birger watched as Lorenzo unclipped his quintri-looking-glass from his belt and held it to his eye. Then offered it to Birger, who grabbed the device to look.

"What am I looking for?" asked Birger.

"Do you see the bolgar?" guided Lorenzo.

"Yeah."

"At his feet."

Birger scanned around the bolgar's massive stompers. Several nikkuni scuttled past, barely reaching above the giant's ankle. The white lion lay to one side, crunching a meaty bone. A faint green glow shimmered on its fur. Birger followed the light and found the shaman speaking to a human...

"Cos damn her," cursed Birger.

"What?" asked Mick impatiently. "What is it?"

"Ulfhild," answered Lorenzo.

She stood towering over the shaman, her scarlet armour and red hair contrasted by the snowy backdrop. Seeing her, Birger felt a lump of terror in his throat mix with an almost uncontrollable rage that made him want to leap past the merlons and charge at her. He lowered the looking glass instead and sullenly handed it back to Lorenzo.

"It would appear that you're correct," said Lorenzo, putting the device back in its place. "What would you suggest we do?"

"I think me, you and Renate should go to the temple for a look." Birger crouched down and rubbed Snow's big head, "Snow, you stay here, keep the others alive." Birger glanced over at Eric, who was scowling at him, and he added, "Not Eric, just Mick and Gunther, okay?"

The weavespider seemed happy, and Birger let the shared experience give him a refuge from anxiety.

Gunther walked up and hugged Birger again. "You better come back in one piece."

Struggling to get out of the big man's grip but not trying too hard, Birger replied, "You're the ones on the wall."

Gunther let go, keeping his hands on either side of Birger's shoulders so he could lock the younger man with his gaze. "If you're right, the Black Wolves are inside the walls. Keep your wits sharp."

48

TEMPLE OF LIFE AND DEATH

Violence erupted on the city walls for the second time since Birger left it behind. Flashes of light, explosions shaking the ground, and the city's usual din became screams of agony. Though the clerics, paladins and militia were better trained, the Wartide seemed able to hurl an inexhaustible supply of bodies to smother the city.

Alongside Lorenzo and Renate, Birger hurried down Pilgrim's March, which was a wide boulevard of crisp white flagstone. Under normal circumstances, the road would've been bustling with friendly people on their way to the temples.

Birger saw another flaming boulder strike a wine merchant's shop a block away, instinctively ducking as it kicked up a debris-laden dust cloud.

That was someone's business, Birger thought. *Did I cause this? Did I set these events in motion by stealing from Foss? Or was this always the plan?*

Probably your fault, Birger's cynic replied. *Even if it wasn't, the revolt that tore Anthir apart sure was.*

Birger had no response. It was true, the war he had hoped to keep away from his home struck anyway, and here he stood in the middle of another he couldn't stop. Bo, Ulfhild and Londel were winning, and Birger was losing.

I'm changing that, Birger thought. *I can't do anything about what has happened, but I can mess up the rest of their plans.*

At the road's end, the Holy Mountain towered over Kindra. The Pilgrim's Rise, with its thousands of steps, led up to the top. Refugees hoping to find safety at the flat summit choked the staircase.

The press of bodies made it hard to move, causing Birger to feel like he was swimming against a riptide, which was rapidly draining his energy. Not to mention, any of these people could be a mutt in disguise.

He tried to distract himself from his aching knee by focusing on the tensions between Renate and Lorenzo. They had hardly spoken since the wall, and Birger could tell Renate was holding back anger.

She breathed heavily, her hair was still perfectly styled, and her dress was unruffled, despite having been in the middle of battle less than an hour ago.

Lorenzo appeared drawn and exhausted. The laceration on his brow from the bolgar attack was bleeding again, and he had a dozen other nicks. His armoured jacket sported several scuffs, but nothing had penetrated it, and grime was smeared across the dark stubble on his jaw.

"...I don't want to talk about it now," Lorenzo was saying as Birger caught the tail end of the conversation.

"So, when will you want to?" Renate shot back, her voice edged with impatience and not at all the mindweaver tone that Birger had come to expect. "Lorenzo, you're not yourself. You didn't even see Ulfhild until I pointed her out to you." Her expression laced with exasperation, more intense than Birger had seen in her before.

"I was occupied, Renate," Lorenzo retorted tersely.

Silence fell over them. Climbing the steps was tougher than fighting on the wall, but the view was stunning. In the south, Birger watched the great windmills of Molt grinding grain for East Rendin.

In the north, he could see the Nord Lake pooling at the foot of the Northern Towers. A giant plume of black smoke billowed skywards; likely it was the Tower under siege.

That thought drew Birger back to Kindra's walls, which were holding, if barely. Eric was having the time of his life, but Birger was scared for Mick, Gunther and Snow. On the south side of town, Devote Hill and the farmsteads of the Jor Blessed Land burned as greenskinned barbarians ravaged it.

"Hey, what are those?" Birger pointed curiously at a cluster of ukthuun attempting to cross the river, to no avail.

"They're called waterweirds," Renate replied.

Birger chuckled, a dry edge to his tone. "I mean, that water is weird alright, but what exactly are they?"

Renate smiled at him. "It's the Holy Spring, which is a fragment of Stillendam. A colossal water elemental that protects the home of the stillari. The entire body of water, being a living creature, exists to care for the Holy Mountain and it aggressively protects the temples."

"Right." Birger looked at her with wide-eyed wonder. After a moment of thinking, he added, "That would explain why everyone – man, woman, child, or even their dog – is trying to get to the top of the mountain. They're hoping the waterweirds would protect them."

"Most likely, yes."

Birger squinted his eyes to get a better look. "What are those things around their necks?"

"Containment collars," said Lorenzo. "Without those, the Holy Spring can't make autonomous units like that. If the collar is destroyed, the water returns to the source."

Birger eyed the constructs a little longer. The water creatures were a solid barrier against the Wartide, and the greenskins hadn't figured out how to destroy the collars yet.

"Couldn't they help on the walls?" asked Birger.

"Too much wall, and too few waterweirds," Lorenzo replied.

Birger pursed his lips in regret, thinking of how many lives could've been saved under different circumstances. He refocused his attention on the seemingly endless stairs. At the top of Pilgrim's Rise, two clerics of Cos questioned people seeking to enter the temple grounds.

To the left of them, Birger saw a platform that reminded him of a ship's deck. A long, flat space with two raised sections on either end. Five temples rose beyond the edge of the bluff. Each was artistically crafted, brightly coloured, and rivalled the splendour of West Haven's Grand Palace.

At the centre of the flat-top mountain, Birger saw the temple of the All-mother Cos, with her pentagram tastefully etched into the façade. The walls of the building blushed with a pearl finish, and its rooftops sparkled like fine jade in the sun.

This central structure was circled by the Holy Spring, feeding into a waterfall. Its banks were studded with succulent, multicoloured plants and well-tended lawns. Birger figured they were meant for monks, scholars, and priests to debate or discuss religious matters. However, they were currently overrun with rickety tents housing refugees.

Taking a deep breath, Renate said, "Look, Lorenzo. I'm sorry about earlier. We're all weary and irritable. I'm concerned about you. Losing your edge in a time like this can be deadly."

Lorenzo nodded and took a deep breath of his own. "I do appreciate that you care so much. And you're right, I am tired... I promise I'll get some rest tonight. Even if it's only a couple of hours."

Renate pursed her lips. She put a gentle hand on the small of Lorenzo's back, sharing a moment as they kept climbing the stairs. Birger let go of a tense breath. He also didn't want Lorenzo to get hurt, but he would be lost if Lorenzo had headed back to the inn now. Birger didn't know what he would do once they reached the temple, and he needed the Shade's help to save Wynn.

Along the outer rim of the bluff, Birger noted the four other temples. Each dedicated to one of the four daughters of Cos.

To the southwest the temple of Mag was poised, keeper of the Magic Weave, or, as Birger now thought of her, Snow's mum.

The temple of the dragon, Aeg, perched in the northwest. She had been a central figure in Birger's life for a long time, and his awareness drifted to the bracelet in his belt pouch.

To the northeast coiled the temple of Jor, the world serpent, while the winter wolf, Lot, prowled closest to the stairs.

Birger swallowed to clear a lump in his throat. *What if Wynn is there? What do I do? Taking her or keeping her from her task could get Neffily killed... Cos, what if she isn't there?*

By the time they reached the end of the queue, the sun already sat close to the horizon, and his belly ached with urgency.

"Next!" called a female cleric in teal-silver armour, her figure slender with the wiry muscles of a seasoned fighter. "What is your business at the temples?"

"We're here to speak with the High Priestess of Lot," said Lorenzo, flashing his ring. "I'm Duke Lorenzo Soto of West Haven, on crown business. These two are with me."

The male cleric was a broad-shouldered man with a pinched face. He glanced at the woman and said, "Your Grace, there is a siege in progress and we need every able body defending the walls."

"I've certainly noticed that," Lorenzo responded, notably keeping his tone devoid of sarcasm.

Birger had to stifle a laugh. *Come on,* he thought, *let us through. We've wasted too much time on the stairs already.*

The woman scowled and said, "Brother Tam means this may not be the time for seeking council with her Holiness."

"If I had any other choice," Lorenzo gave her a thin smile, "I would be on the walls fighting right now. The matter I bring to her Holiness can't wait."

The two clerics exchanged another glance. The woman nodded and then said, "Very well, Your Grace. However, I must warn you, the Holy Council has been called. She may already be on her way there."

"Thank you, Sister. We'll try our luck." Lorenzo bowed, and the two clerics stepped aside.

Lorenzo led them through, along the paved road towards Lot's temple. Most of the clergy on the grounds were tending to the refugees, handing out food, caring for the sick or wounded. Trying to reduce the air of human misery.

Up here there was no acrid smell of smoke, septic stink of gut wounds and metallic tang of blood, but the memory of the battle never left Birger's nostrils. Being surrounded by beautiful sculptures and platforms suffused with sweet-smelling incense only made the horrors in the city more palpable.

"Where should we start?" Lorenzo pondered.

"We don't know which item they're after," said Renate, scanning Lot's temple grounds. "This is the sacred core of the Cult of the Weave. There are powerful relics everywhere."

"Well, that narrows it down," Birger said with a wry smile. "Let's start with the person in charge. We can see if they've noticed anything amiss. That might give us a clue."

Lorenzo and Renate nodded in agreement. It was as good a plan as any.

They entered the temple complex, finding the grounds neatly laid out. The large central chapel sat in the middle. A tower, as tall as the Holy Mountain, stood to the left, and to the right, another tear-shaped building that looked to Birger like a training facility. As was the case all over the mountain, there were solemn looking squatters everywhere.

The trio pushed past the throng of bodies to a wide pearly staircase providing access to the open double doors of the chapel. A pair of statues resembling winter wolves flanked the door. Birger took the steps slowly, his legs weary and his right knee going stiff again. When he reached the top, he leaned his hand on the head of one large wolf statue to catch his breath.

Around the doors, Birger noted the surrounding stonework was carved and inlaid with gold. They depicted Anchorhall on the right side, where the righteous and valiant souls enjoyed a well-deserved drink with the All-mother. While on the left were the souls of the wicked, frozen in ice, their faces contorted into screams for eternity.

Beyond the doors, the chapel looked like a wealthy captain's cabin. A thick red carpet flowed around a pool that had a marble Valkyrie at it's center. The sculpture held a glowing red gem in its hand that illuminated the space thoroughly, and Birger didn't see anyone inside.

"We might have missed her," speculated Birger.

Lorenzo grunted, "Let's look around; we might find something useful even if she isn't here."

Renate and Lorenzo gave Birger a moment to push himself upright, ready to continue. "Right, let's do it."

"Beautiful work, isn't it?" offered Renate as she studied the carved stonework.

"I've seen nothing like it in my life," agreed Birger.

"Timeless art." Lorenzo ran his fingers across the carved stone and walked into the chapel.

"I've been to the Temple of Jor many times, but this is my first time at the Chapel of Lot," said Renate.

Birger returned a smile. "All of this is pretty new to me."

First to enter were Birger and Lorenzo. Lorenzo sagged as he stepped inside, bracing himself at the edge of the pool where two jewel-encrusted collars lay.

"Lorenzo!" gasped Renate and rushed towards the door.

As her leading foot crossed the threshold, her image flickered, followed by a bright flash that blinded Birger. A pang of panic made his heart jump into his throat. Frantically, he blinked his eyes clear. *Had the mutts set a trap at the door? Were they under attack?*

Birger's sight blurred, seeing a turquoise image. He reached for his rapier reflexively. But then he realised it was Renate. He watched as her neck elongated, and her legs melded together, stretching into a tail behind her. A fan of colourful feathers sprouted from her arms, displaying bright pinks, greens, purples, blues, and reds, and forming a pair of vast wings. Finally, her face warped and took on the distinct flat shape of a snake's head, but ending in a beak.

"Renate!" Lorenzo's voice echoed throughout the chapel, his eyes wide with alarm. "Your disguise!"

49

WHAT PLAN

Birger's eyes widened at the alien beauty of Renate filling the huge doorway, decorated in a dazzling mix of coloured feathers. Turquoise ran down her back, a softer pink on her chest and belly. Flapping her huge wings, made the cloth hangings on the chapel walls ripple, and her sharp talons clacked on the stone floor as she righted herself.

The red gem in the marble Valkyrie's hand pulsed. Power radiated from it and Birger felt a tingle running down his spine. Renate moved rhythmically and the coiling of her body looked to Birger like a dance.

"My magic is failing," hissed Renate.

She slipped back out of the building and resumed the coiling action. This time a weave rift opened and thick cords poured out, seemingly on their own. Renate flattened the cords with her body and rolled in them, as if she was spinning herself into a cocoon. Soon, she was fully enveloped in the shell. When it cracked and fell away, Renate appeared, once again, human.

A soothing voice came from behind Birger, "You're welcome here in your true form, jormunger. It's been quite some time since we've had the honour of hosting your kind in Kindra."

Birger whipped around to see a tall woman with sharp facial features. Her almond-shaped eyes locked onto his. Violet irises glowing faintly, her gaze compelled him to bow. Her pink and white vestments of Lot fluttered with the breeze as she came to a standstill on the red carpet next to the pool that housed the Valkyrie statue. Long, pointed ears sprouted from the side of her head, drooping like giant leaves. White hair hung down to her waist, styled with a circlet that sat atop her head, decorated with pink pearls, matching the iridescent texture of her skin. She was the first stillari Birger had ever seen in person, and he found himself awestruck.

Lorenzo gave a low bow, saying, "Your Holiness."

Birger attempted a clumsy imitation of Lorenzo's elegant bow. His right foot slipped, and he teetered on the edge of the pool, barely maintaining his balance. He coughed and put his hand on his hip awkwardly, as if he meant to do that, fooling no one, then he quickly straightened to pretend nothing had happened. Birger caught the stillari woman suppressing a smile as she turned back to Renate.

"Thank you, Your Holiness," said Renate. "I go by Renate Couture, and if you don't mind, I would rather remain in my human disguise."

"Understandable, yet regrettably, not something I can grant inside the chapel." The High Priestess smiled pleasantly. She waved towards the glowing red gem behind her. "The Eye of Winter permits no magic within these halls."

Renate grimaced, her shoulders tight. She, almost imperceptibly, shifted away from the door. Lorenzo joined Renate on the portico, perking up the moment he stepped beyond the threshold.

The stimulant, etherweave, is infused with magic, Birger thought. *Lorenzo must still have some in his system to keep him going.*

Lorenzo straightened and said, "Your Holiness. My name is Duke Lorenzo Soto of West Haven."

"A pleasure, my son." The High Priestess tilted her head in acknowledgement. "And who are you, young man?"

It took Birger a moment to realise she was looking at him. "Oh, ah, I'm Birger of Anthir. May I ask your name?"

That drew a flickering smirk from Lorenzo.

"Nice to meet you, Birger of Anthir. I am Ishyelle Hethnolas of Stillendam, and as Duke Lorenzo has guessed, I am the High Priestess of Lot." The priestess walked towards the door. "You must forgive me. I'm on my way to a council meeting and have no time to entertain pilgrims."

Ishyelle's beauty intrigued Birger as she marched towards the door. The stillari renderings he had seen paled in comparison to Ishyelle. He had also never seen a jormunger before, and his mind reeled with questions. It took a force of will refocussing on their task. There was no time to indulge the curious historian in him. They needed to figure out what was going on if they wanted any chance of getting ahead in this deadly game.

"I apologise for our intrusion on your time, Your Holiness," said Lorenzo, stepping in her way. "We know that your attention is urgently required elsewhere. If you could spare a minute to help us, we would appreciate it. We're working to stop the criminal who caused the attack on the city, aiming to steal something from your temple."

Ishyelle stopped at the threshold and regarded Lorenzo with a tilt of her head, her long white hair flowing gracefully down her back like a waterfall.

With a puzzled expression, the High Priestess asked, "You believe someone would dare to steal from the Lady of life and death? Our defences are rather hard to overcome."

Birger reached for his thoughts like he was looking for his keys in sewage. He had experienced the same with the Queen, his mind blanking in the face of someone so powerful. Taking a slow deep breath, Birger counted to ten on the inhale, blowing it out in five and allowed his nerves to settle.

Birger thought, *Lorenzo is likely as powerful as this woman, if not more, and I can comfortably speak to him. I know this is something I can do.* Birger took another deep breath, and he felt the pressure ease. *I should focus on what I'm good at, puzzling out the best way to infiltrate a mark. They must've come here to gather intelligence, just figure out how they did it.*

"Your Holiness," Birger spoke just as Lorenzo opened his mouth to respond.

The other man closed his mouth mid utterance, ceding the floor.

Birger put on his most formal voice, ladened with a dose of faux bravado, and said, "I know it seems unthinkable, but we have clear evidence that this is their plan. We saw the woman who set these events in motion talking to the shaman leading the Wartide against the city. We believe her people are already inside the walls plotting a way into your temple."

Lorenzo flashed an approving grin.

"Interesting," Ishyelle regarded Birger with a smirk, "and what do they intend to steal?"

"That we don't know yet." Birger shook his head, briefly glancing at his feet. "We've come to see if we can figure that out so we can stop them."

"I see. And what may I assist you with?"

"Just a few answers to our questions?"

Ishyelle nodded for him to continue.

Feeling emboldened, Birger asked, "Have you had any strange visitors recently?"

Ishyelle gave Birger a wry smile and swept a hand over the multitude of refugees on the temple grounds. "It's rather hard to say."

Birger felt dumb. *Of course.* He needed to be more specific. "Right, yes. Has anyone come in claiming to be a noble, expressing a particular interest in any one part of the temple?"

"Winter chokes the roads to Kindra and we haven't had any nobles from outside the city visit us in over a month...until now." Ishyelle's hand drifted up to indicate Lorenzo.

Birger's confidence dropped as his hunch petered out, which must've been written on his face, because Lorenzo stepped in. "Have you seen anything else that you might consider irregular?"

"Irregular?" Ishyelle considered the question for a moment. "Other than the Wartide, spreading across our city walls like moss on an old tree trunk? I would say receiving my first visit from a jormunger in over a hundred and fifty years and meeting a young man that has been touched by Aeg is irregular. Beyond that, everything has been rather routine."

Does she know about Chancebringer? Birger wondered.

"Indeed," conceded Lorenzo with a humorous grin.

Renate gave Ishyelle a pensive look. Birger worried about Renate. She had been more quiet than usual. Like Eric, she must've been hiding her true nature for good reasons. Birger resolved to keep her secret, unless she told him otherwise. Humans weren't known for their tolerance of things they don't understand.

"Your Holiness, what did you mean when you said, touched by Aeg?" asked Birger. He thought he knew what she would say, but wanted to be sure.

Ishyelle's bright violet eyes fell on him and he was again struck by the desire to bow. "I can feel her on you. It's like a part of her is with you."

"Oh, you must be sensing this," Birger retrieved Chancebringer from his belt pouch and walked towards the High Priestess. "I would hand it to you, but it's currently keeping me from collapsing into a heap of pain."

Ishyelle carefully examined the artefact, running her fingers over the surface, and said, "Fascinating. How did you come by it?"

"I took it from the same people that intend to steal from you."

Finally shaking the distracted look, Renate added, "We had Professor du la Rent look at it, and he identified it as Chancebringer."

"Did he say anymore?" asked Ishyelle, looking up at Renate.

She nodded. "He said that it was a 'Piece of Divinity'."

Ishyelle smiled. "It may be one of the most powerful artefacts I've seen with my own eyes. There are only a few genuine pieces of divinity. Items crafted from the essence of the goddesses. Like the Eye of Winter there, which was made from Lot's crystallised tear."

"How many are there?" asked Birger.

"Hard to be sure," replied Ishyelle. "Histories get muddled after a few thousand years. I know of six, though there may be more."

"This is one of only six?!" Birger's mouth hung open.

His cheeks flushed with self-conciousness, and he quickly shut it again.

"Let's just say I wouldn't show this to High Priest Thornfall if I were you." Ishyelle gave Birger a conspiratorial wink, examining the webbing that ran under Birger's shirt. "You said this is healing you?"

"Yes, Your Holiness. Thanks to Renate." Birger was getting uncomfortable with the woman so close to him.

Ishyelle looked at Renate, her almond eyes wide with appreciation. "Very impressive Lady Couture. How did you shield it so well?"

"I used a lattice design. It isolates the magic of the Chancebringer to the healing spell. Then I encoded the cord to allow only energy transfer, blocking all other logic." Renate's explanation made no sense to Birger, but Ishyelle was nodding like she understood.

"Brilliant." The stillari priestess ran her finger along the cord. "The Eye of Winter should've disrupted your healing magic. But your crafting successfully shielded the power source. I'm truly impressed."

"Thank you, Your Holiness," said Renate with a hint of embarrassment in her voice.

Ishyelle looked at Birger again. "May I inquire as to why you choose not to wear it?"

"It doesn't go with my eyes," Birger joked. The question made him feel rather stubborn, but he added, "The cost is too high."

"What do you mean by 'the cost'?" Ishyelle prompted.

Birger resisted for a moment, then swallowed the lump in his throat. He reminded himself of a decision he made not to leave things unsaid, no matter how uncomfortable it might be.

"When I wore this...a friend died and others were put in impossible situations." An overbearing sadness rose in Birger's core. His mouth twisting, he said, "I would rather control my own

317

destiny than let this thing throw me around like I was a boat caught in a tempest."

"It's not the place of mortals to question the will of the goddesses," said the High Priestess. Her tone was matter-of-fact, like a first-mate instructing a sailor in the rigging. "It came to you for a reason. Besides, I doubt Chancebringer directly caused your friends harm. How can you be certain that without it, your friends wouldn't have been hurt, anyway? And instead of setting you on a path to save lives, you may have ended up dead alongside them?"

"I don't know." Birger turned the thought over in his mind.

Ishyelle withdrew and added, "Don't allow misplaced sentiment to keep a tool of the goddesses out of play."

Birger felt the weight of Ishyelle's words and wondered if his stubbornness had caused more problems than he realised.

You can't win, thought Birger's cynic. *Wear it and people get hurt. Don't wear it and people get hurt. You can't control the world. Why try?*

Because I must, responded Birger. *The Magpies' Code says you should help if you are able. I'm able. Hopeless or not, I don't care what the goddesses want me to do. I simply want to do my best and what will happen will happen.*

Ishyelle drew away from Birger and bowed to them. "Thank you for coming to see me, lady and gentlemen. I really must be going. The council is waiting."

An idea popped into Birger's head. "Oh, Your Holiness, one last thing. You said you haven't had any nobles visit, but have you perhaps had any historians that wanted to see something that people don't usually ask for?"

Ishyelle crossed one arm over her fine silk vestments and put a finger to her nose. "Ah, yes," she began, "there was one man like that. He claimed to be conducting a study on King Louis Grengarbane and expressed a desire to see his tomb."

"And where is the tomb?" Birger asked.

"Beneath the chapel, in the deepest sections of the catacombs," said Ishyelle.

"What did this man look like?"

"He called himself Alphred Yale from Larsea, though he had a heavy Sawran accent. His hair and beard were red, and he had a scrunched-up face that looked like he spent time as a boxer or something similar."

"Bo," said Birger with a sneer.

"Bo?" asked Ishyelle.

A harsh, nasal voice interrupted them from the stairs, "High Priestess!"

Birger's head snapped around, looking for the source of the voice. A towering figure marched confidently towards them. It was the same man who had led the cavalry out of the city gates the previous day. His hard, emerald eyes pierced Birger.

The man's shoulder-length white hair fluttered behind him like a flag in the wind, his steps as sure as if directed by divine guidance. Encased in a polished teal-silver breastplate over creamy white greaves, he was the embodiment of military discipline.

He said again, "High Priestess Ishyelle, High Priestess Laquismja requires your presence at the Holy Spring urgently."

The man's eyes fell on Birger, with a distinct air of judgement.

Birger felt a pang of irritation. *Who does this man think he is to judge me?*

Punch the pompous ass, thought Birger's cynic, but he ignored it.

"Brother Hein Witherwood of the Clerical order of Cos," Ishyelle bowed her head. "I'm on my way there now. May I introduce Duke Lorenzo Soto, Lady Renate Couture and Birger of Anthir?"

Hein looked at Lorenzo with what could only be described as ire and didn't even bother glancing at Renate.

"I know who *he* is." The venom dripping off Hein's words could kill if you dipped a needle in it. "You should be on the walls defending the city, you pirate scum." And he spat on the ground.

50

PIRATE

"Brother Hein," Ishyelle didn't raise her voice, yet it resonated with authority.

Lorenzo grinned and said, "That's alright, Your Holiness." He glanced to the east wall, then fixed his sullen gaze on the cleric. "There will be plenty of time for bloodshed, Brother Hein."

"You would know," retorted Hein, his eyes filled with hatred.

People would often use the word loosely, but genuine hatred was as rare as genuine love, Birger thought, and he wondered what Lorenzo had done to earn it.

"Your Holiness," Hein bowed, pivoted, and marched away.

The sun was hanging low behind the temple of Cos, casting a stark shadow on the receding figure in his gleaming armour. Lorenzo's shoulders were slumped and his eyes sad as he watched Hein go.

Ishyelle turned to Lorenzo. Birger thought her expression was a mix of curiosity and wariness. "I really must go. It has been a pleasure." She turned back to the chapel entrance and called out, her voice loud and clear despite not raising it, "Chapel guard! Please secure the doors." To Lorenzo she said, "With your warning, I will lockdown the chapel and increase security."

Lorenzo smiled, but it didn't touch his eyes. The dark circles making him look sinister to Birger. *First etherweave, now accusations of piracy? What else don't I know about Lorenzo?*

Shoving the thoughts aside, Birger stepped in front of the priestess. "Your Holiness, might I be able to go down to King Louis's Tomb?"

"I'm afraid I can't spare anyone to take you, and I really must go," explained Ishyelle, gracefully sidestepping him.

The wind dropped out of Birger's sails. *Another deadend, unless I want to risk the temple defences and break in?* He considered it for a moment, but in the end, he decided it was a bad idea. *I would weaken them, thereby making it easier for Bo to get what he wants, or get myself killed.*

"Thank you for your time, Your Holiness," said Lorenzo, bowing low.

Renate did the same, and Birger hastily followed. He bumped his rear into one of the marble wolves guarding the stairs. Ishyelle tipped her head as she drifted away.

At the base of the stairs, the High Priestess met a pair of lean monks with shaved heads, wearing pink robes bearing the spiral tear of Lot. After a brief exchange, the pair ran up to the chapel and shoved the heavy doors shut, while Ishyelle left towards Pilgrim's Rise.

Standing below the chapel with the other two, Birger exhaled forcefully. He paced back and forth on the path, his boots scuffing the stones. Anxiety butterflies redoubling in his belly, Birger clenched his fists, knuckles turning white.

With gritted teeth, he thought, *I should've done better... Wynn needs me to figure this out, and I have nothing! What the fishers pit was that cleric saying about Lorenzo, anyway?*

"What now?" asked Renate, resting against the bottom rail of the stairway.

"I don't know," said Lorenzo, his hands on his hips and searching the flagstone for answers.

"First, what was with the cleric?" demanded Birger, his jaw flexing and his heart thumping.

Pirates were the antithesis of the Magpies. They killed people for loot and they often took slaves to sell in Apour. If Lorenzo was a pirate, what did Birger get himself involved in?

"What do you mean?" asked Lorenzo, reeling, as if Birger had struck him.

"That cleric," said Birger, "that man hated you. Why?"

"Bad history." Lorenzo's face fell. The spark in his eye was dim, and he swayed slightly, battling against an invisible tide.

"What do you mean?" Birger glowered impatiently. "He called you a pirate."

"Let it go, Birger." Renate stepped protectively between them. "Some things are better left in the past."

"Piracy is an egregious offence under the Code!" yelled Birger. "When you said balancing blood, I thought you meant stopping wars, not robbery, murder, and selling slaves!"

"Birger!" Renate snapped, glowering at him. "You don't know what you're talking about."

322

"It's alright, Renate," Lorenzo steadied himself against a bench by the path. "Birger, we all have a past, and I'm not proud of mine."

Birger continued glaring unapologetically past Renate at Lorenzo. With his arms folded, Birger said, "Abusing etherweave seems quite in the present to me."

Lorenzo's jaw clenched, and he fixed Birger with a hard look. Renate closed her eyes and Birger could almost see the dark thoughts flashing across her face. She turned to look at Lorenzo as well.

"Let it go…" began Lorenzo.

Renate's stare was as impactful as a slap. "So, that's how you've been keeping this pace?"

"I ran out anyway," said Lorenzo defensively.

"I can see that." Renate waved at Lorenzo's rundown appearance. "I was worried about you when you were on two days without sleeping. Three days on etherweave…"

"I know!" interrupted Lorenzo. "I just told you, I'm out. We've been under attack for the last two and a half days. It's not like we're up against amateurs. Ulfhild's as tough as they come. I needed it to gain an edge."

"And now what?" Renate challenged, folding her arms. "You're out? Even if you got more, it would kill you. And look at you…you're on the brink of collapsing."

Lorenzo turned away from them, his shoulders heaving with a deep inhale. "This isn't helping."

Renate mimicked him, appearing to also calm herself down. "Fine. I'll let it drop…*for now*, but me and you are going to discuss this when it's over."

Birger pressed on, "You might be happy to drop it, but I'm not done. I won't work with a pirate."

"Fine." Lorenzo took another deep breath and stood up straight as he turned back to face them. When he spoke, his tone was tightly controlled. "I was born into being a privateer, captaining a ship in the trade wars between Itavia and Korland. I retired after the war and came to live in Rella. That life has been behind me for years."

Birger sneered, "But that isn't all, is it? That cleric looked at you like you smacked him in the mouth with a week-old sea-bass…"

Renate sucked air through her teeth and walked a few steps away from them.

There you go, putting your friends in impossible situations again, thought Birger's cynic.

"No, that isn't all," admitted Lorenzo.

"That kind of hate is personal," said Birger. "What did you do to him?"

"I didn't do anything to *him*." Lorenzo's jaw clenched again, and he closed his eyes. A silent moment passed. "I had a family in Rella, but they were murdered by a nobleman's thugs, leaving me for dead. I lost myself in the grief and took revenge. Unfortunately, a Cleric of Cos was visiting the noble's home when I came. Hein's friend. I didn't spare anyone bearing arms."

The brutal reality of what Lorenzo shared took a moment to sink in. He killed everyone in the building? Including a cleric. Birger stood, stunned. Then he considered how he himself felt after Benny's death. *I might've done the same, if not for Frida, and later Renate, talking me down.*

"I've spent my life making amends for my many sins," Lorenzo said, snorting out a frustrated breath. "While I can never undo the mistake I made, I stop wars, spilling as little blood as possible. I know who I am, and I don't need you to believe me. So, judge me as you will, but I have work to do."

Birger's cheeks burned, and he suddenly felt like a self-righteous fool.

Lorenzo was quiet for a moment, then said, "I'm going to talk to the monks to make sure they're properly prepared. Then I'm going to help on the walls. Do as you please."

Lorenzo walked calmly past Birger. His heart felt like a heavy stone in his chest. Birger ran his fingers through his hair, then tugged his hood over his face, as if hoping the grey fabric could conceal his shame.

"Lorenzo saved a young girl's life that day," Renate broke the silence when Lorenzo reached the top of the Chapel stairs. "She had been taken and held for ransom. Lorenzo didn't know she was there, but he found her malnourished, abused and bleeding. Both her legs and jaw had been broken. He took her home, nurtured her back to health and supported her through the trauma until she could speak again."

"Was it you?" asked Birger. Empathy, sadness, betrayal and guilt still warring in his belly.

"No," Renate smiled mirthlessly, "I'm far from young. That girl's name was Princess Armandine du la Rent. She saved his life as much as he saved hers. Lorenzo was in a dark place after what happened to his family, and saving that girl's life gave him a way back to the peace he wanted."

Who are you to judge anyone else? accused Birger's cynic. *Look at the state of the people that trusted you. Anthir is war-torn, Noxolu has had to fight that war, Benny is dead, Neffily is a hostage and Wynn lives at the whims of a monster.* His eyes fell to his hands, the source of his misery. *It's easy to blame Aeg for it all, but really, it was you.*

"I guess I was being unfair," admitted Birger.

"Me too," added Renate pensively.

The two stood there in silence for a little while until Birger said, "Renate."

"Go ahead, Birger," she gave him a sad smile, "you can ask me now."

"What's a Jor monger?"

"Jormunger," corrected Renate. "My name was once Shrenatelious of the Zhraacias Den. My people have been extinct since the Age of Horror, and as far as I know, I'm the last."

Birger hesitated. "I..." he thought about his reaction when he saw her and regretted reaching for his rapier. He wanted to be honest with Renate and mend his bridges at the same time. She was a friend, and he needed her now more than ever. "You might be the most beautiful thing I've ever seen, and I just saw a stillari for the first time."

Renate blushed, her eyes softening. "Aw, that is so sweet, Birger. I was worried you would be afraid of me, like when you learned about Eric."

"It would be a lie if I said you didn't startle me, but you've been the most consistently positive thing in my life since I met you." Birger kicked at the edge of a paving stone and said, "Look. I'm a hothead, but I want you to know that I appreciate everything you've done for me, and I'm sorry I make things hard sometimes, Shhr... rana... Renate."

She burst out laughing. "Renate is fine. You don't have the tongue for it!"

Birger joined in as they shared a moment of relief.

"I'm going to head back to the Saint's Cup for now," said Renate. "I think I'll do more good, helping refugees than fighting on the walls."

Birger nodded.

"You should talk to Lorenzo," Renate suggested. Then she turned and waved as she left him to ruminate.

51

CONSEQUENCES

Birger and Lorenzo walked in silence, except for the deafening heartbeat drummed in Birger's ears. The breeze, laced with the acrid smell of smoke, relentlessly tugged at his hood. He remembered his decision not to leave things unsaid, despite the embarrassment currently weighing on his lips.

Lorenzo paused near the top of the Pilgrim's Rise, squinting at the gate, his hand tense on Kazania's ornate black hilt. Birger came to stand next to him, clearing his throat to speak, when Lorenzo stiffened, putting his hand on Birger's shoulder.

"What's that?" asked Lorenzo, pointing at the middle section of the northern wall.

Birger followed the finger. He had to squint to see. The battlements were only a mile away, but the writhing chaos made discerning details hard. Until he noticed what Lorenzo was pointing at. Red lightning flashed around a single figure in scarlet armour. The warrior moved so fast that they were only visible thanks to the red arcs trailing behind them. Bang, bang, bang. The figure annihilated three squads of paladins in quick succession. Stepping through the resulting explosions as if they were mere puffs of hot air.

Lorenzo held his quintri-looking-glass to his eye. "By Aeg's tempest! It's Ulfhild."

Terror gripped Birger, his heart redoubling in rate and volume as if trying to break free from his chest. His voice quivered as he asked, "How's that possible?"

Birger noticed Lorenzo's jaw tense and his knuckles white where he held the quintri-looking-glass. He saw Ulfhild pause, hoisting her daggers in the air. With more red lightning flickering around her, she slammed a thundering blow against the top of the rampart.

There was a bright explosion. Charging soldiers were flung to their deaths, great big chunks of stone plowed through the buildings of Saint Armand Borough. Crushing at least two field-infirmaries.

It didn't take long for green bodies to pour through the gap in the wall and overwhelm the stunned defenders.

"The east command tower is fending off an attack. They won't realise they're being flanked!" shouted Lorenzo. "We have to warn them!" He was already moving, and Birger joined, running for Pilgrim's Rise.

The sun was setting behind the horizon. Billowing smoke and the screams of people dying horribly hung over the city like bad weather. To Birger, it was frightening, and a major part of him wanted to run the other way. Catapults added to the indiscriminate destruction as they fired more flaming boulders into the city.

Although it was faster, descending the thousands of steps was almost as physically taxing as the climb. Birger's thighs and right knee ached all the way to the bottom, and despite Lorenzo's condition, he never slowed. When they reached the Pilgrim's March, Lorenzo broke into a jog. Birger found it hard to keep up.

He considered slipping Chancebringer on, allowing Aeg to give him more stamina. As Renate explained, it would mean everything that could go right in a recovery would and anything that could go wrong wouldn't. The healing magic already there would get supercharged. But he wasn't ready to accept that sort of help. Not yet. Instead, Birger dug deep, willing himself to push through the pain.

More refugees flooded past him, their faces twisted in fear, eyes glazed with terror. Seeing a father trying to wrangle his seven children, with the help of their family dog, sent a pang through Birger's heart. He could taste the desperation in the air, a vile mixture that made his stomach churn.

The people of the city had traded oppressive fear for hot panic. He heard a few screams coming from areas he knew hadn't been affected by either the catapults or the invaders. He didn't want to consider the reasons. He had his hands full already.

"We need to get to the watch commander and get him to bolster the defences to the north or they'll be slaughtered," Lorenzo shouted over the din.

"Wouldn't they have seen the explosion?" asked Birger, out of breath.

"It's hard to notice things when someone's trying to kill you," said Lorenzo, ducking into Eckland Street. "And they should've responded by now."

A flaming boulder tore through the buildings just north of Birger and Lorenzo. The two of them dove for cover as debris shot out, shattering windows. A dust cloud rolled across the road.

Lorenzo helped Birger to his feet and asked, "How's the knee?"

"Fine," lied Birger. It was throbbing and stiff.

"Let's keep going," urged Lorenzo, smiling as if their argument never happened. "We're within a mile of the main tower. We can do this!"

How could this man have been a pirate? Birger thought. *A man willing to sacrifice his health and life for the good of others. However,* Birger corrected, *I've seen him in battle. When he says he fights to kill, he's not kidding.*

In Birger's mind, Lorenzo was untouchable. He had been taking that for granted, putting the man on a pedestal. *No, Lorenzo is just a man like any other. He made mistakes, had regrets, and knew how it felt to lose loved ones.*

It doesn't matter if this Hein hates Lorenzo or if Lorenzo has a dark past, Birger challenged himself. *He's trying his best to make a difference in the world. I, on the other hand, spent the last two years on my spiteful quest for revenge against an absent father.* He knew they were heading into extreme danger. *What if something happened, and I hadn't said anything?*

Birger caught Lorenzo by the shoulder before he could turn away. The other man looked at him expectantly.

"I know this isn't the time," Birger coughed from smoke wafting over them. "Excuse me..." the acrid smell was in his nose and the air suddenly felt powdery dry, scratching at his throat and making it itch with thirst.

Lorenzo smiled as Birger took a swig from his waterskin and tried again. "Sorry, the smoke just caught me in the back of the throat. Listen..."

Birger was interrupted by tendrils of ice, wind, and water bursting forth to blast Lorenzo off his feet, smashing him into the wall. Birger gasped in shock, his eyes wide and unblinking as he watched Lorenzo's armour crackle with white frost. Seeing the man's lips turn blue, his hair stiff with ice as he lay motionless, Birger's heart dropped to his stomach.

52

SURVIVE

Birger had no time to think and narrowly avoided Lorenzo's fate. He rolled as the blast of ice sliced into the wall. The yellow plaster and brick of the building melted away, causing the second story to collapse onto the first, much like a horse stepping on a mushroom. The resulting dust rushed into Birger's mouth, nose, and eyes. It stung, and he coughed.

Adrenaline made Birger's heart pound out of control. He ripped his rapier from its sheath with one hand and snatched up a fist-sized rock with the other. Coming to his feet, he blindly hurled the stone at the source of the blast. A yelp told him the shot landed, and the icy torrent dwindled.

"Cos-damned gutter rat!" snarled a familiar gravelly voice, anger surging through Birger like wildfire.

The ground beneath his feet was slick with mud, but Birger's balance held as he charged towards the source of the attack, a narrow alley between a cobbler shop and the smoldering remains of a building.

Bo held a blue crystal that looked like it contained a miniature tornado, spluttering tiny bits of ice and water. His messy red hair was sprinkled with dirt, wearing the mutts' customary black leather armour, a painful welt on his cheek.

Birger thrust his rapier at Bo, but a large block-shaped man with a bald head emerged from the dusty murk, blocking the attack with a heavy wooden mallet. Birger hopped back, his sore knee causing his right leg to lag, but he narrowly avoided a lunge from another mutt wielding a longsword. Someone sat on the ground as if flung there.

Bo skulked forward, a scowl scrunching up his bulldog face. "Not running this time?"

Saliva, turning gritty from the dust, burned Birger's throat. "Trying something new," he said, narrowing his eyes, and spitting on the ground.

The three mutts spread out to encircle him. Bo was to the right, the swordsman in the middle, and the man with the mallet to the left. Each of them wore the same black armour, covered in mud, which was the same colour as Kindra's rocky cliffs. Mallet-man had a sinister leer that sent a shiver down Birger's spine.

"Oh good, the jesters have arrived for the show," jibed Birger. Bo would expect some banter from him. He could use that.

Bo began speaking, the opening Birger was looking for. He pounced forward, feigning a thrust at the swordsman, but at the last second slashed at the mallet wielding mutt. The ploy worked, and the rapier caught the big balding man on the inside of his exposed arm. A squirt of blood indicated that Birger nicked something important. The man cried out in pain, dropping his mallet.

Birger ducked back, parrying the longsword just in time, but his rapier warped around the stronger blade. The air suddenly went a freezing powder dry like before, and recognising the tell, Birger dove behind the cobbler shop for cover. He was too late; his lagging right leg got caught. An intense cold enveloped his foot, rushing up his leg like a wave of icy fire.

A girl's voice cried out in despair, and Birger fell to the ground, uselessly clutching at his thigh. Bo stepped into sight, dragging a girl by her hair. "This little wretch saved you twice now. But I don't need you dead. With luck, the ice won't grow any further and you'll lose the leg. At worst, it'll slowly grow until it turns you into one of Lot's own icicles. Either way, your days of messing with our plans are over."

Wynn struggled against Bo's grip, crying out, "Let Birger go! You said you wouldn't hurt him!"

Bo pulled a hand back to threaten a slap, but Wynn refused to cower. Instead, she just stared him down. When the big man saw the defiance in her, his face turned red and he struck, her head whipping back from the force.

"Wynn!" Birger shouted. A pang of desperation running up his spine as he saw her tear-stained face and bleeding lip.

"Boss," said the big bald man, "this cut is bad. It won't stop bleeding."

"Go get patched up," said Bo, glancing briefly at the man. "Birger's finished."

The balding man turned and vanished into the gloom.

Bo threw Wynn aside, drawing his short-sword, and said, "You stay there and I won't gut him when I'm done."

Birger saw Wynn's eyes flash, but she didn't move.

Bo grinned at her, "There's a good girl. There might be hope for you yet." Then he stalked towards Birger. "I have to say, you've changed since we last fought on the rooftops around Foss's apartment. Striking before we've even had a bit of banter? What's happened to you?"

The burning pain in Birger's foot exceeded anything else he had experienced in the last few weeks by a huge margin, and he barely managed to stay conscious. "I...grew up when...you and your boss...killed my friend," said Birger through clenched teeth, and his body shook from the cold.

He saw sadness in Bo's eyes, but only for a moment before his jaw set. "We've all lost people..." The way Bo looked at Birger felt like an unvoiced accusation. "You've created quite a few problems for me since Anthir."

The mutt swordsman stepped past Wynn, raising his weapon to strike. Birger hefted his bent rapier in a useless defence, but Bo raised his hand.

"No," Bo said with a grin as he walked over to Birger. "Even if he survives, he can't stop us with his leg like that." To Birger, he said, "Now, let's get that bracelet you stole."

"He doesn't have it! The Queen took it from him," said Wynn. Birger thought her voice sounded strong, and her lie convincing.

"So you said," Bo glanced at her. "But I think you're sweet on the mark, and you might be lying; I'll check for myself. No thief would give up that much power so easily."

"Are you alright Wynn?" Birger asked, fighting through his agony.

She smiled weakly back at him. Her lip quivering. "I'll be fine."

"Bo, let Wynn go, or I'll kick you in your ugly dog-face with my ice leg," Birger threatened.

Bo chuckled and said, "I'll take my chances."

When Bo came within reach, Birger swiped his bent sword out, but the freezing cold made him sluggish. With minimal effort, Bo smacked Birger's attack aside, grabbing his wrist.

"Hold still," said Bo as he quickly stashed the blue crystal in his pocket. He forcefully wrenched Birger's rapier from his grip and tossed it into the burning rubble nearby. Bo twisted his hand painfully in search of Chancebringer. Not finding his prize, he took the other arm to repeat the action.

"Are you serious?" Bo glowered at Birger, "I didn't think a puffed-up queen could get the better of you, Light Foot. Though I guess I wouldn't have caught you so easily if you had the thing? Well, Ulfhild's going to be upset with you."

"Sounds like me," retorted Birger, his voice thin and his breath pluming with the cold.

Birger stifled a sigh of relief when Bo didn't check his pouches, and thought to himself, *Thank Aeg for the greedy and the dumb.*

Despite the minor victory, every fiber of Birger's being screamed with a desire to help Wynn. He waited for Bo to look at the swordsman before he struck. His fist connected with the bigger man's square jaw, and Bo staggered back. Birger pushed up. Despite his body weighing a ton, he made it to his feet before Bo recovered and Birger took an awkward boxer's pose.

"You mollusc!" Bo roared, but when he saw Birger ready for a fistfight, he laughed.

A soldier's voice shouted, "Down!" as a flaming boulder screamed through the sky. Bo, Wynn and the swordsman were driven back into the alley when the missile landed in the cobbler's shop with explosive force. Shrapnel cut Birger's chin and brow before he could dive for cover. His eyes stung by tiny pebbles that felt like erupting volcanos.

Birger collapsed on the main road in a weary mass of tangled limbs. The warning had come from a paladin in the colours of Aeg, at the head of a company of troops rapidly marching down Eckland Street.

Bo looked at them and cursed. He yanked Wynn up by the hair. "Time to go."

Wynn shook herself free and bolted past the swordsman, who looked like he might give chase, but Bo forestalled him. "Don't bother. She has nowhere to go but back to base."

"If those bedpans get here, they'll draft us to the wall defence," warned the swordsman.

Bo nodded and turning to Birger he shouted, "I would say next time, but with *that* creeping up your leg, your odds aren't good. It isn't personal. I've got work to do."

Bo tipped his head in greeting, turned and ran, quickly disappearing into the twilight gloom. Birger, shivering from the cold and consumed by concern for Lorenzo and Wynn, barely registered that Bo was leaving him to potentially freeze to death.

"Coward!" he shouted through the shivers.

I have to help Lorenzo, I have to stop Bo, I have to save Wynn...
Birger repeated it over and over in his mind like a mantra to keep himself moving.

Crawling over to Lorenzo, Birger's right leg was stiff and his endurance at its limits. The clatter of running soldiers became deafening. None of them slowed down to look at the pair on the ground. It looked like they were heading to Pilgrim's March to contain the enemy pouring in through the demolished north wall. The soldiers had no time to worry about another couple of dying souls among many.

53

AEG PLEASE

Birger put his hand on Lorenzo's chest and plucked it away from the intense cold. He hissed in pain as some of his skin clung to the frozen armour. Lorenzo's face was pale, with white puffs escaped his blue lips. Icicles tracked up his neck and jaw, reaching for his ears.

"Hey," Birger shivered. "I'm going to get you to Renate. She can save you. Come on."

Using his cloak to shield his hands, Birger tried to pick Lorenzo up, but his own strength failed and they crumpled onto the pavement.

"N-no time, you'll d-die too," Lorenzo spoke through chattering teeth. "Here, take my gear. Kazania. She's an o-oath blade, forged by the stillari, master smith, Quelonje. I made an oath to stop Ulfhild. If Kazania f-fails, it'll, destroy her. T-take her. Finish this."

"Finish it yourself," said Birger, not wanting to accept Lorenzo's impending death. "Don't talk like that. You'll be fine. You'll see. Just hang on, okay?"

"Birger," Lorenzo grabbed him by the scruff of his neck, "I'm, already d-dead. You can't save me. Here," his face was a mask of pain, and twitched as he struggled to unbuckle his belts. Ice cracked and flaked off him.

Finally, Lorenzo pushed his gear with Kazania into Birger's chest, but Birger didn't want to accept it. Taking them felt like giving up, which he wasn't ready to do.

Lorenzo said, "It's your time now. I know you'll figure it out." He gave a wan smile. "Please... tell Renate and Eric that Becka will take care of them."

Lorenzo paused, his eyes softening with regret, "And B-Birger, p-please tell Armandine... I love her. I'll w-wait for her in Anchorhall."

The frost reclaimed the areas that had flaked away from Lorenzo. Birger's heart ached, and he fought back tears. Lorenzo convulsed and shook. Then he stopped shivering.

"Oh, I'm not so cold anymore," said Lorenzo, and the frost continued to climb up his cheek, reaching for his eyes. "Take the sword, please, for my honour, and you'll need her."

Birger put his hand over the sword. "I won't let you down, Lorenzo," he said, clutching Lorenzo's frozen hand with his right, embracing the icy agony as if it was penance for his sins. "I'm so sorry for what I said before. It was foolish."

Lorenzo kept smiling as the frost reached his eyes, and they glazed over. The infrequent white clouds emitting from his mouth ceased, and Lorenzo's hand creaked. His skin felt as cold and unyielding as stone, but Birger couldn't accept that he was gone.

"No. Come on, stay awake, keep talking. You're going to make it."

Birger forced a smile and tried to pick Lorenzo up, but with the bottom half of his leg frozen solid, he couldn't find purchase on the paving stones. He slipped and crashed to the ground.

Two of Lorenzo's fingers snapped off and dashed into shards where they landed. That triggered an uncontrollable rage in Birger, who screamed at the top of his lungs and banged his fists on the wall.

Sobbing, he continued to scream, and when he ran out of breath, he shouted, "Lot, please, bring him back! We need him!"

He let out another roar of emotion, thinking, *I can't do this without Lorenzo. How can the goddesses let this happen?*

You should've listened to the priestess, replied Birger's cynic. *Had you not been too stubborn to use Chancebringer, this might not have happened.*

Shut your rotten-fish's mouth! Birger raged at himself, but that wasn't someone else's thoughts. It was his own. He thought about that. *Maybe if I put it on now, there could be someway I can still bring Lorenzo back, maybe Renate will appear down the street and save him.*

Birger fumbled in his pouches for the onyx band, taking what felt like an eternity to open the buckle with his numb, shaking hands. Eventually, he got the thing out. Slipping Chancebringer onto his wrist, but the cord was still connected to his ribs.

With no other option, Birger pulled Kazania out of her sheath, just enough to run the thread over the blade's edge, and the web snapped. He let the sword drop back into the scabbard and put it down.

Birger grabbed Lorenzo by the shoulders, saying, "Come on, here we go. Lorenzo, come back. I put it on. Okay, Aeg, please, help me."

What did you think would happen? thought Birger's cynic. *He's already dead. It's too late for luck.*

The realisation brought new tears and sobs. He shook. The ice around his leg shattered as Birger dropped to his knees. It burned like a jellyfish had stung him, but his toes could move.

He leaned his forehead against the wall, tears falling to the ground, his strength waning as the cold crept into his body.

Darkness fell, and Birger finally regrouped. The sound of battle echoed from nearby, perhaps two houses to the west. He thought of Wynn being chucked around, like she was only a mooring line. She still needed him.

A scream came from nearby, followed by the yipping of nikkuni. An explosive force shook the rubble behind Birger. The sound of another Paladin falling echoed off the buildings, the Wartide was pushing the city defenders back, inch by inch.

Gullshite! Birger's cynic cursed at him. *You idiot! We failed to warn the command tower. The city is being overrun. Renate is going to be trapped in the Saint's Cup because you were sitting here feeling sorry for yourself.*

The thought brought Birger back to his senses. His legs were stiff, especially the right one. He pushed himself up, and thought, *I have to move; I have to save Renate before she gets stuck.* Birger looked down at Lorenzo's body, shaking his head, and thinking, *I can't leave him here like this.*

He tried to remind himself that what lay before him wasn't Lorenzo anymore. Birger scanned around and then dragged what remained of his friend into a small space beneath the rubble. Pulling his cloak off his back, he covered Lorenzo's face.

He paused for a regret-filled moment.

"I won't let you down, my friend," said Birger, strapping the sword belt on and layering the gadget-filled pouches over his shoulders.

With renewed urgency, Birger headed towards the Saint's Cup to find Renate. It was only three blocks away. Despite the pain and stiffness from his ice-encased leg, he pressed on.

"Pain is penance," he muttered with every step.

54

GOT TO MOVE

Birger stumbled through the green door of the Saint's Cup, the deafening din of battle ringing in the street behind him. A troop of children swarmed around Henry the innkeeper as he hurried to Birger's side.

When Henry placed a hand on Birger's shoulder, he hissed and stepped back.

"Don't touch him," Henry said to the children, pulling the dishcloth from his belt as protection while offering Birger a steadying hand. "By the mercy of the five, boy. You look like you barely escaped Lot's vault."

Birger's leg was frozen solid and ice flaked from his clothes. "R-Renate," he muttered, with a white plume escaping his mouth.

Not waiting for instructions, one of the little girls turned to run towards the stairs. "Lady Renate!" she called out as she went.

Using the washcloth and covering his other hand with his shirt, Henry dragged Birger fully inside. To one of the bigger boys, he said, "Bartholemew, the door."

Birger saw a boy with a mop of red hair, clad in simple farmer's clothes, rush past. The door slammed shut, dulling the noise outside.

"Y-you've got to go." Birger shivered; his words sounded too loud in his own ears. "T-the wall is o-overrun."

"By Cos," Henry invoked, his moustache twitching nervously. He grabbed a tablecloth to wrap around Birger, hauling him to a bench. Henry lifted Birger onto the wooden surface with the strength of a man that spent his life doing heavy labour, and said, "First, let's get you seen to." He hollered to the kitchen, "Tricia, bring towels and hot water, lots of it!"

"Birger!" Renate cried from the stairs. "What happened?"

He watched Renate rush over with her healer's kit in hand, the many people filling the common room parting to let her through.

"By Jor," Renate said as she placed the healer's kit down. "Where's Lorenzo?"

A pang of regret choked Birger as he began. He still wanted to believe it had all been a bad dream, but he knew that was only fanciful thinking. Birger didn't want to talk about what happened, but he had learned his lesson. Leaving things unsaid can end badly.

Finally Birger uttered, "He's gone."

Renate didn't stop what she was doing. She simply shot him a questioning glance, asking, "Gone? How?"

"The f-frost..." Birger struggled to find his breath. His throat felt tight and dry. "Bo shot him with the frost," he tilted his head towards his leg.

Birger saw tears fill Renate's eyes and one trickled down her cheek. She took a deep breath, evicting the emotion. A droplet fell from her chin on Birger's arm. It hissed and turned to steam.

"Stay with me Birger," said Renate, opening a weave-rift with a pop. "I'm not ready to lose you both on the same day."

"Quickly," Henry urged a woman coming into the common room.

Tricia's eyes were dark pools that matched the colour of her curly hair. Her skin, the deep chocolate shade of Korland. She clutched a large basin sloshing with steaming water in front of her, several towels draped over her shoulder.

As she placed the basin on the table next to Birger, Henry nodded to her and said, "Thank you, Tricia."

"Any help I can give." Tricia had a rich smile, her bright white teeth a stark contrast to her dark skin. "By the grand scales, youngin you look like you seen death well done."

Birger wasn't sure if he should grimace or grin at the comment. He was in some respects too cold to care.

"Soak the towels," instructed Renate as she reached into her weave-rift. "I'll be needing them shortly."

Tricia complied, plunging each of the towels into the steaming water and letting them soak.

Renate extracted several long lengths of webbing that she lay down on the table. With a tool that looked like a rolling-pin, she started working the substance into a sheet. "Towels," she requested.

Henry bunched his sleeves to the elbow and extracted a towel from the bowl. He prepared to drape the cloth over Birger when Renate intercepted him.

"Not yet. Lay it down on the sheet I made," guided Renate, helping him place the towel on the spell crafting such that it maximised the space it covered. "Keep layering the towels over the sheet until it's covered completely."

Henry nodded and did as she asked, while Birger watched Renate extract more thick cords from the weave. Seemingly satisfied that she had enough, she snapped the rift shut. Laying the new lengths on another table, she started rolling them flat with the pin.

By the time Henry put the last towel in place, she cast her new crafting over the top and sealed it all like a large blanket. The spell steamed, and a bright blue glow radiated from it when Renate wrapped it around Birger. He could hardly breathe under it's weight.

He felt like an Everwinter Sea char thawing after the seasonal ice. His breathing became less laboured. His hands and feet returned to life with pins and needles. But as the cold fled, excruciating pain replaced it.

A scream burst from Birger's mouth, raw and agonising. For a fleeting moment, he didn't realise that the chilling scream was his own. Pale faces, their eyes wide with shock and concern, were staring at him.

"Tricia," said Renate, not looking up from her work. "Do you have any Korland coffee?"

"Coins of Thash, Lady Couture, of course I do," replied the dark-skinned woman.

"Please, could you make some?" Renate looked up and smiled at Tricia.

"On it." Birger saw Tricia nod before running to the kitchen.

A few of the refugees were gawking at Renate's work while others tried to keep their children from getting in the way. All in all, there were close to a hundred people in the room, and Birger felt the urgency to get them to the mountain redouble.

"They've taken the wall," Birger managed through the pain. At least the teeth chattering had stopped. "We've got to get all these people out of here and back to the temples."

"Easy Birger," said Renate, stroking his brown hair, "you need to rest and get your strength back."

"No time." Birger shook his head. "Got to get people ready to go. Ulfhild blasted a hole in the wall. The greens are in the city. We have to –"

Birger's words were cut off by the loud resonance of bells echoing throughout the city.

"The final defence warning," said Henry, twirling his long grey moustache nervously. "They're calling us to Pilgrim's Rise. I'll get the people ready to move."

The older man walked out of Birger's sight, his voice booming as he began organising the group of refugees. The vibration of feet stomping and chairs moving on the wood floor trilled through the surface beneath him.

"Can you fix me up enough to run?" asked Birger, his eyes closing despite his insistence to the contrary. Sleep was an inviting promise of respite.

Renate huffed in frustration, running her hands through her hair. Then she swept one palm over the spell work that covered Birger. He craned his neck to see what she was doing. Around Renate's outspread fingers, the surface of the spell became clear as glass, revealing down to Birger's skin beneath.

"You have cold burns all over your chest and neck," said Renate as she catalogued the damage, "but nothing too extreme. I can numb the thawing pain, but it'll get a lot worse again tomorrow." She moved her hand down and gasped. "The connection with Chancebringer! It's been severed."

"That was me," said Birger, using his head to point to his right side.

Renate looked at Birger's wrist. "You put it on?"

"Yeah," Birger blushed. "Stupidly, I thought it could save Lorenzo."

Renate continued scanning Birger's body and said, "It might not have saved him, but it *did* save you. The spell that kept your knee together also contained the spreading frost. A life saving stroke of luck."

"How bad is it?" asked Birger, confused.

Renate explained, "Whatever you got shot with was alive, but my spell has smothered it. If you hadn't reached me when you did, hypothermia from extreme cold exposure would've killed you anyway."

With a weak smile, Birger said, "Thanks for saving me again."

"You know this means you can never take it off, right?" Renate asked.

"It saved my life, so luck reclaiming will kill me. Yeah, I get it."

Renate grimaced, the sadness in her eyes palpable as the immediate urgency of Birger's condition waned. "You said Bo did this?"

Birger's lip quivered as emotion welled up in his chest. "He had Wynn. She saved my life, but – by the Code, we have to get these people out."

344

"Henry?" Renate shot a glance at the mobilising crowd.

The old man paused between instructions to direct the refugees. "Nearly ready Lady Couture."

Renate nodded and turned back to Birger. "I'm almost done here. Let's see what I can do to make you travel ready."

Birger watched as the view in the spell crafting deepened to show muscle and skeleton. She checked his ribs. Scar tissue formed a ridge across the bone, where a thread spooled around it like rope.

How did she wind the thread along my bone like that? Birger wondered in awe. *She must've done it last night while I was unconscious.*

Next, Renate scanned the leg and said, "You've done a lot of damage to this knee. I can make it usable for the night, but seriously…pushing it…in this state…you could end up with a limp for the rest of your—"

"I know, I know," Birger interrupted, shaking his head dismissively. The pain suppression of Renate's spell crafting was kicking in, and Birger found himself more functional by the moment. "Not much choice, is there?"

Tricia returned with a steaming ceramic cup. "One fresh life giving coffee, Lady. My, my, don't you look like a happy pig in a blanket there, youngin. I assume the pain has passed, then?"

Tricia had the kind of smile that eased your mood. She and Henry seemed like good people, friendlier than most, and Birger wished he had visited under better circumstances.

Renate took the coffee from Tricia with thanks and put the cup to Birger's lips. The liquid was hot, scolding his tongue, but it tasted refreshing, with a rich, earthy scent that made Birger feel revitalised with warmth. When the cup was half empty, Renate put it down on the table.

"You look better," said Renate.

Birger noted she didn't smile. She usually smiled after helping him, but with Lorenzo gone, he couldn't blame her. He didn't feel much like smiling either.

But then again, Birger thought, *what do we have left if we let bad things happening steal our smiles? Ulfhild and Bo have taken a lot from me. Sten, Benny, Anthir, and now Lorenzo… And they nearly took my humanity, my ability to see the bright side of things… my hope. No, I won't let them take my sense of humour, not today, not ever.*

345

Gritting his teeth through the pain as he moved, Birger forced a smirk. "What do you mean, I look better? I look great," he quipped, popping his eyebrows playfully.

Renate barked a laugh and then shook her head. Taking up a sharp knife from her kit, she slid it along the side of the spell. It peeled away, allowing Birger some room to test his joints. They were all working. For the moment, he found the pain only a distant throb.

Determination flickered to life in Renate's eyes as she handed him the cup of coffee. "Let's get you mobile."

Birger sipped at it, watching Renate cut a strip from the sheet. She knelt and begun strapping the length of spell crafting around his right knee, then brushed her hand over it, shifting the color from blue to pink. He could feel the spell working. Most of the pain was already gone, and more strength filled him with every passing second.

Birger scanned over the group of elderly, mothers and children. "Now let's hope we can still reach Pilgrim's Rise in time."

55

RUNNING THE GAUNTLET

The Saint's Cup Inn exploded as a giant flaming boulder crashed through the roof. It splintered the walls, engulfing the structure in flames that lit up the night sky. Luckily, Birger and Renate, with their entourage of refugees and inn staff, were already hobbling along Pilgrim's March. Birger saw loss flash across Henry's weathered eyes at the sight of his business in ruins, and his long grey moustache twitched with anger.

There was no time to grieve. Henry blocked the serrated blade of a nikkuni's sword with a large iron frying pan. The nik yipped as it hopped about. Its broad, leaf-like ears flapping and spittle spraying from its grinning maw of jagged teeth. Lashing out with his butcher's cleaver, Henry lopped the small greenskin's arm clean off.

The creature squealed in a high pitch, which was cut short as the cleaver lashed out a second time to find the nikkuni's neck. The old innkeeper fought with unexpected ferocity, leaving Birger well impressed.

Kazania sliced through the thick smoke that hung in the fire-lit air as Birger fended off his own assailant. He didn't feel so tired when holding Kazania, like she fed him strength and stamina. The sword was light in his hand, but when the blade connected with a target, it landed with the weight of a heavy longsword. Wielding her was intoxicating – the blade moved with fluid grace, every stroke an elegant testament to perfect balance. It felt like he was dancing.

A hulking ukthuun with red face paint streaked over its green cheeks charged towards Birger. Avoiding the attack with a deft evasive roll, Birger swung Kazania in a wide arc, slashing across the brute's armoured back. The thick hide plates parted as easily as if Birger had struck bare skin.

The uk roared in pain and struck out with a backhand blow, aimed at Birger's head. But ducking underneath, Birger thrust Kazania clear through the bruiser's chest. The towering figure slumped, and Birger pulled his blade free, stepping into the next enemy.

It wasn't just the sword that had enhanced Birger's ability to fight. Chancebringer felt different from the last time he wore it. He figured it must've been thanks to Snow, being a weavespider, eating all enigmites collected on it. The artefact's power was now more tangible. It allowed him to sense things coming, like a distant voice, warning him of what lurked beyond his sight, guiding his steps. It prompted him to duck and told him where to strike. It felt like the world shifted so Birger could stay ahead of his enemies.

With the combined support of Henry, the artefacts, and Renate's healing, Birger held the greenskins away from the refugees. However, he didn't escape unscathed. Knowing what was coming didn't mean he could always avoid it – especially with his numb right leg – and he was tiring. He worried he wouldn't be able to maintain the pace all the way across the city.

At every street and alley, the city defenders lay down their lives to hold the enemy. They held out, hoping more refugees would make it to the safety of Pilgrim's Rise and its defensible mountain top.

The soldiers retreating from the West Wall looked especially battered. Having been caught unaware, they only narrowly avoided being wiped out. Seeing them limp along the road made Birger worry for his other four teammates. Are they even still alive?

This wasn't the time for thinking. Birger whirled and Kazania licked across a nik's chest, splitting its armour to expose the creature's beating heart. Birger put a pin in it and moved on.

"You and Henry can't cover us alone!" cried Renate, clutching at the front of her dress as she stepped over the body of a fallen militiaman. "I have to help."

"No," Birger stopped her, "if you transform here, the defenders might mistake you for an enemy."

Before Renate could reply, a rider drew their attention as they came thundering down the road from the west. They rode a Sawran highlander that trampled several niks under its large hooves. Atop the intimidating beast, Birger saw the long, white hair and intense blue eyes of Brother Hein.

Not this rat-arse...

He swept his spear along like a club, crumpling greenskins as he passed them. The cleric slowed as he reached the convoy. His armour was covered in gore and his features marred with black soot.

"Hurry," called Hein, "get to the Pilgrim's Rise."

"Thanks Sir shouts-a-lot," replied Birger sarcastically as he herded a group of fleeing children through the chaos. "Where do you think we were going? Thornhall?"

Hein didn't hear the comment as he flashed by, but Renate gave Birger a wry smile. The horse passed by a cluster of defenders holding Town Street. Abruptly, a soldier was hurled through the air, colliding with Hein and unseating him from his mount in a cacophony of clattering armour. Another two defenders flew back, and Birger rushed forwards to help.

A towering behemoth, nine feet tall and just as broad, built of solid, pale-green muscle, grabbed a soldier by the helmet. With seemingly little effort, the monster popped the man's head like an overripe tomato. The creature had two thin horns poking out from either side of it's cabbage like head, a long tuft of black hair hung from the back. It had jagged pieces of rusted metal strapped along its forearms. Using the crude armour as a weapon, the monster hacked a man's head off, while another soldier broke their spear on the creature's thick hide.

This hulking piece of muscle was the first siphuun Birger had ever seen in person. The monster's roar smelled like offal. It grabbed a sweeping sword blade in its bare hand and proceeded to beat the owner to death with the pummel of their own weapon.

"Move!" shouted Birger to Henry, Renate, and the refugees. "I'll try to buy you some time!"

Renate clearly wanted to protest, but before she could, a young girl tripped right in front of her. Renate snatched the child up and shouted to Birger, "Stay alive!"

Birger nodded and swallowed hard. He wasn't sure he could promise her that, but sometimes you had to take your chances.

He watched as a militiaman had his arm ripped off by the siphuun. The monster stuck the bloody end in its mouth and chewed on the stump, while the fallen soldier's friends swarmed around to attack it, to no effect, none of them even drew blood. The creature gulped the bloody mess down, proceeding to use its half-eaten meal as a club. Striking the surrounding soldiers down, one by one.

"Cos, give me strength," said Hein from behind Birger.

Birger swung around to see the cleric conjure a weave rift, drawing a cord as long as his spear from it. Hein pressed the weave fibers against his weapon, setting it to glow golden yellow. The rift snapped shut, and the cleric thrust his spear into the air, shooting a copy up in a burst of radiating light. If you ignored the light, it looked the same as Hein's spear but moved under its own power.

The new flying weapon shot forward with Hein close behind it. Chancebringer urged Birger to take the opportunity, and he joined Hein's charge. They struck the siphuun at the same time. All three weapons cut into the monster, eliciting a roar of pain. The creature leapt back into a low crouch, smouldering rage carving the siphuun's face into deep valleys.

"I've never pissed off a cabbage before," joked Birger.

"Go left!" shouted Hein as he darted right.

Birger did as he was told without hesitation, and it saved his life as the giant rolled forward, missing them both by a hair's breadth.

"Keep him busy!" shouted Hein as he popped another rift open.

"Sure, why don't I just let big green and ugly here crunch on my bones while you play with magic?" Birger chided.

Despite himself, Birger pounced forward in a thrust, but the monster deflected the attack, using the plates on its forearm.

Not just strong then, also smart, thought Birger. Thankfully, the autonomous glowing spear hit the siphuun from the side to keep it from focusing on Birger.

Birger struck again. Ready for the defensive maneuver, Kazania had no trouble cutting through the iron armour. A grunt from the siphuun said that the creature felt her bite. Between Birger and the magic spear, they were drawing blood and causing discomfort, but not much more.

The monster exploded into a vicious flurry. But Birger was quicker, thanks to Chancebringer's warning and Kazania increasing his speed. He rolled under a sweeping arm as thick as a mature pine and came up to see Hein strapping a sheet of spell craft over his shield.

"Close your eyes and get ready to run!" shouted the cleric.

Birger didn't appreciate being ordered around by the arrogant man, but now wasn't the time to be stubborn, so he pinched his eyes closed.

The radiant light bursting from the shield made Birger's eyelids glow red, like facing direct sunlight. When the effect faded, Birger risked a look. The siphuun staggered, holding its eyes, and casting around at random, trying to grab anyone he could reach.

"Go, go, go!" Hein was already running, while his magic spear continued to distract the siphuun.

Birger made a break for it. Meanwhile, Hein mounted his horse and kicked it into a gallop, abandoning Birger in the chaos.

With disgust, Birger shouted, "Happy to be a distraction for you anytime!"

He spat on the floor, *rat-arse*. He raced off after Renate. She had already reached the base of the Pilgrim's Rise.

Above, on the platform that looked like a ship's deck, jutting from the mountainside, Birger could see people. They were all busy opening weave rifts, crafting and casting spells that rained down on the greenskins.

Among them, he recognised High Priestess Ishyelle. The stillari woman cast something pulsing bright red into the enemy. It looked like a large ball with a maw of vicious fangs. When it hit, the ball shredded the Wartide warriors to ribbons in a cacophony of screams.

Next to her stood a stout dwan with a long grey beard wearing heavy plate armour embellished with the pentagon of Jor. His hands disappeared into a stone altar, and with each jerky motion of the old dwan's head, Birger felt the earth shake with the sound of rolling thunder. A dust cloud billowed around the sides of the mountain, and Birger saw in the dark a pair of giant stone arms. They slammed hard into the cliffs, crushing wall-scaling nikkuni like an elaborate fly swatter.

Yet another Stillari stood next to Ishyelle, dressed in purple robes bearing the octagon of Mag. With elaborate hand motions, she sent electric purple missiles into the enemy ranks that withered them to dust.

On the landing of Pilgrim's Rise, Renate tended the wounded. Fatigue made Birger's legs heavy as he reached her and he collapsed on the steps in relief. For the moment, nothing was attempting to murder him, giving him a chance to look back at the burning city.

"Cos, did you see that up there?" asked Birger. "That dwan is making arms come out of the mountainside!"

"I noticed." Renate nodded. Her expression was sombre as she wrapped a bandage around an unconscious soldier's arm.

"I would never have imagined something like that when I was living in Anthir," said Birger, shaking his head, and looking over the sour faces of the refugees. Henry and Tricia took care of them, handing out food and water to the children. Birger could hardly believe they had all survived.

"What do we do now?" asked Birger, truly feeling at his wit's end.

Could this be it? No way to save Wynn, because I don't know where she is. A major battle about to swallow us, possibly even kill us all?

"Staying alive isn't enough of a plan for you?" asked Renate, moving to another injured soldier.

"Wynn needs help," said Birger, "I doubt Bo'll keep her alive once he has what he wants."

"Why kill her?" asked Renate.

"Why not kill her?" countered Birger. "They were using her to get to me. I've been gotten to. Why not clip her wings? I wish I knew what the maniac was planning."

"They must be going to the chapel, right?"

"Sure, but how?" Birger looked up the stairs. "Entering the temple area required getting past a couple of stern clerics. Even disguised as refugees, monks guard the chapel. That thing Bo has can cut through a building, but it isn't subtle. He would have holy warriors on him faster than he could say 'gullshite' if he tried from this end." Birger pointed to the side of the mountain that thundered with another stone armed smack. "And climbing isn't an option."

"What makes you think they'll try tonight?" asked Renate, finishing with another patient and moving to the next.

Birger noticed how efficiently she worked, barely showing emotion.

It must be a requirement for the job. If you got teary-eyed over every poor soul, you probably wouldn't be any good at it.

Birger's strength was returning, so he wiped Kazania clean and put her away. He came to sit by Renate, helping dress the wound of an unconscious woman who lost an eye.

"Bo said they had work to do," Birger answered. "Besides, Ulfhild broke the wall for a reason. I'm pretty sure they're moving as we speak. If only I could guess their way in."

"Well, what do you know already?"

Birger held the wounded woman's head up while Renate strapped bandages across her face.

"Is this the part where you do your mindweaver thing?" Birger asked.

Renate glanced at him. As she resumed her work, she smiled. "Carry on."

Birger grinned and began, "One, they want something in the chapel. Two, Bo went down to see the tomb of Louis du la Rent.

352

Three, they have a magical device that shoots ice water. I know! They plan to make snow angels in Louis' tomb?"

Renate looked unamused, and said, "Let's put that on the maybe pile. What else?"

"Well, their clothes were covered in black-grey mud, the same colour as the cliffs." Birger put the woman's head on a cloth bundle Renate had placed on the stone.

An idea glimmered just out of Birger's reach, and he put a finger to his lip. It felt like trying to scoop mist into a bucket, but he could sense something there.

"What is it?" asked Renate, looking him in the eye.

"I...I don't know," said Birger.

Renate kept looking at him, not moving.

Birger looked up at Ishyelle. "The High Priestess said that King Louis' tomb was the lowest point of the chapel..."

"Yes?" encouraged Renate.

"Gullshite!" Birger cursed. "I'm a Cos-damned idiot!"

"What? Why?"

56

CHAPEL OF DEATH

Distance turned the din of battle to white noise. Birger could almost mistake it for rolling waves crashing on a beach.

He stalked up the chapel stairs. Ahead, the twin wolf statues stared sullenly down at him. the lantern-light coming from behind made shadows pool in their eyes. Between them, the massive double door stood open.

Birger gulped.

He had expected this to be harder. Sure, they had to be clever to get past the clerics at the top of Pilgrim's Rise. And Renate handled the obstacle with grace by reminding them of the earlier visit with the High Priestess. She let guards believe she was going to see Ishyelle again. Being pushed back into the city's defense would've made things complicated.

"Looks like you were right," Renate said, trailing just behind him.

"Maybe the monks are on a pee break?" he suggested, with a glance back at Renate.

She still wore the same silvery blue dress from earlier that day. Despite several battles, and treating the wounded, her dress was clean, and her long blond hair styled. Knowing that it was all an illusion didn't make it that much easier to reconcile in his mind. His own grey hooded tunic and leather armour were marred with grime, splattered blood, and sported tears of varying sizes.

"Somehow I doubt it." Renate narrowed her eyes.

"It could happen," shrugged Birger and drew Kazania.

Cracking jokes had always been his way of dealing with fear, but he knew Renate was right. The scent of blood drifted on the breeze, and it wasn't all coming from his clothes.

Kazania's magic gave Birger confidence and soothed his aching legs. He would've carried the sword in his hand up those Cos-damned steps leading to the top of the mountain, but that would look odd.

The pair ascended the stairs slowly. When they reached the top, Birger realised there was no red light coming from inside. Beyond the massive double doors, he could see the pool of water, but the stone Valkyrie was missing.

"The Eye—," Birger began, but a loud scream followed by the crunch of stone smacking into stone cut him off.

He rushed into the chapel; the metallic tang of blood overpowered the sweet smell of incense. A funeral procession was painted on the vaulted ceiling, and the stained-glass windows were flanked by gargoyles along the walls.

On the far side of the large fountain at the room's centre lay two monks in pink robes, with their throats slit. Next to them were four dead mutts in black armour, their gore splattering the carpet and tinting the fountain red.

Close to the back of the room, the stone Valkyrie stalked after five more mutts. Birger didn't see Bo and Wynn among them. However, he recognised the swordsman that helped Bo kill Lorenzo. Anger flared in Birger's gut and he had to resist the urge to recklessly charge the man.

The mutts screamed in terror as the Valkyrie swung its stone sword wide, taking down two of them in one blow. With her other hand, the Valkyrie grabbed the swordsman by his head and snapped his neck with a sudden jerk. The mutt's sword clattered to the marble floor. Losing their nerve, the remaining two ran for it.

The scene sickened Birger, and he choked down a mouthful of bile. "They've got the Eye of Winter, Renate!"

She had a serious look in her eyes. Birger saw her open and close her mouth. Then her posture straightened, and she stepped forward, stating, "I'll handle the Valkyrie. Quick, close your eyes!"

Birger did, and there was a bright flash. Opening his eyes, he found Renate had shed her illusion, allowing her true form, a jormunger, to show in all her glory. Colourful feathers glimmered in the firelight, her vast wings spread wide as she uncoiled her long body and faced the Valkyrie.

The grisly scene surrounding them caught Birger's attention, a pang of worry running through him. "No way!" he protested. "That thing's way too dangerous!"

"I have more power to draw in this form," hissed Renate. "I'll be fine. Wait for me to trap it, then go help Wynn."

Birger's thoughts drifted to Lorenzo with a jolt of sadness. 'Teamwork starts with trust.' Hesitating for a moment, he closed his eyes and offered a silent prayer to Aeg for Renate's safety. I can't bear losing another friend today.

"Okay... but don't take any chances." Birger fixed Renate with a look that made it clear he wasn't having any arguments on the topic.

"You know risk is part of the job," she said with a raised eyebrow. "You better come back..."

Birger nodded and dashed towards the far side of the room. Along the back wall were two doors that he hoped led to the same place. In the only other chapel of Lot he visited, the one in Anthir, that had been the case. Birger touched Chancebringer; it gave him no sense of contradiction, but then, how could he be sure the enigmites hadn't choked up its power again? It wasn't like he could see them.

Birger stole a glance at Renate, her massive wings spread wide behind the Valkyrie. The high chapel ceiling had plenty of room for her to hover. Her tongue flickering, she popped a rift open, pulling long weave cords through it with her talons. She coiled around, allowing the cords to brush against her feathers. As they did, the cords shifted in colour to a vibrant green, sprouting red leaves. Moving in elaborate curls, they began questing towards the Valkyrie like snakes stalking prey.

The stone guardian towered over them, too tall for the doorway. As it started smashing the stonework, each thud echoed, sending jolts of fear through Birger. Thankful for the big altar shielding him, he took a sharp breath and darted through the south door.

He was right. Both doors accessed the same adjoining room. The north and south walls held shelves stacked with books. In the middle of the room, there was a bench with two lit braziers on either side and a short wall around the stairs going down. Rocks blew out from the wall, falling onto the stairs, and Birger dodged a shower of flying pieces.

"Any time now, Renate," Birger murmured to himself. He was sure the wall wouldn't hold for much longer.

Considering his options, he thought, I can either dash past the Valkyrie or chance a jump over the low wall.

Another fist smacked into the door frame. A huge stone block broke loose, falling onto the bench with a loud crash.

"Gullshite," Birger muttered a curse, covering his mouth with his sleeve in search of dust free air. "Renate's plan better work."

Through the growing gap in the wall, Birger saw the Valkyrie. Her face was impassive as she drew back for another strike. Hooked vines shot forward, grabbing the moving statue around the waist, neck, and arms.

The guardian strained against it, but the vines continued to ensnare their quarry. The Valkyrie moved less and less. It tried to turn, searching for the source of the interference, but Renate was well out of reach.

By Jor, thought Birger. *I hope I don't go save one friend, only to find another crushed to slop on the walls. At least for the moment, she seems to have the situation in hand, and let's hope that's the worst behind us.*

With a surge of resolve, Birger dashed forward, his heart pounding as he leapt over the short wall. The moment his boots hit the steps, he realised things could always be worse.

57

ELEMENTAL CHAOS

At the foot of the stairs, the two mutts who had fled from the Valkyrie lay motionless in a pool of water, overshadowed by an animated wave. Adorning the creature was an ornate, jewel-studded ivory collar, and it hovered over the bodies in a perpetual cresting surge. Birger recognised it as a waterweird, like the ones defending the Holy Spring.

The creature saw Birger and rushed towards him. A fist of water shot ahead of it, crashing into the staircase. Had Birger been a fraction of a second slower, he would've ended up like the two mutts. Instead, the liquid washed under his feet, with freezing cold radiating from it.

"I'm a friend!" he protested.

The waterweird didn't look like it understood or maybe it simply didn't care, so Birger slashed Kazania at its core. The blade sloshed through, the waterweird roaring like a flash flood in a gorge, but it appeared unharmed.

Birger had no time to study the creature for weaknesses. Forced to hop back, he barely avoided a second stone-cracking blow. He countered, but to no effect. His heart was racing with panic.

"Listen," Birger began, "you're the go-with-the-flow type, right? Can't we start over and be friends?"

The creature didn't understand or care and surged again. Crashing into the stairs, it rushed up towards Birger. He dove over the top of the gravity defying liquid and rolled onto the floor at the base of the steps. His momentum sent him through a door, and he landed on something soft.

Grinning at his luck, he planted a kiss on Chancebringer. But then he felt dampness followed by the putrid stench of sewage, which wiped the smile from his face.

A glance down revealed a grisly sight; his bedding consisted of two eviscerated monks in blood-soaked robes, a dagger still lodged in one of them.

"Yuck!" Birger recoiled and tried to roll away with as little contact with the mess as he could make.

The waterweird had recovered and was rushing towards him again. Instinctively, he grabbed the dagger from the dead monk's chest and flung it at the creature. The short blade hit the collar and the water creature screeched in a high-pitched whine.

"Aha!" Birger remarked, as he recalled Lorenzo mentioning that the collars were crucial in forming the construct. "Well, then you'll hate this."

With renewed determination, Birger lunged forward, driving Kazania into the collar. The ivory cracked around the impact zone, and he flicked the blade upward to split the band. The guardian let out another screech as the water started whirling like a maelstrom, blasting him with violent wind. Following a moment of chaos, the collar erupted in a brilliant flash. Through bleary eyes, he watched the water fly up the stairwell.

"Sorry," Birger murmured, feeling guilty when the guardian had vanished.

It felt bad for destroying something that was protecting the place, but that ship had sailed. Stopping Bo required wit, not merely brawn. He scooped up the fallen dagger, thinking it could serve as a useful diversion if faced with another one of those.

The underground chamber was relatively small. Birger saw two rooms on the north and south walls. All four of them were living quarters, each containing a pair of dead monks. On the far side, the stairs continued down to another level; it smelled like mold and freshly dug graves.

The distant yowl of another waterweird in battle reached Birger from below. He didn't feel like facing it, but he wasn't going to back down now. The drum of his heart redoubled, with an image of Wynn being run down by the creature flashing through Birger's mind. Wynn needed help and Bo needed killing, so he pressed on, slipping down another flight of stairs.

The first inkling of being close hit Birger when the enhanced vitality Kazania offered him diminished; her magic was being suppressed. Reaching the cold sub-basement, he found it to be a burial chamber. Sarcophagi lined the walls; three to the south and north, and five on the western side, with their feet all aligned towards the stairs.

Birger circled the column containing the next staircase and paused. Looming over four mutts in the middle of the room stood another water guardian. As he entered, the creature engulfed one of the black-clad thugs, only to spit them out a moment later, frozen like a preserved fish.

Bo shook his dangerous blue crystal at the liquid creature with fervor, but nothing happened. "Why is this Lot-be-damned thing not working!" cursed Bo.

Wynn ducked down the next stairway. The surrounding room was lit bright red by the Eye of Winter in her hand.

Birger called out, "Wynn!" but she was already gone.

"Birger!" There was outrage in Bo's voice. His bulldog face contorted into a snarl. His mane of red hair fanned out like flames dancing on his head. "How?!"

"Next time, finish what you started while you can," Birger taunted with a sly grin.

There was a spiteful glee in seeing Bo angry. Part of him felt ashamed at being so childish, but the part that was currently in control didn't care. Birger wanted to make Bo pay for what he did to Lorenzo, for Benny... and for Sten.

"I won't make that mistake again," replied Bo, taking aim with the blue crystal.

Birger continued smiling. Clearly, Bo was unaware of the Eye of Winter's effect, and the throbbing in his knee told him Wynn was still nearby.

I guess I'll be fighting on my own steam down here, thought Birger. He was also pleased that the Chancebringer-aided-healing wasn't temporary. Apart from a lingering soreness in his ribs and knee, bruises from tumbling on the stone floor, he felt relatively unscathed.

The trio of thugs still standing faced the waterweird with eyes wide in horror, frantically trying to evade its grasp.

Finally accepting that the crystal wasn't going to work, Bo said, "I'm getting out of here! Hold Birger back and deal with this thing."

Bo vanished. Clearly in no mood to follow orders, two of the mutts followed, and with his companions gone, the last couldn't avoid the waterweird's relentless advance any longer. The thug screamed, fighting the enveloping liquid, to no effect and soon, they stopped squirming. The creature expelled them as if emptying a brimming chamber pot and then charged after the others.

Birger felt Kazania awaken and thought, *Wynn must be out of range. Oh no! She might already be leaving. Cos-damn Bo for blocking me.*

"Wynn!" Birger shouted. "Don't go, I can help you!"

There was no response, and Birger sprinted down the stairs leading to the deeper chamber. He trailed the swift water guardian, but maintained a safe distance. The waterweird had a good lead, and when he turned the corner at the bottom, he saw the last of Bo's crew go down in gargled cries. That left only Wynn and Bo alive.

The air went a familiar, powdery dry and Birger dropped low behind cover. The confined space reverberated with a loud roar, the temperature plummeting. Stone wall sections burst apart near the waterweird, the debris plunging into it, caused it to wobble.

"Ha! It's working again!" Bo exclaimed.

Bathed in the orange glow of the brazier, the creature looked like liquid fire. Bo appeared in the doorway, grinning. Cruelty glinting in his eyes. He raised the blue crystal. The powdery dry sensation that proceeded the blast caused Birger's throat to burn. He noticed a whitish-blue glow swirling within the artefact, then water and ice began spurting from it.

"Now it's my turn, you walking slush," Bo said, taking aim.

A stream of icy water blasted forth. Birger crawled behind the stairwell for cover. The torrent hit the guardian, freezing it, and then tore it apart. Fragments of ice ricocheted off the walls. Unrelenting, the blast sliced through the stone, tearing into a mausoleum with the ease of a blade gutting a fish. The beam gouged a trench along the wall to reveal the room beyond. Birger's heart fluttered when he glimpsed Wynn on the other side, crouching while covering her head with her arms.

"Stop!" Wynn cried, and the water beam ended.

Wynn rose beside a door that led further into the burial chamber. She looked dishevelled and terrified; her face, marred with cuts and bruises. The image made Birger's heart ache.

Through the gap, Wynn mouthed an apology to him. Tears streaming down her face, she dashed out of sight.

"Wynn, wait!" Birger tried again. "Let me help you!"

"You can't help her gutter rat," said Bo. Despite the insult, there was sadness in his voice. "She belongs to Ulfhild now. You should've taken the chance I gave you."

She's my apprentice for Cos-sakes! Birger thought, frustrated. *I should be the one making the heroic sacrifice, not her.* Burning fury directed at Bo bubbled in Birger's guts.

"You can't stop me if I kill you!" Birger roared at Bo.

362

"Kill me, will you?" Bo sounded surprised. "I've given you every chance to get out of this. Fine. I'm done being nice."

Birger stepped out from behind the wall to look Bo in the eye. The anger ablaze in Birger's chest was more intense than anything he had ever felt. He wanted to see the look on Bo's scrunched-up face when he choked the life out of him.

The waterweird lay on the ground in shattered fragments, covering the dead mutts, like they died in a blizzard. Remarkably, the ivory collar remained intact, anchored to a sizable ice chunk.

Bo sneered. "You're making this too easy, but then, that wall wasn't going to stop Ymir's Breath anyway."

The flickering fire cast a sinister glow on Bo's face, or perhaps that's just how Birger perceived him in the moment. Bo aimed Ymir's Breath, but concealed behind Birger's back, he adjusted his grip on the borrowed dagger, clutching it by the tip.

Birger anticipated the blast perfectly. The air went powdery dry, a tell that the artefact was about to blow. Following Chancebringer's guidance, Birger dropped to his knee and flung the dagger. It whirred through the air, burying itself in Bo's right thigh. Birger rolled back behind the cover of the stairwell.

Bo yelped as the beam veered erratically towards the length of the wall, rending an even broader gash. As Bo staggered backward, the torrent tore upward, punching into the ceiling. The structure seemed to splinter with an earsplitting crack, followed by a shudder before collapsing inward.

58

KILLER

From the far side of the narrow room, a scream of agony pierced the thick dust that hung in the air. Birger's palm scraped against the grit of crumbled stone as he pushed himself upright. The murkiness impeded his vision. To the west, the collapsed ceiling obstructed the passage to the tombs to where Wynn had fled.

Dim blue light glowing ahead drew Birger forward; a glancing blow had numbed his left thigh, making him limp.

Really? Another leg injury? He shook his head, though given the destruction around, it could have been worse.

A few yards ahead lay Ymir's Breath – the powerful blue crystal – Bo's bleeding hand reaching for it unsuccessfully. Birger ducked under a section of sagging ceiling. The structure creaked dangerously.

Birger snapped up the glowing artefact. His eyes caught by the miniature tempest swirling within the crystal.

Pulling away to face Bo, Birger said, "You look stuck."

"Cos-damn you gutter rat!" Bo hissed in pain.

"You've lost." Birger tried to sound angry, but his voice came out tired.

Attempting to tap into the rage he felt over Lorenzo's murder, failed. It was hard to be mad at a man that had several tons of building sitting on his lower half.

Bo plucked and pulled, each movement eliciting a pained yelp. He clearly didn't want to accept the situation for what it was. Halting just beyond Bo's grasp, Birger shielded his mouth with his sleeve to ward off the dust.

For a moment, Birger ignored the bulldog-faced man. *There has to be a way to follow Wynn,* he thought, but the collapse had rendered the tombs inaccessible, even from here.

He turned his attention back to Bo and said, "Clever, cutting your way up here through the rock."

"I have my moments," Bo replied, a sullen grin revealing his blood-stained teeth.

"Oh, come now, there's no way that was your idea." Birger eyed the man doubtfully.

Bo's face contorted in a scowl as he tried to yank his sword from under the debris, to no avail. Meanwhile, Birger sheathed Kazania and picked up a loose sword dropped by one of the fallen mutts near the shattered water guardian. The hilt was icy to the touch, but not unbearable.

Brandishing the weapon, Birger taunted, "Need this? Seems like amputating your legs might be your only way out."

Bo's expression crumpled as the grim reality sank in. "No!" Bo strained again. "It can't end like this! She needs me. I have to succeed. She needs me!"

"Ulfhild doesn't need you. I doubt she needs anyone."

"You don't understand..."

Birger looked down at Ymir's Breath, and then back to the monster that murdered Lorenzo. A simmering cauldron of rage and hatred heating to a boil within him. He wanted Bo to suffer.

Bo flinched away from Birger's gaze, making him realise he was scowling. A talon of self-loathing hooked into Birger's belly, dimming the flames of wrath.

Would vengeance honour the man? he asked himself. *Lorenzo spent decades working to clean the blood off his hands, and here I want to spill more on his account.*

"You can't kill me, I know things," said Bo. "Use the Breath to cut me free and I'll tell you everything."

Birger mulled over the offer. *Perhaps I should walk away. I don't have to kill him. If I walk, he would die all the same,* thought Birger. But then, leaving someone for dead was a bad idea. There were only two real options: kill him or free him. *Besides, leaving me for dead is how Bo ended up in this situation to begin with.*

"You betrayed Anthir." Birger steeled his own resolve. "You murdered Lorenzo, you brought Ulfhild to Benny, and you killed Sten."

Birger had never actually killed a human, and he wasn't sure if he could do it in cold blood.

"No!" objected Bo. "I didn't do that!" There was fear in Bo's eyes as he spoke. "Ulfhild went to Benny looking for you, and I had nothing to do with Sten."

Birger struggled to rein in his anger. He needed to learn where Wynn was headed, and couldn't afford emotions controlling him.

"Benny told me you were there when Sten died," said Birger, scowling. "*You* had him before he died. Tell me what happened, or I'll walk away right now."

"It was Ulfhild's doing. I was merely a guard... I didn't harm Sten, I swear it."

"Tell me what happened!" Birger's shout echoed off the walls, and they creaked ominously.

"A few of the gang nabbed him in the Harbour Ward. Ulfhild had him kept in the warehouses, forcing us to keep him fed and healthy. I swear, I didn't know what she was planning." Bo looked terrified, but not of Birger.

"Spit it out, Bo! What did she do?"

"She... she drank him..."

"She what?" Birger arched an eyebrow in confusion.

Maybe the pain was making him delirious? he thought.

"She drank his essence, like she did with Benny... She drained him to a husk and ordered us to drop it in the harbour..." Bo was turning sheet white; from fright or blood loss, Birger wasn't sure which.

The image of Benny being drained dry like a waterskin flooded back into Birger's mind. His arms and legs felt like they had been encased in ice. He shuddered.

"Why..." the word came out of Birger's lips in a ghost of a whisper.

"The daggers," said Bo. "She took them from some rich idiot who dug them out of Heaven's Peak. They've been driving her insane... Most of the time she's normal. But sometimes... Honestly, she scares Lot's winter ice out of—"

"Imagine the terror of captivity, only to be drained!" Birger interjected; his voice was a tempest of fury as the chilling picture of Benny's death haunted him.

With sudden ferocity, Birger lunged forward, brandishing the icy sword. His face contorted, lips drawn back in a snarl.

"No, please," begged Bo, wincing and blocking with his arms.

Stop! A voice inside Birger screamed, and he froze. *What would I become if I slaughter an unarmed man? What would Renate think?*

Birger lowered the blade slowly. He needed knowledge to find Wynn, and deadmen aren't very talkative.

"I should slit your throat..." murmured Birger, "but I won't — Fine, I'll cut you out if I can, but you tell me what you know first."

"What?" asked Bo, relieved. "Really?"

367

Birger gave a curt nod and lowered the sword. A daemon within him raged on, howling for blood, but he shut it out.

"Why did you betray Anthir?"

"We didn't betray anyone!" Bo's voice rose in protest. "Ulfhild works with the Duke, for Cos-sakes. I work for them both."

"Whatever... what is this all about then?"

"The Feet are coming, and someone has to stop them." Bo's words had a hint of desperation, as though he thought Birger would understand the gravity.

"Who?" Birger asked, but his heart sped up, knowing what the man would answer.

"The Feet of Sarghus –" Bo's words were cut off by a violent cough, speckles of blood dotting the floor beneath him. "They've been behind the gullshite in Azrea for years, the civil war, the plagues killing people every winter. They've been getting at Rendin from the inside. Nobles at each other's throats, too divided to act, while Mura's been sitting pretty, preparing."

Bo wiped sweat from his brow and snorted. Birger felt cold at the mention of the tin-birds, and it triggered an ache in his right knee.

Reminding himself that he was a spy now, he waited to see what else the man would say.

Eventually, Bo added, "The empire is way too strong for us like this. Someone had to do something. Ulfhild and the Duke, some others too, they got a plan."

Birger spat on the ground and growled, "That's gullshite. Who would be so dumb as to destroy the Cos-damned Holy City claiming to be saving Azrea!?"

"We were never going to let them take the mountain!" Bo exclaimed.

"Maybe you haven't noticed, but the uks are giving the defenders a thrashing out there!"

"Listen... Ulfhild has a plan. This was the only way to get the power we need to fight Mura. That's why Ulfhild took–" Bo swallowed, "her daggers, she calls them Kazamung, even though they're driving her insane. She's that desperate..."

Birger was about to make a cutting remark when the building groaned and the remaining ceiling sagged. Falling debris forced him to dive away.

Bo's cry was panicked, "Get me out of here!"

Birger knew Bo was right, but he needed more answers.

"Not yet, tell me how," said Birger.

"How what?"

"How is Ulfhild going to use the Eye?"

"Fine! Her and the Duke are part of a group collecting the 'pieces of divinity'. Things like the Eye. The plan is to bring some old god back from behind the Darkveil and use its power to fight Murapii." Bo convulsed in pain as his legs went into a cramp. "Aeg, blind me! It hurts."

"So the Eye is one," Birger raised his arm and drew back his sleeve to reveal Chancebringer, "and this is the second."

Bo's eyes stretched wide, nodding. "Lying wench!" he spat.

Birger grinned. "How many pieces are there? And what are the others?"

"I'm not sure about all of them. Ulfhild is secretive." Bo's face was wan in the dim light. His eyes looked sunken. "The Kazamung daggers, and the sword of some knight. I don't know the rest."

He's talking about Sir Kallen and Belmung, thought Birger.

Bo sucked air through his teeth. "Lot, it hurts. Come on, man, get me out of here. I told you everything."

"Last thing, then I'll cut you out. Where's Wynn going?"

"Ulfhild's taking her and the Eye to Roviere," said Bo, hurriedly. "Please, Birger, get me out, that's all I know, I swear it."

Birger didn't want to save the slime, but he had given his word, and Bo had answered his questions in good faith. Checking the roof warily, he blinked dust out of his eyes.

"I'll try," said Birger finally.

Despite the evident agony, relief washed over Bo's face. He hurriedly instructed, "Quickly, aim the Breath at the rocks and focus – but not too intensely. The more focused, the more powerful it gets."

Doing as he was told, Birger pointed the artefact at a nearby rock. Something safe to test on. His thigh wasn't numb anymore, instead it throbbed, he ignored it. A trickle of water and ice flowed out, dripping on the muddy floor.

"Concentrate!" Bo shouted.

"That's not helping! Shut-up!" Birger retorted.

He mustered his concentration, pushing through the aches and fatigue. He took a deep breath, counting to ten, and fixated on the crystal. The air became powdery dry, and Birger almost lost his focus when he realised he was succeeding. A torrent blasted forward, cutting a hole straight into the floor. Old buried bones clattered and crunched under the force. The chapel above groaned again.

"Gullshite!" Birger cursed. "The whole place is coming down."

"Quickly!" urged Bo, covering his head.

Birger looked at the man on the floor and swallowed. *How did I end up risking my life to save this scum?* he wondered.

"If this building collapses, I'm leaving. My life isn't worth yours," Birger said, raising the artefact.

He aimed at the rocks trapping Bo and focused. At first, fluid sputtered from it, but as he honed his concentration, it turned into a precise stream that carved through the debris. Soon he was making progress, but then a loud crack and rumble stopped him.

Bo looked up. "Keep going!"

"I think…"

A large section of ceiling came down, forcing Birger dive back. The noise was deafening, and he covered his eyes with his arm, but fragments of exploring rock stung his exposed skin.

When it was over, thick dust and water vapour reduced visibility to zero. The braziers, knocked over, had spilled their coals across the floor, causing them to hiss in the mud.

"Birger!" Bo's voice was desperate. "Get me out! You swore!"

Birger assessed the situation. A massive pile of stones separated them, and any more cutting could bring it all down.

"I'm sorry. The Code says, help if you're able. I'm not able," stated Birger coldly.

"No! You can't!"

Birger retrieved the sword from the ground. "Not sure if this is Lot or Aeg's doing, but luck's not on your side." He slid the sword across the ground to Bo. "Here, for a quick end."

He began climbing the rubble to the next floor, his body weighed down – although he couldn't tell if it was because of his injuries or his guilt.

"Birger!" Bo's voice echoed. "Don't leave me! Come back!"

59

GUARDIAN

A dead monk's body hurtled past, making Birger swerve to the side; once it cleared, he resumed his ascent up the precarious rubble. Occasionally, the entire structure would groan. Fine dust billowed from cracks in the ivory floor, reminiscent of smoke spewing from a smithy's forge. Air laden with the odour of burnt bone and mildew easily overpowered the sweet smell of burning incense.

With his anger fading, fatigue and aching muscles came to the fore. While Renate's magic, empowered by Chancebringer, held Birger's pieces together, like she said, that didn't mean they were healed yet. The pain in his right knee, which had been nagging him since Anthir, intensified.

Not that Birger minded. That particular ache had become a reminder of his purpose and a testament to his commitment to see it through. The fighting, and now the climb, also aggravated his ribs beyond what the magic could dull. Not to mention the mounting injuries he had picked up since his treatment.

Far below, Bo's shouts subsided into desperate sobs. Birger steeled himself, focusing on the climb. He felt a twinge of guilt for leaving Bo, though he knew any more cutting risked bringing the entire structure down on them.

Besides, he thought, *the man deserved it. Bo's a monster. He might not have killed Benny and Sten himself, but he killed Lorenzo.* What pained Birger the most was remembering Bo's harsh treatment of Wynn. He tried to push the intrusive thoughts aside and kept climbing, hoping that time would ease his conscience.

His thoughts raced, *There's still a battle raging in the city, and if I'm going to save Wynn, I must first survive the night.* That thought sent a pang of worry through his gut. *Are Mick, Gunther and Snow still alright? The battle hadn't exactly been going in the defender's favour.*

You should've been helping them, accused Birger's cynic. *What did you accomplish running off to the temple, anyway? You got*

Lorenzo killed; you didn't stop the Eye from getting stolen and you didn't save Wynn.

Birger mulled over the accusation and smiled. These were fleeting thoughts that don't consider the bigger picture. With resolve, he thought, *I acted on the information I had; no more regrets. Besides, I got us new intelligence – that's what this was all about.* If he survived, he could use that information to stop Ulfhild… and maybe the Feet.

Finding the stairs to the top floor intact was a relief, and he gratefully used them instead of continuing his fingertip ascent.

On entering the chapel nave, Birger was surprised by what he found. Renate lay coiled on the ground, her colourful wings drooped around her, eyes partially closed, and her forked tongue hung limp with fatigue. From a weave rift she controlled, a multitude of thick vines snaked towards the Valkyrie, wrapping it in layer upon layer of vegetation.

"Renate!" panicked at the sight, Birger rushed over to her. The kink in his step wasn't serious enough to call a limp. "Are you okay?"

Renate nodded weakly through huffing breaths. "Wynn?" she asked, a glimmer of hope in her tired eyes.

"No," Birger shook his head, "I was cut off. She ran. Bo is still…"

The building shook, and an explosion of dust burst from the doors behind him. He squinted, covering his mouth with his sleeve. The coughing and sneezing made his ribs ache.

Shock stretched Renate's reptilian eyes wide.

"Bo cut the building up pretty badly with this," Birger presented the blue crystal and said, "He called it Ymir's Breath. And the sub-basement just collapsed on him."

"Ishyelle won't be happy," said Renate in a matter-of-fact tone.

Birger shrugged and stowed Ymir's Breath in a pouch. "There's still a war to fight outside. Shall we?"

Renate let out a heavy sigh. "I'm exhausted. Once I close this rift, the Valkyrie will tear through my vines in seconds. I don't know if I have enough left to get away…"

"Can you leave the rift open?" Birger's brow furrowed with concern.

Renate dipped her head, bright feathers bristling, "If I don't close it before I leave, it'll implode into a weavestorm."

"Right." Birger attempted to think of something clever to do, but nothing came to him. "Well, that sounds less than ideal. So...should I try to carry you out?"

"Is there another way?" asked Renate, her half-serpent, half-avian features curling into a wan smile. "I'm pretty heavy. You sure you can?"

"I'll manage," said Birger, shifting Kazania into a reverse grip. He would need to draw on the sword's magic. Assuming a position to lift Renate, he asked, "Ready?"

"Yes."

"Go!"

Renate closed the rift with a pop that caused a spike in temperature. Birger grabbed her under her wings. Supporting her weight was awkward, but Kazania helped, and he pulled. She slithered towards the door. Loud snapping, like rigging broken by a severe storm, echoed in the chapel as the stone guardian overpowered its constraints.

"Faster!" urged Renate.

"I'm trying!"

Stealing a glance, Birger saw the Valkyrie, still partially covered in vines, yet already charging towards them with its stone sword at the ready. By his judgement, they weren't going to make it to the door, and even if they did, the thing would follow them through the enormous frame.

Birger made up his mind. Despite his screaming ribs, he was confident in his abilities. He had grown up working hard in the fisheries and later he built strength climbing as an apprentice Magpie. With his muscles boosted by Kazania, he would surely be up to the task. With as much effort as he could manage, he thrust Renate up and forward. Her wings opened, allowing her to glide through the door.

The exertion caused Birger to slip and stumble, Kazania slicing through his leather armour and nicking his skin. He hissed in pain, but it was only a shallow cut to the hip.

"What're you doing?" Renate called out in surprise.

"Go!" was all Birger could shout before he was forced to roll to his right and avoid the massive stone blade aimed at his head.

Converting his momentum into a dive, Birger was narrowly saved from being crushed by a second blow. The stone Valkyrie was fast, and Birger's legs were much shorter, but with Chancebringer guiding his nimble reflexes, he stayed ahead. That said, Birger was getting tired; the dust-laden air made breathing difficult, and the cumulative toll of his recent injuries was sapping his endurance.

A voice called from the door, "What is the meaning of this?"

60

STONE COLD

High Priestess Ishyelle strode into the chapel with a determined gait. She was flanked by the two clerics of Cos who had previously interrogated Birger and Renate at Pilgrim's Rise. Beads of sweat glistened on the pearlescent skin of Ishyelle's forehead and her fine white hair was disheveled.

"How dare you desecrate the sacred chapel of Lot!" thundered Ishyelle, the shadows around her eyes deepening.

"Your Holiness," Renate interjected, hurriedly slithering in behind Ishyelle. "We were attempting to apprehend those responsible."

As much as Birger would've liked to join the debate, he had his hands full, avoiding another stone cracking blow. The Valkyrie stood twice his height, possessing both formidable strength and, as Birger had come to expect, more speed than made sense for its size. A near-miss sent shards of stone grazing his cheek and narrowly missing his eyes.

"Cease!" Ishyelle's command rang out, and the Valkyrie halted mid-strike.

Birger, already committed to an evasive dive, landing in the pool at the center of the room with a splash. Spitting out bloody water, he sat up, feeling like a fool.

Ishyelle knelt beside the fountain to check on one of the two dead monks while the two clerics hurried to the other.

"She's dead, Your Holiness," the female cleric reported.

"Brother Malcolm as well," Ishyelle responded solemnly.

The stillari High Priestess moved over to a dead mutt for closer inspection. Birger climbed out of the fountain next to her. Squeezing the water out of his clothes didn't help much. The water pooled in his boots; he removed them to pour the liquid out, imagining a sardine being flushed along with it. Finally, he forced his wet boots back on.

Renate slithered forward, her talons clacked on the ivory floor. Her movements were slow, whimpers of pain escaping from her.

"The monks and the robbers were already dead when we arrived, Your Holiness. I'm sorry we couldn't save them. The collapse below crushed the one that led them here."

Birger saw a tear trickle down Ishyelle's cheek, although her expression never wavered. She stood and faced the Valkyrie. "Guardian Vrylis, report," Ishyelle ordered.

The Valkyrie turned and marched over to the High Priestess. It knelt in front of her, with its head bowed. Ishyelle placed her hand on the stone construct's sculpted hair and closed her eyes. A faint red glow pulsed between Ishyelle's hand and the stone surface, running up the stillari woman's arm and pooling in her eyes.

While this was happening, the two clerics each took up position next to Renate and Birger. Neither looked exactly threatening, but instinct told Birger that running would be a mortal mistake.

Ishyelle opened her eyes. The red glow vanished, and she stepped back. Her eyes burned with anger. Pearlescent skin paling and cheekbones prominent with strain, she took a deep breath.

Calm returned to Ishyelle as she spoke to the clerics, "Brother Gard, Sister Frey, to the steps, we have a Wartide to break."

"And these two, Your Holiness?" asked Sister Frey, tilting her head towards Birger and Renate.

"Vrylis showed me the truth," Ishyelle said as she regarded Birger. "Those responsible for this are gone."

Birger sighed with relief.

"Guardian Vrylis," said Ishyelle and the Valkyrie looked up at her, "go with Sister Frey and obey her commands."

The two clerics bowed and left, with Vrylis's heavy steps following close behind them.

"Before we go, where's the Eye now?" Ishyelle asked Birger.

"Gone, High Priestess," Renate responded with a hiss before Birger was able. "One among the enemy escaped with it."

Ishyelle closed her eyes, took another deep breath, and then opened them again. "Losing a fragment of our goddess is a serious matter, but we face a much more important battle. If this mountain is lost, every holy warrior on the continent would be without magic to protect it. The Dead Lands would overrun the Knights of Alba at Lonstad; Rendin would repel the Wartide, only to drown in the undead."

"We'll help you fight," Birger said with as much confidence as he could muster.

"Good," Ishyelle turned and marched to the door.

She stopped at the two wolf statues and opened a rift. Pulling out a cord the length of her arm, she balled it up until it glowed red, then pressed it into the head of the left wolf. The statue stirred and dust flaked off it. Ishyelle repeated the action with the right wolf and both of them came to stand behind her. Their eyes were alive with red glowing orbs swimming in pools of darkness.

Ishyelle led the way down the steps, the stone constructs pawing after her like a pair of well-trained hunting dogs.

Renate looked at Birger, her eyes wide, she said, "That woman is very powerful."

"Good thing we didn't have to fight her then," Birger said with a playful grin, attempting to boost Renate's mood. "Are you able to make it all the way down?"

"I'll be fine," Renate assured him, returning the smile.

Birger's boots squelched with every step as they passed through the makeshift refugee camps that littered the flat top of the holy mountain. He could scarcely believe that only a few hours ago, he, Lorenzo, and Renate had stood on those steps for the first time.

Swallowing down a lump in his throat, Birger thought, *If I had known it would be my last conversation with Lorenzo... Nope... no more should haves. That's not honouring the man. I wish he was here, and I'll miss him. Leave it at that.*

Birger drew Kazania. The oath blade was a symbol of Birger's loyalty to the memory of Lorenzo. He would find Ulfhild, stop her, and do it with this sword at his side. As long as he honoured the oaths made on that sword, some part of the man would live on.

He looked to Renate, sliding her long body across the flagstone. She and the stone wolves had drawn a few gawkers as they passed, but none interfered. Everyone had seen enough outlandishness for the day to accept a jormunger with little more than curiosity.

"Are you going back to your human form?" Birger asked.

"I don't think so," Renate smiled. "I have a feeling I'll need all my remaining strength. Besides, it seems I blend in rather well with Ishyelle and her stone guardians."

Birger smiled and then said, "Renate..."

"What is it, Birger?" Renate looked at him.

"Thank you," Birger said, "for always being there."

"You're welcome," Renate blinked in surprise, "and thank you for saving my life in there."

Birger inclined his head and asked, "I'm curious. Why aren't you more like Eric?"

377

"What do you mean?"

"I don't know, jaded, uncaring, disconnected. I figured it must be an age thing, but you are like…" Birger left that hanging.

"Seven-hundred-and-eighty," Renate obliged with a smile. "We have different histories. I spent most of my life with other ageless beings, like the stillari and my own people… at least until the Age of Horror. Ermenrich wasn't so lucky."

"What happened to him?" Birger asked, turning onto the road to Pilgrim's Rise.

"When Lot blessed the first Wulfher with the ability to transform into half-wolves, they had full control from the outset. They didn't know the gift would be hereditary. Eric was among that first generation to be born with it."

"Oh," Birger said with a sense of foreboding, "and Eric said their young don't have control."

"Yes. One night, he unexpectedly transformed when his father and older brother were away hunting. When they returned, they discovered Ermenrich drenched in the blood of his mother and two sisters. "

Renate sighed, "His father exiled him to the Darkveil Forest to die, but Ermenrich didn't. For centuries, he lived there on his own. Only one person ever came to see him. When Rendin called for support to retake Kindra, Ermenrich heard about it and came. Honed through centuries of combat against the grengar, he had become an efficient killer."

She wet her lips with a flicker of her forked tongue. "Naturally he impressed Louis, who rewarded him with land where Roviere is today. Ermenrich tried to settle down, even had a family, but the problem with being immortal among those that aren't, is that you inevitably outlive them. And you can only watch so many grandchildren die from old age before you would rather not connect at all."

Renate and Birger gazed out to the city, where smoke clouds hung thick over the destruction.

"After the Age of Horror and losing my people, I too felt disconnected. Alone. I wandered the world, journeying through Apour to the far-off continent of Isai. There, among the Jing, I stumbled on an unexpected revelation that allowed me to rediscover my purpose."

"What was that?" asked Birger. A long walk still lay ahead of them, and he allowed himself a moment of respite, choosing instead to prioritise his friend.

Birger saw Renate's eyes soften when she said, "Did you know they don't have goddesses, or even gods in Isai? None. Their deities were all killed in an invasion from the realm of darkness a millennium ago. But the people used wizardry, resolve and unity to repel what their fallen gods could not. When I learned of that, I wanted to understand how it worked. What gave them the power to succeed where gods had failed? I was expecting a powerful wizard or something similar, but you know what it was?"

"A large mechanical boot to kick the shadow demons in the butt?" joked Birger.

Renate smirked and said, "Something like that. They used the Weave to connect their souls, and as one, they struck against the enemy. Everyone sacrificed together, and many knew they were going to die, but they did so willingly, for a chance that others might live. For them, the greater good is all that matters, and that tradition has lived on."

She cast sad eyes over the burning city. "Here we speak of valuing balance, but only the Magpies and the Shade truly embody those ideals. In Isai, balance is life, and one looks after their neighbour so that they and their family would be looked after in return. They have monasteries where people dedicate their entire lives to supporting others to think better, work better and live better. I studied among them for fifty years before I returned to Azrea, looking to bring proper balance to the land I love. That's how I became a Mindweaver."

"That sounds amazing, but how did you end up with the Magpies?"

"When I arrived, they were the only ones truly pursuing my cause, and so I joined to make a difference. Balancing coin sounded like a good place to start. Then I met a retired privateer, smuggling for the guild, trying to be a better father and husband. I taught him what I know, and when he became the Shade, he wanted me to work with him."

"Ah, Lorenzo," said Birger with a pained smile.

A tear trickled down Renate's feathered cheek. "I'll miss him dearly," she whispered.

Birger nodded in agreement. They proceeded in reflective silence from there, drawing near the summit of Pilgrim's Rise. The beautiful holy city lay in ruin below, the smell of smoke billowing up from a hundred fires.

A green tide rampaged through the streets, crushing small scattered pockets of resistance as they went. Spells flew in both directions and explosions rippled throughout. What remained of the defenders made their stand on Pilgrim's March near the landing of the great stairs, the invaders pressing in.

Birger could see Eric battling the Bolgar, both shrugging off the other's blows, but Eric was losing.

61

THE TEAM

Why does Pilgrim's Rise have so many Cos-damned steps? Birger lamented as he made his way towards the press of bodies on the landing.

His senses were assaulted by the noise and stench of battle below. The scene epitomised a last stand. The enemy forces were vast, while the defenders were few and cornered. Running wasn't an option. Each of its defenders knew what losing Kindra would mean. This was a fight for the survival of nations, cities, communities, and families. These soldiers were ready to give their lives to save every other soul living on the continent of Azrea, and so was Birger.

The steps of Pilgrim's Rise were strewn with injured soldiers, tended to by monks and priests. Nearby, several healers lay exhausted, having spent all of their life-energy to save their patients. Birger picked up the scent of death from multiple bodies lying unattended. Most of the injured wouldn't make it through the night, nevermind return to battle.

Renate stayed close to Ishyelle, who guided the pair of stone wolves down the Rise. Birger could see the marble Valkyrie following the clerics of Cos further ahead. No one paid much attention to either Renate's splendor or the three stone automatons. They had seen too much on the extreme end of magic that day to be impressed.

From his elevated vantage point, Birger surveyed the city and concluded that the Wartide held the upper hand on every front. Rage rose from his gut, heating his cheeks as he considered the insanity of Ulfhild's plan.

What sheer hubris could compel someone to permit the annihilation of all faith magic in the region, just to amass power to confront the Feet of Sarghus? How could it possibly make sense?

Birger took a ten-count breath to still his mind. Anger wouldn't do him any good in this fight. He needed to keep his head clear.

"Got to fight smart," he murmured to himself.

Some of the High Priestesses remained on the spell platform, raining death onto the enemy. However, Birger saw a few working as infantry commanders, organising the defenders around the landing.

In particular, a tall stillari woman wearing the vestments of Cos stood out. Her fine pink hair drifted in the smoke laden wind. A bright light emanated from the star embroidered on her robe, blinding the enemy to the northeast as she orchestrated the defense of that flank.

A High Priest with a shaved head and a thick beard adorned in the teal and gold vestments of Aeg stood at the centre of the landing. Beside him, Birger saw three other priests in similar, albeit less ornate, robes. Each maintained an open rift with cords pouring out into their hands. As the material passed through their grip, it vanished to become powerful gusts of wind, blasting volleys of crude arrows away from the steps. However, despite their arrows being rendered ineffective, the small green nikkuni archers kept up their barrage.

Among the defending force, Birger saw something white and splattered with dark red blood, leap on an ukthuun leader. Moments later, the green-skinned creature was abruptly sucked out of existence. A surge of cold bursting out, covering the surroundings in flaking ice.

Snow! Next to the weavespider stood two halberd-wielding men, one broad and one skinny. *Gunther! Mick!* They looked beaten up, but they were still alive, and seeing them sent Birger's heart soaring. He had never been so happy to see anyone in his life and the relief brought tears to his eyes.

Perhaps... A flicker of hope ignited within Birger. *Some of us might still make it out of here alive.*

The defenders rallied around his three friends. Together, they held the enemy at bay and even succeeded in pushing them back from time to time. The trio moved in a choreographed dance of violence. Mick and Gunther lashed out with their pole-arms to create a path to an enemy commander. Then Snow would shoot forward to finish the job.

Alongside them, the gleaming plate armour of paladins dotted the defensive line. They stood tall, serving as beacons of inspiration for the weary soldiers of Kindra.

"Hey," Birger said to Renate.

She paused to look at him.

382

"If it looked like we won't make it…" he gulped, "I need you to fly what I learned from Bo back to West Haven."

Her eyes turned sad, then she nodded, "Alright."

As they descended the stairs, Birger recounted to Renate, all Bo had said. By the time he was done, his hopes that it would prove to be wasted effort dwindled when he saw the defenders on the northern flank buckling.

The siphuun Birger fought earlier that day wreaked havoc, creating gaps in the line for the smaller niks to swarm through. In the monster's grasp, it had what appeared to be a half-eaten horse's leg as a weapon.

Thankfully, Ishyelle and the two clerics were already heading in that direction with the constructs. As Ishyelle closed in on the front line, her two stone wolves leapt over the defenders' heads. Upon landing, they crunched down on a swirl of nikkuni and lay into survivors, flashing stone fangs.

Ishyelle spoke, and despite the din of battle, it resonated throughout the area with crystal clarity. She commanded the defenders engaging the siphuun to make way, and the marble Valkyrie stepped in.

Other greenskins mistook the opening as an opportunity and surged forward into the guardian's path. Vrylis barely slowed to start carving a red trail like a shark fisher chumming the water. Birger watched as it met the siphuun. Their clash splattered niks underfoot, and the battle between the two massive creatures raged, out of control.

With the siphuun finally fighting someone its own size, Birger's attention moved a hundred yards to the northeast, to a pulsing green lantern. Wicked lightning arched from it and struck a paladin near Gunther, causing the soldier to explode in a bright flash. Though each paladin managed to take down five or six enemy warriors before dying, their explosive loss was also dampening the defenders' morale.

And the sickly green bolt kept going, leaping from victim to victim. By the time it stopped, it had killed at least ten. Among the dead were two of the shaman's own.

Birger's gaze returned to the lantern bearer, who perched on a white lion, cackling as she watched the carnage. This wasn't the one Birger had seen talking to Ulfhild. This one wore an icy blue robe and looked female.

Could be one of the two primary leaders, but where is the other one? wondered Birger, while scanning around.

To the east, he spotted a second green glow. Like before, the creature wore a black robe, sat on the same white lion, had a small doll in one hand with the lantern in the other. It worked a constant stream of glowing green thread into the doll as it healed the bolgar battling Eric.

Birger noticed that the nearby Landlor Market and its docks were devoid of fighting. *Oh good,* he thought as an idea took root. Beyond the river, a line of waterweirds held the Wartide on the far bank. The greenskins pouring through the broken walls had no real reason to go there, and likely didn't want to draw the waterweirds back into town.

Birger turned back to the northeast, where the female shaman charged her lantern again. He wracked his mind to think of a way to stop her from getting another spell off, but he had no ranged weapons.

Desperate, he cupped his hands to the side of his mouth and prepared to shout a warning. It wouldn't carry over the noise, but he had to try something.

He stopped when a blur of red lightning cracked past the shaman. The white lion erupted in a gory explosion, hurling the nikkuni off its back. Birger lowered his hands, squinting to make out what was happening.

Ulfhild appeared next to the fallen nikkuni, her wicked daggers humming with power. The nik shouted something in a panic, but Ulfhild pinned her daggers into the creature's skull. Its limbs stiffened before the body went limp, its life force ripped away. The lantern fell from of the shaman's dead fingers, continuing to pulse, growing brighter and brighter.

Looking at Birger, Ulfhild grinned and tipped her head with a flourish. The message was clear: she had what she came for and crippling the assault just as Bo said she would. She had won, and Birger was powerless to stop her. In another flash of red lightning, she vanished towards the hole in the north wall, making her escape with the Eye.

Birger's jaw flexed in frustration. He felt a compulsion to push through the two armies and chase her. Not the most practical urge he ever felt, and he ignored it.

The lantern's steady pulse turned to a flicker. It bathed the area in a blinding green light. A shock wave of power washed out from it, knocking both attackers and defenders to the ground. The green light drew in, turning dark, then exploded into bright purple and teal.

Birger covered his eyes with his arms. The largest weavestorm he had ever experienced ripped open and plucked him a step forward. The thunderous implosion wrenched several buildings from their foundations. Greenskins that were coming in as reinforcements turned to see what was happening. They cried out as the storm sucked them out of this reality in large swathes. The temperature in the entire area plummeted and ice crystals materialised on every surface.

"What was that?" cried Renate, covering her head with one wing.

"Ulfhild!" Birger shouted over the noise. "She killed a shaman over there and caused its lantern to implode into a weavestorm!"

Birger's face twisted into a sneer in the direction that the treacherous woman had fled. Seemingly painting herself as some kind of savior by turning on her own minions. Birger spat on the ground, revolted.

If I had wings, I would fly over this mob, hunt her down and save Wynn, Birger thought, but reality splashed him in the face like cold water. He knew Ulfhild would crush him without trying. Part of him was glad he had no way of confronting her directly.

Birger parked the notion and resolved to settle her ledger another day. Whatever her reasons, Ulfhild had created a gaping hole in the enemy's offensive capability.

"I see Snow, Mick and Gunther over there," Renate pointed with her free wing.

"Yeah." Renewed strength filled Birger when he drew Kazania, and he said, "You sure you're up for this?"

Renate smiled weakly. "I have a lot more in me when I'm not constantly holding an illusion. Don't worry about me, focus on winning this thing."

Birger nodded, then started towards Snow, Mick, and Gunther.

Ishyelle and her stone guardians were supporting the weakened flank, while a weavestorm guarded the northeast. Leaving the east most in need. While Eric had the bolgar in a deadlock there, the giant still limited any gains by sheer size.

Birger broke into a jog, ignoring the chafe of his clammy armour, squelching boots, and sore legs. Now wasn't the time for weakness. Chancebringer's awareness allowed him to time his approach. When an ukthuun broke through the line behind Mick, Birger shot forward and skewered the large green brute before it could harass

385

his friend. The uk fell to the side, and he drew Kazania back out from its ear.

"Birger?" Mick gasped in surprise, his blistered hands dripping with dark blood. A cut ran from his temple to his cheek. "Don't worry..." he sucked another exhausted breath, "we left a few... for you." Mick lashed out, ending two incoming niks with a sweep of his halberd.

"Drop back and get patched up," said Birger. "I'll hold your place in the line for a while."

Snow leapt on top of a nikkuni pack, bowling them over, his mandibles working as he crunched into them. Birger joined the weavespider and quickly killed three while Snow took care of two more. Gunther slammed his halberd down on another one's head. And then there was a moment where no one was trying to kill them.

"You too Gunther, Snow," Birger called, "take a rest!"

"So glad to see," Gunther gasped for air, "you."

The three of them did as Birger said. Renate approached them, and Birger glimpsed Gunther's eyes going wide.

"It's Renate!" Birger shouted as he prepared to enter the fray.

"Just your friendly local healer, here to take care of the wounded." Renate's snakelike mouth curled into a smiled and her feathers rustled.

"By Cos," cursed Mick, but that was all Birger heard as he stilled his mind. Mick would be rude, Gunther would understand, Renate would be diplomatic and in the end, they would work it out. Birger couldn't take part, he had a gap in the line to hold.

Two green-skinned niks lunged at him. A flurry of butterflies danced in Birger's stomach as he realised he had a choice: to let his nerves turn into terror or exhilaration. He chose exhilaration, brandishing Kazania into an outside guard position.

Fight to win, the words echoed in Birger's mind. Poised, he sensed the movements around him through Chancebringer. The first nikkuni sprang towards him. He dodged aside, flicking Kazania out, catching the creature along the neck.

Without pausing to see the first one fall, Birger executed a precise spin and thrust, spearing the second one through the heart. After those first two well timed blows, everything became a blur. Birger flashed in and out, green bodies withering as they came near. Amidst the adrenaline and pounding fear in his heart, there was a sense of freedom, immersing himself in the rhythmic combat.

It had been a long day. Birger hurt all over, and no matter how many he killed, there were always more. When a couple of stout paladins took up his flanks, he accepted the help.

The battleground grew confined as the dead piled around his feet. Blood-slicked flagstones made balancing arduous. Weariness gnawed at his muscles as time blurred, the minutes dragged on like hours, and soon Birger could no longer maintain his flow.

Momentary loss of focus saw hot agony explode across Birger's upper arm. An ukthuun brute flashed him a wicked grin, his axe blade laced with fresh blood. Birger grinned in reply, before stabbing the green hulk in the eye.

His pain and fatigue became too much. It forced him to withdraw, and the paladins closed ranks to fill the gap.

"Gullshite!" cursed Birger. "They're relentless."

"Been like that all day," agreed Mick, already looking fresher, with a bandage wrapped around his head.

Behind Mick, Renate had an open weave rift, and she pulled thick cords from it. She thinned and empowered each by running it through her talons, turning them into bandages. Once clipped, they took on a life of their own, wrapping wounds on Gunther's leg. Snow also had a few cuts that breached his exoskeleton. The weavespider's old leg wound was spotted with fresh blood.

Mick's voice thundered above the clamor, "Reserves, rotate! Relieve the front line!"

Activity rippled through the double line formation. Battle weary soldiers dropped back to receive treatment for their wounds. Calling the replacements fresh would be a serious overstatement; instead, a somewhat less recently battered second line advanced.

"We need to break their resolve," Birger said to the others. "Or we won't last the night."

"Wonderful idea!" Mick's voice dripped with sarcasm. "Why don't you go over there and convince those uks who outnumber us ten-to-one, our faltering force isn't worth the effort?"

Birger arched an eyebrow and countered, "I don't hear you coming up with anything better."

Mick shrugged, "Where's Lorenzo?"

Birger's heart sank and his mouth felt dry as he answered, "Didn't make it."

Mick's expression and shoulders sagged, his weapon teetering in his grasp.

"You're serious?" Gunther's voice came out in a shocked gasp, his face draining of colour.

"Listen..." Birger exhaled, bracing himself against the surge of emotions. "Lorenzo was a man of action who left a mark on each of us. How about we honour him by winning this fight?"

No one said anything. Each still reeling from the news. Birger couldn't blame them. He wasn't sure how he would've reacted in their shoes.

Snow nuzzled Birger's hand, which he reciprocated by stroking the weavespider's head. He could sense Snow's weariness and his hunger. So, he held out Chancebringer for him to feed on. Snow dove straight in, his sweepers playing across Birger's arm.

"Finding you three was such a relief," Birger admitted, his smile genuine and weary.

"Been a long day," agreed Mick. His sunken eyes were downcast with sorrow. "Alright. Let's survive this arse kicking together then."

"What's the plan, Birger?" asked Gunther, as a magical bandage wound itself around his bleeding forehead.

"Eric, a bolgar, and Landlor Market," said Birger.

62

BIG PROBLEMS

A potent magic wind howled overhead and dismembered bodies lay strewn across the urban battleground in pools of blood. The cobbled streets were aglow with a sickly purple hue in the eerie light of the weavestorm. The pungent odour of decaying flesh and acrid smoke caused Birger's eyes, nose, and lungs to burn. And coughing did little to clear it.

Next to Birger, Snow's wounds had been cleaned, and he was now intently watching the battle unfold. His dog-sized body bucking as though he were amidst the turmoil.

Birger rubbed at his arm. Renate had applied a magical bandage to his cut to numb the pain, though the rest of his body still ached. Renate looked drained after healing everyone else, and concern for her weighed on him. He downplayed most of his other injuries to prevent her from expending more of her energy. Besides, holding Kazania was already revitalising him – an advantage he knew the others didn't have.

However, Chancebringer channelled every detail of the dynamic environment into Birger's mind. During the fight, his instincts helped him sort through the mess, but waiting around with everything going crazy was too much.

Birger tried to focus on the plan he had devised. Soon they would enter the press of defenders on the south flank, but even thinking about it sent terror creeping up his spine. He began to quiver uncontrollably... and then he vomited.

What am I even doing here? wondered Birger. *I don't know anything about leading an assault team.*

Mick came to stand by him with Gunther and Renate on their way.

"You okay there, boss?" Mick asked, putting his hand on Birger's shoulder.

"What?" Birger looked up at Mick through tear-blurred eyes.

"I asked, are you alright?" Mick repeated more gently.

"I was just getting ready to boot a bolgar in the backside and possibly piss off a werewolf in the process," Birger said, wiping his face with a grimy sleeve.

"Oh, don't worry about it mate," said Mick. "If he eats you, it'll be over quickly."

Birger gave Mick a humourless smirk and said, "Thanks."

"Let's go," Gunther chimed in from behind them, with Renate in tow. "I can't stand all this waiting around. Makes me nervous."

"I know what you mean," said Birger, ruffling the gore matted fur on Snow's head. "Right, I'll take the lead, and listen, this is going to be dangerous, so if you don't want to come, it's alright."

Everyone gave Birger a flat stare and Gunther said, "It's dangerous to stay here. Besides, my heart can't take standing this close to a fight without being in the Cos-damned thing. I would rather die with my friends trying something crazy than staying here to be slowly ground down."

"Same," Mick agreed.

The two donned their usual matching silver chest plates, though they were battered and smudged with soot. A full day of fighting was messy business.

Gunther grabbed Mick in a tight hug, pecked him on the cheek and said, "Live together, die together."

Mick grinned, "Always."

Renate smiled too. She shook her vast wings, turning her brightly coloured feathers dull, until they darkened to a deep purple. She would be close to invisible in the night. Snow padded over to her and crouched at the ready.

"Dying isn't part of the plan, Gunther." Birger winked at the broad man. "Okay," he put some effort into sounding like Lorenzo as he said, "this mission is complex. I need you to be both committed and self-reliant. This isn't a battle-line where you just follow orders. To survive this, you'll need your wits."

To himself he added, *And being rigid could cost you your lives.*

Birger inhaled deeply and faced the defenders on the southern edge. "I'm going in. Once I have the bolgar hooked, I'll make my way to Landlor."

He braced himself as he pressed between the soldiers, trying to appear confident through a barrage of doubts. *Perhaps Aeg is with me, but how far would her protection go? And would Ymir's Breath even work in this chaos?* Birger used a ten-count breath to slow down. *I need to focus.*

Armour scraped as soldiers made space to let them pass. Those still standing against the enemy were hardened veterans. The greenhorns were all either nursing wounds or dead. When Birger reached the front line, a mound of uncleared bodies confronted him, redoubling the reek of blood and filth.

Ignoring his revulsion, Birger scanned for options. First, he needed to make space for him and his team to break through the enemy line.

He guessed this was as good a time as any to test his plan. Drawing out Ymir's Breath, he brandished the artefact before him. A nikkuni cutthroat lunged at him, forcing Birger to defend himself. In a fluid motion, Kazania intercepted the attack and, overbalancing his opponent, Birger hacked the creature's weapon arm off at the elbow. The small greenskin let out a deafening scream as it fell away.

Ice trailed from Ymir's Breath as Birger ducked under another rough steel blade. He replied with a quick thrust. Kazania pierced through armour like it were flesh, stopping the next nik dead in its tracks.

Focusing on Ymir's Breath in all the madness was impossible.

Birger spotted the bolgar lumbering towards them, its fiery red beard matted and bloodied. Part of its pauldron was cleft away, revealing the rippling muscles below as it grabbed a soldier near Birger and bit the man's head off.

The behemoth stepped over a line of ukthuun, crushing several defenders. Birger ducked away, his heart pounding with fear like a galleon drum. A thundering blast of yellow light knocked the giant's foot back, toppling the beast. It crashed down like timber.

The bolgar, clad in heavy metal plate armour, tore through a building like it was made of twigs. A paladin's mangled body lay at the centre of the explosion, but the incident had opened a gap in the offence.

Pocketing his artefact, Birger yelled, "Come on!" and leapt over the heaped bodies.

The others followed, hot on his heels. Birger cleared the front, while Mick and Gunther took care of the flank. Renate remained in the middle of the pack, and Snow brought up the rear.

"The bolgar's recovering! I'll lead it away first!" Birger had to shout over the din of battle. "Where's Eric?"

"Maybe he got his honorable death!" Mick replied.

391

Eyeballing the wreckage and bodies the bolgar left in its wake, Birger's plan suddenly seemed daft. *What were they going to do about an invulnerable monster that can wreck a house by tripping?* he thought... It didn't matter; he had to try. They would soon run out of those paladin explosions and the Wartide would flood every nook and cranny till none of Kindra's defenders remained alive.

"We stick to the plan!" called Birger. "Find a place to keep our backs secure! The waterweirds are holding the river, that's still our best shot! Meet you there!"

"Stay alive!" Gunther shouted back.

He, Mick, and Renate split off at a brisk trot. The southern side of the city was clear thanks to the Holy Spring, with most of the enemy concentrated in the north.

Birger noticed Snow stuck with him.

"Off you go!" Birger yelled at Snow, gesturing towards the others.

Snow cocked his head innocently.

"Really? Playing dumb now?"

There was a crashing sound behind Birger, and he whipped around. It was coming from the destroyed building, which now served as the bolgar's bed. A set of roof tiles came free and clattered to the flagstone. Birger flinched at the sound, but he reminded himself that he wasn't on some rooftop in Anthir.

A colossal hand gripped the crumbling wall. As Birger watched, it heaved a hulking body from the debris. The bolgar glared at him with a bloodied sneer and rose.

"Gullshite," muttered Birger, "It's on."

63

CATCH

As the bolgar reached its full height and roared, Birger had only a split second to act. Sword ready, he charged the lumbering behemoth. It shoved against the surrounding building's remains, causing a collapse. Birger veered away as a massive stone section crashed before him. He leapt over the rubble, his aching legs powering him towards the creature. Snow trailed him but hesitated at the building's edge. Confident in the weavespider's resilience, Birger pressed on.

Kazania sang through the air as Birger slashed at the bolgar's exposed foot. She bit deep with a brief moment of resistance, blood spattered as he dragged the blade across the calloused skin.

The bolgar's roar of pain was followed by a swipe of its massive hand, forcing Birger to dive for safety. His shoulder collided with debris littered on the ground; his armour absorbed most of the impact, but the pain in his injured rib intensified. Gasping, Birger turned behind the building, heading south at a high-speed hobble.

It's working! he thought with mixed celebration and panic, but the monster was already back on its feet.

Snow reappeared, and Birger felt a pang of worry when the weavespider paused to do something at the corner of the partially demolished building.

"It's coming!" shouted Birger. "Move, Snow!"

The weavespider glanced back, then scaled the wall, running parallel to the road. Birger noticed a purple and teal trail glistening behind Snow in the weavestorm light. He realised what the weavespider was up to when the bolgar let out a thunderous yelp, tripping and flopping onto a second building. Snow leapt away as the wall crumbled under the tension created by the giant's weight when it pulled the webbing tight.

The weavespider landed near Birger, who whooped, "Good boy!"

As they raced towards Landlor Market, Birger noted that most of the nearby buildings were still unscathed. *We'll soon change that,* he thought.

The bolgar rose more quickly this time, bellowing in an unintelligible language, but Birger knew frustration when he heard it. The giant's thunderous footsteps rapidly closed in. At this rate, Birger wouldn't make it past Short Street. Aware that looking back could cost him, he risked a glance to gauge the distance and time remaining.

He cursed. He needed options, fast. The adjacent building had a torn roof, and its north wall caved in like it was hit by a catapult. Ahead of him, he saw Renate beside an open rift near the distillery. Mick and Gunther raced across the road, laying lengths of weave in a lattice pattern above head height.

The group had already done a lot of work, securing several lengths of cord to the solid stone smithy on the other side. Renate had explained that the Weave was versatile, and she could encode behaviours into it. Here, she was encoding it to latch onto anything except living skin.

But there's a potential flaw, thought Birger. *If the bolgar realises it can escape by shedding its clothes, that'll be an eyeful. That's if I even reach them in time. The last part of the plan might end with me as a mess at the bottom of that thing's foot.*

Birger needed more time. The heavy footsteps thundered closer. Turning, he prepared to dart between the bolgar's legs. It was madness, but he saw no other way. Adrenaline mostly masked the pain in his right knee, but he favoured his left as he prepared to dive.

Movement on the broken roof of a nearby building caught his eye. There was a man standing on it with an axe in hand. *Not a man,* he corrected himself, *a werewolf.*

Eric leapt from the roof with inhuman strength. The axe swept smoothly through the air, and it sank into the bolgar's neck, eliciting a roar of agony.

The massive bipedal wolf scrambled onto the giant's back, using the axe for leverage. Eric then propelled himself upward with his hind legs, driving the blade in again as he fell, sliding down the bolgar's back. Blood spurted out, splattering around him when he landed.

The bolgar thrashed, and to Birger's astonishment, its wounds started to close.

"Runt musk!" Eric growled. "What're you waiting for? Run!"

Snapping out of their shock, Birger and Snow turned to flee. Eric joined them at what looked like a casual jog to his long, lupine legs.

"You're a sight for sore eyes!" Birger shouted. "I thought you were dead!"

"Not for lack of trying..." Eric shook his enormous head, his jowls flapping. There was a treble in his voice, as his mouth clearly wasn't shaped for speaking. "Don't think that'll hold it, but worth a try." He gestured forward.

"What?" Birger asked, confused. Then realisation struck, "Oh, the trap! You don't think it'll hold?"

"That runt shaman is elusive, and it's giving the bolgar a lot more endurance and strength than it should have. Unless we find and neutralise it, our chances are slim," Eric said, his yellow fangs bared in a grin.

"Gullshite." Birger's heart sank. "That was our best shot."

A voice, reminiscent of a tidal wave crashing against the docks, barked as the giant's booming footsteps resumed in pursuit. Birger couldn't see the rest of his team, but knew they were hiding nearby. Though the cables overhead weren't visible, he ducked under the space they should be, and Eric dropped to all fours. His usual towering nine-foot frame would've definitely got caught.

When they reached Kindra's river harbour, Eric stopped. He turned to face the bolgar, saying, "Your plan is going to work, or me and this biggen are going for round ten."

"Round ten?" Birger asked, slowing down as well. "You've fought him ten times today already?"

"It would be nine. How does your math work?" Eric growled with a questioning glare directed at Birger.

"Sorry, my mind is a little pre-occupied right now," Birger said sullenly and reached for Ymir's Breath.

The wolf had a point. Aeg only knew if this would see success or catastrophic failure. Birger pointed the crystal at the bolgar. His hands shook. He lowered his aim to the floor below the lattice work. Focusing on the artefact, water and ice began sputtering forth.

Birger steadied his mind with deep breaths, but the crystal jerked, releasing an overpowering blast that tore through the flagstones. He eased off, just soaking the ground with ice-laced water.

"Shut your eyes!" Renate cried, hurling a pulsing ball of weave into the air.

As a bright explosion lit the sky, Birger shielded his eyes. When he looked again, he saw the blinded bolgar collide with the lines at breakneck speed. The distillery's copper tanks screeched and the tension on the cords wrecked one tower. The smell of yeast mixed

395

with the stench of carrion. Fortunately, the second tank held, and
the smithy stood firm.

64

DOOMED

Birger watched as the weave cables coiled around the bolgar's massive thighs, squeezing the skin like dough between a baker's fingers. A piece of copper piping flew across the road with a clatter. The cables held, though they groaned under the strain. Finally, the bolgar toppled forward, crashing onto the latticework. The tightening cords cocooned the giant in a tangled heap.

Eric loped towards the bolgar. His enormous axe looked small in his grip, each claw a dagger capable of disembowelling a shark. Birger looked around in search of the others. He found Mick and Gunther charging from the door of the smithy. They let out battle cries, their halberds thrusting forward as they closed in on the flailing giant.

"Tangle its legs!" Birger shouted to Snow, and the weavespider obeyed.

Eric hacked into the bolgar's torso. To keep it off balance, Mick and Gunther struck at the monster's colossal fingers. Snow darted around its ankles, ensnaring them in cords of strong weavespider-silk.

Birger glanced up and saw Renate flying above. She yelled, "Look out, north!"

A greenish hue shimmered off a dozen menacing ukthuun advancing towards Birger and his comrades. A large white lion walked casually among the mob, with the dark-robed shaman sitting on its back. The shaman's voice pierced the air as he gestured towards the bolgar, propelling the greenskins into a charge.

"Gullshite!" cursed Birger. "Incoming!"

With Renate's spell empowering the cords to cling to the bolgar's armour, each lumbering thrash constricted it tighter. Eric could contain it for a time without help. Birger maneuvered around the flailing giant. His legs throbbing, his muscles drained; he needed to muster every ounce of strength remaining to fend off the ukthuun onslaught. Mick and Gunther also left the bolgar to Eric and Snow.

Each taking an opposite flank to cover Birger and the three shifted into a battle stance.

"With you, boss," said Mick, his voice tinged with a smile.

"That's right," added Gunther.

"Let's make these cod-faced slug eaters rue the day they set foot on this road." Birger flexed his right arm holding Kazania and took aim with Ymir's Breath.

"Cod-faced slug eaters?" Mick shot Birger a quizzical glance.

"Cut me some slack... I'm exhausted."

"Clearly!" Mick's laughter boomed, and some of Birger's anxiety fled as he joined in the mirth.

"You two..." Gunther smiled and shook his head.

Birger focused. When the powdery sensation in the air scratched at the back of his throat, he grinned. The blast shot out in a powerful line, cutting down three ukthuun. Seeing what he had planned, the shaman vaulted from his mount and kept the green lantern from falling as he landed gracefully on the flagstones. The small character bared his teeth at Birger in a sneer.

The frost beam hit the white lion, and it roared, rearing back, the ice rushing up its giant paws. The shaman dropped the doll to reach into the burning lantern. He drew out a long cord, and swung it to lash at the frost on the lion's chest, halting its spread. Then the ice turned black and flaked off the animal's fur.

Birger had to swerve to the left when the first ukthuun reached him. He cut down another three with the Breath before his focus was disrupted, forced to use Kazania as defence in the ensuing melee.

Gunther and Mick each impaled an ukthuun warrior as they defended the charge. However, Gunther took a blow that tore his breastplate open and sent him sprawling. Mick ducked under an axe swing and ensnared his assailant with his halberd; they tumbled into a heap, grappling for an advantage. That left Birger with the two remaining brutes.

Gunther was in trouble, and Birger saw an uk looming over him, about to strike. Gunther wasn't ready for it. Chancebringer told Birger the move would expose him, but Birger shot Kazania into the back of Gunther's attacker anyway. The price came due as searing pain erupted on his left side. He felt his shoulder blade crack under the blade's weight, and he collapsed to the ground in a cry of pain. Ymir's Breath clattered to the flagstones.

"Birger!" shouted Gunther as he recovered and stabbed Birger's assailant in the armpit.

The ukthuun cried out and toppled to the side. The second went for Gunther, and using Chancebringer to guide him, Birger struck out with Kazania. With a loud sickening snap and a cry, the uk's Achilles tendon parted. The large green brute hit the flagstones next to Birger, who rammed the sword through its eye. The uk jerked and then lay still.

Birger's left arm hung lifeless, his back ablaze as though hot coals were smouldering inside his armour. He rolled and tried to get back on his feet, but only made it as far as kneeling.

He looked up to see that, having shaken off the ice, the lion was charging towards him. Knowing he was powerless to stop the impending onslaught, he bowed his head. *I'm sorry, Lorenzo.*

The white lion lunged, its gaping jaws wide and tongue lolling, but Gunther barrelled into Birger, hurling him to safety. The beast's monstrous claws tore into Gunther's thigh, ripping it into a bloody mess. He let out an agonized scream.

Having won in his scuffle and killed his opponent, Mick dashed towards the lion, crying out, "Gunther, no!"

Mick's halberd sank deep into the lion's neck, but it wasn't an instant kill and the animal reared back, slashing out with its claws. It raked across Mick's breastplate, tearing it with the screech of bending metal and he went flying a good twenty feet before crashing into the stone wall of the smithy.

The lion emitted a feeble moan of pain, and Birger lunged forward to plunge Kazania into its skull. The animal's death spasms almost killed Birger and forced him to fall away from more lashing claws.

"Mick!" Gunther's voice cracked as he crawled towards his fallen husband, leaving a trail of blood in his wake.

The shaman approached Birger, hoisting the green lantern, tending to the doll once more. Speaking in a heavy accent, it said, "Good try, human. Siphok hisself would be impressed. It will bring me honour to kill you." The shaman smiled and turned to the dead white lion. It spoke a few words and ripped a tuft of hair from the beast's mane.

"I'll kill *you* for what you did here," Birger snarled through gritted teeth. Kneeling, he held Kazania pointed at the creature. Blood was running down the small of his back and tickling the top of his buttocks.

The shaman narrowed its glowing red eyes and cackled, "This one no die so easy. This one thinks you die first." The small character tucked the fur into a beaded bracelet on its arm.

Behind Birger, a clamour of shattering stone echoed through Landlor Market as something big collided with a wall. Moments later, Snow soared over the nikkuni shaman's head.

"No!" Birger called in anguish. The weavespider landed in a limp heap near Gunther and Mick. "You toad scum! Leave my friends alone!" Birger's voice erupted in anguish, eliciting a cackle from the small, green figure.

"I think no. And yous has strong soul, this one can use," retorted the shaman. The nikkuni raised the lantern, and it pulsed brighter.

Birger saw movement in the sky above the creature. Overhead, Renate opened a weave rift to draw green vines from it. The rift closed, and she started gliding down towards them.

Need to buy time, thought Birger. "Why?" he asked.

The shaman cocked its head, regarding Birger with a puzzled expression.

"What drove you to attack us? Why did you come here?" he continued.

"Same as all war," uttered the shaman, its mouth pulled into a rictus grin, showing sharp crooked teeth. "We's hungry. Yous has food. Strongest take food and live. This is way of Frost Wild. Hunter or prey, strong or dead."

Deeming the conversation over, the nikkuni hoisted the lantern again. That was when Renate struck. The vines hooked onto the shaman, and the small creature whirled around to see what was happening.

A concentrated beam of searing green fire erupted from its lantern, punching into Renate and hurling her from the air. The vines wilted under the ferocious intensity of the inferno, and Renate hit the ground with a chilling thud.

A surge of fear and rage invigorated Birger. He lunged at the shaman; despite the pain in his shoulder and rib, he drove Kazania through the creature, the blade grating against bone and busting through its spine. It went limp, its weight pulling Kazania out of Birger's hand. As she fell, so did his strength, and Birger himself followed. He couldn't even move to retrieve Kazania from the shaman's corpse.

Rolling onto his less injured side, Birger let out a breath. He needed to check on his friends.

"Renate, are you all right?" Birger called out.

There was no answer.

"Gullshite! Gunther?!"

"I'm here," Gunther's voice quavered, "but my leg is ruined. I can't move."

Birger saw Gunther sitting against the smithy wall with Mick stretched out next to him. Gunther was tying a belt tourniquet around his own torn leg.

"What about Mick?" Birger checked.

"Unconscious, still breathing," replied Gunther, his voice crackling with emotion.

"And Snow?"

"He isn't moving."

"So help me Cos, I'm going to make that bolgar pay," said Birger, drawing on the intense fury for strength.

He struggled onto his knees and hoisted himself upright; his left arm dangled lifelessly at his side. With his right hand, which was still somewhat functional, he picked up Ymir's Breath and turned to see what had happened with the bolgar.

A towering, naked giant with a bright red mane stood watching him. The bolgar's armour remained entangled in the latticed webbing. There was no sign of Eric, other than a hole in the side of the distillery building.

It's up to me, thought Birger, as he took a resolute step forward and squared off.

Birger sighed, drew in a breath and shouted at the naked bolgar, "Your master is dead! Give up!"

The bolgar didn't seem keen because it stomped forward, and Birger raised the blue crystal, aiming it at the monster's core. The terror Birger had experienced before was gone, replaced by a different kind, something so deep that it focused his senses.

"You aren't invulnerable anymore," Birger grinned wickedly. "You look hot. Let me help you cool down."

Ymir's Breath kicked in almost instantly. A powerful torrent of ice flooded out and crashed into the giant, knocking its legs out from under it. The bolgar crashed down, ice splintering from its skin on impact with the stone, but Birger kept going. The bolgar raised its head, smirking at Birger. Then it stood, the ice cracked, but not doing much more.

The monster spoke in its own tongue, and Birger got the distinct sense that it was thanking him. The ice simply flaked off the bolgar.

401

Birger deactivated Ymir's Breath. "Cos-damnit!" he cursed.

That was when the distillery front door burst open. Eric marched out, with half his skull exposed and one eye dangling beside his cheek. He was missing several fangs and walked with a limp. He still held his axe firm in his right claw.

"Hey you!" Eric shouted. "I'm not done yet."

Without waiting for a response, the werewolf sprung forward, his loose eye swinging and smacking against his forehead. Eric grabbed it with his left claw and plucked it out before throwing it at the bolgar. The eye bounced off the giant's chest at the same moment Eric pounced.

The bolgar snatched at him, but the werewolf was too quick. Eric pushed off the giant's clutching hand and flipped himself, tail over head, clear of the grab. The axe slammed into the top of the bolgar's massive head. The blade cutting away half its face.

In a smooth motion, Eric landed on the flagstones and spun, his axe slicing across the bolgar's belly. A cascade of coiled intestines spilled out. The bolgar collapsed to its knees.

"Never hurt my pack," Eric snarled through clenched teeth, spun and hacked through the bolgar's spine.

65

CLEAN-UP

Landlor Market, with its quaint shops and moored sailboats, would've looked tranquil in the purple and teal light of the weavestorm that illuminated the night sky. That is, if one could overlook the blood, entrails, and corpses strewn about.

Birger was exhausted. He yearned to collapse to his knees, but the fear of not being able to rise again held him up. The battered form of a werewolf crouched over the bolgar's remains. Eric's skull was half-exposed. Blood clotted his grey fur, and he panted with his tongue lolling out.

"We're your pack?" asked Birger, his face breaking into a wide, albeit weary, grin. "Wow, that's…quite touching."

"Don't make a thing out of it," Eric growled. When he shook his head, blood spattered the surrounding flagstones.

"Sorry you didn't get your honorable death." Birger touched his sore shoulder tentatively.

"There will be another," Eric replied, turning his head towards the landing of Pilgrim's Rise. "More work to do. The others are in terrible shape. I'm not good at caring for wounded. I mostly make them, but I can help you get them on a cart."

"Thanks," said Birger gratefully; he had to admit he was feeling a little overwhelmed.

It had been the most gruelling day of his life, with many moments where he doubted his ability to make it through.

Eric had stepped up when it mattered in a big way. *They all did,* thought Birger. *Each of them saved my life over the last few days at least once.*

Eric walked behind the distillery, and Birger turned towards Gunther. The burly man had tightened his belt around his thigh. Flesh protruded from the ragged wound in his leg, blood pooled around him. His skin looked sickly in the weavestorm glow. The sight sent a pang of worry through Birger's gut.

"Mick first," Gunther insisted, gently caressing the other man's mussed, brown hair.

Mick's face, though marred by blood and bruises, had a serene quality to it. His breastplate sported four long furrows plowed into it, and Birger could see the skin below. There was no blood. The armour had taken the punishment.

"You're bleeding pretty badly, man," Birger grimaced, putting a hand on Gunther's shoulder.

Gunther shrugged him off with a hard look, and repeated, "Mick. First."

"Of course... We need to get you both onto a cart. Eric's fetching one." Birger and Gunther fell silent, then Birger said, "Look, stay alive till Eric gets here. Thank you for saving my life. I'm sorry for what happened to Mick."

Gunther's eyes softened as he said, "It's not your fault, Birger... We were here fighting for a worthy cause. Dying to defend this city is worth it five-hundred-thousand lives over."

Birger returned a sad smile. The wind plucked at his tattered hood. "I'm going to check on Snow and Renate."

Gunther nodded, continuing to run his hands through Mick's hair as he whispered in a soft, melodic tone.

Was he singing? Birger wondered.

Limping over to Snow, the big man's words stayed with him. He stooped to stroke the weavespider's thick, blood-matted fur. Muted groaning noises emitted from Snow, eyes opening to focus on Birger. He sensed Snow's joy at seeing him, but also felt the weavespider's pain, fatigue, and hunger.

"You did good, boy," said Birger, stroking Snow's head. "Rest. You deserve it."

Birger allowed Snow a brief feed from Chancebringer. Content, Snow laid his head back down. They both knew Birger had one more check-in to do, and Snow didn't protest when he moved on.

He walked over to the dead shaman and pulled Kazania out of the creature's neck. He wiped the blood on his greaves and sheathed her, then secured his limp left hand to her guard, maintaining contact to draw on her power.

Birger continued to Renate's side. She lay still and Birger gulped back raw emotions at the sight of her. The dark purple shade she used for camouflage had reverted to a vibrant mix of blue and pink. The burns looked severe; they covered most of her upper body and part of her left wing.

How do you check a jormunger's pulse? Birger wondered. *Cosdamnit, I told you to run if it came to this... What would I do if she's dead? No, she can't be dead.*

Birger knelt next to her and put his right hand in front of her nose. Slow, shallow breaths blew heat against his skin. She was still alive.

"Thank Aeg, and Lot and, and...oh gullshite...thank all five!" Birger felt his emotion rise and turn his cheeks hot.

He closed his eyes, choked back tears, and took a moment to compose himself. They were all still alive, and if he acted swiftly, they might stay that way. He had managed to avoid letting Lorenzo down a second time, and perhaps he could still salvage the first.

Behind him, he heard the cackle of wagon wheels rolling over flagstones. He looked over his shoulder. Eric, back in his human form, but looking no less beaten up, pulled the cart. It took all of Birger's strength to get back to his feet, and despite faltering twice, he wouldn't be stopped. He had friends to make safe.

They used a wooden plank from the smithy to secure Mick's back. It didn't take long for Eric and Birger to get all four of the others on the cart.

"Get on," Eric said to Birger, when they were ready to leave. "I'll pull you in."

Birger protested just enough to be polite, but he was thankful for the offer. He didn't have enough left to reach the landing on foot.

A few minutes later, they arrived. The defenders held firm with the bolgar gone and the weavestorm divided the attacking force. The stone Valkyrie had also overcome the siphuun. Leaderless, the discipline of the Wartide faltered. Too many were distracted, looting instead of fighting. With their offence so watered down, the defenders countered.

The southern side was safe to approach. Eric pulled the cart up to the steps.

"Get them help," said Eric. "It's time to break these fools."

Eric turned towards the battle, howling as his muzzle stretched to fill with fangs; his hind legs lengthened, and his claws extended. His specially tailored armour adapting to the transformation of his body.

The Wulfher warrior was ready for another bout. He charged into the enemy, leaping over the defenders' heads and proceeding to rip the greenskins apart. Eric's ferocious onslaught quickly shattered the remaining greenskins' resolve. With no one to rally them, it started with a pocket of deserters that turned into a stream, then a river, and soon they were all running away in a flood.

Meanwhile, Birger climbed off the cart and limped in search of a healer. The only ones still standing or remotely able to cast spells were the High Priestesses. He approached Ishyelle, who was directing the defenders to hold the landing, while her stone guardians joined Eric in the chase.

"Your Holiness," called Birger, "I have wounded that desperately need help."

"Help is needed everywhere," retorted Ishyelle, her eyes icy, fixing on him. "What sets yours apart?"

"They killed the general leading the Wartide and saved everyone that're still standing here from being slaughtered. Doesn't breaking your body to keep the holy mountain from becoming a nikkuni den count for something?" Birger asked with a tinge of bitterness.

Exhaustion stripped him of tact, and concern for his friends left no room for worrying about the woman's opinion of him.

Ishyelle stared at Birger, the stillari's violet eyes shocked at his tone. He half-expected her to strike him down for his insolence. If she did, he hoped she would at least still see to the others.

"Where are they?" asked Ishyelle finally.

"This way, Your Holiness." Birger gestured, thinking it prudent to show some deference. Leading her to the cart, he explained, "The enemy shaman burned Renate with a strange green flame."

Gunther sat next to Mick, checking the slender man's pulse as he held his hand. Tears streaked down his face, cutting through the grime. Snow crooned over Renate, spinning a web over her wounds.

"Oh my," exclaimed the stillari woman, "a weavespider!"

"That's Snow," explained Birger, "he's hurt too."

"What happened?" asked Ishyelle.

"We fought a bolgar in Landlor Market, but luckily, we had a werewolf."

406

66

FAREWELL

Birger put his hand on the casket, and a tear trickled down his cheek. He stood at the rear of a wide black carriage with a pair of Sawran Highlanders ready to go, a transport coffin in its trunk.

The sun was warm in contrast to the chilly wind, and Birger felt the difference in weather phenomena mirrored his internal state. It had been four days since the slaughter; he felt grateful to be alive when many others weren't, but Kindra was still far from normalcy.

Birger walked gingerly to the carriage door. His right knee remained stiff, despite Chancebringer expediting his healing. His left arm, however, was in a sling; it appeared that for fractures in a mechanically significant area, even luck, magic, and proper binding had their limits.

"Stop that!" ordered Gunther. "Honestly, you're behaving like a child. The High Priestess said you must rest, or your back might never recover."

"Stop fussing over me," countered Mick. "I'm fine."

"No, you *aren't*," retorted Gunther. "Settle down so I can buckle you in for the trip."

The carriage interior boasted a velvet red lining, cushioned panels, and comfortable seats. Gunther sat sideways in the seat. Although only a bulge of bandages was visible through his trousers, Birger knew that Gunther's right leg was a mess. It was barely functional, and even with magical aid, recovery would take weeks or months.

Mick sat beside Gunther, trying, and failing, to strap himself in, while Gunther adjusted Mick's legs to a more comfortable position.

Mick's back had broken when he hit the smithy, and he no longer had control over anything below his sternum. The thought sent a pang of guilt through Birger. His plan had resulted in his friends paying such a dear price.

Birger cleared his throat and said, "You two are going to drive Becka mad before you get to Thornhall and she's gonna kick you out to sleep in the Nord."

"Birger," Mick's brow twisted into a grimace, "tell Gunther I don't need him to wipe my nose like I'm a child."

"You tell Mick," Gunther countered, "that he better stop fighting me and let me look after him."

"Fellas," Birger smiled, drawing on the mindweaver training Renate had given him. "Both of you, take a step back and think. What, would you like, to have, happen?"

"I want to feel like I'm not a Cos-damned invalid," said Mick, his voice laden with emotion.

"You aren't..." started Gunther, and Birger stopped him with a raised hand.

"What about you, Gunther?" asked Birger.

"I want to make sure Mick gets better and back on his feet," replied Gunther.

"Well, it sounds to me like you have common goals, gentlemen." Birger looked each of them in the eye. "So what is possible for you here?"

"Listen, Gunther," Mick said as he looked at the larger man, "thank you for trying to help me, but I need some space to do things for myself."

Gunther sat back and said, "I guess I've been a bit overly worried about you. Sorry, I'll let you do this."

"Nah." Mick shook his head in surrender. "It's me. I'm taking this out on you again. I can't get the buckles in, anyway. Can you do it?"

Gunther smiled and started working on the straps.

"There you go," Birger said, wearing a broad grin and feeling helpful.

"Sorry, Birger, I'm sure you didn't come here to save our marriage," said Gunther. "How can I help?"

Birger handed Gunther a note. "It's for the Queen," he said, his smile giving way to a solemn frown. "Lorenzo's last words."

Gunther paused a moment, allowing the silence to settle between them.

"I'll miss the man," said Gunther after a while, "I don't know if I'll ever get used to the idea that he's gone." Gunther gave Birger a wan smile, and added, "Consider it done. It'll be delivered to the Queen's own hand."

"Go save Wynn and make Ulfhild sorry she ever crossed paths with you, Boss." Mick offered a salute.

The smile returned to Birger's lips. "You got it."

408

The three exchanged pleasant goodbyes, and Birger closed the door. He turned to find Renate standing nearby in human form, wearing her usual blue dress. While her skin looked unmarred, Birger knew that her actual body was covered with blistering burn wounds.

With a knowing smile and her head tilted slightly to the right, Renate asked, "What's that in your hand?"

"I'm just finding a place for Lorenzo's things so they can go with him to West Haven," Birger explained. "I see that amulet High Priestess Ishyelle gave you is working."

Renate nodded, "It does. It puts a lot less strain on me than constantly holding a body morph spell together."

Slowly, Renate moved to Birger's side, each step drawing a wince of pain. She took the pack from him and began sifting through the contents. "We still have a lot of work ahead of us; your armour and clothes are in tatters. There's no way they would make it through another battle." Renate split the pack in two, placing some things aside and leaving others where they were.

After a moment, Renate pressed the new bundle she had assembled into Birger's hands and said, "Here, go get dressed. You can't walk around looking like you've been living in the Wild Lands. I'm meeting Eric near the Pilgrim's Rise. He said he found something we have to see."

Birger accepted the bundle with a nod of appreciation before Renate turned and left. He made his way to the house where they had set up temporary lodgings. The inns were all either bursting at the seams or reduced to rubble, while the battle left many houses unoccupied.

The lime-green building, with its red-tiled roof, was in poor condition, and the main room had an enormous boulder sitting in the centre; at least the three bedrooms that connected to it were still intact. But Birger found the familiar smell of dust comforting. It reminded him of his dilapidated warehouse in the Squat.

"Hey Snow!" Birger said, happy to see his seven-legged friend stretched out on the bed. He rubbed the weavespider's head with affection. Snow had continued to grow and now stood at the size of a pony. "Have I told you that you grow way too quickly?"

Birger sensed Snow feeling simultaneously embarrassed and proud. The weavespider disengaged and curled up on a spot where a few blankets lay in the shape of a comfortable nest.

Birger laid the gear on the bed, a lump forming in his throat that he swallowed hard to suppress. It didn't feel right to wear a dead man's clothes. Birger wondered if it would be easier to consider it a tribute?

On Benny's word, Lorenzo had taken him in and offered him a new life with a legitimate purpose. Lorenzo stood for ideals that Birger wished he could live up to.

Naturally, Lorenzo was not perfect and sometimes struggled to live up to his own ideals. Nevertheless, he always gave his best, and Birger aspired to follow in his footsteps. It gave him hope that a bastard thief from Anthir could become something else, something more.

Snow shook himself and watched Birger closely. He opened the leather satchel that again held the original encoded documents that had started all of this. Seeing them made Birger wonder about Wynn. There had been no sign of her since the temple, which was both disappointing and a relief because a body would've been worse.

What use could Ulfhild still have for the girl? Why keep her around now that the deception was done? wondered Birger, but he parked the thoughts. He had already spent a lot of time thinking about that over the last few days.

At the bottom of the bag, Birger found something glowing. It was barely visible, stuck under the leather lining. He extracted it and held the small glowing vial up. Etherweave... It must've fallen out of Lorenzo's stock.

Had Lorenzo not lost it, he might still be alive, lamented Birger. *Or perhaps he would've died of exhaustion the next day.* He shrugged and placed the stimulant into a pouch. He would figure out what to do with it later.

Birger slipped out of his sling and then took his old leather armour off. In this case, old was relative. It had only been a little over a week since he bought them in Stella. Holding it up with one hand, he saw what Renate meant as the light from the window shone through the holes. He tossed the worn gear to one side.

"Well, I guess all considered, I got my money's worth out of those," Birger joked, but Snow didn't respond.

Fortunately, Birger was roughly the same size as Lorenzo. He donned the green leather jerkin, threading his arms through. The left was more challenging and painful. While the jerkin wasn't tailored

410

for him as it had been for Lorenzo, it was close enough and looked neat.

He then slipped on the cedar jacket, adorned with floral embroidery, and fastened the bulbous buttons. Before long, all the straps and their many pouches crisscrossed his body. Maybe he looked like a paler version of Lorenzo, except for a worse haircut. The thought made Birger smile. His hair had turned into an unruly mop atop his head.

"A tribute," Birger said to Snow. "What do you think?"

Snow approved with a low purring sound.

After securing the buckles and placing his arm back in the sling, Birger headed out, with Snow lazily rising to his feet and follow.

Once outside, he paused by the carriage, placing his hand on the casket at the rear, and murmured thanks to Lorenzo. From within the cabin, he could hear Gunther and Mick bickering again. Birger sighed and then smiled. *Those two*, he thought, shaking his head.

From across the road, the driver came walking towards the carriage. Behind the man, Birger could see the crooked distillery tower in Landlor Market. The driver, a skeletal figure, wore a charcoal grey suit that seemed far too large for him, and his long grey beard sagged to his navel. He carried a bag of horse feed on his shoulder, which dusted his suit with particles.

"Lord Birger," the man said in a polite greeting. "Top of the morning to you. I hope all's in order."

"Yes, Henk. Everything is fine," Birger smiled, "and for Cos' sake, I'm not a lord."

"Excuse an old man, sir," Henk said with a slight bow. "I've never seen no ordinary folk dressed so fine."

Snow approached the old man, seeking a pat that Henk graciously provided. Snow was becoming skilled at looking non-threatening; after people got over their initial surprise, his reassuring aura did the rest. Even Gunther had come to tolerate, if not *like* Snow.

Birger gave the man a weak smile. "Please make sure the two in there have everything they need on the trip." He put a gold coin in the driver's hand.

"I surely will, sir," said Henk, taking the money with a toothless smile.

"Stay safe on the road." Birger felt a pang of concern and added, "The stragglers from the Wartide could still be out there."

"Oh, the convoy has a company of paladins as an escort. Don't you worry, sir," Henk placed the bag of feed on the footrest of the

411

driver's seat, ripped it open, he scooped some into two feeding sacks. He then hung them on the heads of the mares.

As Henk returned to the driver's seat, a stray dog emerged from a nearby alley. Strays had become a common sight in the city since the battle. The driver grabbed a piece of jerked meat from his supplies and tossed it to the dog, who devoured the morsel with eager whimpers.

Snow crouched and jumped playfully around the pup, waiting for it to finish its food. Once satisfied, the dog accommodated the weavespider in a game of chase.

Birger laughed at the display, and said, "All the best to you, Henk, and if I don't see you again. Thank you."

"Happy to serve, sir," Henk nodded, "and you stay safe, too. Oh, before I forget. Spy Master Black said she would come to find you soon. She's up at the temples in a council or some such."

Birger felt his hackles rise at the thought that Lorenzo had already been replaced. However, he reminded himself that he rather liked Becka and that Lorenzo himself wanted her to be his successor. A part of him still harboured the feeling that Lorenzo would come back. It was a silly thought, and he knew it.

Birger grimaced, "Thanks again, Henk."

The old man recognised Birger's expression and offered a sympathetic smile. "Do rest, young sir. A battle can leave you with many terrible ailments, not all physical."

Birger pursed his lips and said, "I appreciate your concern, Henk. Please, travel safely."

The two men exchanged nods, and Birger turned away. Snow broke off from his new playmate and joined Birger, walking towards the Pilgrim's Rise to find out what Eric had discovered.

67

IN PLAIN SIGHT

"Seeing the experience of another as if it were your own is the path to unified action, a path that leads us to balance and harmony." First Jing Emperor Lenri Oanti

Despite the cleaning efforts, the flagstone surface of Pilgrim's March remained stained with dried blood. Moving the bolgar's body proved particularly challenging, leaving a charred spot on Landlor Street where it was put to the torch. Simply walking past the ravaged buildings triggered a flood of terrible memories for Birger.

The colossal weavestorm implosion caused by Ulfhild left a vast gaping hole in the ground. Many surrounding buildings were still missing sections of wall or roof, and the storm itself persisted for two full days before subsiding.

So many lives lost right here, thought Birger, as he placed his hand on Kazania, feeling his heart throb in his chest. *I used to think I was untouchable, that I could find my way out of anything.* Again, Birger's thoughts turned to Wynn. And then Bo, the man's bulldog face, desperately calling for help. That was what haunted his sleep the most. Leaving a man, even an evil one, to his fate. *Am I cruel? Was leaving him trapped down there an evil act?*

Snow brushed against Birger, drawing him out of his rumination. He felt a wave of reassurance emanating from his companion. He forced a smile, and the weavespider hopped playfully, still lithe for his size.

Ovia Laquismja, the High Priestess of Cos, hailed Birger, Mick, Gunther, Renate, and Eric as heroes for taking out the enemy general and the bolgar. High Priestess Ishyelle even helped protect Eric's identity. She proclaimed the werewolf as an avatar of Lot fighting to defend the city at her behest. Despite the public celebration, Birger got the feeling there were politics at play that could just as easily have gone the other way. He wasn't sure that they wouldn't turn on him and his team now that the public eye had moved on.

413

Birger stood on the blood-stained landing, scanning for Renate among the people coming and going. He hoped that Eric's discovery didn't lead them up to the temples. He had more than enough of those steps for one lifetime.

To the north of the landing, a grand grey-stone temple with a blue roof stood tall. It bore many scars from the recent battle. The barricades had been cleared, but the hollow frames of shattered lead-glass windows glinted with fragments. Before the battle, Pilgrim's Grove was a lush park for weary travellers to rest. It lay behind the building, ravaged by fire, its lawn churned to mud.

Snow scuttled off in that direction and Birger noted movement between the trees. Eric was resting his shoulder against the back of the temple, and Renate stood nearby with a black cane for support.

"Birger!" Renate exclaimed when she spotted him. "You look splendid."

Eric grunted, pushing off the wall, walking north, "This way."

His left eye had mostly regenerated in its socket and a layer of thin pink skin had formed over the wound on his skull. He refused to conceal the gruesome healing process, much to the discomfort of onlookers.

"Good day Eric," Birger greeted.

Eric replied with a sullen shrug. After learning about Lorenzo, Eric had retreated into a less talkative disposition again.

"Becka was looking for us," Birger mentioned to Renate.

She came over to straighten Birger's lapel and tilted her head to the side. "You really do look stunning, you know." Her comment made him feel self-conscious. "She was at council. They're still deciding what to do about us. I hope she can appease them. Getting arrested, or having to escape, would be inconvenient. Either way, I'm sure she'll find us when she's ready."

Birger sounded more bitter to himself than he had intended when he said, "It's still hard to accept that she's the new Spy Master. My oath was to Lorenzo, not her."

"Yes," Renate fixed Birger's hair like his mother used to do when he was five. "You're free of your promise, but I encourage you to remember that Lorenzo wanted her to succeed him," she said, with a touch of reassurance.

"It's not right." Birger frowned.

"Which part?" asked Renate.

"The Queen chose Lorenzo's replacement so soon. He's only been gone a week." Emotions welled up in Birger; his cheeks grew

414

hot, his ears rang, and his vision tunneled. He inhaled deeply, as Lorenzo had taught him, regaining composure.

"What will you do?" Renate finished fixing Birger's hair and looked him in the eye.

"Don't know," admitted Birger. "Come, we'll lose Eric."

Eric was guiding them along the cliff face of the Holy Mountain. Above, Birger could see the top of the towers from the Temple of Lot poking up at the sky. He had avoided going back there since the battle. When asked, he blamed it on his knee, but in reality he harboured an irrational sense that Bo haunted the place.

Snow was trailing behind. Birger could sense the weavespider growing restless until a blue jay landed nearby, and Snow eagerly began stalking it. His initial pounce missed, but that seemed to spark a newfound zeal as he began to hunt any bird or flying insect in range.

Birger found himself smiling. Watching the display made it easier to keep the anxiety at bay.

"The Queen did it with a heavy heart, Birger." Renate gave him a compassionate smile as they walked and said, "Becka's up to the task. She's a competent leader and spy. Lorenzo personally trained her for this specific role."

Birger shrugged. His emotions couldn't be rationalised away; he had already tried. They just were what they were.

Eric sauntered on without care, and Birger wished he could be as stoic as the big Wulfher. Then again, maybe Eric felt it as much as anyone, but buried it in silence.

Snow made a sudden lunge for a beetle scuttling across the path. A large creature being so playful was an amusing sight, even drawing a grin from Eric.

A few hundred feet ahead, Birger spotted some houses. One nestled against the mountain, and Eric headed towards it. He noticed the house had piles of mud heaped around it.

Seeing his curiosity, Eric remarked, "The mounds seemed out of place, considering what you mentioned about them digging up to the chapel."

Shielding his eyes from the sun with his hand, Birger asked, "Did the mutts live there? How did no one notice they were doing this?"

"The dirt smells fresh," said Eric. "Two weeks at most. People don't care if their neighbours are digging holes."

"Less than two weeks – that's just before the siege. And by the end, the chaos outside the walls must've been too distracting," Birger guessed, speeding up despite his troublesome knee.

Renate struggled to keep pace, but she was well ahead of Snow. Finally, realising he was lagging behind, Snow abandoned his sport to dart after them.

Birger and Eric reached the brick house. The odour of death hung in the air. The front door was open. Dried, charcoal-grey mud, akin to the colour of the nearby cliffs, trailed into the main living area. Birger stepped inside, his hand on Kazania.

"There's no one alive inside," assured Eric with a shrug.

Birger let Kazania drop back into her scabbard. The stink of a days-old dead body multiplied tenfold, and his heart sank with dread. "Someone dead?"

"It isn't her," said Eric, his voice uncommonly gentle. He didn't follow Birger inside. "It's a man in black leather armour, deep cut on the inside of his arm. Has a wooden mallet next to him."

Birger pursed his lips. An image flashed through his mind, *Ice creeping up Lorenzo's cheek, reaching for his eyes ...*

He took a deep breath. These flashes were unpredictable. Birger had hoped that getting over Benny's death had put them behind him, but since the battle, he had a whole new array to draw on.

Pressing on, hoping no one caught his momentary pause, Birger offered, "Probably the thug who attacked Lorenzo and me."

Trying not to think about the man he killed, Birger began his investigation. The small room had a simple wooden table in the centre. Several half-eaten meals were on plates next to a burnt-out candle. A basin of muddy water was on a low stool by the entrance, facing an empty cabinet.

Snow darted in behind him, scrutinising the place with obvious curiosity. Amused, he watched the large weavespider snuffle things.

Birger turned to the corridor, heading left. A short hall led to two rooms facing the front of the house, and on the opposite side, a stairwell connected to the basement. He checked the rooms first. Each contained bedrolls from wall to wall, and on one lay a bloated dead man.

The revolting stench sent waves of nausea over Birger. He fought down the urge to vomit and closed the door. It didn't help much.

The basement was next. On hyper-alert, he carefully scanned for traps, but found none. It smelled damp and mouldy as a ship's bilge, mounds of damp mud heaped in every corner. A square table holding papers huddled in the dark next to the stairs. He struck the candle with his flint and steel.

In the dim light, Birger identified the four forgeries they had let Wynn steal. The fifth with false information was missing.

It appeared that someone had made multiple unsuccessful attempts to decipher the remaining documents. A sheet of paper that caught his eye looked crumpled up, tossed in the mud, then flattened, cleaned, and reused.

Written on the paper, the words 'Death comes'.

Birger slipped the note into his pocket and discovered an opened letter beneath it. Tucked into one corner of the page was a lock of mouse-brown hair, secured with a seal of red wax. He read it:

Bo, just do what you're told! Your incompetence in letting the street rat escape Anthir has jeopardised more than you know. This lock of hair came from your living daughter within the hour of writing this letter. If you bring the Eye of Winter to Roviere, you'll see her again. If not, my next letter will contain a finger. You'll use Wynn to get under Birger's skin. Force a mistake and exploit it. I don't care if you like it or not. We can't let Lorenzo figure out what we're doing. Kill Lorenzo if you can, but don't send any more pigeons. You're endangering our mission. Get it done.

– The Grand Priest.

Birger swallowed the lump forming in his throat. *Bo had a daughter?* he thought to himself. *I had no idea.*

Grief swelled in his belly as he realised he had orphaned a child. *Bo wasn't particularly old; his daughter couldn't possibly be an adult yet, could she? Would the Grand Priest consider the task fulfilled even though Bo hadn't survived?* He stroked the lock of hair. It felt soft, and he remembered the wooden doll Ulfhild took from Bo on the rooftops near Foss.

Reading the letter, Birger's self-righteous justification for letting Bo die under the temple felt hollow, and guilt gnawed at him. He had to make it right somehow. He didn't even know the girl's name. He only had a lock of her hair.

Then something struck him about the letter... "Interesting," murmured Birger. "Why not kill me?"

Something to consider later, he decided. Putting the letter aside, Birger scanned the room. Opposite the table was a tunnel entrance carved into the mountain. He recognised the scar pattern. *Definitely Ymir's Breath.* He stared into the dark tunnel. In his mind's eye, he could see Wynn running towards him, heading out of the city.

417

"Find anything?" Renate's voice echoed off the walls.

"Yeah…they were here," Birger said. "I found more of the code. 'Death comes'. Very dramatic. They cut through the mountain and tunneled up from here."

"Clever. Nobody would've suspected they could do such a thing," said Renate. "They've certainly made a mess."

Birger reached into his satchel and withdrew the original documents, flattening them on the table. Then, he retrieved Lorenzo's custom pince-nez from a pouch, trying to recall how it worked. He held it up to his eye. Some letters had a black square flipped over them with a white letter in the center.

Birger examined the gears on the device. A series of tiny flip cards read 'Death co'. Birger tested the gear switch that was furthest forward, and a small metal frame shifted from 'o' to 'c' in 'co'. He clicked the gear back, and the frame shifted back to 'o'. An additional click positioned the frame over an empty slot.

Rotating the gear next to it, he saw the space change to '0', then '1'. He cycled through the alphabet until he reached 'm'. Testing his hunch, he held the pince-nez up to his eye. More black squares appeared with letters on them. He shifted the frame to the next blank spot and entered 'e', then 's'.

"What do you see?" Renate asked, her footsteps echoing on the wooden floor as she approached.

"I can read the first document now. Instructions to steal the Eye of Winter from Kindra. It says there would be an attack on the city as a distraction. It also mentions that Ymir's Breath would be delivered by a courier and to use it to tunnel through the mountain." Birger rubbed the short stubble on his chin. He needed a shave. "Things we already know."

Renate smiled at him. "Good thing you cleared that up…" she remarked with sarcasm. "What about the other documents?"

"Almost there, bear with me," Birger replied as he turned the page. The first eleven letters made sense, but the rest was gibberish. "It seems to be deciphering only the first eleven letters."

"You might need to add more blanks because this document's key is longer," commented Renate helpfully.

Birger checked the pince-nez once more to see if that was possible. It had a third gear. Recalling Lorenzo explaining how to add more characters, he adjusted the device, moving a metal arrow one space right of 's'. He held the lens to his eye and looked at the document. Still no change. He continued clicking the gear. After eight more clicks, a sensible pattern emerged.

Renate, noticing his pause, asked, "Is it working?"

"Somewhat. It's hard to say. It's talking about a crown in Lorilla. I can only read fragments of the sentences." Birger squinted as if that would help, but it didn't.

"Lorilla?" Renate considered it. "I thought you said that Wynn was going to Roviere?"

Birger nodded. "That's what she said. Bo was to take the Eye of Winter there."

"I guess there might be something happening in both locations." Renate glanced at him with concern before adding, "Roviere is on the way to Lorilla if we take the ocean route. We can look for Wynn while we pass through?"

Birger gave Renate a grateful smile. Despite Wynn's betrayal, he knew Renate cared for her, or she cared for Birger caring for Wynn. It hardly mattered which, the result was the same. He began packing the documents into his satchel. While returning the pince-nez to its pouch, Snow scuttled down the stairs, a mouse clutched in his mandibles.

"Seriously?" Birger shot a grimace at Snow. "Can't you find a less messy toy?"

Snow tilted his head to the side and wiggled his body, signalling he wanted to play. The weavespider set the dead mouse on the floor, nudging it towards him.

"No." Birger shook his head. "I'm not going to play fetch with that."

He sensed Snow's disappointment and felt bad. "I'm working..." he explained.

"Should we go and find Becka?" Renate asked, a broad smile betraying her amusement at the comical exchange.

68

A NEW JOURNEY BEGINS

Birger appreciated the fresh air after being enclosed with the potent scent of death inside the building. Eric was leaning against a splintered tree, fiddling with the leather straps of his unusual axe, as Renate and Birger emerged from the mud-caked house. The sun cast a gleam on the fuzzy ring of hair surrounding Eric's bald patch, giving it a halo-like appearance.

Snow darted past Birger's legs, almost toppling him over.

"Hey!" Birger called out to Snow.

However, the furry white weavespider ignored him, as it set off in pursuit of a squirrel.

He observed workers mending the section of the wall that Ulfhild had demolished during the battle. He shuddered to think that he was chasing someone with that kind of power. Thanks to that breach, this area took the brunt of the Wartide's assault, with the desolate shells of broken homes lining the streets.

"Does your axe have a name?" asked Birger.

"What?" Eric fixed him with his half-formed, exposed eyeball.

"Your axe," Birger pointed. "It looks special, does it have a name?"

Eric nodded. "Her name is Bonereaper, and yes, she *is* special." He perked up and asked, "Found what you were looking for in there?"

"We found something," Birger acknowledged.

"Birger managed to decipher part of the second document," Renate said, her tone laced with praise.

"He did?" Eric nodded approvingly. "Maybe you'll fill Lorenzo's boots after all."

Birger's mouth dropped open, not knowing how to respond to the comment.

"So…" Eric scowled. "What was it?"

Birger fumbled with his words briefly, before saying, "Their next target is in Lorilla. As before, we can only decipher half the words because of the encryption."

"Lorilla is full of wizards... I detest wizards," Eric uttered, his gruesome scowl intensifying.

"Why don't you like wizards?" Renate wondered. "You didn't seem to have a problem with priests?"

"Priests get their magic from the goddesses," explained Eric. "Wizards steal it from others. They take what isn't theirs and then use it to power their spells. You know better than anyone, Renate. A wizard would be happy to lop off your tongue, or pull my fangs for their spell pouch." Eric spat on the ground.

"How's that different from hunting a bear and hanging it over your shoulder?" Birger pointed at the fur pelt that made up much of Eric's armour.

"No one asked you, smart arse," Eric grumped. "Hunting isn't the same. I kill to eat and warm myself. It's the natural order of things, and any trophy I take is a tribute to the beast I killed. This bear fought well, and I proudly carry his bravery with me. Wizards take specimens to study and for experiments. They have no respect for those they take it from and they kill with traps. No sense of honour."

Eric's face became a storm cloud, and Birger sensed he had struck a nerve.

"Totally different," retorted Birger, failing to hide the sarcasm.

Eric opened his mouth to speak again, but shut it, glaring at him. The Wulfher had a good glare; it got under Birger's skin almost instantly.

"Good afternoon," Becka startled them as she stepped out from the grove. Brother Hein marched at her flank. His shield was scarred, and he had a bandage wrapped around his head that bundled his white hair together.

"Becka!" Renate exclaimed, spreading her arms wide with her black cane in hand, enveloping Becka in a hearty embrace, followed by a peck on each cheek. "How are you?"

"Doing well, thank you, Renate." Becka pulled away, smiling. She had cropped black hair, donned a fitted maroon coat adorned with white angular stitching. Her hands were resting on a pair of long daggers that almost qualified as short swords. "I hope I'm not interrupting anything."

Eric huffed at her, and Birger considered himself lucky that she intruded, because he was close to making things worse.

"We were just debriefing after investigating the mutt's hideout," Birger stated, casting a sidelong glance towards Hein.

"Oh?" Becka looked eager. "What did you find?"

"The mutts are targeting another artefact in Lorilla. All I could get was that they wanted a 'crown' there. And it looks like the Eye of Winter will travel through Roviere," said Birger. "They've aggressively pursued these 'Pieces of Divinity', and have at least two in hand already. Before he died, Bo said that they were going to use them to summon an old god from beyond the Darkveil to help them stop the Feet of Sarghus from invading."

Snow approached Becka and nuzzled against her leg. Stroking the fur on his head, she exclaimed, "Oh, hello, Snow! I hardly recognised you. You've grown huge!" Still petting the big white fluff ball, she said to Birger, "A righteous cause makes for the most dangerous enemies. When you believe the ends justify the means, laying waste to a city seems worth it."

Birger became acutely aware of the surrounding destruction. The memory of Ulfhild slaying the second Wartide shaman flashed through his head.

"Is it true?" asked Birger. "Have we known that Murapii were coming and ignored it?"

Becka's mouth turned into a thin line. "I believe so, yes."

Birger cocked an eyebrow. "Why?"

"It began quite subtly," explained Becka. "Duke Londel brought it up, fought to seek them out and stop them. However, the other nobles, including the Queen, assumed he was employing scare tactics to amass political power. Only a few other nobles rallied behind him. Roar, Earl Irthan, and so on. Both Queen Armandine and King Ferdinand refused the claims."

"But they *are* here... We saw them in Thornhall," Birger insisted.

"Yes," agreed Becka. "It would seem they were right. Our spies in Mura tell us they've mustered a large army and fleet. Itavia and Murapii are engaged in a border war. The group you encountered were scouts. Similar ones have been causing problems throughout the kingdom. We're already mobilising to counter."

"Gullshite," Birger blurted out. "Well, Ulfhild first, then the tin-birds."

"It appears events have set your mission, isn't it?" Becka's tone indicated she was seeking confirmation rather than making a proposition.

"I gave Lorenzo my word that I'll carry Kazania to fulfil his oath. So, by the Magpies' Code, I must stop her," Birger stated. His tone left no doubt about where he would go. He had no time for games and this was his mission now.

"I own a place in Lorilla. It's high time I dropped by to ensure things are in order." Renate wrapped an arm around Birger's shoulder and gave a gentle squeeze. He was thankful she remembered not to do that on his left.

"I have no interest in the wizards," said Eric.

"Oh, that's unfortunate. I'm sure Renate and I will handle the next bolgar or dragon the mutts throw at us," quipped Birger.

"Dragons?" Eric cast a sceptical glance at Birger. "There haven't been dragons in Azrea for hundreds of years."

"Neither had the Wartide attacked Southern Azrea in hundreds of years...before now," Birger countered.

Eric smiled and said, "That's true, Birger. I like the way you think. Okay, I'll come."

"You have one more," interjected Becka. "The Council of the Five are sending their own agent with you to recover the Eye."

The Council of the Five was the name for the united church of the Cult of the Weave. Kindra might have been located in West Rendin, but it didn't belong to Queen Armandine in any way. The Council, religious leaders of the entire continent, held supreme authority here.

Birger glanced at Hein. *Oh no, not him.*

"We don't need a priest," Eric rumbled disdainfully. "I don't have time to wipe some snot-nose bookworm's tears off their cheek."

"I'm afraid it's not negotiable," said Becka. "The Council wanted to hold Birger responsible for the damage to the Chapel of Lot. Their envoy coming along was the only way to keep their wrath in check."

"Let them try." Eric's lips contorted into a feral snarl, and Birger could almost swear the man's teeth grew longer. "We saved their precious hill, and *this* is the thanks we get."

"It's alright, Eric," Renate interjected. "Let's hear Becka out."

"I thought Ishyelle was on *our* side?" Birger asked.

"She is," agreed Becka. "But there are five temple leaders on the council, and she's only one voice. The other four weren't as understanding. High Priestess Ovia, in particular, wasn't happy."

"Who are they sending?" Birger thought he knew the answer.

"That would be me," said Hein. "I'm your snot-nose priest with tears on his cheek."

Eric and Hein locked eyes.

"We accept," Birger cut in. He didn't want to, but having Eric rip the man apart would force them to flee the city, and that seemed less than desirable in their current state.

Eric growled, but he let it drop.

"Looks like you have a team, Birger." Becka remarked with a smile. "Lorenzo was right about you."

A flush crept up Birger's cheeks at the remark.

"There is one more thing," said Becka. "Lord Caoimhín was taken by ukthuun when his caravan passed the Darkveil along Lake Water Heart. Sir Kallen and an envoy from Stillendam are in pursuit."

"Lord Caoimhín was taken?" Renate furrowed her brow. "They targeted him specifically?"

"My sources tell me that during the ambush, Lord Caoimhín and Sir Kallen were the targets, but Sir Kallen proved too hard to take, and they settled for his father. Though I imagine there to be a connection between Caoimhín's knowledge and the artefacts Ulfhild is after." Becka looked at Birger.

He nodded, then he tilted his head and popped an eyebrow at Becka. "So now that you've baited your hook, why're you telling us this?"

Becka smiled, and said, "Aren't you a clever one?" She turned towards Eric. "I need to know if the Grengar King would ally with the Pogtor Wartide?"

"Zholani?" Eric looked sceptical. "Not likely. He only works with those that subjugate themselves to him and the uks don't seem inclined to do that."

"So how would Zholani feel about the uks being in his domain?" Becka asked with a sly smile.

"That depends how the uks went about it. If they paid tribute, Zholani would've allowed it. If they didn't, he likely already knows and aching to rip a few heads off." Eric gave her a look that said, where are you going with this?

"What would it take to get an audience with Zholani?" asked Becka.

"I didn't spend much time *visiting* him. Grengar tea parties aren't as posh as the ones that West Haven nobles like to have," said Eric, oozing with sarcasm. "I don't know. I know he likes gold. Perhaps with a big enough tribute, he won't eat you or your messenger."

"Not getting eaten sounds like a good start." Becka scratched her chin as she considered her options. "Thank you. I can work with that. What would it take to get your father to go with me to see him?"

"That pig-headed tyrant wouldn't go speak to Zholani if you could drag him there by his tail," Eric uttered with a palpable sneer.

Becka offered a tight-lipped smile. "I guessed as much. Anything you can think of that could help me?"

Eric regarded her in silence for an extended time. Then his face split into a toothy grin. "You said that a stillari envoy was chasing the uks? Well, my father hates the stillari more than anything else. If you convince him that the stillari would do it instead of him, then his pride won't allow him to say no."

"Interesting, Lord Walt hates stillari?" Becka tapped her nose thoughtfully. "I can work with that. Thank you, Eric."

Eric shrugged.

"Birger, do you still have Ymir's Breath with you?" Becka asked.

"I do. Why?"

"I would like to have it, please," said Becka.

"It's good for cutting holes, but I wouldn't suggest it as a source for cold showers. Why do you want it?" asked Birger.

Becka chuckled and said, "I'll keep that in mind, but no. It'll be handy for dealing with the grengar. They can only die by fire, so freezing them should be safe and give me space to negotiate without the fear of being eaten."

"Well, be careful. It didn't work on a bolgar." Birger smiled. "Alright." He reached into his satchel and extracted it.

"Thanks," said Becka. Snow protested when she stopped rubbing his head to stow the artefact.

"Right," Birger extended his functional arm, acutely aware of the stiffness of his many injuries. "I guess we're ready to go stop Ulfhild from summoning a god."

Epilogue

WINTER, 733A.R.M. POGTOR, WILD LANDS

The fist struck Caoimhín so hard that his toes started tingling. He could taste the coppery tang of blood, which told him that his teeth had cut the inside of his lip. He feigned unconsciousness, hoping the large ukthuun standing over him would lose interest. But the brute kicked him in the ribs anyway.

"Humans weak," said the ukthuun warden.

The female ukthuun towered over Caoimhín, standing taller by two heads and having shoulders twice as broad. He had heard his ukthuun cellmate, by the name Kubaal, call her Wari. Kubaal uttered something in their language, laden with heavy syllables and intriguing clicking sounds. Caoimhín had been paying close attention and figured out a few key words.

Kubaal was conveying to her that there was no honour in assaulting the defenceless. Caoimhín thought the big ukthuun referred to a god by the name of Ukthu as a reason.

Wari spat on Caoimhín. An indignity, but hardly the worst he had endured during his capture. The female ukthuun walked out of the small dark hole in the ground, locking the cell door behind her.

"You can stop pretending. Wari gone," Kubaal said in a voice so low that it almost sounded like a pestle grinding against pewter.

Caoimhín coughed in pain and spat blood onto the floor. Kubaal was naked, save for a small cloth that matched Caoimhín's, and the ukthuun offered him a cup of water.

Caoimhín sat up and took the water. "Thank you."

"Wari angry with not going on Siphkuwa, Wari thinks you're to blame," said Kubaal.

The ukthuun's broad frame was heavily muscled, and his skin marred with plenty of scars. He had waist-length blue hair with a streak of white.

Leaning against the stone walls of their cell, Caoimhín cast his eyes upwards to a small hole in the ceiling. These allowed light and water to trickle in from the melting ice outside. He sipped from the cup and placed it back under the drip.

"So, you were telling me about the gods of your people," said Caoimhín as if they hadn't been interrupted. "Let me see if I understand correctly. Siphok is a black woolly rhinoceros that protects you in war. Nokkuwa is a giant serpent that keeps your magic flowing and... Help me understand Ukthu better. He seems at odds with your society?"

"At odds?" asked Kubaal with narrowed eyes.

"Doesn't fit," explained Caoimhín. "You mentioned he's a white lion that brings tranquillity. Yet, all I associate with the ukthuun is a desire to hunt and fight."

"All warrior fight and all warrior want peace. Not your soldiers end their war and come home?" asked Kubaal.

"They do," said Caoimhín, rubbing his bruised ribs.

"Nobork clan wants to see peace. We wish for Ukthu to guide all, and other gods to protect. Pogtor wants Nokkuwa to rule, and Ukthu to obey."

"I see, so your clan and our host's differ on religious grounds. Is that why you're here?" asked Caoimhín.

Kubaal nodded.

An alarmed shout with a clash of weapons came from outside. Kubaal shot to his feet and walked over to the thick ironwood cell door to see if he could make sense of the commotion. Caoimhín tried to follow, but getting up was hard with a broken left foot.

"A fight outside," said Kubaal as he dropped down to flip their cup over on the ground.

With a big bare-foot, he smashed the tin cup flat and picked it up.

"What are you doing?" asked Caoimhín. "That's our only water."

"Need for escape."

Kubaal set to work on the door, wedging the flattened cup between the locking mechanism and the frame. Caoimhín watched him as the big green character worked. His tongue sticking out at the corner of his mouth as he did.

"Even if we escape, with my broken foot and being in the Wild Lands, wouldn't we freeze to death?" asked Caoimhín. He had learnt that the imposing green ukthuun was far more clever than he appeared.

"Steal clothes on the way," said Kubaal, his scowl of concentration transforming into a triumphant smile as the door swung open. "And I carry you."

428

Kubaal didn't wait for Caoimhín to answer; he simply picked him up and started out of the cell. They found themselves in a wide hall lined with multiple doors and a stairwell at the end. Kubaal unlocked cell after cell as he went, shouting something in the ukthuun language that Caoimhín believed meant, 'It's time to fight.'

Caoimhín felt like a sack of potatoes as Kubaal carried him out into the cold air. The ukthuun camp was primarily constructed of wood and thatch. Blanketed in snow, the biting wind threatened to peel Caoimhín's skin off as they sprinted.

Smoke was billowing well outside the walls and greenskin warriors in armour carrying weapons rushed towards the gates.

Behind them, the prison was carved out of stone. Only a foot of the flat-topped building rose above ground, nearly naked ukthuun from the Nobork clan flooding up the steps.

Screams were erupting from the gate as Kubaal set Caoimhín down, the snow biting at the skin of his exposed feet.

"Pig poops!" exclaimed Caoimhín, reeling from the pain.

"Sorry," replied Kubaal. "Get clothes, wait here."

Kubaal dashed towards a log cabin with supplies piled in front of it. An armed soldier bolted out of the building, only to collide with Kubaal's fist; the warrior's horned helmet was sent flying back indoors.

Kubaal grabbed the other ukthuun by the face and smashed the back of their head into the stone floor, before taking the warrior's axe. He vanished into the shop and a moment later came out with a stack of furs.

Caoimhín shook uncontrollably by the time Kubaal draped the thick fur over him. The boots he offered were far too large. On the bright side, his broken foot had become too numb from the cold to ache any longer.

"What now?" asked Caoimhín. "And where has everyone gone?"

"Dunno," shrugged Kubaal. "We run." With that, the big ukthuun scooped Caoimhín up and started heading for the gate.

It was ajar, and from beyond, mist rolled in, accompanied by the cacophony of an intense battle. A hundred ukthuun warriors remained at the palisade to guard the walls.

"How are we going to make it through that?" asked Caoimhín.

"Stop here!" cried Wari, running towards them.

The ukthuun female wore red hide leather and had feathers braided into her long red hair. Kubaal called and his fifteen hastily clothed Nobork warriors rushed to his side. Wari followed suit, rallying fifty Pogtor brutes to hers. Caoimhín and Kubaal found themselves outnumbered, and most of the newly-liberated Nobork were unarmed.

"Pants," cursed Caoimhín.

A tumultuous uproar erupted at the gate as blue lightning tore through the ukthuun guards. Bodies exploded into pieces and blood painted the snow. Wari turned to look at the mayhem and her green skin went pale.

"What's happening?" asked Caoimhín.

Kubaal simply shrugged and adopted a battle-ready stance. Blue arcs of energy tore through the ukthuun as though they were no more than dandelions, culminating in a strike landing on Wari. In an instant, she was reduced to a scarlet mist against the white ice, with a towering figure looming over the spot where she once stood.

Caoimhín had to rub his eyes to make sure he wasn't seeing things. In front of him stood his son, but it wasn't Kallen. His face was the same, but his eyes burned with blue fire and his blonde hair drifted upwards as if lifted by the heat of a flame. Blue lightning danced over his body, originating from the long ornate two-handed sword that hung loosely in his right hand. His armour barely covered all seven-and-a-half-foot of him.

"Father," Kallen said, his voice echoing as if spoken in a cave.

"K-Kallen?"

430

Glossary

MAGIC SYSTEM

Terms	Description
Weave	An arcane web, a vibrant ecosystem pulsating with the harmonious flow of magic. Magical cords, known as the material, stretch in all directions with streams of energy running through them. In the section that connects to Azrea, the goddess Mag nestles at the heart of this sprawling network.

Untamed, neutral magic run along the cords of the Weave that function like veins of raw, potent energy. Celestial entities like Mag continually crafting and regenerating the complex web, and fortifying the network.

While connected to the Weave, this magical power is at its peak. But, once a part of the web is taken to a different realm, it starts diminishing. Keeping a crafting connected to the Weave is hard. Only the most skilled people who understand magic can make objects that keep their magic and it usually requires orillium. This involves making a persistent rift to the Weave within the item. These items are very dangerous to make and when they're destroyed cause weavestorms. Lesser creations lose their power fast, and rarely can spells last more than a day without a connection to the Weave; most lose power in a few minutes. The web material is malleable and can be shaped easily, especially by someone with the right tools and skills.

Rift	Magic users spend their life force to rip a tear from their realm to the Weave and must continue to spend more in order to keep the rift open. Rifts have to be carefully controlled or they can escalate into a Weavestorm. Rifts are the primary way to retrieve neural material for crafting spells.
Spell Crafting	Materials from the Weave are filled with energy, but they are blank slates. Spell crafting is the art of taking this material, encoding it with a behaviour, and then powering it with life essence. The more complex the encoding, the more time and effort it takes to create the spell. Spell crafters can template spells for later use, which allows them to cast complex spells more quickly.
Natural Magic	Creatures that have essence with an innate tendency towards a particular behaviour. An example would be a Jormunger which has a natural tendency towards life. Their essence permits spell crafting to grow, regress, heat, cool, brighten, darken, dull or enhance the natural properties of an object or person. Every entity has different properties, and some are more powerful, while others may be more diverse.
Divine Magic	Deities are Natural Magic Users with extensive domains. They have the ability to grant their Life Essence to their agents to empower spells through conduits like holy symbols. Since the connection between follower and deity is managed by a much more powerful being, their rifts are more stable and their spells more predictable.
Arcane Magic	Wizards study the properties of other life forms to understand their interactions with

magic. They harvest the Life Essence of those beings, carrying them in spell pouches to use in crafting. This means that Wizards are able to cast a much more diverse set of spells as long as they have access to their components.

Encoding

A verb that describes giving a spell crafting a particular behaviour or set of behaviours. It requires physical contact between the crafter and the material draw from the Weave. The material must still contain enough neutral magic to encode, and the user needs a clear mental image of their intent to project into the material. Finally, the crafter spends their own Life Force to fuse the behaviour into the weave.

To dispel the encoding also requires physical contact. While it's easier to dispel than encode, some spells are inherently difficult to dispel. For instance, touching a fire spell can be deadly. A spell crafter could also have encoded a counter measure, like an explosion triggered by a dispel.

The crafter can set trigger conditions, provide instructions in terms of how energy should be spent, and use logic to dictate other conditional behaviours. Each behaviour the crafter adds to the spell must be powered with Life Essence that can create that kind of effect.

For instance, a fireball would require a spell crafter to use Living Essence with a heating component and a kinetic energy component to mix into the material. The spell crafter would then set a trigger such as "on contact with a surface other than my own hand, ignite and explode".

The more complicated the instructions, the more time it takes to craft the spell and the more likely it is to go wrong.

433

Life Force	Simply put, it's a soul. Energy that allows an object to resist entropy. Any living thing in the realms has it. Draining too much of something's Life Force allows entropy to overwhelm it and leads to death.
Life Essence	The way that something's physical existence interacts with its Life Force, leading to its particular nature, pattern of life and nature of its death. The essence types are Light (modifies brightness), Life (modifies natural properties), Weave (modifies sentience), Shadow (modifies desire). Light combings with Life to modify temperature. Life with Shadow modifies energy consumption. Shadow and Weave imparts control, while Light and the Weave affect gravity. Everything is tied to one or more of these essences and as such is able to learn to modify themselves accordingly.

RELIGIONS

Terms	Description
Cult of the Weave	The religion honours the cycle of life, death, creation, and destruction, as well as the natural order of things. It emphasizes maintaining balance, delaying entropy, compassion, charity, honesty, integrity, duty, and responsibility.
The Ladies	The five goddesses of the Cult of the Weave are sometimes called the Ladies. They are Aeg, Cos, Jor, Lot and Mag.
Aeg	Domains of power: Oceans, chance, change, travel. Holy Symbol: A crescent wave. Avatar: A dragon. Personality: Aeg is a capricious goddess who is connected to the oceans. She is seen as the embodiment of chance and change, and is believed to control the fates of those who travel the oceans. With her twin sister Mag, they see different possible futures. Preferred weapon: A trident.
Cos (All-Mother)	Domains of power: Light, protection, healing, motherhood. Holy Symbol: Pentacle. Avatar: A beautiful woman standing in the sun Personality: Cos is a compassionate and nurturing goddess who is connected to the needs of her followers. She is the embodiment of light and protection, and is seen as a loving mother. Preferred weapon: A spear.
Jor	Domains of power: Nature, land, earth, agriculture. Holy Symbol: Upsidedown Pentagon inside a right-side-up Pentagon. Avatar: Feathered flying serpent.

Personality: Jor is a wild and untamed goddess who is deeply connected to the earth. She is seen as a protector of the land, and is believed to be able to shape the earth to her will. She is a goddess of mining, agriculture and is closely associated with the cycle of the seasons.
Preferred weapon: A scythe.

Lot   Domains of power: Winter, summer, life, death.
Holy Symbol: A spiralled tear.
Avatar: A great winter wolf.
Personality: Lot is a goddess who embodies the cyclical nature of existence. She is a goddess of winter and summer, life and death. People see her as a force that brings balance to the natural world.
Preferred weapon: A sickle.

Mag   Domains of power: Magic, balance, knowledge, divination.
Holy Symbol: Octagonal Web.
Avatar: Giant Purple Spider.
Personality: Mag is a wise and powerful goddess. She is seen as a guardian of knowledge and the balance of magic. With her twin sister Aeg, they see different possible futures.
Preferred weapon: A wand.

Belmung   Enlightened God of Destruction trapped within a sword that is named after him. It's currently with Kallen du la Rent.

Kazamung Twisted God of Creation that is trapped inside a pair of daggers, which are with Ulfhild.

Hazmothane The First Son, god of the Cycle. Trapped in the Realm of Shadow behind the Darkveil.

Anchorhall The Cult of the Weave believe this is where the righteous and valiant souls go to enjoy a drink with the All-mother.

Ice Vault Those who disrupt balance and cause entropy weaken their own souls and cannot be sustained in Anchorhall. Instead, Lot keeps them frozen in her vault.

Holy Council	The five High Priests and Priestesses of the Cult of the Weave that preside over the faith from Kindra.
Realm of Magic / Weave of Magic	A place that exists parallel to the physical world. For the section that connects to Azrea, Mag sits at the centre of the arcane web, known as the Weave, and maintains it. The Weave touches both the light and the dark realm simultaneously while physically existing in a dimension between them. These realms run parallel to the world wherein humans live.
Realm of Light	The home of the Ladies that few mortals have ever visited. Most deities are born in the Realm of Light.
Realm of Shadow	A realm of dangerous predators, often called daemons, that crave to feed on light and life from other realms. Some entities in the Shadow Realm rival the power of any deity.
Darkveil	The barrier that keeps Hazmothane and other creatures from the Realm of Shadow out of the physical world around Azrea.
Cult of Sarghus	The Cult of Sarghus has a long and complex history on the Apour Continent. It's believed to have originated in the ancient kingdom of Sarghus, which existed over a thousand years ago on Apour. The religion focused on the worship of a single deity named Sarghus, whom they believed created and protected the world. After the collapse of Sarghus, it came to be adopted by the empires of Kurhan and Murapii as their primary state religions. However, as the cult spread and grew in influence, a significant schism emerged between the two branches.
Cult of Sarghus: Divine	Practiced in Murapii, focused on the worship of Sarghus as a divine being who could grant favours and blessings to his followers. This branch of the cult placed greater emphasis on ritual and ceremony, and favours the ruling class and the aristocracy.

Cult of Sarghus: Beacon	Practiced in Kurhan, focused on the worship of Sarghus as a beacon of hope and guidance for the people. This branch of the cult promoted personal spiritual growth and self-improvement. It placed an emphasis on the importance of morality and ethics in daily life.
Frost Wild	Revered by the savage races of the Wild Lands as powerful and an unpredictable force of nature. Its deities are worshiped with bloody sacrifices and rituals to gain their favour in battles and hunts.
Nokkuwa: Goddess of magic and death	Domains of power: Death, magic, and the underworld. Avatar: giant serpent with scales as black as night. Personality: She is a mysterious and powerful goddess that is known for her volatility. Preferred weapon: Curved dagger with a blade made of ice.
Siphok: God of War and Conquest	Domains of power: War, strength, and conquest Avatar: Black woolly rhinoceros with a pair of razor-sharp horns. Personality: He is a fierce and relentless god who only respects the strong. Preferred weapon: massive two-handed axe.
Ukthu: God of Peace and Tranquility	Domains of power: Life, light, and nature. Avatar: White lion with a mane made of radiant light. Personality: He is a calm and wise god who is respected. He is invoked on all agreements as a fair judge. Preferred weapon: long staff adorned with white gems.
Jing Belief	A religion with no deities where the people of Isai believe in the power of their unity as the primary power that protects them. The people of Jing are not Humans.

GENERAL

Terms	Description
Alexander Epicoch	Murian author who wrote a critical opinion about The Isle in his treatise "The Power to Dominate a People".
Age of Horror	A period in history when a cult of powerful people invested Azrea with an undead plague that nearly overwhelmed all its nations. A combined force led by heroes, Vernum, Karrigan Trent and Amythine, were able to reverse most of the damage, but the Dead Lands remains as a permanent reminder.
Anthir	Birger's home city. The ducal seat in Sawra, it's a free city along with all the other cities in the former duchy that declared independence during the Rendinian civil war.
Apour	Large continent to the south, from where humans originated.
Armandine du la Rent	Current Queen of West Rendin.
Ayrul	The name for the entire world.
Azrea	Northern continent that is mostly within the arctic circle.
Barrel Side Inn	The original Magpies guild headquarters based in West Haven.
Becka Black	Number one spy working for the Shade out of West Haven.
Benjamin 'Benny' Bolton	Former Magpies guild leader in Anthir, member of the Shade spy network and Birger's friend.
Beruehrt	A term for one touched by Lot, who can turn into a werewolf. They originate from Kings Fort, called Schutzfort by the locals.

Birger 'Light Foot'	A young thief in the Magpies of Anthir who is the bastard son of Duke Roar Fordson.
Black Wolves	Brigands, footpads, extortionists, slavers, and assassins. They trade in blood and will work for anyone with enough money to pay them. They're the antithesis of the Magpies.
Bo Cyclin	A Black Wolf captain in Anthir who is known for his stern attitude, hard-work and short temper. Few dare to mess with Bo. Birger and Bo have had a rivalry that stretched over the previous few years. It started when Birger pick-pocketed him while he was still a gang enforcer.
Bolgar	Giants that live in the Wild Lands. They pride themselves in physical endurance and strength. They believe they descend from a noble race called the Titans that once sculpted the world. The Bolgar society is divided into several castes, each one responsible for mastering a specific element. High Caste handles the mastery of air, Middle Caste for earth, and Low Caste for water and fire. No Caste are ones that cannot wield any elemental power and often leave their tribes to work for others that follow the Frost Wild.
Caoimhín du la Rent	Royal Archeologist and explorer who dedicated his life to finding the city of the Titans from stillari legend. He is the Queen's uncle and has the royal family name.
Caper	A criminal or illegal activity.
Castra	The Murian name for a military camp.
Chancebringer	A piece of divinity, this artefact was crafted from one of Aeg's scales and empowered with luck, which manifests as the ability to sense things before they happen. The artefact bends events around itself to serve the greater good. However, once it's removed, the universe reclaims what was taken in the form of sluggish response time and bad luck.

Cryll	Small squirrel like creatures that hibernate in the summer and come to life in the winter. Their blood can only flow in extreme cold.
Dagger and the Bird Tattoo	The mark of a Mapgies thief. Every member carries one on their left shoulder and it's burned off if someone leaves the guild.
Dead Lands	Territory in the easternmost part of Azrea that is overrun with the undead. It was formerly known as the Jorman Plains.
Dwan	A dwarven people who primarily follow the goddess Jor. They have a connection to the earth and stone. They believe that by studying and mastering the properties of different types of stone, dwan crafters can create a better future for themselves and their people. They originate from the Northern Towers and it's capital, The Tower.
East Rendin	A kingdom formed when Rendin was torn into three by civil war over the succession of the crown. It's located on the east side of Azrea. Known for its focus on local industry and trade relations. The culture is feudal in nature with a harsh class divide.
Empire of Murapii	An empire on the continent of Apour that follows the fanatical Cult of Sarghus: The Divine. The empire is militant and led by a role called the Head of Sarghus and an Emperor. Murapii stretches around the vast Murian sea at the heart of Apour.
Enigmites	In the Weave, enigmites and other insectoid creatures eat magic, which are in turn eaten by weavespiders, and other similar critters adapted to feeding on the magic eaters.
Ermenrich 'Eric' Wolfanger	A Wulfher from Schutzfort who works for the Shade. Known for his brutal efficiency in battle, he wields the legendary weapon named Bonereaper.
Etherweave	A highly addictive stimulant drug. It allows users to ignore fatigue and pain while

strengthening their bodies and healing injuries. 72 hours of continuous use burns out the user's organs and brain.

Ethrium Roviere	The Duke of Roviere.
Exploratores	A Murian term for military scouts.
Eye of Winter	A piece of divinity, the artefact was crafted from a crystallised tear of Lot and blocks magic in a radius around it. Since dispelling magic usually requires physical contact, it's considered incredibly powerful.
Feet of Sarghus	An elite, fanatical wing of the Cult of Sarghus: The Divine, who are woman taken from birth, trained and physically mutated to become super soldiers.
Fence	Someone that buys illicit goods and finds buyers for them.
Foss	A fence that works for the Black Wolves in Anthir.
Fridarium 'Frida' Pastuli Werareta Mumsinu Technochal Ruwal	The quintri, captain of the Airy Bell. A smuggling vessel that often works with the Magpies. She was the former head of research for the Technomancers Guild.
Frey	Cleric of Lot in Kindra.
Gelreton	A small town in Sawra that supports farming, lumber and orillium mining for Anthir
Gertrude	The innkeeper of the Yellow Yoeman in Stella.
Grengar	A type of troll found in the Darkveil Forest, which is named after the barrier that is between the Shadow Realm and the other realms. They were created when an evil stillari created a temporary hole in that barrier. The grengar worship their ancestors and in particular their king, whom they see as a living god. They can only be killed with fire and heal any other wounds.

Greenskins	A derogatory term humans use for the people that live in the frozen north of Azrea, known as the Wild Lands.
Gunther Jenkins (Harper)	Member of the Magpies that works for the Shade. He is married to Mick Jenkins. The pair are known for being efficient in battle.
Hamish 'old'	Old Hamish was once a proud and respected soldier, fighting for his country during a civil war where he was blinded. He lives as a beggar where he became one of Birger's most trusted informants and friends.
Hein Witherwood	A cleric of Cos, he is a capable spell caster and military leader stationed in Kindra.
Henry Ollich	The innkeeper of the Saint's Cup in Kindra.
Hersir	The highest ranking dwan in a mining company.
Iron Caster	The inn in Thornhall.
Ishyelle Hethnolas	The High Priestess of Lot in Kindra. She is a stillari know for her wisdom and skill with constructs.
Isaac Irthan	The Earl of Irthan who is known for his ambitious nature and ruthless court tactics.
Isai	A continent attaching to the west of Apour that is inhabited by a people called the Jing and where all the local deities perished a long time ago.
Itavia	A mercantile nation that facilitates trade between the great empires of the east and west on the Apour. They were once part of Murapii. Their culture is expressive and romantic. Despite being mainly on Apour, they follow the Cult of the Weave as Sarghus' power is weak in the area.
Jing Empire	The largest nation on the continent of Isai and the primary exporter of silk. It's populated by a people named the Jing. The Jing Empire follow the Jing philosophy which has no

deities and pride themselves in the mastery of the mind.

Jing	A tall humanoid race, the Jing possess a unique triple helix DNA and requiring three parents in reproduction. Known for their vibrant skin with luminescent markings, they have psionic abilities and a communal culture centred around "Nexus Points". Their society values interconnectedness, showcased by their ability to physically and mentally connect through "Weave Nexus Pillars". Economically, they are prominent traders, with their naturally-produced silk being a key commodity. Despite their powers, they uphold a pacifist nature and are sensitive to emotions.
Jormunger	A now extinct society of crafters, diplomats, and traders with minor telekinetic abilities. During the Age of Horror, their homes in the Jorman Plains were reduced to a festering sore in the landscape called the Dead Lands. Of the surviving Jormungers, some chose to return to fight and die with their people, while others took their own lives. Only one is known to survive.
Kallen du la Rent	Son of Caoimhín du la Rent. A knight of West Rendin. He is a well-trained and capable soldier who is the current holder of Belmung.
Kazania	A powerful oath blade that channels energy from the Weave through the wielder's soul while they continue to honour a sworn oath. If the sword is used to act against the encoded oath, it is destroyed. Destroyed magical items usually cause Weavestorms. An active oath grants the wielder enhanced strength, agility and endurance.
Kindra "The Holy City"	Built around a mountain that serves as the seat of power and primary point from where deities of the Cult of the Weave channel power to their followers.

Knights of Alba	An organisation pledged to hunting and killing evil in all its forms. Founded during the Age of Horror when the Jorman Plains were laid to waste by an undead plague. They're stationed in Lonstad in East Rendin. They keep the Dead Lands at bay with ranks of paladins, clerics, fighters, rangers and more.
Korland	A maritime trade empire on Azrea with a monopoly on the dye trade and, most notably, purple dye. Purple silk is one of the most valuable trade goods in the known world and a way that most royal families or wealthy merchants show their riches.
Krunak Pogtor	A powerful ukthuun leader from the Rotog Clan. He envisions a future where his people can live beyond the frozen wastes of the north.
Kubaal Nobork	A powerful ukthuun leader from the Nobork Clan. He envisions a future where his people can peacefully co-exist with the peoples of the south.
Kurhan	A vast and powerful empire. It stretches across the western side of the continent of Apour. Governed by a monotheistic religion known as The Cult of Sarghus: The Beacon. The people of Kurhan worship Sarghus as the one true god and believes Sarghus is a guiding light for humanity. They're opposed to the fanatical version of Sarghus followed by the neighbouring empire of Murapii. The two have a long-standing rivalry with many conflicts throughout history.
Larsea	A duchy ruled by the Larsea family who are nearly equal to the du la Rent's in history and influence but are fiercely loyal to the crown of the west. They watch over Lake Waterheart, as well as mining in the Rockwall and Assmorans. Larsea is also home to the Caoimhín du la Rent University.
Lonstad	Formerly a large city built around the bridge between the Jorman Plains and East Rendin,

but it has been reduced to a heavily fortified castle standing between the living and the undead. The Knight's of Alba fight a never ending war to keep the monsters on the farside of river Parton.

Lorenzo 'The Shade' Soto	West Rendin's master of spies. He holds the title of Duke of West Haven under Queen Armandine. He is a former Itavian privateer and Magpies smuggler.
Lorilla	The city famed for its magic university is a duchy that holds vigil over the undead east.
Louis 'Grengarbane' du la Rent	The king that brought civilization back to Azrea and became the first human ally of the stillari in Stillendam thanks to his victory over the Grengar. Driving the Grengar King Zholani back to the Darkveil Forest.
Lucinda Rose	Innkeeper of the Barrel Side Inn, from where she serves as the current leader of the Mapgies of West Haven.
Magpies	A thieves' guild that has been around for hundreds of years. They follow a strict code under which members operate, and they believe their function is to funnel wealth back to the poor. The Magpies' Code strives to minimise human suffering. Due to the popularity of the Code, the guild has expanded to nearly every city in Azrea and some of Apour. Every member bears the Dagger and Bird tattoo on their left shoulder.
Marco Petty	Famous Murian painter. Among his works are the Eave El' Grande and Mangelo Ire.
Mick Jenkins	Member of the Magpies that works for the Shade. He is married to Gunther Harper and the pair are known for being efficient in battle, having won honours for their service. Mick is a smart mouth who often gets himself in trouble.
Mindweaver	Someone trained in psychological practices by the Jing monasteries. Renate Couture fills this

	role for Lorenzo Soto, building his teams and supporting the members.
Mutt	Slang for Black Wolf gang member.
Neffily Rhys (Cyclin)	Wynn's best friend that works at the Rusty Tankard. Neffily is a member of the Magpies, but not an active thief. She works on the administration side with Noxolu.
Nikkuni / Niks	A form of goblin, short green-skinned people that live in the Wild Lands. They're known for their cunning and resourcefulness. They worship the three gods of the Frost Wild. Their culture has developed a strong spiritual connection to the land. They see the gods as tools to achieve their goals rather than spiritual beings.
Noxolu	The leader of the Magpies in Anthir. She's a former Korland privateer that retired in Anthir. Thanks to her strong leadership and her inn the Rusty Tankard, she quickly became an important figure.
Nobork	An ukthuun clan who wants to peacefully co-exist with the nations of the south. They value honour, strength and fair trade. Their leaders, Kubaal and Oraana, are powerful figures in the Wild Lands.
Northern Towers	A nation in the cold, mountainous region in the frozen north. It's home to the dwan. Their capital is the Tower and ruled by King Ducan Anvilheart. Their society is governed by a consortium of clans, each led by a council of leaders who are elected every five years to advise the King.
Oraana Nobork	The Nobork clan's powerful witch-doctor and spiritual leader. She is a follower of Ukthu and desires peace for her clan.
Orillium	A rare stone that is formed when a Weavestorm opens undergrounds and triggers a methane gas pocket detonation. The stones are able to sustain a connection between an

447

	object in the material plain and the Weave. Given how rare these events are, and how powerful orillium is, these stones are incredibly expensive.
Ovia Laquismja	The High Priestess of Cos in The Holy City of Kindra and leading member of The Cult of the Weave. She commands the armies of Kindra.
Patrick 'Pat' Marias	Sergeant in the Roviere guard, on assignment to protect Lord Roland Alfgabond, owner of the Alfgabond Bank, on a diplomatic mission to West Haven. Pat and Birger have found themselves in a bitter rivalry. Pat plays Grenguard for the Crimson Elite team.
Petra Black	Becka Black's sister and a shade working in Lorilla.
Pieces of Divinity	Powerful artefacts that were crafted from the essence of a deity of the Cult of the Weave. There are few of them in the world, but those that exist are very powerful.
Quan	Ruled with an iron fist, the nation is militaristic and constantly at war with its neighbours. They're tasked with defending The Isle and will cease all hostilities with others to turn their attention on any that threaten it. The culture of Quan is vicious and brutal, and only the strong win respect. Despite their duty to The Isle, many people in the nation detest magic users and some actively hunt them.
Quelonje	A stillari master smith who forged the oath blade Kazania. She lives in Etmenja.
Quintri	A gnomish people from Quintrom who follow Mag: the goddess of Magic and Balance. They love magic and technology, striving through the secretive Technomancers Guild to weave them together. They shape the world to create a better future for themselves and their people.
Quintrom	A society that values intelligence, knowledge, and innovation above all else. They're

governed by the most competent and proven person, holding the title of Professor. Their government is a technocracy called the Technomancers Guild. Their economy is post-scarcity, and export rare mechanical goods, silver, platinum, gold, magical items, and spells. They have a strong sense of community and cooperation, respecting knowledge and innovation. To them, pursuing knowledge and innovation is a sacred duty.

Renate Couture / Shrenatelious	Lorenzo's mentor, she is a member of the Shade, Magpies and a magic user. While working with Lorenzo, she is responsible for diplomacy and the psychological health of the team. Formerly of the Zhraacias Den.
Rella	A small riverside town on the border between Quan and West Rendin. Lorenzo settled there with his family, where he worked as a Magpies smuggler.
Roar Fordson	Duke of Anthir and Birger's father. The Duke lost his family at the start of the Rendinian civil war and has been negligent in the upkeep of his city since.
Rotog	A notorious ukthuun clan who are constantly at war. Their leader Krunak is a follower of Siphok and believes that only the strong should live. He and his clan are the current leaders of the Wild Lands' Siphkuwa or 'Wartide' and want to claim the world for the Frost Wild.
Roviere	A powerful duchy, ruled by Ethrium Roviere. The city is responsible for most of the food production in Azrea and even supplies a considerable portion of Murapii's imports. The city is renowned for the Red and Green sports rivalry, which also double as political factions within the city.
Rovskia	Clansmen on horseback, raiding and pillaging rival states in their native Apour and neighboring Murapii. They have established

cities and food production settlements by the Korland Sea. However, they maintained a massive mobile cavalry that move like locusts over the lands to the south. One of their people who loses their honour commits ritual suicide.

Rusty Tankard An inn located in the Squat of Anthir that belongs to Noxolu. Considered the local Magpies headquarters and doubles as a soup kitchen for the poor.

Saint's Cup An inn in Kindra owned by Henry Ollich.

Sarghus The deity that created humans and reigns in Apour. He's known as a jealous deity who permits no others in his domain.

Sawra Before Louis du la Rent settled Azrea, there were already humans living there. The Sawrans were a loose collection of tribes that traded with one another. They were incorporated with Rendin when Ferdinand Larsea conquered them. Due to the cultural divide between Rendinians and Sawrans, they declared independence during the Rendinian civil war. Korland has influenced Sawra's culture by proximity. Their city-states follow the same general structure of unified defence as their neighbours. Anthir is the lead city. Sawran culture is stoic.

Sawran Highlander Powerful horses with thick matted fur that can handle extreme cold. Used throughout Azrea.

Schutzfort Also known as Kings Fort, is home to the Wulfher. A group of renown warriors that guard West Rendin from the grengar in the Darkveil Forest.

Siphkuwa / Wartide The tribes of the Wild Lands name themselves Siphkuwa when they group together in mass under a single leader to go to war. They start small and gain momentum as the tribes flock to join. They're most common when resources in the north are scarce, and the people of the

	Wild Lands are forced to take what they can or thin their numbers to survive.
Siphuun	A type of ogre that lives in the Wild Lands and worships the three gods of the Frost Wild. They're known for their physical strength and resilience. Their culture emphasizes the importance of physical fitness and endurance. Honing their bodies and minds, allow them to survive and thrive in the harsh tundra.
Stillari	A type of fey that lives in Stillendam. They follow the Cult of the Weave and many high-ranking priestesses are stillari. Their forests are holy places and they guard it jealously. They don't cut down trees or harm the forest, using magic to shape the forest to their needs. The forest provides for them in turn. All stillari are both male and female but present as female so humans refer to them as female.
Stillendam	An ancient and established stillari monarchy. It's a place of mystery and wonder. Magic and nature are intertwined, and the boundaries between the living and the dead blur. The forest itself possesses a will of its own. At the heart of Stillendam lies Etmenja, the capital, where Queen Ellamji Reethnia and Prime Minister Cilcye Faelynn rule. The government of Stillendam is a monarchy, but making changes to laws requires both the Queen and the Prime Minister.
Stella	A small town within a day's ride of West Haven. A popular stop over for land traveling merchants on their way to or from the Capital.
Sten Thornson	Birger's mentor who trained him to be a thief. Sten adopted Birger after he tried to burgle the old thief and got caught. Sten died shortly before the start of the book under mysterious circumstances.
The Isle	A mystical island located off the coast of Azrea, home to a community of wizards. It is governed by a magocracy, where those who

are able to wield Magic hold the highest positions of power and make the important decisions for the island. The wizards of The Isle are dedicated to protecting Azrea from supernatural threats, and stay out of politics beyond their borders.

Thornhall | A barony surrounded by cattle farms and lumber camps.

Tin-birds | Slang for the Feet of Sarghus.

Ukthuun / Uks | A type of orc living in the Wild Lands. They follow all three gods of the Frost Wild. They see them as the embodiment of the harsh and unforgiving tundra and have strong spiritual connections to the land. The tribes are diverse, but all are fierce warriors and hunters with a long verbal story telling tradition.

Ulfhild 'The Blood Queen' | The leader of the Black Wolf gang. She's rumoured to have been a slave in Voeterland, blood thirsty sea raiders. She's a known associate of Roar Fordson, the Duke of Anthir and feared by most.

University Lorilla | The University of Lorilla, also known as "The University" is a long-standing institution of Magic in Azrea. It is in the city of Lorilla, East Rendin. It's an arm of the Knights of Alba, and helps them defend against the threat of the Dead Lands.

Vernum Salja | The most powerful wizard in Azrea. He was originally trained at the University of Lorilla. Vernum, Karrigan Trent and Amythine were the key players in the Age of Horror. After it's conclusion, the King of Quan adopted Vernum who was an orphan, giving him the family name Salja. Vernum convinced the nations of Azrea to grant him an independent Magocracy on The Isle. The King of Quan swore that all kings of Quan would protect The Isle's independence.

Vrylis	The name of the guardian of the Chapel of Lot in Kindra. It's a sculpted Valkyrie that watches against intruders.
Wandor Londel	Duke of East Rendin and third heir to the throne. He is in his late 70s. Londel is a ruthless and cunning political animal, willing to do anything to protect his family and country. He's known for extreme methods.
Warjah	A nation in Isai that is known for its tropical jungles and the deadly giant lizards that inhabit it. Warjah links trade between Apour and the Jing Empire. They also export spice, exotic jewelry, and animal products.
Waterweird	A type of water elemental that serves as guardians of the Holy Spring in Kindra. These creatures are autonomous units created from the Holy Spring and controlled by "containment collars." They're aggressive protectors, capable of enveloping and killing enemies.
Weavespider	Also known as "Arachnida Magi," are magical creatures that resemble furry spiders. They have feathery appendages next to their mandibles for feeding on Enigmites. Ranging in size, some are small as tarantulas, while others get as massive as elephants, depending on their age and how well-fed they are. They live within the Weave.
Weavestorm	They start with a flash of purple and teal light, then the brightness dims a moment later into a steady pulsing cloud that swirls. They can appear anywhere, but are more prone to happen in areas where the Weave is being accessed excessively. The event occurs when the Weave (Realm of Magic) collides with the Physical Realm. It causes temperature drops, extreme gravitational pull and strange light effects. Sometimes creatures from the Weave escape through them into the Physical Realm.

Weavestorms don't usually move, but they can.

Weldon	The second most powerful city in Sawra. They maintain security in the Wide Canal and house a substantial standing military. Their port is a primary trading point and they maintain close relations with Korland and Larsea.
West Rendin	Nation ruled by Queen Armandine du la Rent. It was formed after the Rendinian civil war and contains Rendin's former capital, West Haven. Which is a bustling metropolis, with a diverse population of artisans and merchants.The people are expressive and wear their emotions on their sleeves. They follow the Cult of the Weave.
Wild Land	An unforgiving frozen wasteland in north Azrea where only the toughest can survive. The Frost Wild gods are worshiped by its inhabitants. Ukthuun, Nikkuni, Siphuun and Bolgar each have their own distinct customs, based around these gods. It's a land of snow-capped mountains, vast glaciers, and icy rivers that carve through the landscape. Fierce storms and blizzards are common occurrences and temperatures regularly drop to bone-chilling lows.
Wulfher	Inhabitants of Kings Fort who are a proud and fierce people, deeply connected to their history and the land they call home. Clan loyalty is a big deal to them and they have their own king despite being in Rendin. He's seen as a living god and protector of his people. Many families have lived in the area for generations. Their culture is martial, with an emphasis on training and discipline.
Wynn 'Feather Touched' Leigh	Former farm girl who moved to Anthir after her parents died. She is best friends with Neffily, who convinced Birger to accept Wynn as his apprentice.

Yellow Yoeman	Stella's inn run by Gertrude.
Zholani	King of the grengar in the Darkveil and first of his kind. Zholani is nearly six-thousand years old, cannot be killed, and stands twenty-five feet tall. He is a walking calamity. Powerful and immortal, Zholani is not unbeatable, and the Wulfher clan who have been fighting him for a thousand years know how to neutralize his efforts. Zholani is confined to the Darkveil Forest and rarely leaves it. The grengar of the Darkveil worship him as a god.

The Magpies' Code

Written by Kepler Winkelman, Eva Herzog, Gabriel Michaels, Renwick Gibbons, and Lilia Warwick ratified in 500 A.R.M. in West Haven.

Agreed to by every man, woman, or child bearing the Dagger and Bird upon their left shoulder.

Introduction

The Magpies are a criminal order, but we are an organisation with a purpose. Our role in society is the fair redistribution of wealth from the haves to the have-nots. It's the way of the world that some have much and can turn what they have into goods to sell and gain more wealth. On the other hand, some have nothing and, therefore, can make nothing, so they remain destitute. Therefore, our moral obligation is to redirect the flow of having such that those with nothing, gain a brighter future.

Nature of the Code

This Code seeks to regulate the conduct of thieves, burglars, swindlers, con artists, and smugglers. It aims to facilitate collaboration, deign the proper flow of wealth reallocation, and minimise suffering. When one takes the oath to uphold this Code before Aeg, they may reap its rewards, and be held to its rulings as decided on by the local judicator – a Guild Leader. Upon initiation to the Code, the initiate will show their dedication by taking the Dagger and Bird tattoo on their left shoulder to become a full member. All past Indiscretions are forgotten at the point of becoming a full member.

Induction under the Code

To become a full member of the Magpies, one must first prove worthy. Members gain access to guild networks, resources, protection under the Code, and the support of the local guild.

An initiate must work under a full guild member as an apprentice to learn the trade for a period no shorter than 12 months and no longer than 36 months. After this time, if the initiate can't pass the criteria for full membership, they are dismissed and must seek a new mentor.

To complete the initiation, the initiate needs one full member who can nominate them for membership. They must then complete a caper of notoriety.

A full member of the guild must be present during the act to verify it, and the local guild leader will judge if the level of infamy is sufficient. If authorities identify the perpetrator as the culprit within one month, the initiate fails the test. A guild leader may reject any membership application.

Punishments and Fines under the Code

The local guild leader judges Indiscretions and all rulings are final. Indiscretions comprise four levels of Code violation.

1. *Minor indiscretions*
   a. *Fine*: The local equivalent of one month's wages for a commoner to be given to the guild leader for distribution among the poor. 10% stays with the guild.
   b. If the misdeed can be rectified, the perpetrator must make all reasonable efforts.
   c. If the deed can't be rectified, the fine is doubled, and the additional funds are given to the aggrieved party.
   d. All payments must be made within thirty days of the final ruling.

2. *Indiscretion*
   a. *Fine*: The local equivalent of one year's wages for a commoner to be given to the guild leader for distribution among the poor. 10% stays with the guild.
   b. If the misdeed can be rectified, the perpetrator must make all reasonable efforts.
   c. If the deed can't be rectified, the fine is doubled, and the additional funds are given to the aggrieved party.
   d. All payments must be made within ninety days of the final ruling.

3. *Major Indiscretion*
   a. Stripped of membership.
   b. All property is forfeited to the guild to be redistributed to the poor. 10% stays with the guild.

4. *Egregious Indiscretion*
   a. Death to be carried out immediately after the final ruling.
   b. All property is forfeited to the guild to be redistributed to the poor. 10% stays with the guild.

Definitions

Caper: A deed where something of value is procured from another without the original owner's consent, and something of equal importance wasn't exchanged.

Initiate: A junior member of the guild, working as an apprentice under a full member.

Full member: A person beholden to the Magpies' Code and bears the Dagger and Bird upon their left shoulder.

Guild Leader: A person elected by the local thieves as the leader of the guild.

Indiscretion: An act that directly or indirectly breaks the Magpies' Code.

The Code

1. Wealth must flow down. 10% of every share from any activity that is considered a caper under the Code must be given to the guild.
   a. Failing to give the guild its due is an Indiscretion.
2. The guild leader is to see that half of all funds received by the guild from its members are distributed among the poor of the local area.
   a. Failing to distribute the wealth is a Major Indiscretion.
3. No Member or Initiate or Guild Leader shall commit a caper against another Member, Initiate or Guild Leader of the Magpies.
   a. Committing a caper against a Magpie is a Minor Indiscretion.
4. A Magpies' word is their bond. Once a Magpies' word is given, they must complete whatever was agreed as per their exact agreement.
   a. Failure to deliver on one's word is a Minor Indiscretion.
5. Magpies don't trade in blood. A Magpie is expected to keep the human cost of their caper to a minimum. Doing physical harm to another should be avoided. It's terrible for business.

Killing in self-defence or in defence of another is permitted, but it must be proven necessary for the continued survival of the person in question.

    a. Killing in self-defence or in defence of another is a Minor Indiscretion.

    b. Killing in cold blood is a Major Indiscretion.

    c. Partaking in slavery or human trafficking is an Egregious Indiscretion.

6. Failure to pay a fine as laid out by the Code automatically graduates the Indiscretion level of the offence to the next level.

    a. A Minor Indiscretion becomes an Indiscretion.

    b. An Indiscretion becomes a Major Indiscretion.

    c. A Major Indiscretion becomes an Egregious Indiscretion.

7. All participants in a caper are entitled to a share of the bounty equal to their contribution. The shares are to be decided and agreed upon upfront during the planning. If the plan changes and one member does more work than anticipated, the other members are expected to accommodate the change in good faith. The local guild leader will decide on the shares if a disagreement can't be resolved.

    a. Failing to award a fair share is a Minor Indiscretion.

8. Initiates are entitled to Half Shares. While they are learning, half their share goes to their master as payment for training.

    a. Failing to award an Initiate their Half Share is a Minor Indiscretion.

9. Helping those in need. The Magpies are a service to society. If someone is in trouble, a member of the Magpies that is aware and able is expected to help, especially if the victim is of meagre means.

    a. Failing to help the poor when the Magpie was able and aware is a Minor Indiscretion.

    b. If failure to help results in that person's death or serious physical harm, including incarceration, it is a Major Indiscretion.

    c. A Magpie isn't obligated to help any who trade in blood or has made an attempt on said Magpie's life.

10. Once per year, all Magpies of the local guild must gather to elect a Guild Leader. The guild leader must be nominated

by at least two other members and carry the day with a majority vote. In the case of a tie, there must be a re-vote. If there is a tie three times running, the leadership for the year is to be shared.

11. The Guild Leader must ensure the fair distribution of wealth in the local area and look out for all members. If a member can't make enough money to live at a reasonable level, the guild must take care of their essential needs—food, water and shelter.

12. The Guild Leader is compensated for their efforts with 5% of the monthly income of the guild.

    a. A guild leader who takes more than their due is considered having committed an Egregious Indiscretion.

13. Any member may call a guild leader to trial by initiating Defiance. All local members are expected to attend the trial if a guild leader is officially Defied. The accuser may present evidence of the guild leader's abuse of the Code, and the guild leader will be entitled to one month to muster a defence. Once the evidence and counter-evidence have been provided, the assembled members will vote and determine if the Defiance is Legitimate by a majority vote.

    a. Any guild leader found guilty of abusing the Code is held to have committed an Egregious Indiscretion

Any breach of the Code which doesn't have specific repercussions associated with it is an Indiscretion by default.

The Oath

By Aeg, I solemnly swear to uphold the Magpies' Code in all my dealings and subject myself to its rulings as laid out by the duly elected judicator. I won't deal in blood or knowingly bring an innocent person to harm. I'll do all within my power to see that riches are fairly distributed in society and that those who are of meagre means can live. I swear to uphold and enforce the Code upon all that take the Dagger and Bird. I won't abide a false Magpie, and I'll always help a fellow Magpie in exchange for my fair share, should they ask me. All these words are true, or may Aeg send rats and buzzards to feast on my entrails.

Technical Notes

Renate (and to a less refined extent, Lorenzo) is a Transformational Coach. The way she speaks is crafted intentionally to generate awareness with the other characters by reflecting back the way they think, based on the words used, and then she asks Clean Language (by David Grove) or Open-ended questions to evoke understanding.

This technique is combined with the concept of Gain Frame (Coined by psychologist and economist Daniel Kahneman and studied by Alison Ledgerwood, a professor of psychology) to direct the conversation, and thereby the minds in the conversation, towards the positive possibilities so that the other party might shift from a Closed Mind (Narrowly Associative State) to an Open Mind (Broadly Associative State) which is a more creative way of thinking that allows new ideas to arise (See the work of cognitive neuroscientist Moshe Bar).

In addition, the breathing technique taught to Birger by Lorenzo for grounding himself during stressful moments, is another way of shifting from a Closed minded state to an Open minded state. This kind of breathing helps the person to focus on something in their present moment, creating a separation between themselves and the ruminative thoughts distracting them. By observing the thoughts as birds flying overhead, and simply allowing them to be, the person gains much needed perspective that can alleviate anxiety.

The approach Lorenzo takes to his team, aligns with a high functioning, small group that have existing paradigms for resolving conflict and making decisions. While Birger is new to the team, the others have been developed to a state where they can quickly support new members to do the same through role-modeling.

Renate works actively behind the scenes to build this capacity and ensure that the team remains operational. This mode of leadership is essential for a gorilla squad like this group of spies, because (As shown in the narrative) leadership can easily be disrupted during a mission and it should not cripple the team.

463

Acknowledgements

I want to appreciate all the amazing people, family, friends, players and colleagues for the time they gave to support my quest! Thank you for making this huge undertaking possible.

Here are some of the people I want to call out for significant time contributed, reading and giving feedback so I could improve this book:

Laura Smit, Liam Smit, Nelia Smit, Francois Smit, Paulin Prifti, Gustav Seymore, Earlie Rose, Danielle Kleffmann, Hendro Smit, Stephen Logan, Mariska du Preez, Gabriel Ruiz, James Bateman, Rick Stemm, Dale Pugh, Clinton Keith, Tracy Meyer, Nicolas Espinosa, Florian Garcia, Jo Lanigan, Sarah Devereaux, Nicolas Espinosa Turgues, Tyrone McAuley, Tim Chapman, Helen McEwan, Pierro Smit, Koos Smit, Nicola Smit, Claudia Smit.

About the Author

In 2009, in the thick of a difficult period in my life, I started a book. It was inspired by the pen-and-paper role-playing game world that I created. But soon I ran into a roadblock. Though I love storytelling, due to difficulties with ADHD I was not very well read, which affected my work.

I went on to travel the world as a game designer, got married and had a son. Then I discovered coaching and Positive Psychology. What a wonderful gift, I thought, enabling others to excel! So, I dedicated myself to learning all about it and, through it, I refined my purpose. But it also brought me something unexpected.

I was a creative for most of my career, and now I spent all my time enabling others to create. I missed being a creator myself. What's more, I was working so hard I was getting drained. I needed to find balance.

Through it all, I never gave up on my book. I continued to read, research, write and play. After all, you get better at what you focus on. And if there's one thing ADHD is great for, it gives you hyper focus!

When I thought of that first amateurish attempt, I knew I could do better. I'm not saying I'm great now. You begin to decline when you think you are. I strive to consider myself a forever beginner because embracing this mindset opens up my thinking.

I sat down to rewrite the story and wanted two things. First, a setting worth playing in. I prepared the maps, so that one day, players could walk in the streets of Anthir and hoping that the Magpies' Code might live in another Game Master's world.

Second, I wanted to bring into the book my personal vision of creating a world where every person feels valued, purposeful and empowered. I laced my story with concepts from Positive Psychology, hoping to galvanize a Positive Fantasy movement.

Back on the topic of fantasy, allow me a moment to share the story of a seven-legged jumping spider who made its home in my hallway. It was a hardy soul, hanging around for weeks, becoming something of a family pet. My young son Liam and I named it Bob.

Since my son was a fan of my writing, I decided Bob should be in the book.

Bob would later be renamed Snow as he took shape in the pages, but this little bit of inspiration became a defining factor in how my magic system came to life and evolved – giving birth to the ecology of the Weave and all its unique features.

Creating this book has been a long journey. At times draining, but most of the time it was life-affirming.

VERDANT
HEART

TEARING THE DARKVEIL

Book Two

Snippet

1

SPIES

Herma pulled her hood up and sat on the bench by the door of the Hung Sailor. It was the cue. Limping, Birger sped towards the tavern, pushed the door open and sidled in.

The place was humid and smolderingly hot. The reek of stale beer and sweat hit him like a tidal wave. It was full of dockworkers, playing cards and engaged in bouts of banter as they clinked their mugs of beer. They all wore something green. *No one would dare wearing red in here,* thought Birger.

He noticed one person dressed in black leather – the signature look of the Black Wolf gang – was sitting by the bar. It was his target. S*eriously?* wondered Birger, *how could a gang of cutthroats be so blatant?*

Birger wore tan dockworker attire. Mindful of his green bandana, he shrugged off his fur coat and hung it near the door. He ambled to the bar, black cane in hand, where two women cleared out. Birger took one of their stools, and while shifting around to look casual, he waved to the bartender.

Casting a glance down the bar, he saw his hooded target was a man. Birger's brow furrowed into a hawk-like scowl, accentuated by his high cheekbones. He thumbed his button nose and leaned back against the counter. Birger had dark brown eyes and even darker hair. His build was slender, fitting for someone in his profession, and the fresh scars on his face could fool some into guessing him to be much older. In reality, this was only his twentieth winter.

His onyx armband, Chancebringer, hidden under his sleeve, let him tune into all the surrounding movement, and with effort, it let him sense what someone was focused on. He closed his eyes to block distractions.

The man in black was watching him, too.

Birger opened his eyes and waved impatiently at the young, lanky bartender, who was busy with another customer. "One Verdant Brew!" he shouted, when he finally caught the bartender's attention.

471

The young man nodded, his expression saying, In a moment. Satisfied, Birger swiveled in his seat and felt his target's attention drift to the crowd.

A week in Roviere and still no sign of Wynn. Luckily, ships to Lorilla were scarce too, buying him time. With the Mid-Winter Festival in full swing and Murapii scouts haunting the seas, captains were being cautious.

The tavern featured a bare stage, tightly packed tables, and two glowing hearths. Smoke billowed into the room now and then, likely from a blocked chimney.

The aroma of cooking pork brought memories of burning homes, screaming soldiers, and dying friends. Birger felt sick. His appetite had been minimal since Kindra, causing him to lose a few pounds. He took a deep breath to steady himself. No room for distraction while on a job.

Glancing down the bar again, he cursed. His target had vanished.

A door slammed shut, jolting him upright. Not the front door. He looked around. Losing his target wasn't an option. Birger dashed for the back door leading to the harbour. His stiff right knee made him stagger and collide with a cluster of patrons.

"Your Verdant Brew!" the bartender shouted.

He shoved the door open. A biting wind sliced through his thin clothes, the shock ripping the air from his lungs.

He saw a multitude of snow-covered ships moored in the lamp-lit harbour, but there was no time to take it in. Chancebringer warned him to duck, and he did, just as an oar whizzed overhead, exploding into splinters as it struck the Hung Sailor's brick wall.

He charged the attacker, ramming his shoulder into the man's gut. They both went down in a ball, ice soaking Birger's clothes and stinging his exposed skin. The man's rough stubble scraped against his neck as they tussled.

Despite his opponent's superior strength, Chancebringer let Birger anticipate and counter each move. Soon, the wrestling match turned in Birger's favour.

But then came a second attacker that was impossible to avoid. A blow to the temple struck, and stars filled his vision. Suddenly, he found himself adrift in ice-cold water. Thin cords pulsing with teal light ran in all directions. No, not water, a void.

A dream then... he didn't have time for this.

There was someone with him. Birger found a girl close to his own age suspended above him, reddish-brown hair adrift behind her.

472

Crystal blue eyes studied him, and he felt guilt, betrayal, loss, and longing flush through him all at once.

Wynn, he thought with a mix of excitement and dread.

He reached out. She smiled and touched his cheek. It burned. She kissed him, lips soft and hot as smouldering coals. It hurt. Then something shook him and the lights, along with Wynn, flickered, then vanished, replaced by devouring darkness.

His whole body shook, and while his head was throbbing, the cold made it seem trivial. Birger was unsure how long he had been out, but it felt brief. The world came to him in a mix of black, white, and orange blurs.

Something silver caught his eye. Blinking his vision clear, he found it was a sword blade under his chin. His gaze trailed up to a gnarled hand on the hilt, behind which was a grim-faced man in black leather armour.

It wasn't his original target, but Birger didn't mind. Anyone in the Black Wolf gang would do fine.

Good, Birger thought, but made sure to hide his relief.

"Who're you?" the swordsman asked.

Birger rubbed his sore temple, trying to think clearly. "Just a drunk, looking for a place to piss."

Oh no, Birger cringed, *I butchered that.*

"Why were you following me?" another voice came from behind him.

Birger turned to see who it was. *Oh, there you are.* Birger made sure not to smile. He realised that his original mark was just a kid, maybe even younger than Birger.

Both spoke in Sawran accents, confirming his suspicions. These were definitely, mutts. No one else from Sawra would dress like that.

"I wasn't," replied Birger, feigning innocence while trying to gauge how to best play this, "I was going to take a leak off the pier. I didn't expect to get jumped."

"That's gullshite!" sneered the man holding the sword to Birger's throat.

Any doubts if the man was from Anthir were laid to rest. The curse was rarely used anywhere else. Birger noticed the man was missing an ear and there was a murderer's hardness in his eyes. "You don't have a whiff of drink on you."

"Please, mister, I didn't mean you any harm." Birger tried to look scared. It wasn't entirely an act – one-ear seemed ready to kill him and there was a sharp blade tucked under his chin. "How about I buy you each a drink at the bar, and we forget all about this?"

The kid tilted his head to the side and, with a cocky grin, said, "I could do with a drink."

"Thank Aeg," said Birger, feigning relief. He was well aware that one-ear hadn't lowered the sword. "I thought maybe you were Magpies, here to rob me. I heard they pulled off a huge heist last week... or was it the Black Wolves? I always get those mixed up."

He was hoping the comment might get under their skin. The Black Wolves hated the Magpies. Not only did the two guilds have a two centuries long rivalry going, the Black Wolves were considered inferior. Birger hoped the dig would prod one of them to slip up.

But in doing so, he needed an exit strategy. This was a very dangerous game. He used his peripheral vision to scan the surroundings and spotted his cane lying nearby. He wished he had Kazania with him, but a dock worker carrying a sword would've been a giveaway, and the ironwood cane could block a blade well enough. He continued scanning, then he found what he was looking for. That time, he nearly did smile.

"Magpies!?" the kid spat on the ground. "More like pigeons. They don't hold a candle to the Wolves."

One-ear smacked his partner with a backhand to the shoulder. "Shut it! He might be working for the Duke, you foolish child."

"Hey! I'm not a child!" The kid's cheeks turned red and his scowl almost made his brow wrinkle.

Aeg, how young is this kid? thought Birger.

"I haven't said anything important," the kid huffed, "and besides, we can just kill him."

"Wait, wait! I'm not working for the Duke! I swear!" Birger's teeth began chattering from the cold, but he didn't try to stop. It would help sell the scared victim act, and he needed all the help he could get. He had never been good at cons and, had it not been for the dim light, he was sure this whole thing would have backfired already.

"You're not a very good liar," one-ear shot back, baring his teeth and tapping his nose with his free hand. "Even if you were, I can smell lies."

"Please, I don't know anything," said Birger, spreading his hands wide in surrender. He considered his options. Maybe playing to their egos was a better way forward. "Even if I were working for the

Duke, he wouldn't dare to mess with the Black Wolves. They're a legendary outfit." One-ear's sword shifted and pinked Birger's exposed skin. He hissed. "Hey, hey, hold on. You already have me at sword point. I'll tell you anything you want to know."

"Maybe he really doesn't know anything," suggested the kid. "Should we let *Her* decide what to do with him?"

"Emrys! Shut your fool mouth!" snapped one-ear. "He could be noting down everything you say."

"I'm just saying," shrugged Emrys sheepishly. "She got real upset with us after we killed that last fella without letting her ask the questions first."

A kid named Emrys? I've always thought of Emrys as an old man's name, mused Birger. *And are they talking about Ulfhild?* He needed confirmation.

One-ear grit his teeth. "No one questions punters better than me."

One-ear spat on the ground, then closed in on Birger and said, "Who are you working for?" he paused and with a deadpan stare he added, "If you don't tell me, right now...I'll pull your tongue out through your throat."

The one-eared man leaned in a bit more and his sword bit into Birger's bare neck. Warm blood started trickling from the wound.

"Wait! Alright!" Birger shot the man a defiant snarl. "You caught me. My name is Roar, but I'm just a messenger. I was told to look for a man in black. He was meant to know about...something valuable. Look, I don't want trouble. I don't even know who the guy is exactly. I think he was working for the Blood Queen."

When light flashed as one-ear struck him a blow with the sword's pummel, Birger guessed he was right about Ulfhild. More blood ran down his chin. The cold made it hard to tell where the skin had broken. Another scar for the collection.

"That's for lying to us earlier," he said. "Do you work for Elise?"

"I can't tell you that!" Birger objected, and he winced as he prodded the fresh wound. He had to flip this around, make them say something to get him to explain. While he didn't know who Elise was, that they were expecting someone from her told him she was bad news.

"It's alright. We're the ones you were looking for," said Emrys reassuringly.

"Look, I know you might kill me if I don't tell you what you want." Birger edged away from the sharp blade. "But my mistress will do much worse if I give her up."

"She won't be. We're the ones helping to secure the Verdant Heart," explained Emrys with a wink. "Elise must've..."

"Emrys, I swear!" one-ear cut his partner off. "Screw it. If Elise sent you, she can send another."

One-ear drew back his sword. Birger didn't need Chancebringer to tell him the chit-chat was at an end. But Birger was ready.

2

ALLIES

Birger rolled onto his cane. He caught the one-eared man's descending sword, slapping it aside. He struck out, nipping the man's whole ear with a smack.

A gust of icy wind whipped through the harbour and plucked at Birger's thin linen clothes, but adrenaline dulled its bite. The sound of snow crunching under the second man's boot drew his attention. Emrys had drawn his sword.

Birger smiled. Behind the man in black armour, a pony-sized, seven legged weavespider, covered in thick white fur perched on the roof. Snow, his best friend, had a couple of months ago sacrificed one of his eight legs during a desperate battle to defend Birger.

Snow launched himself forward; his front legs struck hard and sent the black armoured man sprawling into a pile of white powder. Emrys grunted as the weight thumped him to the ground, and Birger thought he heard a rib pop.

One-ear shrieked when he saw Snow. Very few people knew what a weavespider was. They came from the Realm of magic, or simply the Weave, and Birger had to admit, seeing one pounce on your friend was terrifying. One-ear grabbed Emrys and pulled the man up into a run. Emrys cried out in pain, and Birger winced in sympathy. He knew the agony of broken ribs too well.

Beside him, Snow crouched low to stop from slipping on the icy ground. Birger reached out to his companion and ruffled the tufts of fur on his head.

"Good work, Snow," said Birger with a wide grin, shivering now that the fight was over.

The tavern door creaked and a seven-foot man stomped out. His grey hair circled his head like a lorel, and he fixed yellow lupine eyes on Birger. The broad slabs of muscles under his bear-hide armour rippled as he tossed Birger a fur coat. The big fella had a massive double-bladed axe strapped to his back. It's handle looked like it had been made from a giant's femur, and strapped with red leather for grip.

"Thank-Cos, you're a lifesaver, Eric," Birger said, gratefully slipping into the coat.

"You done?" Eric asked, closing the door.

Snow's big pink eyes stared expectantly in the direction of the fleeing men, as if questioning why they weren't in pursuit.

"Yeah, we're done here." Birger leaned on his cane and dusted the ice from his clothes.

A gust of wind rippled through the canvas sails of the ships that lined the docks, cooling Birger's pants and reminding him they were still wet. "I got what we needed and I don't care if Ulfhild knows I'm in town. If they come after me, that'll make finding them easier. Besides, we need to get back to the Empty Barrel and meet up with the others. They'll be back by now."

Snow sent him a jolt of disappointment and nuzzled against him so forcefully that Birger almost toppled back onto the floor. The weavespider was huge. When they first met a couple of months before, he could fit in his satchel. Snow had initially been lured to Birger by the enigmites gathering on his magical bracelet, Chancebringer. The invisibly small insect-like things ate magic, and Snow ate them in turn.

"I know, boy," said Birger, "chasing them would be fun, but they won't head to their hideout after an encounter like this, and now we know what they look like, so we can find them again. Let them think they got away."

"They were a talkative pair," noted Eric, leaning against the wall.

"You heard that?" Birger asked.

"Wulfher ears, remember." Eric pointed at his head.

To Birger, who had grown up on tales of mythical creatures, Eric was a werewolf, and a thousand year old one at that. The big man could tear a company of soldiers to shreds single-handedly. Birger had seen him disembowel a fifteen foot tall bolgar after a gruelling fifty hours of nonstop combat. Calling Eric scary was like calling a blizzard chilly.

Somehow, the old Wulfher had taken a liking to Birger and treated him with more respect than he did most, even recently training him in swordmanship.

Herma Pont stepped around the corner of the Hung Sailor with a lantern in hand. The older Magpie had hard grey eyes and short grey hair that swept right like a bird's wing. She wore a green hooded coat with a grey leather jerkin over a white shirt, and a rapier dangled at her side.

478

"I saw a couple of whipped mutts tuck tail and run," said Herma. "That your handy work?"

"Yup," answered Birger, pulling the fur coat tight and trying to think warm thoughts. "Cos, it's cold tonight."

"Don't let Hein hear you talking like that." Herma gave him a mischievous grin. "Tell me you didn't waste six hours of me wilting in the Weave-cursed snow following that vermin..."

You messed up, thought Birger's cynic in Bo's voice. *You almost lost Emrys in there because you let yourself get distracted.*

Birger knew he got lucky. Emrys could've bolted by the time he came out.

"Firstly, I don't care what that miserable book thumper thinks," said Birger, his lip twisting in distaste at the thought of Hein. The cut on his cheek throbbed in response, making him wince. "And yeah, I know what those two were after. Let's get back to the Empty Barrel. Hopefully, the others' had as much success."

The local Magpies had taken Birger and his team in once they confirmed the Dagger and Bird tattoos – except Hein, but three members vouching for him bought temporary Guild clearance. Herma volunteered to help, for a healthy pay, of course. The Magpies were only a charity to the poor, and Birger's team hardly qualified for that with the Queen of West Rendin backing them. He found it comforting that he could always rely on the thieves' guild wherever he went on the continent.

"While you were playing ignorant interrogator with your friends, I found this," Eric handed Birger a letter.

Birger read the content.

"How in Aeg's wide blue ocean did you get this?" Birger asked, his mouth hanging open.

"Wulfher," Eric shrugged, as if that should explain all the mysteries of the world.

Birger blinked at the big man, screwing his face into a look he hoped would communicate exasperation. "Tha...I...what?"

Eric didn't explain. The man often did things like that. Birger figured Eric wanted to seem nonchalant, but that didn't make it any less frustrating.

"What is it?" Herma asked, holding up her lantern to see.

"It's a missive asking for a meeting with Ulfhild, signed by Lady Elise de Valois," said Birger.

Herma's eyes went wide, her voice incredulous when she asked, "The head of the East Azrean Trading Company wants to meet the Blood Queen?"

The tavern door opened, and the young bartender stuck his head out. "What's going on back here?"

The entire group turned to regard the man, and Birger answered, "Just sorting out a misunderstanding."

"Right..." the young man looked them all over with suspicion, "you owe me five silver for that Verdant Brew."

"Sorry about that," replied Birger with a smile. Fishing in his pockets, he extracted a gold coin and handed it to the man. "Here, get yourself one."

The young man's face lit up. He pocketed the coin and withdrew his head back into the tavern.

"Meet you back at the Empty Barrel in ten minutes," said Birger and hobbled towards the door.

"What?" Herma asked, looking over Snow and Eric. "Where are you going?"

"To finish my Verdant Brew!" Birger shouted, striding back into the Hung Sailor.

Full Maps

Get them all at http://www.ayrul.com/maps

Apour& Azrea

Southern Azrea

Anthir

West Haven

Kindra

AZREA

OSTRE

MORTESHALLA

STELLENDAM

NORTHER
TOWER   QUINTROM

AZMURIAN SEA

WEST RENDIS
QUAN   EAST
RENDIN

LAND

VERTO

OVSKIA   ITAVIA

APOUR

RTA CHANNEL

MURIAN SEA

BREHIN

VIHN

ANKAL

ISALLA

APOUR, AZREA

HUMAN POPULATION: 37,000,000
DATE: 735 A.R.M

PYXIOS

THANARC

THE MIRROR

WINTER
WOODS

ANGLEWEIR
FOREST

WILD LANDS

FROZEN HOOK

THE VAIL

DARKVEIL

EVERWINTER
SEA

ICEDRIFT

ARGIL

KINDS END
KINGS
FORT

HEAVEN'S PEAK

ANTHIR

ARGILBORN

KINGS REACH

HELGAN
FOREST

HEAVEN'S RISE

AZREA

WATERHEART

ASSYEN

WEST RENDIN

GELRETON

THORONSTAD

WHITE

ASSMORANS

WARDENS
POINT

SAWRA

WELDON

WIDE CANAL

TREND

LAKSEA

CRYSTAL

KALRA

KORKUSU

HELGAN

CRYSTALFALLS

ROCKWALL

CARN

SOCHAR

KALARI

FORNATUNA

KALARIM

QUAN

PASTIN

MKU BAY

MKUU

SHINAS

SOKO

U'GALO

VAHSORMAN

KISANE

BEKKIMO

SALJ

SHIKA

ALMAS

SELAL

NEHIRVADI

SELAWA

KANGA

SHAMBA

GUMUSOVA

KORLAND SEA

KORLAND

ISINBAI

PWANIHATUA

BAWANA

MIR

THE ISLE

AVANZ

OPAN

THASH

MONTORO

FLURTIAN

AZMURIAN
STRAITS

VALI

VI

ROVISKA

ROVSKIA

APOUR

SCALE   100 MI.   200 MI.

IGLE

LUDZIE

WASKU

MAVIGRA

SKALA

OCHRANIA

GOLDEN TREE HILL

GALON ROAD

TEMPLE OF COS

GRAND DOCK

FERDINAND KEEP

COEDENIUF AVENUE

CAER ROAD

GALON ROAD

CETYL STREET

MERCHANT WARD

ARIAN STREET

BACH ALLEY

PINSTED ROAD

JOR SIDE

WAREHOUSE DISTRICT

OBELISG

FERDINAND STREET

WITCHWOOD

TEMPLE OF JOR

CYTO LANE

PATTER STREET

HUD LANE

PACIWR LANE

THE APARTMENTS

PATTER STREET

ICHMAN ROAD

THIRSTY TRAVELER

HIR BOULEVARD

WEST GATE

PACIWR LANE

WEST GATE REPRIEVE

LOGGERS LODGE

ANTHIR
FREE CITY - SAWRA
GOVERNMENT: MONARCHY
POPULATION: 15,000

EVERWINTER SEA

ANGLERS MARKET

DEAD END

FERDINAND STREET

AEG CIRCLE

TEMPLE OF AEG

McEVAN BUROUGH

TAKSIG BOULEVARD

MOREMILL LANE

SYLVER ISLE

MOREMILL LANE DEAD END

THE SQUAT

CROSSGOD

PASGOD CRESCENT

ARBOUR WARD

FERDINAND STREET

TEMPLE OF LOT

DEAD END

PONT AVENUE

LOT ROAD

LONG KENT STREET

KENT STREET

THE GUILDS

MYSERY CLOSE

THE RUSTY TANKARD

WHITE SEA

PLE
LAG

CRESCENT

SHORT KENT STREET

FISHERS NOOK

EAST GATE

ANGLERS WING

HELGAN FOREST

SCALE   0.5 MI.   1 MI.

WEST WALL ROAD

WALVER BOULEVARD

SILVER SPOON CLOSE

THE DEAD

TINKER ALLEY

LITTLE SAWRA

BEGGAR LANE

RICHARD LANE

DU LA RENT PARK

BIG SQUASH STREET

THE DITCH

MORIART AVENUE

WEBSTER STREET

MERCHANT WARD

BLOOR STREET

STOCKTON STREET

MILLER STREET

WEST GATE

ANGLER ALLEY

PACKER STREET

FISHMONGER COVE

LARK LANE

QUISTRELL STREET

LESTER LANE

WEBSTER

FISH BOTTOM

FISHERMAN ROAD

PORTEGEE CRESCENT

MARKED WARD

MERAK STREET

DOCK WARD

RIGHTEOUS WAY

HARBOUR WARD

NORTH KEEP BRIDGE

WEST KEEP

THE MOTE

WEST HAVEN
CAPITAL CITY - WEST RENDIN
GOVERNMENT: MONARCHY
POPULATION 20,000

FLAVEL'S CLOSE

CHAPLAIN WALK

TOWN

WAY

SLIGLAN AVENUE

WEST SLIGLAN BRIDGE

THE DITCH

DU LA RENT AVENUE

WILTON LANE

EAST SLIGLAN BRIDGE

SLIGLAN AVENUE

EAST GATE

CRANFORD BOULEVARD

MANOR HILL

ROYAL CANAL   ROYAL BRIDGE

DU LA RENT BRIDGE

PATTON STREET

GRAND STREET

DU LA RENT AVENUE

ROYAL AVENUE

PARLIAMENT HILL

HEMMING STREET

LIST STREET

KEEP BRIDGE

PARLIAMENT CRESCENT

ROYAL GATE

UNION STREET

SCALE   0.5 MI.   1 MI.

TEMPLE OF JOR

TEMPLE OF LOT

TEMPLE OF COS

PILGRIM'S

HOLY SPRING

TEMPLE OF AEG

TEMPLE OF MAG

NORD FOREST

NORD HILL

KINDRA
THE HOLY CITY — WEST RENDIN
GOVERNMENT: MONARCHY
POPULATION: 7,500

UPEND AVENUE

ORTHANE AVENUE

SAINT ARMAND BOROUGH

SIMPLE ROAD

ORTHANE HOOK

WILL WAY

im's
T.

MANER STREET

KIN ALLEY

TOWN STREET

ULSTER CRESCENT

WALLACE STREET

FOSTER STREET

PILGRIM'S MARCH

BORLAND STREET

MARCH ROAD

TOWN STREET

WALLACE STREET

BORLAND STREET

ART ALLEY

SUN STREET

WIDE ROAD

HORT STREET

LANDLOR STREET

TOWN STREET

TOWN HALL

OPLAN STREET

DLOR MARKET

LONG STREET

TRIM STREET

SAINT'S CUP

CUP ROAD

PILGRIM'S GROVE

WIDE ROAD

PILGRIM'S GATE

JOR BLESSED LAND

DEVOTE HILL

PILGRAM'S MILL

SCALE   0.5 MI.   1 MI.